MOSQUITOES AND MEN

MOSQUITOES

Mark Alan Polo

# AND MEN

DEVIL'S PARTY PRESS, MILTON, DE

MOSQUITOES AND MEN

ISBN: 978-0-9996558-6-3

# DEDICATION

Nothing is created in a vacuum. Art, whatever its discipline, absorbs its environment, translates its emotion, and molds the result into a shape like clay in the sculptor's hand. To that end, I wish to dedicate this novel to the "pieces of the quilt" of my life and the support that I have consistently received from them.

Deborah Emin prodded and pushed my story in its infancy with enthusiastic loyalty.

Throughout the many years, Anne Early encouraged me in everything I did and never failed to help me reach as high as I could.

Johanna and George Sturm gently watched the air come out of the balloon, sometimes holding the string.

Lorraine Antine guided and counseled my past, so the present could make sense.

In this journey, I met Dianne Pearce and David Yurkovich when my husband and I moved to Delaware. They created the supportive environment to gently guide and allow my ideas to flow in my literary style.

Bayne Northern, David Dutton, Carrie Sz Keane, Judith Speizer Crandell, and Bill Crandell have become the group I depend on for conference and support.

Ellen Roller assumed I would conquer this and never let me forget the goal and the value of the prize. And all this on every Tuesday, and by tragic accident of birth was born north of the Mason-Dixon Line.

Reverend Barry Stopfel shows me what strength of character looks like in life's turbulent transport. He kept me focused.

Randy Shore Dower, my cousin, keeping us all together.

Joe Hanlon, although farther away than I prefer, together we are like the Statue of Liberty–visits are few, but knowing it's there is comfort enough.

Debbie Kay, with whom I share a seat in the back of the "intellectual" bus as part of the "bad kids", is a woman of personal introspection and integrity. She has counseled and supported my journey.

And finally, I dedicate this book to my husband, Norman Cohen. He gifted me the freedom and support to take the flights of fancy and necessary isolation that I need to be creative. His life shows me what courage looks like every day and, with his consistency and love, always guarantees me the promise of a safe place to land.

From this day forward called "My posse," thank you all.

A family is one of nature's solubles;
it dissolves in time like salt in rainwater.

Pat Conroy

MOSQUITOES AND MEN

# 1

I SAT PERCHED on top of my Samsonite for what seemed like hours, staring at the house of my birth. The taxi's abrupt dump capped my grueling fourteen-hour trip to get here from my studio apartment in New York. Overcrowded subways, missed airplanes, transfers, delays and, finally, rural taxis seemed to be fitting transport punishment for time travel back to a world that started for us, an Italian immigrant family, in 1822.

Where's here? Here is Greyhaven at Salt Marsh, in a town called Peaceable, just far enough from Beaufort, South Carolina, to be considered nowhere. Greyhaven is a different "nowhere" now that the edges of development scrape the rusted gates of this, my ancestral home. These gates, forged many years ago, signaled the majesty of thousands of acres of a plantation, known throughout the South as the model of an industry built from English vision and American slavery. Now, these same gates were the only thing holding back the outside world.

I looked down the long drive still covered in a mixture of gravel and dust, feeling apprehensive about my return. Sweat, memory, and trepidation covered my entire body because of the heat of the day, the season, and this place where I grew up. Every thought, every alarm sent by my nervous system, warned me not to open this door again. I felt the sweat mount, large drops of salted water leaving a trail between linen and skin. It lay differently than the heat of an ordinary sweltering August day, heavier than the wet within folds of skin or matted hair dampened by summer perspiration, or clothes thicker than this season allows. It warned me always, as it does an animal sensing the hunger of its predator.

Wet, in all its shimmer and glisten, on my hands and at my brow, signaled not only August heat but dread. Silent and breathless, always at the ready, my alarm triggered, tripped at the break of a glass or a motion unexpected, waiting, just waiting, wired in me all my life. The deafening ring of panic pierced my core when dealing with my family.

Now, staring down this familiar driveway, the dust, heavy and wet, covered everything: the trees that lined it, the house that faded in the distance, the very air, almost too hard to breathe. The gravel, unevenly scattered at the edges of the path, bore the weight of history and a succession of carriages, Model As, and old Volvos, a style and pretense lacing harshly into the haphazardly mown grass that replaced the rare specimen flowers and the manicured lawns, the evil of this place no longer masked by beauty.

I pressed my weight solidly on my suitcase, looking alternately at my home and the telegram that had summoned me, wondering what toll five days would take. What would I have to do to cut my sentence short? What penance, what behavior, what emotional trickery, would I have to devise to negotiate what was left of my illustrious family?

This telegram, a gracious means of communication from the past, stubbornly prodded at the gadgets of the twentieth century. Telephone, e-mail, fax, cellphone, all avoided to maintain a pretense. The telegram that summoned me had simply read…

### FAUSTUS…FATHER IS DEAD…CORNELIUS.

And still I sat, telegram in hand, playing imaginary scenes of dare, alternating with snippets of truth, resisting the work I needed to do to negotiate my family. I watched the gathering breeze push past the rows of moss-laden trees, only to be stopped by the thickening drape midway, even wind refusing to work that hard.

I stood up, displacing the wet, steamy air that swirled around me, grabbed my luggage, and began to erase my twenty-five-year absence, slowly, stumbling right foot after left.

It was August, it was sourly hot, my father was dead, laid out for viewing in a house that was barely alive, and I was back.

—

Though I walked forward, the house refused to get closer. The drive had always been endless, a remnant of its former glory and grandeur. The cornerstone of ten thousand acres of rice and cotton, the

"Pride of The County" melted in the heat of too many summers. It shrank into a tract of land not much wider than the city block that I had become accustomed to jogging around in Manhattan. The house, now framed by a northeastern experiment called *the split level*, whose popularity soared in the 1950s, became the only other component still awkwardly visible of our immense plantation, except for Back Bay and Crumpet Island. Row upon row of these awkward houses dotted the landscape, tightly surrounding my house like gauze around a mummy, suffocating the very life out of our land, preserving its very own decay.

In 1953, my father, Titus Madigan, broke off pieces of our property, in smaller parcels than had ever been sold in our region since the depression. He sold off two thousand acres under the name Greyhaven Gardens to maximize the land and gather cash. Titus, attempting to ride the post-war building boom, built a development of low-cost, high-profit tract housing, thirds and fifths and eighths of an acre, some even smaller, where houses scraped up against each other, separated only by inches and the available colors.

However successful elsewhere, this building experiment never sat well with Southerners, no matter how cheaply our family built these awkward houses. Although people reluctantly bought these colored boxes, our family ensured that their success would be short lived by its own actions, proving to us again that we would remain outsiders and would never be *let into* their club. For our family it would be just another venture with another bad ending. Although designed to make the once proud and wealthy family moneyed again, it failed. There had been the assumption that money could buy social standing and wealth could capture status; it instead resulted in further isolation, landing our history and our family digs into the epicenter of suburban sprawl, creating our own ghetto, the high-class "Never Weres" living in the middle of the low-class "Oh, my Gods."

In another part of the world, Levitt built instant success with his formula for thousands of houses, fulfilling the post-war dreams of the masses to own homes in the cornfields of Long Island. We built, instead, instant blight, ensuring continued depression in the already depressed cropless fields. The blight that we caused eventually bubbled and oozed from the earth. The land spit back at us angrily in protest for having ravaged it. The houses we built were actually a side business, a direct link to our mother, Ivinia. A natural progression from our vinyl products-manufacturing plants, she thought; and Titus, our father, relented again. The blight, the waste from vinyl byproducts, contaminated everything. Her business savvy never gave a thought to the downside, just the upside and her need for power. The newest of products that she latched onto quelled her desires for power for that moment, like a fancy necklace or new hat that would satisfy her female contemporaries. But because of her unquenchable needs, Mother never thought things through. The waste from the vinyl production grew and grew, mounting without a plan. So, in an effort to clean up the debris, she spilled it into the streams and buried it in large pits, dug deep. Out of sight and out of mind, her hands were never dirty. This set the stage for our destruction, ending the long line of experiments to regain our family influence in the town of Peaceable for quite some time. And with my twin brother and my sister at the helm of the family, glue, gum, and spit would be all that would hold the parts together now.

Walking down the drive, I picked a hardened tire rut that felt comfortable, much like the one I had designed for my life before I left for New York so many years ago. I wanted nothing to do with illustrious. I wanted to blend in and be unnoticed, a departure from the tumultuous wake my family left in the Southern stream of society. I chose this same course in my beginning years in New York, contributing nothing more or less than necessary to survive. But in the Big Apple, I could take my desire for anonymity and protection, and work in a huge corporation, becoming like the man in the cubicle adjacent to me and the one adjacent to him, our degrees of boredom the only thing shading our individual color. We all waited, waited for the next office memo to appear in our in-baskets, written by a grayer suit than ours in the corporate food chain, in his vain attempt to tweak and adjust our malleable work ethics.

What do I do? I process complaints in the offices of Vastigone Ribbon and Trim Company, at the very end of Wall Street, an odd place for trim to be brokered. We are centralized, computerized, and organized, with offices in all the major cities across the US and China, where our product is made. I never see the trim, just the complaints. They pour in daily by fax, phone, and e-mail, though certainly not telegram. I resolve them the same way, everyday: anonymously, impersonally, efficiently.

Living in Manhattan, I never adjusted to the passion required for business life. I knew how the power plays roared and injured and saw their result in my own family and I wanted none of it. So, instead, I lived for the times before and after the punch of the clock, those moments of fun, camaraderie, and companionship interrupted only by the nine-hour stretch of paperwork, problems, and solutions. I loved Manhattan immediately; it was the center of my world. I fell into the lovely notion that nothing existed beyond its watery borders. It became my plantation and

I lorded over it. Except for required trips abroad which kept my conversation full of interesting facts and witty repartee while dating and living the single life of a citified gay man, I swore I would never leave its island ends to return home…until now.

With this reluctance, I reached the porch where we had spent all the years of our lives since moving onto this land and into this house in 1840, running fox hunts, sipping lemonade, plotting local revenge. Peering over the remaining lands, I absorbed the decay. The wide columns that surrounded the house peeled vertically to reveal fashionable colors for every season gone by. Climbing the steps, I noted the floorboards of the front porch, warped from the excessive (then nonexistent) rain, which never seemed to fall gently or appropriately. A line of rockers stretched down left and right of the entrance, cocked in angles of two as if engaged in pleasant conversation. All in high-gloss white, they still perched crisp on this crumbling backdrop.

Standing there, I no longer felt easy enough to just walk in. I slammed the door on that ease many years ago on my way out. Inches away from the front door, I remembered its segmented glass and carved panels, now weathered gray instead of the rich mahogany that had shone always like a fine piece of furniture. It discolored and baked from the heat of what burned inside and out, never designed to withstand the intensity of my family. I touched it and it seared my skin, bacon sizzling on a skillet. This front entrance, the door to my past, considered the heart of the Southern home and hospitality, showed the age of its grain now, its lifelines shortened over the years by stress and neglect. I stood there for a moment, tucked the telegram inside my jacket pocket, and hammered the large knocker in the shape of our family crest.

I heard the pounding resonate within the house and felt the stirring from within. It took several moments for the thump of the approaching patter of familiar feet to resonate, and I supposed, the rustling of mourning attire. The door opened.

"Faustus, you're not dressed," Cornelius, my twin, looked me over immediately. He stood in a morning suit with cravat and cummerbund, as I had expected. What didn't divide us emotionally, his attire certainly assured.

"Hello to you, too, my dear brother."

We embraced, a gesture just warm enough to separate us from strangers.

"I see you received my telegram," Cornelius said, an edge of surprise in his voice. "I didn't think you would come."

"Yeah, life's full of firsts. Why didn't you just…um….call? Never mind." I changed tactics. "Good to see you, Cornelius. Is Madeline here?" I hadn't seen my sister in a few years and missed her wit and our antics.

"She's still preparing. You know your sister, even black has its details to attend to. She'll be down in a pregnant minute," Cornelius continued, poking fun at our sister's dressing habits, while every bit as fussy as she. "You're all dusty. Put down your luggage and we'll get you a libation."

It was only 11:30 a.m., and Cornelius' start had been earlier than that, as witness the half-empty martini glass on the entry hall table.

"Why wouldn't the cabbie drive me to the door?" I felt compelled to ask, knowing that it would take much more maneuvering to get the full story.

"Huxley's Service?"

"Yeah, what's up with him? The minute I told him the address, it was as if I had called his mama ugly. He'd go no further than the front gates. Asked me if I was kin. I looked at his license photo posted, you know, on the dashboard and recognized him," I could see by the look on Cornelius' face that I was not forging new territory. "I reminded him that we played in Salt Marsh Pond together as kids. I guess he didn't recognize me, at first; that was so many years ago. It was all I could do to get him to drive me here. He was going to leave me on Route 111 near Maybelle Sinder's chicken farm. I had to pay him double."

"That low life, he's never been reliable. His whole family's worthless!" Cornelius practically spit out the words. "Just never you mind. You're here now and that's all that's important. I'll show you upstairs. God, listen to me go on. You know where your old room is. Go and freshen up. Guests won't be arriving for the viewing 'til one, so we'll have time to talk. Can you believe that Father was almost ninety-five years older than Addie?"

"Where is she? Where's Momma?" I've called Addie "Momma" for as long as I could remember. Addie Waters, more formally Adela Waters, is the continuation of a long line of Waters that have lived, rather, *survived,* on the Greyhaven property since 1820. The first Waters, Hit and Besha, were bought at auction in Charleston to serve the original owners of Greyhaven.

They hailed from a little coastal town in Senegambia named Portudal and were sold to slave traders, along with countless others, by their own elders. Hit and Besha, more educated than most in European customs, were purchased to be the heads of staffing at the plantation, replacing two slaves who were killed by the original owners when they tried to escape to the north because of a rumor they had heard about a path to freedom. That started the history of the Waters and Greyhaven and, ultimately, the greatest in the line, Addie.

"You're still calling her Momma. How cute. Addie's at the house on Crumpet Isle, you remember, on the Back Bay Inlet." Cornelius continually jabbed at my absence by stating the obvious.

"I know," I said impatiently, "Is she coming today?" I asked as if just a formality.

"No, she's coming with Jedidiah…at the third viewing."

I could not believe that Cornelius was still holding onto the old cultural pecking order. "I'll call her and ask if Jed could bring her today. I want so much to see her."

"Now Faust, don't mix everything up on your first minute back. Everything's been arranged." Cornelius never took direct blame for much of anything. "There just isn't time to confuse matters, okay, brother?" he said.

That word—brother—became the signal many years ago to stop me in my tracks, so he could assess the lay of the land and re-chart its course, if necessary. Cornelius used it deliberately. He looked straight at me, not blinking, assuming I would go no further. I complied, awakening the games that we played, as if only yesterday.

"Of course you know the way," he said dryly, pointing in the general direction of up in gracious consolation for not burning a path with me to my old room. He established the right of possession with this aura of ownership, presence being nine-tenths of the law. He stayed and, therefore, had greater stock. I became the stranger in my own house.

My immediate itinerary in place, Cornelius grabbed his cocktail and sauntered off to the salon.

"Well, I must run; things to do, you know."

He adjusted flowers and corrected the fall of the fabric portieres that framed all the doorways of the public rooms on his way out.

"Your luggage is heavy enough to have something appropriate to wear, I pray?" he said, without turning, as he floated away.

We didn't look alike, Cornelius and I, at least to me. We had shared the same womb but used the time differently. He, dull-haired and thicker; I, thinner and brighter faced with deeply shiny hair like my father, flecked with a silver glitter—the same path that my father's mane once took. So, we approached "identical" with resistance. Wherever we went, although the similarities on the charts balanced the sheet, people were always surprised that we were born within hours of each other; that surprise started right at the beginning.

Neither Mother nor Father had expected twins. The combination of 1952, the built-in prejudices of South Carolina, and my family's inability to lose its outsider status, had made the "oops" all-the-more possible. Addie, Mother's sidekick, lackey, and unemancipated slave, had tended to her needs as a midwife, since no doctor would touch her.

Mother's demeanor left a lot to be desired. She had gone through three local physicians at the birth of my sister, Madeline, four years before, and would have had to drive clear down to Memorial General in Savannah for doctoring. In spite of Father's imploring, Mother insisted that, "No one in my family will be born in Savannah! No one! We are born Carolinians and will die Carolinians. None of my children will be born in that backwater town in Georgia! Do you hear me, none! Sherman lost his mind when he let that place slip through his fingers!"

She would go on and on, speaking of Georgia, in foreign terms. She'd invariably mumble something about "needing passports."

Mother hated Savannah and added it to her list years ago, a list already long and detailed, filled with people and places that shunned her, the tradeoff not only for partaking in Madigan wealth, but for her earlier, less-successful career.

I arrived first or escaped the womb first on that blustery day in 1952. It was so sudden, Mother said, that Addie could not be raised. She was tending to picking up some important documents for Father.

Wide eyed and hands moving in the air, Mother said that a most unusual windstorm rocked the trees so hard that I got scared and ran for cover. My brother, Cornelius, took another tactic and stayed in the belly of the beast for three more hours. And yes, Mother bore the mantle of the beast very well. She even spoke of herself as being "this side of the devil's left cloven hoof" when one-too-many martinis loosened her truths. She loved and nurtured it, honing the skills required to be a survivor, which often got confused with evil, depending on the perspective. She died exactly two months before Father, two months to the day that I received a similar telegram about my Mother's passing.

Ivinia's death could never be construed as "passing gently into that good night." I learned from Madeline that Mother had run headlong into a grove of pecan trees clocking ninety in her '67 Thunderbird convertible, affectionately known as "Two Quarts Low," because it continually burned oil. Father said that Mother could always "push that 'Two Quarts Low' when she was two quarts high."

My sister and I mourned her passing at the age of seventy-five and blessed the peace this sadness brought. I did not attend her memorial service.

On the way to my room, I walked past the salon and the dining room, shifting my eyes, not turning my head. I thought better of curiosity concerning the whereabouts of my father's temporary resting place.

But, as I passed the library, there he lay, Titus, spread out in full metal coffin with a backdrop of books that we never read, just showed. The coffin glimmered in the candlelight from the votives placed all around the room. The flickering candles made the griffins that supported the corners of the casket appear alive. Draped silk flags covered my father's torso like a patchwork quilt, emblazoned with insignias of the Masons, the Confederacy, and the Italian Nationals. He loved these flags no matter how insignificant they became or how embarrassing the connection, for Titus did not love incompletely or without contradiction. To complete the dramatic setting, he lay perched on an ornate platform that had our family crest once again emblazoned on it. I recognized the old placard, the bronze and the paint of it. It had been ripped off the door of my father's old construction office at Greyhaven Gardens before the *incident.*

Fitting that he lay beside it, both fallen.

I couldn't help but stop at the French doors of the library, just to gaze at the scene. I remembered father sitting in this room in his easy chair, its mohair worn to a shine, now pushed to the side, displaced by his metal cocoon.

The room loomed darkly, absorbing all the candlelight. The clutter of books and mementos created shadows, confirming the mysteries of his life. His library seemed a fitting place to store his body, I thought. It still had the sweet after-scent of his pipe, locked in all the volumes, woods, and wallpaper. I warmed to the memory of my father playing on the floor with me and an old set of jacks on the even older Oriental rug, and yet bristled at the times in that same room that I hid behind his easy chair to avoid my mother's martini-induced wrath.

He lie there now in the silence of that memory. I saw his face, waxen, hollow, and old, smaller than I remembered. Titus seemed dwarfed by the display case in which he slept. I dared not get closer. The reality of this event was not necessarily unexpected at his age, but not prayed for either. I knew that his passing would soon unleash a torrent of change. At that moment I felt nothing more than apprehension. Stepping closer to his coffin may have opened more emotional doors than I was prepared to deal with at that moment. I wanted to stay with simpler, understandable fears for as long as possible.

# 2

CLIMBING UP THE wide stairs, I stopped midway on
the landing, where the largest of windows billowed in darkened white
sheer silk, gossamer in gloom. It overlooked the back of what remained
of the property. We would often stand there, Madeline, Cornelius and I,
to watch the local upper class practice crew in the shallow marsh water
that almost completely surrounded the house. Greyhaven was built on
one of several peninsulas that extended helter-skelter into the salted waters that collected the summer rains, eventually feeding the Atlantic
Ocean. On early mornings we could see the shrimp boats in the distance.
Father would tell us of the time when we would lease the inlets to the
shrimpers before we sold off the land that edged all of these grassy ram-
parts. Now they own it, a collective called Gay's Shrimp Company which,
since the twenties, slowly bought up all the rights to the privately owned
waterways.

I passed my sister's room, my brother's, then my parents' double,
and arrived at mine. My room shared the upstairs veranda that wrapped
the house to let in the night marsh breezes and overlooked the path to
the large front gates that were now at the edge of a county road. The
ancient oak trees that lined the drive, overgrown with moss, squandered
the view and I could no longer see to the end. I could no longer see the
business of our house at work, at play, or at battle, the Civil War but a
small skirmish within the genetic pool of my family.

I stood at the threshold of my youth and peered into the room that
Ivinia prepared for my arrival almost fifty years ago. It all looked the

same. The wallpaper, a simple silk stripe, had stood the test of time. Mother had decorated only her son's rooms at birth. She avoided tradition when it came to Madeline.

Mother had insisted on grown-up decor for her children, not childish themes.

"You will leave this world with the same wallpaper that you had when you came into it," Mother would say continually, knowing the history of the house, assuming who would stay, and all the work that had been done to ensure its preservation. She believed in continuity and financial conservatism, unless it was personal.

The draperies in my room matched the walls, a pale green and cream. The chest of drawers had been made here on our plantation in in 1817 by Augustus Grove, a slave owned by the original family that gave birth to this place. An Italian settee from the mid-1700s sat facing the French doors, enabling its occupant to enjoy the view, and a writing table from one of the French Louis's lazed under the side window. A Tiffany lamp with green dragonflies, a leather desk pad with sterling corners, and an ink blotter and writing box from Cartier, all containing my initials, filled the desk. The bed cover, painstakingly hand embroidered by Ellie Sutton from Charleston, laid a little flatter than I remembered. Ellie had studied French stitchery in Paris and, after all these years, the bed cover was still beautiful. I peeked under the cover to see if my favorite blanket and crisp linens still lay taught on the bed. They did.

I placed my suitcase on the bench in front of my four-poster bed and looked up at the carved pineapples that English craftsmen perched on top of the narrow pillars some two-hundred years before. My bed, as well as my brother's, were from Fallen Timbers, another plantation one-hundred and fifty miles inland, whose principal crop became tobacco around 1870. The owners, fifth-generation Delbartons, had switched from cotton to leaf after cotton prices plummeted, part from Northern punishment, part from lack of infrastructure to bring product to market after the war. The Delbartons sustained irreparable damage from the Northern scourge. To make matters worse, none of their slaves stayed on after The Proclamation. So the decision to switch to tobacco, although risky, seemed to be the right move, because it grew easier and faster, and could be processed by others.

A commodity that sold in good times and in bad, the Delbartons thrived for several decades, 'til a rumor spread of customers dying because of a new tobacco product from Paris, the cigarette, that hit American shores around 1915. Roman Delbarton, in a struggle with conscience, switched to corn and Berkshire pigs from England in 1928.

Family friends of the Dukes, he followed their divestiture from tobacco. The Dukes had much more security to back up such a cavalier gesture. Their transition, not only seamless, proved to be lucrative. The Delbartons, on the other hand, lacked the collateral to weather yet another transition.

Mother purchased their furniture at a bankruptcy auction on the front lawn of Fallen Timbers in 1959, when the Delbartons' debts outran their assets. She approached Abigail Delbarton, the matriarch of the family and seventeen years her senior, with sarcastic superiority.

"Are you sure that these beds are worth their minimum bid?" She followed with, "And did you really purchase them from Charles Pendleton, the prominent antiques dealer from Providence, Rhode Island?"

Mother had often told this story when touring the house with guests. "Delbarton's mammy would still be polishing these beds if his conscious didn't win out." She would then turn to us in front of the guests and say, "Never let what's right get in the way of what's necessary to survive. Remember, the survival of Greyhaven is paramount."

She made every visitor uncomfortable by the second floor. That way, they ate less at supper.

I started to unpack, fiddling with the latches on the armoire, when suddenly, the door to my room flew open. It slammed the brasses into the wallpaper, widening a dent that had already been placed there by my sister years ago. It was still my sister, Madeline, draping herself across the doorway, leaning in a "vapors faint." Black poured over her from head to foot. Her face, her entire body, was sheathed in a sheer silk chiffon mourning veil.

"Pater is dead," she put her wrist up to her forehead, "What *will* this family do?" She paused for a moment, noticing my surprise at her dramatic entrance, "Let's bury the bastards and have some sour mash!"

"Maddie! For God's sakes, he's in the library! And what do you mean *bastards*?"

"Don't worry, Faust, my love," Madeline chided. "Titus can't get any deafer. And while we're at it, I say let's club Cornelius to death and do a two-for-one viewing! I dare say that a lot of people coming today feel the same way! There isn't a jury of twelve in the county that would convict us!"

She moved with lightning speed, grabbing me in a bear grip. We fell onto the bed laughing and hugging. "Where have you been? You little shit! You left me alone for so long in this Southern swamp," Madeline reprimanded me.

She always resented being born first, which never was an enviable position for the females of the Madigan clan. But mostly she blamed me for leaving, feeling it caused her further isolation.

She conjured a notion that if Cornelius and I had been born first there would have been no reason for Mother's disregard, and the transfer of Greyhaven could never have been disputed, passing to the first male heir, as written in the original deed of 1760, with twins parlaying a double header.

But, since the reverse was true, Madeline bore not only Mother's social disappointment at having a female firstborn, but, more importantly, the guilt over weakening the right of succession and inheritance of Greyhaven, so specifically designed, a tradition not unlike King Henry's troubles so many years before. Madeline's birth set the stage for the rest of my father's family to file suit after suit in every level of court to challenge the right of inheritance.

"Business is business," was heard at every family gathering, of which there were many, where everyone showed up as much to keep close as to smell weakness. All this aside, Madeline never forgave me for running away, leaving her exposed to Mother, Father, Cornelius, and others.

Seeing my sister again reminded me of just how long I'd been away. "Where have I been? You know what I'm doing, working long hours and barely living in the Big Apple, as always."

"New York, New York," she sung it half in southern drawl and half like Ethel Merman. "How long has it been? Let's see. It's been two years since I visited you with Addie."

She stroked my hair and planted kisses on my cheek as if laying seeds in a furrow. "Wasn't that tops! Didn't we have the best time?" She giggled. "All of us piling into your apartment, all those sleeping bags, like when we were camping in the Black Hills as kids. Addie purrin' like the Queen of Sheba or something, in your down-filled bed. So posh! She never got over it. We certainly spoiled her that week. She still talks about it and I still have a back ache from sleeping on the floor!"

"You were the one who wanted to turn it into a slumber party. I was perfectly okay with everyone staying at the Four Seasons. So don't blame me!"

"Oh pooh, I'm pulling your cart, Honey," Madeline withdrew.

"I just remember getting nervous," I said. "When Addie didn't come back for four hours from her shopping with Jedidiah. I never really understood why she didn't want us along."

"You've always been such a worry wart. You know she brought us back gifts. She wanted to surprise us. What's to understand?" Madeline could never focus on the bad or the dangerous, or the oddly curious, just the playful and fun. She always took the "what is" and turned it into her liking. It's why she married Harris Delbarton.

The marriage of Madeline to Harris was a classic scheme made famous by Mother's need for power. She manipulated the event and, to please Mother, Madeline found the means to help her survive it. She liked Harris' manner—quiet, understated, and reserved, so unlike her own clan.

She'd never noticed that Mother stayed up nights plotting this merger. She hadn't grasped the meaning of all the attention that Mother showered on her. She'd failed to understand that it was not a new chapter in their lives, but a continuation of need and use, designed by Mother to get what she desired. Ivinia wanted the status that Madigan money could not buy. The Delbartons were the oldest family in the region, from fine English stock. Landed gentry before they arrived on these shores, they claimed vast land holdings from the Crown long before they'd even unpacked.

So, Madeline, at that moment, had become important to Mother, but it was too brief for her to notice. She was oblivious to Mother's schemes, having designed herself that way.

"So, Mads, where's Harris?" I asked.

We were still on the bed. I held her face in my hands like I had done so many times before in this very spot. Her face, now slightly wrinkled, slightly puffy in the adult places that we try to hide, still retained the joy that a Southern life, however designed, engenders.

"He's up in Chicago, attending a meeting. Something about the splits and the land. You know, lawyers and their need to win, it never ends."

"Still? We settled that, my God, over twenty-five years ago! Don't tell me they're going after us again?"

"Oh, no, my dear, absent brother, this is not about the settlement. You're right, that's over. This is about reopening the land. Honey, I just write children's books, so I don't know nuthin' much about it, but we're going to reclaim the land, or something."

Madeline always hid behind her career as if it meant nothing. She was second in line, in popularity, to, as she puts it, "that English woman who writes those books that go on and on about sorcerers."

"Reclaim the Land!" I shrieked.

And the reason for my absence came sharply into focus once again, with the words of my mother flooding back: *remember, the survival of Greyhaven is paramount.*

The ugliness of the struggle stiffened my spine and I sat up. "Not again."

"What's 'not again'?" Cornelius stood in the doorway of my room, holding a tray of libations. "You two kids catch up yet?"

He never joined in with our fun, whether we were nearer to ten or fifty. Always, he removed himself and his emotions from our equation. Most times superior, often times distant, he remained apart.

"I thought some drinks might soften the day."

He walked over to my desk and balanced the tray on top of my writing box, covering my initials. I felt the affront, the sand kicked in my face by that subtle move. The nervous competition awakened between us, swelling up like an intentional bruise.

I never felt like a twin, the ones that I have heard about, the ones that think thoughts together, finish each other's sentences, wear the same clothes, and feel things happen to the other though miles apart. Miles apart, I felt safer, only safer.

"Yes, twelve noon, and drinking, I had forgotten the need. Hand the glass over, Cornelius."

"Scotch still your drink?"

"Better make that a double. What's this about reopening the land?"

"I see you've been telling tales out of school, Madeline," Cornelius' tone ashened her face.

"Well, Cornelius, he's going to know eventually. What's the harm in having this conversation now?"

"There is time for it, I suppose, just not now and certainly not all at once," he cautioned. "I thought we should bring Faust up to speed gently."

"Maybe this is the right time for it," Madeline suggested softly. "He's been gone for so long."

"Yes, Madeline, he's been gone a long time," Cornelius made drama out of sipping his Martini and his stance, "It's not as if he's a player in this."

"Yes, Brother, I've been gone a long time," I said, "but, it's amazing how quickly I can remember how the family secrets swell the knots in my stomach." I took a big gulp of single malt, gritting my teeth at the alcohol's assault. "Not much has changed; my room, Madeline's perfect charm." I raised my glass to her and she winked and returned the gesture and turned to Cornelius. "Or your manipulation. You certainly took after Mother in that regard."

"I'll take that as a compliment. After all, if I had left like you did, where would we be today?"

"Ah, dear Brother," tipping my scotch-filled Baccarat tumbler, "Therein lies the mystery. Where would we be? I am the only one who tried to find out. One thing, I know…"

"Don't go there, darling," Madeline warned me, stroking my face and throwing herself between us, a scene that had occurred over and over so often before. "Let's just drink to our reunion, under less-than-happy circumstances, and we'll sit down later and start this all over again."

She turned to Cornelius, took her Cosmopolitan and tapped her glass against his, staring at him to go along with her plan.

"Time is getting short. Faust needs to get ready, so I'll leave you both. Madeline?"

"Yes, dear?"

"Come downstairs when you've finished catching Faust up," he started to leave but instead turned around. "Oh, and don't let Harris see you drinking. He made me promise to keep you and your blood sugar even. Remember, we need to tend to last-minute arrangements, so I need you coherent," he paused no less dramatically. "My wife is coming with the twins and…just look at the time!"

Cornelius pulled a gold pocket watch that had belonged to Father from his pants pocket and sprung the cover open. "It's late."

As he turned on the heels of his patent leathers to leave the room, I decided to extend the courtesies that are intrinsically linked to all genteel Southern families.

"By the way, Cornelius, how are Sarah, Rollins, and Benton?" He stopped at the door, turned, and narrowed his eyes. I swear that I sensed a surveying of a situation before he answered.

"Thanks for asking, brother. They're fine. Sarah's days are very long at Memorial General and the twins are sprouting up past their roots. They're twenty-five years old already. Benton's toying with the idea of getting married; lovely girl, good family. It seems that Rollins is a confirmed bachelor. I suppose like you."

We always spoke in code when it came to bachelorhood and its reasons. We just made the statements and moved on.

The only connection that I have ever had with my nephews began and ended in FAO Schwartz or Bergdorf's, trying to plot their age without cutting into their limbs to count the rings. Asking for appropriate gift selections from a mildly interested clerk, I would answer his few questions. After a short rundown of what I knew about them, I finished our exchange with "gift wrap and send, please."

"Can't wait to see how they've grown," I said to the back of Cornelius' head.

"Well, see you downstairs." Gone he was, smooth as unruffled silk in the morning breeze.

"Shit, now he's pissed!" Madeline quickly adjusted her dress, wiped her cheeks, and placed the veil back over her face.

"So, this is familiar territory when it comes to us, isn't it?"

"Oh, Faust honey, you don't know. It's much different now that everyone knows Father is dead."

"What do you mean, 'knows'?" She put her hand up to my mouth.

"Hush, Honey, not now. The walls can't hear this yet. You know Southern superstitions. Never go against the family."

I wasn't sure if that was Southern loyalty or Italian immigrant reflex. "I hope Cornelius will tell you soon. Until then, my darling, let me go downstairs and smooth things over. I love that you're here." Madeline adjusted her attraction and her calculation. "We'll go to Gorman's for a frozen hot chocolate," she pulled out of the air as if just discovered. "Yes, that's what we'll do. Tomorrow."

Her eyes shifted back and forth in a fit of gathering confidence, looking for more than a fun date, "Yes, tomorrow! Meet me there tomorrow morning, puleeese," she drawled.

"Sure, of course." I couldn't refuse her; I never could.

"Oh, fab! Toodles," she said, as the pressure that filled her head evaporated and she waved off her words in a grand gesture. "See you downstairs."

And as she ran off, she said, "Remember. Gorman's, 9:30 sharp, so we'll have lots o' time. Kisses."

She vanished in a floaty black blur.

# 3

I FINISHED GETTING ready and as well timed as the crow of a cock, the pounding of the knocker on the front door began precisely at the stroke of one. I wanted to stall my appearance for as long as possible. This first round of visitors, the family, felt like the toughest. If Cornelius invited Addie to attend on the third day, then it was assured that the rest of our traditions would hold firm in death, for days one and two. On the first day Titus' younger brother and older sisters would sleaze in with their offspring. The second day would be the business partners. The third day would be everyone else involved.

Friends came and went, but in the heyday of the plantation, there were six-hundred workers—slaves—who tended to the needs of this family and to its business. Madeline and I found hundreds of diaries written by the former mistresses of this plantation deep within the eves of the silent parts of the house, even back before our family owned Greyhaven. Their pages told stories of deaths and acquisitions, friends and enemies, and life every day within these walls. Back then, the third day of viewing would last for hours, each of the staff walking past the open casket, each showing his or her respect or disdain. The structure of the slave population, layered like the services available in a small town, answered all the needs of our working plantation. Except for a few supplies and some raw materials, everything was produced, manufactured, or fixed on Greyhaven property.

Today, when we need help on any level, we advertise in the paper, visit an agency, and interview and select from the applicants, talking about salary and perks. Prior to Lincoln, as the diaries told us, they would ride in to Charleston for a day or two. The mistress of the house would make her stops at Feona Eggleston's dress shop for a fitting, then off to Biddles and Banks for a redesign of a jeweled necklace that had gone out of fashion, and finally to John Sergeants, to pick up a sterling butter server created by Paul Store from England.

All of this pleasantry occurred while the master of the plantation went to the auction house at the docks to purchase a slave. He'd look around at the merchandise on display. Those unfortunate men, women, and children who did not succumb to the fright, horror, or exposure to the ships' condition, stood side by side in the shadows of dim, misty light surrounded by the wealth whom they would service. The head of the plantation would feel the muscles and assess the bone structures of the available stock, check the teeth and the attitudes of the current selection, and inspect their limbs for rickets while shifting the shackles that bound their legs and souls to this new land of freedom and opportunity. All this activity occurred while the transfer agents boasted about the origins of these wretched individuals, their history, their health, and the prospects of their work and their abilities, and how they would be an asset to any working house.

The buyer imagined the result of a good purchase and the added ease and productivity ascribed to the purchase while the seller weaved a story of possession and power, puffing up the buyer's ego to create an absolute need from a cursory interest. The power, the swell to the ego, using the purchase of another human being as a testosterone ploy, white man showing muscle to white man, comparing their tools in a locker room. *Mine is bigger than yours. How many do you have? I have more.* All this layered and intermingled in the dank atmosphere of the auction house. The sounds of the slaves moaning and grunting their last resistance, the auctioneers selling and upping the bids, counting in their heads past the line where profit is made, and the masters bemoaning the rise in prices and the memory of better stock in years gone by, talking to their sons, showing them the ropes, occasionally letting them make a bid. Fathers laughing and feeling proud at their sons' first steps, first words, first slave purchases. Ah, the tradition!

African men, women, and children, standing there, skin colors a kaleidoscope of bronze, mahogany, and chocolate, shiny and deep, tears and sweat beading up, falling down, raw jewels on their backs and faces and arms, seeing what remained of their families, being ripped apart and divided into parcels of property so that families of milky complexions and European backgrounds could preserve their own way of life while destroying the lives of others. Plantation or Walmart, the slave is a necessary part of the greased wheel.

All men are created equal, excepting these by twisted Bible verse, filled with loss and hopelessness. And so, life lived on without a thought that this twisted status quo would change. And, it didn't; not for some time. But it did within the time of my family's history, enough to resent the change. The feeling that this engenders when you read it in a history book or an innocent diary, the author unaware of the future shame, reads like unbelievable horror. Live it, and hear it spoken of, politically correct within your own family, but with a twinge of sorrow for the extent of the past wealth and the loss of the ways to make it without slavery, on the backs of people *not* created equal, good-old days, Lincoln dead again in the undercurrent of this family's disappointment.

From this, I ran away to New York, as much from the history and the diaries as from the present. I felt ashamed of my family's past on so many levels and the distortion that it took in my generation that it seemed as bad, if not worse, than the history from which it evolved. I ran as far as I could, knowing that my family would stop my finances, for rebellion and disrespect breeds punishment and financial isolation.

I saw an article in an old Sunday *New York Times*, in the heat and wet of August, sitting on a rocker on the front porch, facing down the drive watching the familiar black faces even then paid not enough, and certainly free, but not enough, and integrated, but not enough. The paper read of the involvement of Lee Iacocca and the bicentennial, happening within just three years, in 1976. It happened then, looking at the yellowed pictures of New York Harbor and its sleek ships, the skyline and its majesty. In yet another UPI photo I felt the titillation of fear in Manhattan's size, saw the smallness of the windows in the tallest of the buildings. At that moment I was struck with the contrast of New York City's enormity despite its many tiny parts, a puzzle of sorts where all the pieces fit. In that enormity, I suddenly saw the possibility that I could be anonymous within that contrast. Then still in another photo, I saw a street, where a tall woman—taller than the statue of Dionysus in our salon, taller than my father when he stood defiant and proud at his board meetings, taller and prouder than anyone that I had ever seen—roller skating down the street while waving a flag. She held a sparkler and a book and wore a Statue of Liberty costume. Her name was Rolla Rena, the caption to her photo said. The sweetest of houses surrounded her as she rolled down the narrow tree-lined streets. She worked at banking by day and blossomed from moth to butterfly at night, touring her domain and blessing her flock 'til the wee hours of the morning.

Turned out, *she* was a *he*. The small brick houses comprised the tight little streets and it was aptly named the Village. He glided strangely, eccentric and captivating. I was home. The Village, how quaint, how small town, caught within the context of a massive city, how perfect for my escape. It called to me, a city of extremes not unlike the environment from which I came, lacking only the wet heat, the measured accent, and my family's complications at every turn.

I wanted to melt into this melting pot of which I'd read. The teeming masses, the opportunity, and the freedom, without the shackles of my family, liberated not by Proclamation but by determination. I needed to enter and disappear, for a while if not forever. And I did.

—

Extending icy formalities and excruciating pleasantries took forever emotionally, and I needed to slip away from my family soon after their arrival. Hiding behind the shadows of my father's books, I stood next to him in the corner of the library, both wallflowers at this first day gathering. I hadn't seen most of them since I left Greyhaven in the seventies.

I stared at Titus Madigan, prone in front of me, remembering his effect on the universe that he controlled. A tall man, he stood well over six feet tall in life and taller in ego. He towered over everyone and spent his time in the sport of bulldozing his successes and failures, pushing everyone where he needed them. There were only two categories of people in my father's life—those he liked and those he disliked. Family for family's sake held little glue for attaching his emotions. His circle small, it included Mother, me, and Addie.

Titus by all accounts lived his life as a narcissist. He had little room for emotional alliances, only business ones, and he felt no shame in executing his benevolence or wrath with swiftness and impunity. Often the needs of our family coincided with his, but there were times when they didn't. And when they didn't, I had my father as an ally, always. Cornelius had Mother as an ally, always, but Madeline had no one, always.

Her lack of importance to this family, plainly evident in so many memories: I recalled the time when Madeline was sixteen and had her Debutante Ball, a "coming out to society" event. She'd met a boy, Thomas Kinley Tinsdale, "T.K.", who was brought to the party by Madeline's best friend, Linifred Wallingford. T.K. snuck sour mash into the party at our home, fed it to Madeline, and made her so drunk she passed out.

Mother found them in the boathouse on Back Bay, after an embarrassingly long absence, naked under a toppled service dingy. She woke Madeline, asked no questions, and beat her bloody. Father finished the job and Madeline went under cover for two months to heal from the wounds. She visited no local doctors. No police were summoned, just internal family justice.

Her ensuing pregnancy was aborted in Washington, DC, by a personal friend of Congressman Wilcox, who became my father's partner in his horse breeding business. Favors, no matter what the import, could be gotten with the right phone call or reciprocation. In return, Mother convinced Titus to open a small hotel in Beaufort, a large house conversion, with T.K.'s father, Kelsey, as his partner, keeping friends close and enemies closer still, punishing Madeline with a permanent reminder. From that day, not only did Madeline know her abuser's location, so close, but Mother insisted that she work at the hotel during summer break and winter holidays with T.K.

No one asked Madeline if she'd been conscious, or if she knew what had happened, but me. She wasn't, and she didn't. I spoke to Titus about what I had learned and came to know him on that day. He would never go back on a plan, a decision, or an act.

"Father, I need to talk to you about Madeline." I rushed into his library and saw the smoke twist and curl from his pipe as he sat in his easy chair. "There are things that you don't know."

"The things I don't know," he said back to me without looking up from the business ledgers in his laps, "are the least important to me, Faust.

"But, Father…"

"There is nothing more to say on this topic, Faust," he said, as if reading it from the book that transfixed his eyes. "Now please, Son, leave me be."

It was done, and he shed a blind, cold eye on my concern and the welfare of my sister. We never spoke of it again, he and I. It was as if the incident never happened.

At that moment, Madeline and I bonded completely. She would hide out in my room, sometimes in the armoire, sometimes under the bed covers, and I would hide with her. We would tell stories, weave tales, conjuring up swamp fairies, frogs, moss princes, and golden alligators with jeweled tails so long that they were our rudders for lily pad flyers where castles looked like the houses of our history, where family listened and thwarted evil, protecting their young, going to the ends of the earth to vanquish their children's pain and enemies. It was here, with Madeline at sixteen and me at twelve, that we retreated into a childhood that we never had. It was here that her life and career as a writer began, within the abuse of our family. A place to look at and say, "Here is where the inspiration came from." Here in a secret's whisper that would translate time and time again, in interviews with editors and columnists and critics, weaving a base of achievement, a source, that it was the Mythical Land of Madigan, a serenity and peace that needed to be shared. Madeline could not leave and blow the cover of her success. She stayed at Greyhaven, the only retaliation she imagined, ever, so she could bask in the glow of their squirming from a truth so close to revelation. Her fame starting at nineteen, so young they said, so young yet so secretly old.

I walked to the casket where Titus lay and touched his full mane of silver hair, silver, it seemed, since the day he was born. For as long as I could remember, I wanted to touch that silvery torrent of hair. It was captivating. Even at the age of five, I always wanted to climb on his shoulders and hold onto his flowing mane. Though nearly ninety years old, there were remnants of the features of the Emperor of Rome for whom he was named. He knew the power of his physical appeal. He worked it. Everyone adored the view of him, the style and the power of him. Even Grandfather adored Titus to distraction. Grandfather wouldn't end or begin a sentence without interjecting his son's thoughts, observations, or perspective. He was proud of his son, my father, and always showed it. 'Til the day my grandfather died, we all knew where he stood. He only had enough emotion for one son, the first. The other children who came before or after Titus, my aunts, Hannabelle and Matilda, and my uncle, Marcus, would go from uterus to grave unnoticed. Outside of this room where my father and I held each other hostage, the offspring of that resentment festered and oozed their puss.

Some of the puss oozed into the library where my father and I were hold up. A familiar voice assaulted my father's and my rebonding. "Once upon a time, there was a man and his *boy*." Josilyn Benoit, my cousin, stood rigid, brittle from years of hatred. I hadn't seen her for at least two dozen-odd years.

"If it isn't Josilyn," I responded, without turning around or suspending my affection for the man I sometimes knew. "I'd recognize that shrill, contemptuous voice anywhere."

"Is that any way to greet your closest cousin?"

"The margin of error on that one is greater than you think, my dear."

"Don't be sarcastic, sweetie."

"Don't be acerbic, Josilyn," I smirked. "It doesn't suit you. Sort of goes against the total look that you've achieved."

She wore a bib dress with an electric-blue cotton blouse, the sort of color that could divert air traffic. Atop her head sat a Southern bubble hair tease, a blonde football helmet. I guess someone told her it would make her appear taller. Truthfully, it just made her hair higher. Her forehead still only barely hit the five-foot mark.

Some time ago, I had heard from Addie that Josilyn had joined the Junior League of Charleston and was drummed out because she contributed a recipe to their annual cookbook that had caused thirty people at the Junior League Charity Taste Off to report food poisoning to the local poison control center in Santee. The source was traced back to a recipe for slow-cooked jalapeno blueberry-encrusted capon, Josilyn's signature dish (page thirty-five of the *League Cookbook*). Turns out that the cooking temperature of that God-awful capon was much too low to fully cook the dish, but just enough to incubate botulism.

"How's our career in cooking, Josilyn? You didn't do the catering here today, did you?"

"That was five years ago! It wasn't my fault! Besides, how did you ever hear of it?"

"Josilyn, I live in New York, not Albania."

"So what brought you back," she said, trying to regain her composure. "The reading of the will?" She adjusted her dress and her attitude and moved on.

"Good one, Josilyn. You've gotten right to the point. Um...no," I shot back. "My father's funeral brought me back. But how could I pass up seeing my illustrious aunts, uncles, and cousins at this momentous occasion? Don't you people ever die?"

"Not often, dear," she snapped.

I saw that my cousin hadn't held up well over the years. Josilyn Benoit aged much differently than anyone in my immediate family, especially my sister. Where Madeline had grown into her style and captured a surety of speech and step, Josilyn had taken what was and withered, soured, and grown into a narrower version of herself, a pinched sort of Bible-Belt narrowness.

"How are the kids?" I decided I would ask everyone that, after the mild success I'd had with Cornelius. I wanted to deflect their attention with no requirement to give up anything of myself. I never paid attention to the answer. I didn't find it necessary.

Josilyn was married to a man of French derivation, Christian Benoit, from the Bayou in Louisiana. His family had festered there since the late 1700s. He was a smooth talker who wove a web of big prospects, partnerships, and benefits to the family—ours, not hers. While we resisted his less-than-tantalizing offers, Josilyn spawned three children with this man—Bennet, Barbara, and Bettilyn. You could stammer and still get their names right. And, they begat and begat and begat in biblical proportions, creating little towns of close-eyed relatives with low IQs, living in tin houses, in rooms lined up like the wheels of inline skates, plopped at the edge of a section of Greyhaven property closed by the Feds because of the pollution. Somehow it didn't affect them. Thousands of split levels abandoned, in shades of puce and pomegranate, because children were born either defective or dead. It didn't affect them.

"We're not dead yet. We're going to stay around until we get our share. And we want it soon."

Josilyn became a widow four years earlier, after Christian died selling used cars off Route 95. He managed to sell a Cadillac Seville to a local drug enforcer who discovered a stash of heroin, worth a half-million dollars, under a false bottom of the trunk. The discovery made the papers, since the bill of sale was a forgery and Christian wouldn't reveal how he took possession of the car (or six others on his lot, for that matter). The car's true owner, one Billy Russet, a drug dealer whose name would not be mentioned by anyone for fear of reprisals, had been missing the drugs and the car for months. Josilyn surmised that Billy had read about the used car scandal in the newspaper and decided to seek the money for the drugs from Christian. To this day, Christian turns up piece by piece when area farmers till the land or construction crews break ground for new developments. Billy was never linked to Christian's disappearance or the drugs, but he did get his car back.

"You want your share. Share of what? This mess?" I paced around the library as if caged. "What share? You want the house, these books, this coffin? What? Look around you. Haven't you noticed the decay, the shadows left on the walls and the ghosts remaining on the tables of things gone? Or, do you hold such animus for my family that you can't see that things have changed? What am I saying? Why am I having this conversation yet again with you? You have no hold on us. We went through this before I left, and ten years before that, and ten years before that. It's cyclical with you people, like pestilence and disease. You keep assaulting and we keep winning. The will and the deed restriction stood up in court three times and it stands today. First male born of the last owner, not the relative, is the rightful heir, you persistent little gnome."

"You keep sayin' that, but you know we will win," Josilyn said, becoming riled. "If we persist, and we will, I know we will get something!"

"You want a piece of this? I'll tell you what. Cornelius and I will send you a bill for the debt that you helped us incur. How's that?"

"Cheese and crackers! That's all you ever yap about, the debt. You don't know what's been going on here," she said.

*Cheese and crackers* was Josilyn's way of substitution to sidestep taking the Lord's name in vain.

"Oh, for God's sakes, just say it! Jesus Christ! Say *Jesus Christ*, not fucking *cheese and crackers!*"

It always annoyed the living hell out of me that Josilyn could despise people and their lives out loud, condemning their very breath exhaled, and yet be unable to say the name of her distant notion of the God she championed. All this fed to her by a small-town minister in a shark-skin suit, bought with her pennies, so she could have a place of superiority in her life. She disliked wealth, she disliked color, she disliked difference. She eventually even disliked the French. I was not at all surprised by that. Josilyn easily despised all creatures on this planet, grouping them according to a single facet of their lives, not connecting God to the creations, but various *sins* to His offspring. She could devise a way to hate difference, reasoning choice not random selection, as told to her in a snippet of a Bible verse.

The messenger, her purchased minister, spewed these conjured and manipulated words through the airwaves, like a lightning bolt, piercing molecules of air grabbing onto and traveling down her antenna attached to the tin box in which she lived, rusting precariously on the edge of a precipice of a notion that she held onto in desperation, fighting for the rights to someone else's life. That was always and still is my cousin, Josilyn Benoit, and her minister, the Reverend Ray Blacksol.

"Don't you talk to me that way," she said. "We see 'em. Even Reverend Ray and Bettilyn see the bulldozers, and the payloaders, too. We all see 'em. They come at night and work till the sun cracks a rip. You're up to something. So don't pull this…this crap…oh, my God!"

She made the sign of the cross at the sound of her own harsh words.

"Aha! You said *crap*," I exalted. "A little bit of humanity just slipped out of those tight lips. When are you going to just let it rest and take care of that brood of yours, maybe even spend some time raising money for Reverend Ray, so he can move the congregation out of the trailer that you all spend Sundays roasting in and praising God. Oh, wait, you *live* in one of those, don't you?"

She was smart enough to recognize sarcasm and swung at me. I ducked, and Josilyn slammed her hand on the bindings of *The Complete*

*Works of William Shakespeare*, which sat at attention, neglected, on the shelves of this tomb. The books hadn't been touched since my great grandfather put them there, and now one volume lay in brittle pieces on the floor.

"You know, Josilyn, maybe if you spent less time with Reverend Ray, your husband wouldn't have been hanging around those special blocks in Charleston looking for 'a little.' Such a shame he died wantin' some."

"At least he wanted *women*!" Josilyn went for my throat. She was tiny, but she packed a wallop, especially when she drank too many toasts to the dead. We fell to the floor and performed for my father yet again. Not an unfamiliar scene, it repeated itself at family functions, public meetings, outside courtrooms, everywhere, over the years, so the solemnity of this occasion never would dissuade Josilyn from these emotional calisthenics.

"What the hell is going on here?" It was Madeline.

She stood in the doorway, hand high on the edge of the French doors, looking quite Audrey Hepburn in Chanel sunglasses. "For Christ's sake, Josilyn, when did you start wrestlin' on dry land? I always thought you needed a mud hole and an audience."

Josilyn stood up as if caught by her mother. "Y'all will never change. I hate you and this house and that…that *man* lying there."

She spat freely into the air, trying to hit everything and everyone she despised. "You won't get away with this, I promise you! My family is just as connected to this land and its business as you. We are blood and you have been horrible to us. Reap what you sow!"

"Speaking of sew my dear," Madeline called out to Josilyn as she bolted, "it's time someone told you. You need to stop making your own clothes or make 'em bigger. Memory is not a good mannequin for fashion, dear."

Josilyn's face reddened with a mixture of embarrassment and rage. She left dust in her wake as she stormed out of the room, the house, and the drive, never stopping, mumbling about revenge, religion, faggots, and damnation. Her family lined up in unison behind her, like ducklings following the butt end of a waddle, and disappeared.

"You really need to bone up on your people skills, darling," Madeline said, smoothing her hair and her dress. We both looked on after Josilyn to make sure she was gone, and then burst out laughing, falling against the bookshelves, each of us remembering the resentment that had come at us from every direction like cluster bombing. It would have felt empty and lacking that special familial animosity without it. I then turned serious.

"Josilyn blurted out something about bulldozers. What bulldozers, Madeline?" I noticed that she wore more rouge than earlier. On closer inspection, it hid a bruise on her left cheek.

"What happened to you?" I held her chin and touched the raw spot that summoned the past.

"I told you, later, darling." She pulled away, adjusted her glasses, and turned. "Cousin Althea, Ray, there you are! Don't you look positively precious in those matching shirts!"

She nodded at me and was gone, lost in a pool filled with piranha, swimming strong.

I stayed in the library to compose myself and clean up the mess of Shakespeare on the floor and noticed that more than a book had fallen from the shelf. An envelope lay in the heap of high English debris. It was addressed to Cornelius Madigan and written in Mother's handwriting. I placed the envelope in my pocket and headed out. Cornelius met me at the door of the room,

"What's going on? I watched Josilyn and her faction pull up stakes like the Confederate retreat."

"I don't want to do this, Cornelius. There are too many layers to get through. Josilyn told me about the bulldozers, and connecting that to Madeline's little confession earlier, oh, and just out of curiosity, Cornelius, what did you do to Madeline?

"It wasn't time for you to know."

"So you hit her?"

"What are you talking about?" It was a badly played response.

"Don't even try it. You hit her for telling me. I know, and not just because she told me, this time." Cornelius was silent. "You've done this continually to her, and you think that I don't know."

I swung at him, hitting his jaw with an open hand. His face reddened, not so much for the strike but the humiliation. The shot stunned him for a moment and then he struck, grabbing my lapels and pushing me up against the books.

"Don't think for a moment that you know what's going on or, for that matter, that you can get in my way. As for Madeline, we have developed a more, how do I say, *energetic* relationship over the years. Don't worry, she gets in her share of the hits before the bell sounds."

He whispered so close to my face that I felt the moisture of his words. "It is what we do, how we communicate."

He looked me in the eyes and then up and down as he pinned me to the books. "Listen to me right. I've taken care of bigger problems with a lot less bother and even less remorse." He composed himself and smoothed out my lapels, and gave me a little push. "You've been gone for too long to be of any concern to me. Complicate matters and I'll make sure that you become a fond memory. 'Dear Uncle Faustus always sent great gifts.'"

"You're threatening me?"

"Be sure of this: it's not a threat. But..." He paused and started to carefully scan the books as if suddenly interested in their arrangement, "...know this, Brother, the land *is* opening up again. Get in our way this time, and you will not be able to run." He turned his full attention toward me. "I will hunt you down. Better yet, if I sense any inkling of a problem, I am going to be a lot more proactive than I was twenty-five years ago. I couldn't get old Titus here to do what was necessary. He didn't listen to reason back then. But now, guess what? No problem. He loved you, though I don't know why. He got spineless as he got older. Wouldn't listen to reason. Now it's my turn." Cornelius looked around again. "I really should go through these books," he said as he left. "I bet that there is some value here."

He was gone. I took a minute to recapture my composure in the security of the shadows and the silence. When the air settled, I walked over to the casket to take a last look at Titus for the day. "What have you done? Couldn't you see that some people are just not meant to be breeders?"

I joined the *party*.

# 4

THEY CONGREGATED everywhere but in the library. In the salon to sit, commiserate, and drink; in the entry, to stay near an exit; in the dining room, to scoff down free food. My bloodline stood before me, some successful, most not. They congregated in the steamy stillness around the house. The summer heat added a mist that slowed the pace down to a crawl; even the sound dragged in an exaggerated southern drawl. They all fit in this caricature of a place, tattered, elegant, timeless. The brocade and the accolades touched each other with the raised glasses and hands of the Bible Belt fringe, the lost, and the successful.

In the midst of varying degrees of insanity stood my father's two sisters, Hannabelle and Matilda, still alive at eighty-five and eighty-three. Matilda had married a philanderer, James Arbis Thaniel, in the grand tradition of this family. Moderately successful in the lumber business, he had long-standing affairs with women local to him. He never ventured far, an economy of movement. He continually tried to keep hidden from Matilda his other life, but she knew of his dalliances and the humiliation kept her stoic, loud, and the center of her world. Josilyn, her only child, became estranged from her immediately after her marriage to Christian, in part because of this stoicism and, in part, because she had inherited her father's lack of regard for this little woman. Matilda never said a disparaging word about her daughter or her grandchildren, the three Bs. Connected to them by spirit if not by presence, she created her own mythical world of connection, though she was despised by her daughter.

Hannabelle, the quiet one, was the elder sister. She had tended to their mother for as far back as I could remember. She kept the secrets of the last generation. The service vehicle to the war ships at play in this skirmish, she listened, held confidences, and never denied her assistance to anyone provided it was for benign purposes only. Not an educated woman, she had a sophisticated radar for both good and evil, knew the difference, and never crossed the line for anyone. The wisest of the lot, she never married, knowing that little good would be done by furthering the line.

Marcus, the younger brother to my father, held court at the buffet table in the dining room. He and his wife, both 80, stood there from the minute the doors had opened and wasn't going to leave 'til the closing bell rang. He mingled with his ten children, their wives, and thirty-odd indistinguishable grandchildren.

All of Marcus' children and grandchildren filled the balance of the categories that a county generally encompasses. Since there were enough lawyers, merchants, and gas jockeys to go around, they generously filled out the balance of thieves, charlatans, and scoundrels. All, except for one, Marcus' fourth son, Nasby Worthinton Madigan. Nasby took advantage of US Marine discipline, rose to colonel, and left with a full pension. He studied to be a mortician, ultimately opening a funeral parlor in Parner's Green, about fifty miles west of Santee. He tended to my father's remains. He stood on the main staircase as I walked toward the salon. Nasby gently scanned the crowd, perusing the scene, separate and away, like Cornelius.

"Hey, Nasby."

"Hey, back at ya!" Always affable, he raised his glass, bourbon, not sour mash. He had his standards and his prejudices.

"You made it. Cornelius said he wasn't sure that you were coming. I'm glad to see you." Nasby shook my hand and smiled gently. I remember as a child that he had more reserve than the rest of his brood. He married and divorced, early, having one daughter, always troubled, as he was. His demons were kept close and bottled, coming out only when drunk through plaintiff phone calls to the rest of the clan, asking for acceptance, love, understanding, or all three.

"I assume you prepared Titus?" I started to fish.

"Yes, everything meet with your approval?"

"Well, don't take this personal, but he looks like day-old bread. Know anything about it?"

"There is a chain of command, you know," Nasby explained. "Why don't you start at the top?"

"I understand that we'll be having a meeting tonight?" A strong possibility existed that he would be there. I gambled that he knew.

"Yup, at twenty-one-hundred hours." His military training never let him tell time like us.

"Great, see you then." I walked away ticking my cheek and raising my thumb. I had no drink to raise but desperately needed one at that moment.

Cornelius attached himself early to the bartender in the salon. He was instructed to constantly search out my brother's glass and keep it full. I bellied up to the bar next to him and caught the tender's attention and, hopefully, Cornelius'.

"Scotch, neat." I turned to Cornelius, "Truce?"

"Sure, at what price?" he asked, not turning his head.

"That's my line. So we *are* related." I tried to lighten the mood.

"We're twins, how lucky for us," he said, more dryly than the pour of his martini.

"Yes, how lucky for us."

Mission impossible. Nothing could change. I always felt that he wanted the eggs and sperm that created the both of us all to himself.

"So, what's the meeting about?"

"Well, if you must know now," Cornelius laid out the plan, "we need to discuss the future of Greyhaven."

"I'm actually glad we're doing this tonight. The faster we get it done, the faster I can return to New York."

"So, you *will* be going back, right?" This felt too exploratory. There was no question that I wanted to get out of this hell as soon a s possible, but at this moment, I smelled the blood of insecurity thicken. I wanted Cornelius to feel as unsure and tentative as I had felt on my first day back home, so I adjusted my position.

"Most likely. I bought an open-ended ticket, though, just in case. It's been a tough year in Manhattan with the Twin Towers coming down and all."

"That must've been something. Nothing like that happens here," Cornelius said. I didn't want to admit to him I still felt safer there than here.

"I saw the planes hit the Towers from my window at Vastigone," I wanted him to know. "After seeing that, you can handle anything, y'know?"

"I imagine you could." He spoke to me in automatic pilot, a game we played. He knew I was ready for anything.

"So, after the rough landing here, I may need a few extra days," I lied. Truth was, I could steal Addie, leave now, and never look back. But, at this moment, I was ready to turn the table and get inside this mess in a hurry.

We are twins and that means that we share the land portion of the estate. He needed me to be compliant as much as I needed him to be kinder and gentler. He, however, held the notion that possession is nine-tenths of the law. He was here; I, in New York. Cornelius banked on me, and the miles between us, to give him the home court advantage. Madeline kept me up to date and what I didn't learn from her, I learned from Addie, including some corrections. Still, to be a contender in this family, especially with Cornelius here, twenty-four seven was the order of the day.

"I always thought that you couldn't be pried away from Wall Street."

"Actually, Wall Street is becoming claustrophobic. All that fake ticker tape and those smart suits rebuilding their lives and careers. I'm feeling a bit of a change coming on. Maybe for my fiftieth birthday I'll treat myself to a new career and a climate change. Those long winters are starting to get under my skin. Perhaps something warmer is in order. What do you think, Cornelius?"

"I think we both have been drinking too much. When we sober up, life will begin again, and we'll continue as we were, twins controlling the Eastern seaboard."

I viewed Cornelius' attempt at humor a poor cover for the beginning of a negotiation at the bar, in front of Dionysius, and the tender, an unwitting witness, to our separate resolves.

Then I realized what he'd said about controlling the Eastern seaboard. I had heard it before; it felt familiar. And then I remembered that it was what my father had said when he told us the story of Adlai Morrisette, his business partner. It was the same phrase that Adlai had said to Titus, during the Great Depression, while they devoured stocks of underestimated companies that had survived the crash.

"We'll buy up every stock of value, Titus, and we'll control the Eastern seaboard by the end of the next decade," Titus would tell us in a tone mimicking Adlai's fervor and drama as he sat in the library, the drifts of smoke from his tobacco pipe curling through his silver hair and the books. We'd watch him for hours, sitting there, telling us with a glimmer how the man he'd called friend and confidant would spin his tale of fortunes and dynasties and convince him to weave the legacy with him. This personality trait existed in many of the people around Titus. He needed them to be that way, and he chose them deliberately for that trait so they would react to his satisfaction, and he would respond, in kind, by making them feel as if *they* were the movers and shakers. He would grow richer by their energy and, in return, earn their gratitude. This was a bond almost greater than family.

Fond memories—only a glimpse—faded quickly. And, there I was, negotiating life once again with Cornelius. Time melted in between skirmishes—thirty years, thirty minutes. I looked up at the statue holding court in the salon and prayed to the god of wine and song to let the games begin and to let me be the victor.

"Return to New York?" I said with exaggerated pause. "We'll see."

"Bartender!" Cornelius nervously switched gears. "Two more drinks for these thirsty twins!"

"Y'all are twins?" The bartender blurted in innocent surprise. He didn't understand the arena in which he was working. "I never would have guessed it."

# 5

THROUGHOUT THE DAY, toast after toast filled the air touting the marvels, kindnesses, and excesses of Titus' life, all the public statements, measured, and predictable. It was the undercurrent and the spaced breathing that gave the real tone of the afternoon. No one mentioned the premature death of Ivinia, Mother. No one connected their souls or their reunion in the great beyond. No one toasted their lives together or the children of that union. No one but Madeline.

"As a special honor to my parents," Madeline raised her gimlet with a less-than-steady arm, spilling it down her limb like a dribble fountain in our gardens out back, "…and this illustrious family, I am penning a tome to document our history." The buzz of voices increased as if a swarm of African killer bees had just landed. "I have spoken to my publisher," she slurred, "and he is very excited by my transition to adult novels. We've already planned the marketing, and I've submitted the first chapter roughs." As if that wasn't enough, she critiqued it herself. "It's gonna be a humdinger! You're all going to be in it…my nearest and dearest!"

Madeline staggered and lost her balance as she raised her glass a second time. She had not eaten anything and her sugar level was out of control. The revelation of the book signaled the end of the funeral reception. Every face blanched white and, in locked step, the lot of them headed for the door.

Marcus was the last to leave, with a chicken bone hanging out of his mouth, pockets filled with cornbread and Sweet 'N Low packets.

Harris entered as everyone was leaving and as his Madeline fell into the potted palm tree near the bar. He ran to his wife's aid.

"Madeline! Are you alright?" He picked her up gently. "Madeline...honey." His was a practiced motion.

"This happens every time I'm gone and she's surrounded by too much family." His face reddened. "Cornelius, I asked you to watch her." Harris's words slipped out buttered and easy, the smoothest of our familial drawls. His style was impeccably Southern. Even his trousers never wrinkled behind those linen-covered knees.

"I lost track of her." Cornelius turned to the barman. "I'm sorry I don't know your name."

"My name's Rick."

"Richard, would you see if there are any dirty glasses in the other rooms, please?" Cornelius turned toward Harris in moderate disinterest. "I got busy."

"You were busy alright. Busy drinking!" Harris was furious. "Is there ever a time that martinis are not appropriate? Faustus, help me get her to the divan." Harris and I carried Madeline to the sofa.

"I guess they don't like my idea of a book. Well...fuck 'em." She slurred, swinging an arm.

"Yes, dear." Harris tried to placate her. "She can think of little else lately, ever since she had this night sweat of an idea. It took her less than two weeks to write the outline and send it to her publisher."

"Harris, no one told me." Cornelius adjusted his cravat. "Aren't we concerned about the exposure and the implications?" Cornelius leaned against the bar in an unfamiliar, relaxed stance.

"No, Cornelius, I'm not," Harris said in Madeline's defense. "She won't expose anything that isn't already out there. Besides, the stuff that you're afraid of wouldn't make for a good novel. It would be too unbelievable."

"And who will be the judge of that?" Cornelius dead-eyed Harris.

"For Christ's sake, Cornelius, I'm living this shit and I don't believe it. And, like I said, it's a fucking novel. She's just using this family as the character base; the rest is made up." Harris said it, but even I didn't believe it.

"You know the lines get blurry," Cornelius countered.

"Fiction, remember?" Harris reminded Cornelius of Madeline's literary strengths. "You know her better than that. She was just yankin' their chain. They deserve it."

Harris ran to the kitchen, removed Madeline's insulin from the refrigerator, and gave her a shot that was always at the ready.

"Good, I knew I could count on you to control her." Cornelius left the room.

"Welcome back, Faust." Harris said, looking up at me.

"Yeah, it's been such fun, so far. Where the hell were you?"

"I had several private meetings with some Feds in Chicago." Harris threw around the legalese. "I was up there pow-wowin' with a Contam Swat Team from OSHA."

"A what?"

"Oh sorry, I forgot a…civilian." Harris glimmered around his insider talk. "It's an 'in the field' team that investigates toxic clean-ups and inspects superfund sites around the country, along with suspected new ones. The site in Chicago needed a quick remediation before the land could be developed. They dispatched the team."

"And you know them how?"

"Ahhh, a little politics and a little elbow to elbow with the right people. You know, the DNA of who knows who. Anyway, the agents compelled me to fly out and meet with them to, I sensed, put out feelers about our project, 'cause it's high on their list of destinations to visit."

"Ah, yes. I keep hearing little tidbits about *our project*. It's high on *their* list?"

"Yeah, we've been making noise for quite some time and they want to get to the smoke before the fire gets too big, if ya catch my pitch. And…" he paused for effect, "greasing the wheels with pre-emptive information puts them at ease." Harris paused again, looking up from his insulin jab site. "It was important to provide that ease."

"This redevelopment is a lot more along than I imagined," I said, looking at Madeline with a changing eye. "How'd you get a meeting in Chicago for them to review it?"

"Remember Wilcox?"

"Our congressman turned horse breeder?" It brought back a flood of memories about Madeline's unfortunate encounter with T.K. Tinsdale—the Sweet-Sixteen rape and a partnership in a horse-breeding business between our family and the congressman in an attempt to thank him for the favor of quietly eliminating an unwanted pregnancy.

"His son's a representative now. I got hold of him and he pulled a few strings at the EPA, found out who would be the best team to deal with. And lo and behold a new mall was necessary where some undeciphered waste had been bubblin' up for a few years. Arsenic is such lovely colored ooze. So does this sound at all familiar?"

"You mean there are other places where they bury chemical secrets?" My sarcasm was never wasted on Harris.

"Funny. Anyway, I brought them copies of the legal briefs, only selected shorts of course, and the engineer's report on some of the locations of the intensities. Turns out OSHA was in Chicago because a few metal workers on site were using torches and the dirt caught on fire. Can you believe it?"

"Oh, I believe it, because I saw it right here." I remembered the fire and the destruction caused by a Sunday afternoon barbecue by one of the owners of a house in Greyhaven Gardens years earlier. An overuse of lighter fluid had left four injured—one fatally. "Doesn't explain how you got the call, Harris."

"Their union called them in. One of their delegates used to be a liaison to my office in Santee. I hit a double; both of them there."

"Well, Harris, you certainly pulled off a coup."

"Yeah, fuck man, I did!" He was caught up in the adrenaline of the score, the rush of the competition, making the machine pump and whine smoothly.

"You showed them everything?"

"The hell, I did! I rented an eighteen-wheeler in Charleston, dragged the shit up to Chicago, and loaded up a warehouse on Jane Street with fourteen-hundred boxes of what they thought were briefs from the trials, meeting transcripts, the background research, everything."

"What do you mean 'what they thought'?"

"Wait, wait, listen. So, the 'paper' was only a few blocks away from where they were holed up in the Marriot."

"Coincidence, no doubt?"

"There are no such things as coincidences, only well-planned manipulations."

"Wilcox, I assume?"

"Yeah, Junior again. He got the info from the travel agency that the bureau uses. So, I checked in and casually ran into them again at the bar. Five of them. Had a few drinks. Two of them, grainy veterans, remembered the case and the findings, but only vaguely. I got them to agree to look at some of the paper. It's amazing what flipping for some drinks and Buffalo wings can do."

"You brought everything there for them to see?"

"You don't think I'd risk bringing all of the information, do you?"

"I guess not," I admonished myself.

"I brought the most benign info, and thirteen-hundred and seventy-five boxes of empty paper."

"You've got to be kidding? Why would you ship empty paper to Chicago?"

"The devil's in the details, Faust. You know that. You need to cover the money and the tracks. Remember, the trail has to lead from here, not Chicago. If I had arrived in Chicago empty handed, and all of a sudden the paper was there, eventually it would raise a question. Following the money buries the tracks. I kept everything here in rented storage. Even went through the motions of emptying the warehouse here."

"Why would you risk them seeing empty paper?"

"Do you really think that they were going to go through all that shit? They're government employees, for God's sakes! When they saw the warehouse and the stacks of boxes, they asked if the info was on disk. I said that the original transcripts were from the seventies, so it is all transcribed, typed, and shorthanded. I played 'em, Faust. They opened a few boxes and basically read several first sentences and last paragraphs. They saw what they were up against and, even if they could, they weren't going back to their offices to dig up and dust off the old microfiche."

"'Even if they could'?"

"Faust, some big corporate man you are! You know that the best technology available was microfiche. Platform shoes, select type typewriters, and microfiche. There were big, crude computers but they were not available to many government agencies. Thank God for bureaucratic red tape and political infighting. By the time a reasonable technology was available, all the trails and the case were over.

"Weren't there fax machines then?

"Yeah, they had 'em, again infancy of fax technology, but you know what happens to thermal fax?

"Oh yeah." I remembered from Vastigone's archives. "It turns yellow, then brown, then voila, it disappears. Oh, my God. It disappears!"

"Right. It disappears. And even if there was someone there who was integral to the case, it would all be a memory thing, and the memories worth worrying about are all retired or dead. So guess what? They want me to get all this on disk. I told them that it was a tremendous job, but with a little time I thought we could accomplish it."

"Why would you endeavor to convert all of that stuff? It's too damaging."

"Not all of the info will make it to disk. Don't forget, some the rules are different now. There is precedence for what we are doing, Faust."

"Precedence for all of it?"

"Well, for some of it. The rest, well…we…how do I say… adjust."

I sat there, not believing what I was hearing. I thought I knew Harris. I thought that the things that his family went through were enough to keep him simple and unencumbered. I was wrong. Suddenly, Madeline was held with different hands, hands I didn't know, hands Mother knew better, hands Mother banked on, gambled on, and cashed in on.

We sat there, Harris and I, speaking of old deeds and new intrigues while Madeline slept off her sugar rush, awash in newly installed insulin. She stirred.

"Hi, Harris. Honey, when did you get here?" Then she turned dazedly to me and tried to adjust her vision. "Faust, darling. My two favorite men, how lucky for me!"

"Are you feeling better, dear?" Harris stroked Madeline's head in a protective motion, established slowly over the years.

"I had a wonderfully fascinating dream, Harris." Madeline stared beyond. "I dreamt that I grabbed Father by the shoulders and begged him to tell me why he married Mother and why he stayed with her. He just smiled at me and turned away."

"Okay, Madeline, just rest a bit, it'll pass." Harris fussed over her, supporting her need to be perfect at all times.

"Yeah, Father turned away and then Elvis appeared in his batwinged and glittered pantsuit and we had fried chicken and sex on a leopard skin carpet in the den in his house in Memphis." She focused her eyes on Harris. "Sorry, Harris...only in my dreams." As she faded, Madeline reached to touch Harris on the cheek, studying him as if the typography of his skin had changed. Cornelius returned to survey the damage.

"I'm leaving for a while. Y'all will have this under control?" Cornelius spoke of the scene as if it was a highway accident and he was due at the precinct to write the report.

"Yeah, it's fine. Go ahead," Harris off-handed Cornelius. "Come on, Faust, let's get her up to her room and we'll all take a break, okay?"

"Fine with me, Harris!" I grabbed Madeline's shoulder and helped him carry her upstairs.

I hadn't seen her room in as long as I could remember. It reflected a mood that was deliberately orchestrated but never lived up to in real life. The wallpaper sung its tune in the sweetest, softest pink. I recalled one of the stories that Madeline wrote and published, *A Mother's Promise*, that explained the story of her room. It was about a princess and her good Queen Mother who gave her daughter a birthday gift of building– a play castle with towers and moats, maidens in waiting, and knights in shining armor to protect her. It had pop-up pictures and colorful characters.

In real life, Mother had promised Madeline that, for her sixteenth birthday, they would go down to Charleston and pick out everything for her new room with Barbara Johns Fieldston, the society decorator that Mother had used, so that her room would be done for her coming out party. The way Madeline tells it, she had picked out a very bright shade of purple flowers with a moss green stripe behind it, quite bold but in an English way. Madeline said that Mother argued with her for hours over the paper. Truth is, Madeline fought for the wallpaper as much for the fact that Mother had hated it. Mother rose to her very persuasive anger but it did not move Madeline, who'd argued that Mother had promised that she could pick it out herself.

Seeing this, Barbara had taken Madeline aside and showed her lovely pink silk wallpaper with little delicate flowers on it. She'd spread the silk out all over her showroom in a very grand way, telling Madeline what could be done with other fabrics, the new furniture pieces, and paint. Then Barbara had told her a little story about how her own mother and she had had the same argument, but that her mother had said that she would have this paper a long time and it would be there through her growing up, her changes, her joys, and her sorrows. It would be there during many boyfriends and birthdays, many Christmases and New Year's. She had then asked Madeline again which paper she would pick for Barbara if it were reversed and Madeline was helping her. It was the pink silk with the little flowers. Barbara Johns Fieldston had become the Goodly Queen Mother and her staff, the other oddly whimsical characters in the story—the guards, the maidens, and the knights. It was magic woven from the threads of a much more tenuous and tragic existence because, in actuality, Mother had refused to decorate the room after all. After the skirmish in front of Society's Decorator and Gossip, the argument had dragged its way from Charleston to home.

"You won't listen to me, will you? Embarrass me in front of Barbara! She is everyone's decorator. The news will travel so fast it will probably get back to our staff before we even set foot in the door. I will be the laughing stock of the season."

"You already are..." Madeline hadn't even finished that sentence and the next thing she knew she was looking for a tooth in the backseat of the car. We'd hunted for it the next day, she and I. We'd giggled about how Mother would have to wear gloves instead of jewelry for the next week because, we surmised that Madeline's teeth marks had been imprinted on the back of her hand. Madeline wasn't sure whose blood she'd spat out, hers or Mother's. As it turned out, after the argument and the missing tooth passed, Mother still wasn't done. She'd had the paperhangers tear off the old wallpaper, hanging nothing in its place and leaving

Madeline's room in a tattered mess.

Addie, hearing of this, had convinced Father that Madeline's room should be repaired and redone. Redeemed from Mother's rage and vindictiveness, it was then that I knew Addie looked after me. She'd understood my need to protect Madeline. She'd also known that protecting Madeline comforted me. Father then went to Barbara Fieldston and purchased everything. Even so, Madeline had been devastated by the hurt and disappointment. It was then that she had her first insulin episode.

We didn't see Father or Addie for days afterwards. They had to go to Memphis to check on the progress of the building of an industrial site we owned in partnership with Adlai Morrisette, another venture with my father's closest friend and partner. Mother had seethed in anger because of the end run, and had punished Madeline for the loss of this round and the overall competition. But it would not matter to Madeline; the contest quieted and this round had ended, with Madeline victorious. However, Mother's resentment had simmered for being unable to punish the one she wanted to punish. Addie was above reproach.

Harris and I brought Madeline to her bed. Gently, Harris took her from me and laid her down. We silently left her protected in the pink of the Goodly Queen Barbara and walked downstairs.

"We'll wake her up before the meeting. Do you remember where the coffee is? I want to make a pot."

"Butler's pantry, I think." If time really stopped after I left, that's where it would be.

"How do you take it?"

"Come on, Faust, I like my bourbon neat and my coffee black."

"Harris, what's this meeting about?"

"You know Cornelius. He controls everything around him."

"*Everything*, Harris?" I was no longer sure of this.

"For the most part." There was a hesitation in his voice that was palpable. I reached up to the top shelf for the coffee, almost without looking. It was there as if it had made its own choice not to change. As I stretched, the letter from Mother to Cornelius dropped from my coat pocket.

"You dropped something, Faust." Harris reached down to pick it up. "What's this?"

"Nothing special, Harris. Just a letter that fell out of one of the books in the library."

"It's addressed to Cornelius."

"Yeah, I forgot about it with all the commotion going on."

"What is it?"

"I don't know; it's not mine,"

"Open the goddam letter, Faust."

I needed Harris to be complicit in *our* inquisitiveness. I ripped at the yellowed envelope.

"It's just some pages from a...Bible?"

"Any handwriting on them?"

"No, just the pages.

"Where from?"

"Let's see. Looks like Genesis...um...chapters 16 and 17." Out of the corner of my eye I glimpsed some writing on one side of the pages and avoided showing it to Harris.

"Well, Ivinia was getting a little crazy toward the end." I was successful in the camouflage, and Harris went on. "She ranted and raved at the slightest provocation, sometimes without provocation." Harris reminisced, simultaneously filling in the holes created by my absence.

"Dare I ask this, Harris, but why was there only a memorial service for Mother?"

"What else can you do when there's no body?"

"No body? Mother was presumed dead?"

"I thought you knew." Harris looked caught with his hand in the cookie jar. His blood rushed to his face.

"I just assumed you all decided that she was largely hated, so 'let's skip the formalities.'"

"No, Faust, she disappeared," He looked around as he said it, though no one was there.

"Disappeared?"

"In the last year of her life, she wandered around. Turned up in some of the strangest places. We even found her in one of the vacant split levels on Bradburn Court. Actually, it was the one owned by Ardent Huxley. You know, the guy who owns the cab service here."

"That's right! I had forgotten that he moved in after he got married to Rosalie Charmers. That explains the rough cab ride from the airport," I said.

"Didn't he lose a child while he lived there?"

"Yeah. Leukemia, I think. Sad. One of twelve in a ten-block cluster."

Harris continued. "Anyway, she was digging in the backyard with her bare hands. Wouldn't tell us why. We looked around and found nothing. We assumed she was just off her rocker. Then one day...gone. We dragged Back Bay the next morning...but nothing. Found her shawl a few nights later by the inlet behind the house."

"Why didn't someone tell me the truth? Why did everyone tell me that she died in a car accident?"

"That was Cornelius' decision, I guess." He seemed to hedge. "Sorry, I didn't pay much mind to those details. Come on, are you surprised that he controlled everything and everyone?"

I didn't buy the reiteration.

"Besides, what was the point? She disappeared. Gone. The reasons don't matter, well, at least not to Cornelius. Just the result. Besides, it's not like you cared about her."

"Wow. Very lawyerly, Harris. Stiletto to the heart."

"Sorry, Faust. Automatic," he apologized.

"I cared, Harris, but I needed to care for Mother at a distance. Ivinia rarely acknowledged my existence and was not the least bit saddened by my departure. In actuality, quite the reverse. She made sure the trust stopped paying me. I received money from Titus. Did you know that?"

"Really?"

"Yeah. Never saw it coming. It just appeared in my checking account. Titus never wanted to discuss it when we spoke. I tried to confirm it was Titus, but the bank had the information sealed and it would take too many of you lawyer types to open the privacy seal. So I let it go. It appeared every month like clockwork, and I needed it.

"Money. The great motivator." Harris set the tone of justifiable actions. "I guess I'm connected to this family after all, aren't I?"

"Yeah, by a gene or two," We clinked our coffee cups as the tall-case clock in the hall struck five.

# 6

THE TRAIN WHISTLE blew its sound in the distance. It had announced seven o'clock for as long as I could remember. The stillness on the veranda forever captured me. Pushing against the curve of the rocker, the tempo of the day slowed to the fading clang of the metal wheels against the tracks. Chechung…chechung…chechung. Back and forth I moved and the air resisted me, like velvet brushing my cheek. It was complete.

I felt the magic the gloaming brings to the South that makes window panes glimmer pink gold, that makes dogs forget to bark, that reminds all creatures to pause and pay reverence to creation. That moment when all things slip slowly from sight. In the distance, green to russet, then russet to black against an intensely iridescent copper sky, the edges of the trees turning in a quiet tumble of fading color. Whether we claimed our inheritance or not, whether we drew another breath, this would exist, beyond us, without us. This silent transformation purifies the twist of what men do, laying silent the struggle. It was a peace, for a moment, that told the story of the South.

I needed this time alone, away from my family. Madeline asleep in her room, Harris in the salon, on the phone designing the outline for battle. Everyone had a place here. Cornelius, picking up his wife at Memorial General, cautioned us to be assembled in the dining room promptly at nine.

"We have a lot to go over before tomorrow," he said. The business partners and their heirs, amassed over the years, would be paying their respects and feeling us out for information. Cornelius said it was "very important that we all be on the same page."

Thinking about all of this and looking at the sun descend over these complications, I yearned to see Addie. I couldn't wait 'til day after tomorrow to see her. I needed to see her right then. I ran around the back of the house, jumped into the service dingy that was tied to the mooring in the closest inlet to the house, and motored to Crumpet Island. I could have taken Towbridge Road over Back Bay, but making it known that I needed a car would have blown my cover. I wanted to slip away unnoticed and return the same way.

The motor hummed as I wended my way through the marsh, cutting through the brackish waters as much as through the thick twilight air, past the tar pits, past the tall grasses peaked with clouded plumes bursting at their tops as if they were the origins of the twilight mist. I passed where Mother's shawl was found, sitting in the same dingy under which Madeline had lost consciousness, her insulin, and her virginity. Quiet and still, this spot held its many secrets, so Southern and misted gray. Approaching Addie's house, my anticipation grew. I wondered how she had been since I had seen her last. Our time in New York seemed like so many years ago. I would stay just for a little while and be back before nine o'clock.

Approaching Crumpet Island, Addie's house peeked through the lush plantings of Bougainvillea, fan palm, wild rhododendron, and azalea. Built in the middle 1700s, it was the original house on the property prior to the main house, which was constructed in 1810. Crumpet Island got its name from the English. It was the first place in the region to bake English crumpets, the traditional flat muffin from the motherland. People came from as far away as Atlanta to buy the delicacy. The original bake house was incorporated into the living quarters when it was built. The house had a simple Palladian construct built on a split staircase. Known as a Low Country house, it was built high up because of frequent and sudden flooding, sweetly growing over the years, room by room, wing by wing, when needs changed, rambling organically as if grown out of nature's need to house. Painted the palest of yellows, it had dark green shutters accenting the window frames which were painted a shiny white.

The front door came into sight as I approached the dock. Painted a brilliant red, it reflected light and welcome and was guarded by two ornately carved stone pots filled with birds of paradise blooming bright orange and red. Standing perfectly crisp and neat, Addie's house glowed as the sun sank behind me. I docked the boat, climbed the stairs, and ran to the front door. Already opened, I entered the house and called out Addie's name.

"Addie. Momma, where are you?" I'd called her *Momma* from the beginning, as she had given us those things that our Mother could not attempt to offer.

Silence. I kept going, remembering the path to Momma's room. I'd run there so many times, whether it was to hide out for a while, or to watch her sew, or to listen to her weave her tales, conjuring up the spirits of her family late at night when the crickets beat the sound of their mating against the silence and the stories. Into the entry hall, I hurried through the living room, through the summer gathering room to the connecting gallery, then to Momma's bedroom.

"Momma. Addie?"

"Yes, dear?" It was her voice, fragile and soft, "I was expecting you." Her long silver-white hair glistened, reflecting the sunset. She didn't turn.

"You were running. How many times did we speak of the proper way to enter a home?" she instructed, a timeless routine, still facing the mirror. Her hair caught the light as she separated each strand, curled naturally into tiny ringlets as if woven with diamonds, brushing the ends into a fan, counting, "ninety-nine, and one-hundred. There, done." A ritual started by her mother some ninety years ago.

"I thought that I would never get to see you." She smiled through her clever guilting.

"I would have gotten here sooner, but it became a little complicated back there." I caught her profile. Its detail had not changed from the softness that I had remembered. Her skin, not black at all, but tanned, almost faded, like overly creamed coffee, wrinkled and folded in billowing swells and hollows, puffy and gentle, honoring the roadmap of age and the memory of her and me.

"I can well imagine. The Madigans are a complicated family." She turned and smiled at me and I became ten again, embracing the woman who had watched me grow, who had guarded and nurtured me. We embraced, and I felt her arms delicately around my neck and her hand on the back of my head. She kissed my cheek slowly. It was something that still comforted me. I was finally home. I sat next to her at her dressing table and she smiled at me.

"I have something for you," she said, as she rose from the bench at the dressing table and carefully pattered to her trousseau chest under the window that looked over to the main house.

She used deliberate, four-score and five-year-old steps, careful not to fall. Slowly leaning over, she opened the heavily carved wooden cover, leaning it against the lace curtains framing the view. Highly polished and rich in color, the carving depicted a mythical couple standing next to each other within a heart. She dug under her collection of quilts made by many generations of indentured and hired Greyhaven women. She pulled out a large, leather-covered book tooled in gold. It was bigger than she. She held it like a newborn and, gingerly placing it in my lap, almost tipped over before reaching me. My name was stamped on it. An ornate sterling silver picture frame, mellowed from polishing, sat embedded in the center of the cover. It framed a picture of me in a Christening gown, passed down from the first Madigan born on this property. I was held in two pairs of arms coming from either side of me. Cropped close, you could see the fineness of the lace that edged the embroidered vest coat and the long, hand-pleated silk under gown spilling to the floor. It was me. It was beautiful, preserved by the keeper of my history.

"I made this memory book for you, anticipating your birth. It's high time that you have it."

"That was a long time ago, Momma."

"Seems like yesterday." She paused for the tiniest of moments and looked down, lost in a page of her own memory. "Yes, over the years I filled it. I collected pictures, news clippings, school and graduation no- tices, everything. I want you to have it now. You need to remember some of the good things that you took from here. You left in such a hurry." Her eyes twinkled in a question.

"Momma, that was over twenty-five years ago!"

"Yes, I know, and it feels like a hundred. But, you know, y'all left a lot of good memories behind," she said, wistfully touching the edge of the book.

"Were there any?" I played devil's advocate and chided her as I turned the yellowed pages of the album. Each page held a memory. I revisited my commencement speech when I graduated from Honea Path High School, typed out badly by me many years ago. It was May 21, 1970. I read the gift notes from birthdays, holidays, and graduations. I saw the news clipping touting, "Juniors to Use Spring Theme for Banquet." I was on the party committee that year. I turned the page and read another article. "Campus to Dance From 9 PM to Midnight at Cotillion Club's Spring Formal Saturday." A family friend and columnist, Gene Wilson, wrote this piece when I attended Emory and as well as the Agnes Scott Spring Cotillion with B.J. Crowthers, my friend, debutant, confidant, and social cover. Everything was here. My history had continuity, edited by Addie.

"You cannot know what was bad unless you see what lays good." Addie could always put everything in perspective. "I kept your history, what I knew. You need to fill me in on the rest. And judging from what I see in this here mirror, I haven't much time." She turned and looked long into my eyes and smiled.

"How do you do that?"

"Do what, child?" She held back a smile. She knew.

"Get me to say what you need to know, do what you want me to do, think well of this place?"

She stood, took my hand, and pulled me toward the window. "Look out. What do you see?"

"I see the main house, the dock, and the place where I was born."

"You know what I see?"

"What, Momma?"

"I see the colors, the richness of the land, the way the sky meets the earth in an uneasy stitch. I see power and possession, the house where you grew up, complete with its shadows." She chose her words carefully, she always did. "I have learned a few things in eighty or so years, give or take," she winked, "and I've learned that it's all about understanding what you see, not just seeing it. Life's a mess, a jumble. It wants to be, I don't know why. Look at the trees. Just when you get used to the color green, they turn red and gold. Just when you get used to that, the leaves fall in a brown spiral. All this happens in its own time. Nothing to be done 'bout it. It's their secret. Everything has them, you know…secrets. I have 'em, too." She paused, searching for words that, years before, would have come instantly. "You have, too. I got used to seeing you a certain way. And I knew what you wanted me to know while you were here. And then you left, and the person I needed to know left with his quiets." She called all hidden things "quiets."

"My quiets? I don't have any quiets." I protested in vain.

"Listen here, I've looked into your eyes for, well, you know how many years. I look deep into them and see quiets that keep me from you. Nobody should be held at such a distance." She challenged my feelings as if hurt. "Some nights in the fog's stillness just before a heavy rain I can feel your sadness way up there in New York City. I can feel your loneliness up those narrow stairs through that locked door, and into the bed of my child, as if he is lying in the next room from me. Your quiets haunt me…hurt me…like the ghosts trapped in that house you grew up in. I can hear 'em, loud."

"Momma, I'm fine, really. I'm a grown man. It's all settled. It's all okay."

"You go and stay away over twenty-five years and you call it set-tled? No." She shook her head in defiance of me. "No, not settled at all. Buried maybe, but not settled."

"Momma, buried quiets...settled quiets...either way. Done. Over. Past."

"No, no, no. Buried or past, not settled. Still quiets. They're strong, and they haunt you. Secrets, just like the leaves. Just like rest of the Madi-gans and," she hesitated, "the Waters." She gave up one of her own qui-ets right then. She stared out the window at Greyhaven in the distance and did not look at my face to gauge my reaction. She continued, "And just like this plantation," she dismissed the notion with a sarcastic chuckle, "silly word for this thing that's left—plantation. But secrets it has, and secrets we kept from each other. They are different ones, and before your time here is over, I want to know yours. I need to know what kept you from me." She grabbed me by my shoulders as much to steady her-self as to emphasize her goal. "I know too much about this place, child, and not, I think, enough about you. Tell me, this time, this place." She bent over me and the scrapbook and I felt five years old again. She sat down on the bed next to me, gently reached for my hand, and held it to her chest. "We will trade histories, make the last entries into this memory book, final and complete. We have a distance to go, you and me. We'll hold nothing back. Let's fill in the blanks, my child."

"I'm almost fifty. You still call me child?"

"You'll always be my child, as long as you still call me Momma." She laughed, heartily.

"I wish that Mother had cared enough to do this," I said, as I closed the cover of her laborious creation.

"Ivinia did the best she could, and that's one of the reasons I stayed here, Faust. I stayed around to do all those things that a mother should do." She spoke of Ivinia gently, so rare an occurrence.

For years, I was satisfied and comforted by the fact that I got what I needed, that someone cared enough to give me a place to run. I just wished that Mother had thought to do it, had thought enough of *me* to do it. More than that, right now I wished I could trust that Addie would stay loyal to me upon the trading of our souls. This mistrust was not as much about Addie as it was about me. I had a built-in mechanism, honed over many years of self-preservation. I wasn't sure that I could risk it ever, and certainly not then. I would have to think about it.

"I'll be here for a few days. Let's talk again, okay?" I wasn't ready to make that exchange.

"Oh, my love." She backed down a notch. "Of course, let's talk, you and me, as soon as you can. Promise me." A thought rushed across her mind. "Oh, my." She looked at the mantle clock on the bedroom's fireplace. "Y'all need to go. They'll be waiting for you to start the meeting."

"How did you know about the meeting?"

"Cornelius and I spoke earlier this afternoon about the arrangements for Titus' viewing. He told me that there was going to be a meeting at the house this evening. He needed Jed to get a few provisions but his phonin', clever man, was designed to prevent me from coming."

"Was he at least gracious about it?"

'Well, to his credit, he always steps around in good shoes. But we are all extensions of the plantin' seed, are we not? He was very clear. He didn't want me there."

"I apologize for him, Momma."

"No need to apologize for a Madigan. I have seen the one I wanted to see. Just be careful. He's twisted into a poison wood." As she said that, Jed appeared outside her window, watering the garden that framed and bordered the house.

"Ah, there's Jed. How is he?" We had our language. Addie and I turned our corner.

"Well, he's out there. Wanted some 'lone space. Doesn't abide commotion the way he used to." Jed saw us watching him, waived, dropped what he was doing and disappeared. We waved back. "He retired last June, you know. I cannot believe my baby brother's retired. He took his horn, packed his bags, and said goodbye. They called him 'sweet blow' in the clubs. Did you know that? He left the late lights of New Orleans and hasn't looked back, except for the nights that are the stillest, and he needs the 'old sounds.'"

"He gave up being a sideman?"

"Nah, you're always a sideman, you just give up the gigs. He sometimes plays till the wee hours. Instead of B.B. King and Lady Day, the cicadas have backup now." She smiled and drifted a moment in Jed's direction.

"Jed played for Billie Holiday and B.B. King?" There was so much I didn't know.

"Truer than a plumb bob," Addie swore. "He played for 'em. In fact, many others. Been in all the big cities. Loved Chicago the best. He lives out back in 'Little House' now."

Jed had moved into one of the few remaining sharecroppers digs turned offices, turned guest house for Addie's visiting relatives, when he returned from New Orleans two years ago. She called it "Little House" to wash it clean, but also, to remember.

"I want him close by now. You'll need to see him before you go. He asks about you all the time, you and Cila and Ti."

"How are your daughters?"

"They're fine, all way past growin' like you. There are some pictures of you with them in the album. Their lives are complete," Addie said, by which she meant removed and safe.

"I must go. I'll see you tomorrow night after the viewing. I love you, Momma.

"I love you, too." She touched my cheek. "Go now."

I fled. I placed the album on the seat next to me in the boat and looked back at her house as I chucked the motor. The glow of light through the lace of Addie's bedroom window surrounded her silhouette as she watched me watching her. Behind her house, a sound pierced the air, willowy and intense in its delicate rhythm. It was Jed's 'sweet blow,' weaving through the thickets of night air and bougainvillea, and it caught the rhythm of the cicadas. Addie blew a kiss. She caught mine and drew it to her heart and I felt close to that heart, some of the good she spoke of, out of what was bad.

# 7

I RAN UP THE PATH that led from the dock to the garages and heard a great commotion coming from the front of the house. As I rounded the side veranda, a white-hot light glowed above the roof like an intense halo. The scene drew me to an instant halt. I had been gone less than an hour. I started to run to the front of the house to see what was happening. A crowd of people descended on the place like locusts before a Biblical dust storm. I stood in the middle of a Hollywood set transformation. More big lights spotted the driveway, flooding the house with surgical brightness. I started as no less than ten men dragged huge matured shrubs and flowers on dollies and wheelbarrows, planting them hurriedly down the driveway. Landscapers, like gnomes, edged the car path with mulch around the groundcover of ivy, indigenous grasses, and mature wild rhododendron of red and pink, forced to bloom in a season that their flowers never see.

Fine gravel, dumped by a pay loader, had five men pushing it evenly down the drive from the front gates to the front porch. Six more men painted the columns surrounding the house with shiny white paint. In amazement, I bolted through the front doors into the entry. The vases on the heavily carved entry table gushed and spilled with exotic flowers, cascading like a petal waterfall. The richness of the colors reflected off the shiny, black-gold marble top that had been missing from the day before. Two men busily changed the portieres that framed all the archways of the rooms off the main foyer from the somber, dark-putty cotton brocade that set the tone of the first day's viewing to jewel-toned, ruby silk velvet with long bronze fringe hanging from all edges. Antique porcelains, family paintings, English tomes, and tea and tobacco boxes were sprinkled throughout the house by uniformed women holding not only the rare antiques but diagrams and numbers as to where they belonged. I had just assumed that most of these collections had been sold off. Machine-made rugs were rolled up by men stuffed into khaki uniforms boldly printed with letters spelling Matley's Carpet Service curving across their backs, the letters pinched into submission by their extended shoulder blades. They laid the priceless Persian rugs that my great grandfather had purchased from many auctions of other plantations throughout the South.

I spun around in the middle of the hall, clutching at my album, watching all the business of every kind turning this house into the home that I remembered. Metal clanged against wood. I looked up to see three men taking the plain brass chandelier down from the ornate plaster surround on the ceiling. The one I remembered waited impatiently on the floor to be reinstalled. Reported to be from one of Ludwig's many castles in Germany, it glistened with ruby, amethyst, and topaz rock crystal dripping from a lyrically forged skeleton of Dore bronze.

I looked up the staircase. Two men hurriedly screwed in the old hand-twisted brass stair rods with carved stone finials at their ends on each step of the staircase. The sheers at the platform window fell to the ground, dropped by two men on ladders., while two more men standing at the bottom of the ladders held the original Austrian shades, ready to go up. Made from iridescent silks that were brought from India, the silks were the result of a trip that my grandfather made with Ivan Tolome, his frequent traveling companion from New York. He preferred Ivan to grandmother. They were very close.

Four more men dragged in twelve-foot fichus and bird of paradise trees in huge Chinoiserie urns. They pushed them on dollies into alternating corners of all the rooms. The rest of the corners were filled with marble pedestals topped with bronze Remingtons, Degas, and Boteros, of a more recent vintage. Cornelius was on the balcony overseeing this project aware of my stunned entrance.

"Faustus!" Cornelius' commanding voice filled what remained of the empty spaces in the house. "What do you think?" he continued, as if trying to wake me from a coma.

"Um…stunning," I said, as I slowly twirled in disbelief.

"Do you like the transformation?" he asked, arms waving in a Caesar gesture. He looked like Mother at that moment.

"You certainly have a flair for the unexpected."

"You are unimpressed?"

"To come here in the morning to a house on its ass, then voila–dressed to the nines! I don't know–call me a little taken aback."

"You are unhappy," he mocked me.

"'Unhappy'? You think that this expression is the telltale sign of unhappy? No. Actually, I am incredibly underwhelmed that this is all you are doing. I'm surprised you aren't trying to put another floor on this fire trap." Cornelius ignored me as he surveyed his accomplishments.

"What's that you're holding?" He focused on the album I'd received from Addie. I ignored the question. "Well, Faust," he sighed, "Pull in your claws and help me."

"What can I do?" I asked, astonished that more help was needed.

"Put down whatever you're holding and take this." Cornelius swept down the staircase carrying a box. "I want you to put these items where they belong. The diagram will show you where they go. It's right on top." I dropped the album on the settee at the bottom of the stairs and grabbed the box from him.

"What's that, again?" He wouldn't let the thought of the album go. His curiosity overwhelmed him.

"It's a gift from Addie, that's all."

Later, in the privacy of my room, I took the box, opened it, and paused a moment to focus on the contents. It was a box of gilt framed relics. I remembered them. On the top of all the things was the original deed to Greyhaven, written on sheepskin and signed by the King of England in 1760. It was the original description, borders, and reasons for the land transfer. Under that were local maps from 1716 when the French laid claim to this land. Originally part of the region designated Caroline, it reverted to English ownership and became part of the land parcels granted to Loyalists. And finally, beneath all this gold-framed history laid buried a painting of the original owner of Greyhaven, Wolsley Harcourt IX, an English lord and barrister. Rewarded for his loyalty and his decision to accept a commission to come to America, he contracted with the Crown to cultivate and export products either fashionable or necessary to English society. In one of the diaries that we found in the attic, Harcourt's wife explained a bit about the grant:

*He was granted a tract of land that gently rolled and twisted, laid wet and dry with timber and grasses, webbed in channels of brackish and fresh waters, covered in the delicacy of a shadowy mist, so like the bogs and lake shores of the north country of England, our home and estate called Grey Mist.*

As legend had it, Wolsley Harcourt had stood at the mouth of Back

Bay Inlet and said, "I have found my truest mission and love, this place, a haven of protection and delicacy, both. It has the odour of sweet gum and the rolling mist of my homeland. It shall be called Greyhaven and stand forever more as the symbol of family, strength, and honour."

Although Wolsley Harcourt IX began the history, he now lay on his back ornately framed in a cardboard storage box. He began the legacy that for all his good intentions would be reduced to a painting and an effect. His destiny was less grand than his designs. His destiny, sadly, allowed only to be hung tidily back in his place of honor. The Madigans felt it gave weight and substance to the studied seriousness of the salon. Wolsley Harcourt IX, a prop for the designs of Cornelius.

# 8

"LET'S GET THIS meeting started," Cornelius barked, as he gathered us into the dining room. He looked at his watch, aware that nine o'clock had come and gone several minutes ago. Madeline, although brighter than hours earlier, looked like she had gone three rounds with the referee asleep. Cornelius' wife, Sarah, back from her shift at Savannah General, seemed impatient and disrupted by this gathering. She nervously paced back and forth in front of the limestone fireplace.

"There you are, Harris. Hey, Faust," Sarah said, greeting me with a kiss on the cheek before politely embracing her husband. We entered the room, oddly stiff.

"Cornelius, dear, can we get this thing going? The kids are at home with Marigold and they really want to see us before they leave." Sarah didn't want to believe that this meeting was important and the look on Cornelius' face bore that out.

"This is really important, honey, and your lifestyle knows the reason why." Straight shot. Cornelius honed the art years ago. "I want to remind you that the partners are arriving tomorrow for the viewing. We all need to be up to speed on what to say, how and when to say it. One slip and the whole thing can come crashing down."

This statement started to fine-tune my anxiety about being home as well. There was never a time when we did not have to be brought *up to speed*. Our constant state of family affairs was wound tighter than a seven-day clock. We always needed to be ready to go the distance whenever an assault happened, whether from family or partners. It appeared now to be rougher around the edges since Titus was no longer here. That would change with practice. We had all taken notes.

Sarah, Harris, Madeline, and I sat down as if the teacher had just announced the start of class. The walls that surrounded us in the dining room appeared to stiffen, as if knowing the solemnity of the meeting. We had shared many meals in this room, and this solemnity was all-too familiar. During countless family dinners, Mother had orchestrated some scenario, an event or scheme that needed to be "discussed" at the all-important Supper Table. I remember a Sunday some forty years ago, when Mother had dressed the table in an extra-special way. Sterling egret place card holders had been laid in front of all the best porcelain and crystal from our pantry. Madeline and I had been suspicious, for no important guests were on the roster. It was just the family. With something brewing, we'd stood behind the doorway just to listen to the housekeeper and maid gossip about the pretense of Ivinia's traditions. We were sure that they knew something.

"She's up to something, I knows it," Della had said to her charge, Freda, the upstairs maid. She was brought downstairs to do special things whenever necessary. "Every time I polish these blasted card holders, something dreadful happens," she'd said, head shaking. "I been here too long. I gotta find me a new situation."

"What d'ya mean, you leavin'? I just got this job. You can't leave me."

"Oh, don't listen to me. I'm just slammin' my shutter a bit. I can't leave. I owe Addie so much."

Madeline and I had looked at each other and quietly documented these little bits of brain fodder between us.

Addie had become head housekeeper to Greyhaven some fifteen years before and had delegated much of the work to others. She controlled the house budget and project schedules. Titus would deal with her. Mother stayed away unless she lobbed a complaint Addie's way. However, Mother always needed a rage to muster up the strength.

"I knows it. She's helped me, too. I don't know what I would've done without her. She saved my family," Della said, confirming Addie's behind the scenes maneuvering.

Madeline and I would not know what that meant 'til years later. But Addie helped many people in the county and never ceased to get involved when she saw a problem. So, unlike Mother, where Addie saw need and fixed it, Ivinia saw opportunity and used it. And that night, so long ago, another opportunity had embraced her. As we dined on an impressive array of foods, Mother plotted her *opportunity*. She had started to pontificate about turning the land that she'd decimated years earlier with waste water from manufacturing into a building development. Her face, flawless in its beauty, had brightened as she spoke about a dinner that she had with people who invested in the big development that was so successful in Long Island. She'd met them in Ashland, at a benefit for the Biltmore Estate, built by the Vanderbilts. She'd learned numbers, ways to manipulate financing and profit projections. Father had sat there, tired but resistant, listening to her roll her words, "Levitt…cape cods…new styling…we should try…split levels."

Madeline and I had listened with one ear each. We'd mimicked the conversation and played and giggled. In between Mother's tirades, she'd intermittently reprimanded us. Continually frustrated by the interruption of her flow of words, she'd screamed us down, retarnishing the silver with her acid tongue.

"I have had enough from you little beasts! When you sit at this table you will conduct yourself with proper decorum or I will hang you over the wash line and beat you like a rug 'til your nap comes out! Have I made myself clear? Della! Freda!" Even though she had a bell buzzer by her foot, she would scream at the top of her lungs, while she would incessantly slam the floor bell with her foot. She was out of control, again.

"The children are wanting more vegetables and milk. Hurry, so, they can be excused!" Freda had then spooned a heap of buttered broccoli in both my and Madeline's plates.

"No, not Cornelius, Della. He's full. No milk for him, either, Freda. Just bring cake for Mr. Madigan and Cornelius when they are ready. Madeline and Faust won't be having any."

Once again, we would be excused from the table without the children's reward for a finished meal. Madeline and I sat there, yet again, our demeanor melting into a somber puddle. Mother was on a mission and we all knew the outcome, maybe even before Mother knew it.

We'd gulped the broccoli down in a chewless swallow and forced the milk down.

"Now, you can leave," she'd said, emotionless.

"But what about the ca…?" Before Madeline had finished the sentence, Mother threw a knife at her, nearly missing her head and landing, point in, piercing the gold frame of the Degas.

"Ivinia! Enough! Children…just go." Titus had dismissed us in a calmer, protective gesture, pressing his hand against his head. We often thought that he desperately wanted to go with us. "Cornelius, you may leave as well."

"No, Cornelius stays," Mother had shot back. "He needs to hear what is going on and learn. There needs to be someone here who knows the workings of this place. The others are useless."

As we left the table, cake-less, Cornelius bowed his head and smiled a smile that became his subtle signature. He'd known even then that he was different from us, special to Mother, and that made all the difference in the world in our family food chain.

She started these "special" dinner conversations with Titus, almost monologues, with an apparent apprehension as to their success. She was the only one who was unaware that her success was a given. So even though she always won, she attacked hard and swift. Across from us, we could see Cornelius, studying Mother's mannerisms, looking at her in awe, absorbing her every mood, her every motion, her every contemptuous response. We eventually ate in silence. Father would inevitably say, "Darling, if this project is so important to you, I'll make some phone calls and we will get it going," as if from a script. But it never failed that Mother would drag him through the process. On this occasion, the dialogue, usually written in stone, had assumed a more intense tone. Father, always willing to listen, resisted her, seeming to sidestep her reasons.

"Ivinia, let the land rest a bit." Madeline and I were again behind the portieres that draped the edges of the doorway. "Haven't we done enough to that parcel without scarring it with a development?"

"We need to maximize our profit, Titus, you know that."

"Ivinia, dear, aren't we doing well enough without bringing profit to that bit of land? It's only, what, seven hundred, maybe one thousand acres. Please, let's let it rest. I love looking out the windows and seeing green and mist and wet, no matter how poisoned the soil is." Titus had been truly connected to this place, a lineage and love unbroken. "Isn't there something else that could occupy your time?"

"You promised that I would control the production of this place, and I will be damned if you will go back on your word. Just remember what happens if you do," Ivinia had said, very close to grinning. "And it is well more than a thousand acres, just a blush shy of two, so don't do a back door whittle on me."

We heard that beginning phrase a lot, "Just remember, if you do…" It never seemed to have a finish, except for the result. Silence would always fill in the gap between these words. Madeline and I had glimpsed the diamond clips holding Mother's hair glimmer tensely as she arched her back at the end of the table. Cornelius would move closer to her. Father, at the other end, initially looming, diminished as his back lost its arch, stolen by Mother and Cornelius. Watching her, Cornelius had grabbed a piece of that bravado and victory and sat taller in his seat.

These memories stayed with me, so much so, that I fashioned my life in New York in defense of these moments. Since leaving home and moving there, I set up my apartment with no dining space, never again sitting at a dinner table. I shuddered at the thought. I remained busy and on the run. I would meet friends at restaurants, where confrontations over food could be contained, at movies and theatre, or at parks and museums, never inviting anyone to my home to eat. Madeline, in similar fashion, sculpted a parallel defense. When she married Harris and they started to build their own home, she insisted on building a house that had no dining room. Instead, their house had a huge room that encompassed a kitchen, a gathering place for the family, and a gigantic table…everything together…as much for lack of formality as for ensuring witnesses.

The only one to carry on the tradition, Cornelius, reveled in the "head of the table," and that was where he sat this night. We sat, Madeline in her childhood position and me in mine. Cornelius adjusted his position, with his back arching against the archway. Mother's place.

Whenever we were summoned to the dining room there was tradition to follow. Breakfasts were served on the demi-lunes that, when put together, served as a traditional breakfast table during the day and became the extensions to the main table at larger dinner parties at night. At full capacity, we could serve a sit-down dinner for forty. Around us, now, the little gnomes that Cornelius had hired were putting back the sterling and porcelain accoutrement. On the mantle appeared the sterling cornucopia that spilled fresh fruit daily. On the main table, the seventeenth-century Scottish candelabras, eight wicks each, glistened as the gnomes placed them according to their little cheat sheets. A majolica bowl made by Josiah Wedgwood sparkled on the breakfast table in the bay window. Only three of these bowls were known to exist, with one in the Victoria and Albert Museum. It was a richly painted, Cobalt blue, soft paste pottery piece circa 1850, footed by four clown-collared dogs holding it up in comic reverence with even bigger clown handles in bright colors of yellow, russet, and green. The clowns developed a different meaning than when they were created. Instead of paying homage to the wildly popular Punch and Judy of early Victorian England, they laughed at the farce that was before them now, like chorus and siren both, warning and bemusing the events unfolding in front of them. Now, in its laughter and alarm, I remembered its sweet lilac pink wash buttering the inside hollow with color. Serving as the cornerstone to the room, lilac pink draperies were being reinstalled in place of the drab cottons that had hung somberly in the bay earlier this morning. The walls responded in kind, rising gaily in glazed printed chintz, bolstered by the reassembly of the house, mocking my family's folly even more loudly now.

"Excuse me, people. People, go somewhere else. There are other rooms to finish," Cornelius commanded the troops with a triple clap of his hands. The little uniformed gnomes scurried away to other parts of the house, where Humpty Dumpty needed additional shoring up. Cornelius' claps made us all jump, putting percussion to the tense scene as we watched the workers vanish. I wanted to go with them. I was catapulted into childhood, sent in a time machine magically back to the fear and apprehension of my past. Each of us was on a different plane of knowledge in this saga. Cornelius, I instinctually knew, held all the parts. It was corporate cake, made with each of us knowing enough of the ingredients to aid, but not enough to steal the recipe.

Cornelius looked around to ensure that the hired strangers were gone.

"Good. Now, down to business." His voice became determined and low. "Here's the list of guests for tomorrow." He handed out photocopied sheets of a list of businesses and partnerships in which the Greyhaven Corporation held major holdings. "You will need to familiarize yourselves with this list. Y'all know these people from over the years and they will all be here tomorrow."

We looked down at the papers, and each of our heads rose and turned at different times in recognition and puzzlement of the many names the list contained. Heading the fifty-odd names on the list were Adlai Morrisette, market partner when only acquisitions were necessary, and his daughter, Sophie Morrisette; and Johnston Picket, the partner in South Sector Construction Corporation, the company responsible for our major development of housing and commercial construction for the family. Adlai and Titus set up and used South Sector to develop many commercial and residential projects including Greyhaven land and the fiasco of the split levels. Ivinia was the major stock holder in that venture. And, not of lesser importance, T.K. Tinsdale, of the Hotel Madingdale fame in Beaufort. When Madeline read his name, she looked at me and shuddered. Also included on the list was Senator Wilcox's son, Wally Jr., still breeding happy horses in a part of the state further west from our core on about two thousand acres of land left from Delbarton holdings, now absorbed.

As we read the list, our cousin Nasby entered the room, beads of sweat frosted his military buzz cut.

"Sorry I'm late. Accident victim took me longer to piece back together than I thought it would. Did I miss anything critical?" Cornelius handed him the sheets of paper and said nothing in response.

"The list of prominents." He spoke at Nasby not to him, a subtlety not noticed by this ever-needy fringe member of our family. It became apparent to me that Nasby was a tool and not a permanent participant. If all went as family history bore out, Nasby would be bought off and eliminated when his usefulness and guard were no longer needed by the family. Money would be doled out as if a royalty for services rendered.

"We need to put on an air of normalcy and success." Never turning his head to acknowledge Nasby, Cornelius continued, "You know that we are embarking on a plan to reopen the land adjacent to this house. We have found a way to redevelop the land that the Feds closed on us, that would follow the new guidelines of toxicity…to a degree." Cornelius chose his words carefully. "Any smell of impropriety and the hounds will ascend upon us. I have given this much thought and preparation as you can see." You could depend on Cornelius to stroke his own ego when no one stepped forward to do it. We nodded numbly. "Any questions so far?"

"Okay, I'll bite," I said. "Why the intrigue? Why this transformation? You are going to open the land? Do it. Why this stage setting?" I blurted out these questions with little forethought, which was more style than accident. Madeline inhaled cautiously.

"I plained up the house for the relatives so that they would not be wanting a piece of the pie."

*Plained up.* I'd not heard the phrase since Addie dressed Madeline for her coming-out party when she was sixteen. *"Honey, you gotta be less plained up when you meet the boys. Now go through these magazines and pick yourself out something pretty. Addie'll make it for you."*

"I'm redressing the house now so that the partners smell success and business as usual. I don't want questions of instability to arise. Titus didn't run as tight a ship as he could have the last few years. And we need passively quiet support from the partners…because…well…" Cornelius showed his first sign of fear. "We have leveraged a lot of the assets from the other corporations to do the reopening. The partners need not know the details." And there it was. The twisting of the Feds and OSHA was just the small piece, little problem with that.

Government, especially this regime, slid over anything that made corporations, especially those with the right conservative connections, more money. Trickle-down economics, we all know, just…trickles down…into the lower pockets of the powerful. It was never designed to go further. If it did, it was accidental. But now I saw the larger problem.

"I can't believe this shit," I said, bolting out of my chair. "Not only are there debris around us, but now there is fraud and a potential bout with the SEC. Wonderful. How did you think you could pull this off, Cornelius?"

"Calm down, it'll work." Nasby tried to lower the pressure of the steam within me.

"We have a way to develop the land. You know that, Faust; I told you that earlier," Harris chimed in as if adding something that would comfort me. Madeline touched my hand and looked at me and winced our sign of *Quiet down and let it pass*. I didn't understand her compliance.

There was no one left. She was an equal and now in a position of power. Maybe it was just old behavior, used when dealing with Ivinia. I didn't know. Maybe, *lay back and let it happen, fight and you have more to lose* was her mantra. I felt unsure of her, right then, and it stunned me. I pulled my hand away from Madeline. The line had moved so slowly and steadily that she did not see this venture for what it was going to be. Or did she? My absence from this place kept me unaware of the changes that time and my family would orchestrate.

"This meeting isn't for all of us. I think that it is being held solely for me." I stood as a reflex to this potential threat. "I cannot believe that all this has been going on and I am first hearing of it tonight. The cadaver in the library, as old as the incident that probably killed him, mother's disappearance." I listed everything I had just learned. "...And not killed in the car accident at Pecan Bend...the fake funeral, the set changes in this house. You're all in on this! I cannot believe that this has been going on and not even one of you let me know."

"None of us could risk it," Harris said. "I'm sorry Faust, we needed to have this happen. Cornelius, tell him. *Now*, Cornelius!"

"The past few years, prior to Father's death," Cornelius paused deliberately to choose his words, "Mother and I had been trying to convince Father to work with us to devise a plan to redevelop the land. Actually, Faust, it was because of you that this all came about."

"Me? You must be out of your mind, Cornelius. I had nothing to do with this debacle."

"Ah, but you did."

"How?" I asked incredulously.

"I'm sure you remember the memorial you put in the Sunday *New York Times* about Mother's death."

"Yeah, I thought people would want to know about her demise. There are a lot of Southern expatriates up in my neck of the woods. I thought it appropriate to make the announcement. It was the least I could do."

"Do you remember sending me a copy of *The Times* containing the memorial column?"

"Absolutely. I felt you should know what I said so it wouldn't come as a surprise."

"I wouldn't have read any of it, except that when I searched for the memorial, I found a small article on a cement construction factory building in a little hamlet south of the George Washington Bridge, in, I think, Undercliff, New Jersey. In fact, the article read, 'Toxic Hamlet Redefined.' I'll never forget it."

"This is news to me, Cornelius." Sarah's surprise was not acted.

"Dear, it just slipped my mind…"

"Right." Sarah looked away to the garden being reconstructed outside.

"And what does that article have to do with this little gathering?" I asked, feeling a little defensive that I might be implicated.

"The article noted that the factory, formerly a metal products plant, had for years been left vacant because, as redevelopment for residential use had revealed, it was loaded with PCBs and arsenic. The building was left in limbo for many years because it could not be developed nor taken down. Even waste dumps designed to accept toxic refuse declined to take it. Years later, faced with pressure from developers and local politicians, not to mention the scarcity of land close to cities, the rules for toxicity were relaxed.

"Well, let's not say *relaxed*, let's just say *adjusted* to the new political perspective and technology. What was previously severely toxic became marginal, and what was marginal became acceptable…and… voila! The building was taken down and they started constructing high-end rentals."

"Oh I get it! So, armed with this little ray of hope, you embarked on this latest venture." I was finally caught up to speed. "Harris, you and Madeline knew this all along? Why didn't someone tell me?"

"We couldn't, my love." Madeline looked at me and Cornelius, her demeanor unchanged.

"Why, Madeline? Why?" I needed to know.

"I can't take this shit any longer." Madeline summoned a resolve.

"Madeline, don't," Cornelius warned.

"Yes, now, Cornelius. You see, Faust, we all have something at stake here; not just Cornelius. Very important things." She chose her words carefully. "So, you see, my dear brother, we are all locked to this venture."

"Why did you let this happen?" I still had to read meaning into her words. Brother? She said brother. Couldn't be.

"The line kept moving, Faust. With each turn, we thought it would be over, but we just kept getting in deeper and deeper," Sarah lamented.

"Sarah, why you? I expected more from a Delbarton, and you too, Harris." They both locked stares then turned from my direction.

"Didn't you hear, Faust? All of us. All of us, Faust," Sarah lowly, slowly repeated. The bright lights from the outside kept shifting to new places of necessity as the shadows kept shifting inside on the walls of the dining room, across the table, in high and low streaks across our faces.

Silence filled the table for a moment before a little gnome scurried in, carrying a bust of Ivinia and Titus created by a local artist named Arland Russel. He put it on the vacant pedestal that stood between the front windows.

"I told you, not now!" Cornelius' voice showed contempt for the help and the meeting that he was conducting. The gnome dropped the sculpture the last few inches before it reached its proper resting place. It rocked back and forth, lending animation to their heads. The gnome quickly left.

"How do we end this, Cornelius? How do we make this quick and get it behind all of us?"

"Act."

"Act?"

"Yes. Pretend that you have been involved. Pretend that you love your history, your family, and your future in it. Convince everyone who comes tomorrow that we are a family, united and strong. Can you do all that?"

"Why do you need my help, Cornelius?" I needed to know what the bargain was.

"I said, *everyone*. You have been away for years and have left the survival of these businesses in my hands. Mother tried to get Titus to move on all of this. He wouldn't budge. Death has freed us up."

"How convenient!"

"Yes, convenient." He agreed too easily.

"So, what did you do, Cornelius, kill him?" I said, mockingly. The room was silent.

"You've got to be kidding." I looked at everyone, but no one met the glare of my eyes. "His death was planned? How? Who? I want answers!"

"No, not exactly *planned*. Mother took something that she and I talked about, somewhat of a wish list, and acted upon it." Madeline bowed her head in the shame of her admittance. I couldn't believe what I was hearing.

"You can't be serious. She…murdered Father?"

"We're not sure," Sarah chimed in. "She drank more and more as the years progressed. If she didn't suffer blackouts, she raged out of control, and she drove that horrid car." Sarah shuddered in disbelief of the past.

"That's when it happened," Madeline interrupted. "She and Titus were driving home from Charleston. Yet another charity event in which Mother embarrassed herself…"

"Yes, and I was there." Sarah shook her head at the memory of it. "She *did* have the accident at Pecan Bend, but was thrown clear of the car and uninjured. It was Titus who hit the trees head on. She was driving," Sarah repeated, still stunned by the memory. "He hit the trees. I was following them home from the event and saw what happened. It looked as if they were arguing. They were supposed to stop at Johnston, Shaddie, and Murkle, you know, the trust lawyers. There were papers to sign. I don't know what it was about, neither did Ivinia. Titus caught her by surprise while she downed her final martini at the event. You know how hard that was to do. You know, staying with them and watching it turn uglier. Then as we drove back, they turned left at the fork on route 111 and went in the wrong direction for the lawyers. I saw Titus waving his hand, alternately grabbing at the steering wheel. The top was down and the struggle wasn't long. I was beeping my horn to warn them, but they didn't hear me." Sarah started to cry. "They didn't hear me. Ivinia drove the car into a tree, pushing in Titus' side of the car. I got on my cell phone and called Harris. He called Cornelius and then it all began."

"Titus died at the scene?" I asked, wanting to wake up from this nightmare.

"No. I ran to Titus. He was bleeding," she touched her own head and winced at the phantom pain, "from the side of his head. The dashboard pinned his legs and the door catapulted open from the impact. He was conscious, though barely. Cornelius arrived. He tended to Ivinia. He put her in the car and the ambulance arrived. I heard some conversation back and forth, and then they left."

"They left?"

"Yes, they left."

Cornelius broke in. "Why? It was only a head wound, or so it looked," Cornelius said. "Titus was conscious and Sarah was there. She was the attending doctor on the scene. So, I convinced them to leave." He stuttered just a little, maybe unsure if he should continue. "That, and two thousand dollars, contributed to their favorite beer charity and the records of the emergency were, how'd you say, lost. I helped Titus into my car and we drove home."

"Why is he dead, Cornelius?"

"Funny thing about internal injuries, sometimes they just don't show up at first. Sad, isn't it? It was a bad judgment call. I will always feel…well…something about it." He searched the air for what he was missing for a moment and then there appeared that smile. The arched back, the bowed head; it was all there. It chilled the room, and the flowers on the wallpaper seemed to wither from the cold.

"You have created the fifth ring of Hell, Cornelius," I said, shaking my head as a silent pallor washed the room.

"Well, start stoking the fire," Cornelius arched his back in defiance, "because Hell and August just ain't hot enough."

Time and silence sifted together in the room. No one could say anything. It was out there, placed on the table like roadkill for dinner. I needed to process the story around me. I began to feel that I was the freak and everyone else was normal. They each spoke of this as if it was just an unfortunate story told about someone else. My years away from this horrid place changed that perspective. I'd spent twenty-odd years dealing with inner-city problems: late subways, terror attacks, cold latte, and drive-by muggings. Nothing prepared me for reentry into this steamy hellhole that enveloped my family. After what seemed like an eternity, I changed the course of the conversation just to lead us to a momentary conclusion to this evening. I had little energy left to hide the mixture of fear, rage and disgust that I held deep inside for all of them. I needed to take charge. My stomach knotted.

"Let's get back to the money. How did this happen without the partners' awareness?"

"There are so many companies that money could shift from left to right with intricate paperwork, and the partners would be none the wiser."

"How could you justify all this on the annual reports?" Even I knew that there had to eventually be an honest accounting.

"We own the accounting firm in Savannah with only one silent partner and one visible partner."

"Who, pray tell, are they?"

"You mean, *were* they. Mother was the silent partner and Abigail was the public partner. They formed a trust holding for the corporation," Sarah said, looking hatefully at Cornelius at the sound of her own mother's name. All the venom built through the years spilled out over him. He bathed in it, and in the recognition. Cornelius loved that the plot was so complicated and ruthless. I now recognized why Sarah was married to him. I saw the relationship of Cornelius and Sarah now for what it was.

"What you are telling me by inference is that control of the Delbarton stock and of the accounting firm went to…and the winners are…Harris and Sarah. Have I guessed right?"

"Yes, you're right. For Christ's sake, let's just say it!" Sarah's voice shook the room. "Let's get this out in the open and over! We are all trapped in this whirlwind of debris. We need to open the land to development. We still own it; we bought back every acre and every house, so the Feds wouldn't take it over and make it another Love Canal debacle. Let them have what they want!" I thought I misheard Sarah, that she'd just misspoke. I thought it was only Cornelius to whom she was gifting her soul.

"Years of desolation," Madeline quickly countered, seething, "and eventual redevelopment and reoccupation at the hands of strangers. Don't you remember the residents storming the development office that day? Don't you recall the chaos? My God, you remember the settlement. We almost lost everything. And the buy-back plan! The Feds kicked in some funds, but we fronted most of it, many millions of dollars. It had to come from somewhere. I peddled countless pages of mind-numbing children's crap to front that loan. But more was needed." And at this one moment I saw a glimmer of happiness in Madeline's eyes.

"Guess what?" Madeline had found her little pleasure, "Little T.K. and the hotel are mortgaged way past their chimneys." Her eyes narrowed. "If Wilcox ever found out that his land and semen rights were limited to the cups that held the little swimmers, his horses would never get another erection. And let's not forget–"

"Enough, Madeline. Enough." Cornelius swept in to stop the hemorrhage.

"No! Not enough. Let's not forget Mother's little foray into waste management."

"Madeline, I'm warning you…"

"What, Cornelius? Are we gonna duke it out again?" Madeline started to get into Cornelius' face. She lost that tired beaten look with which she had entered the dining room. Harris suddenly lunged at Cornelius, pinning him against the entrance to the dining room. "You son of a bitch! You hit Madeline?" He grabbed at the front of Cornelius' chest, their faces almost touching.

"Mother has nothing to do with this," Cornelius said with a smirk, chuckling at Harris's bravado. "Besides, Madeline usually wins the rounds."

"Touch her again and I'll…"

"Kill me? Not likely. You haven't got the–how does one say that up north, Faust–testicular fortitude. Besides, I'm worth more to you alive and happy than disappointed and dead, don't you think, Harris?" He stared Harris down.

Reluctantly, Harris lightened his grip on Cornelius.

"He's not worth it, darling," Madeline said. She had a cool demeanor. I was unaccustomed to it showing itself here.

"No, *darling*, I'm not worth it. Now take your hands off me." Harris released his grip. "Never, but never, touch me again. Don't make me reconsider my silence."

We all stood there for a moment reassessing our part in this potential crime scene and made no move to change it.

"Okay. I think we're done here. Everyone knows what to do. We all have risks and liabilities, so I guess we're all on the same page. It's all out in the open, Cornelius," Madeline stuttered.

"Why is it that you didn't want me to know all this 'til now? Why, Cornelius?" My words became heated all over again, as I directed my anger toward Cornelius.

Suddenly, Nasby summoned his marine training and took control. "I think I've heard enough!" Nasby positioned himself in the middle of this intense circle of family. "We all know why we're here. Sorry Faust, you represented a threat because of the distance, so we kept you out of the loop. We had no visual or ideological control or surveillance. I take responsibility for that; it was my suggestion to isolate you."

Cornelius smiled as the storm passed and watched as his concert of people jelled, like a puppeteer whose schizophrenic characters worked out the story that he created in his mind. But, as if the puppets had a choice to do something different, and as if they could catch the meaning of the story and reverse the outcome, they all struggled with the pieces, whirling about in the windstorm, to no avail. After all, puppets are just that–puppets. No, they would make no good ending of this story that could bring them any peace. Not these puppets, not this story.

The meeting dragged on with skirmish after skirmish. Finally, exactly what needed to be accomplished, the Bible according to Cornelius, was accomplished. He honed the details that he deemed necessary in his script that was to play out at the partners' viewing for our father. He survived all the truth telling, the exaggerations, the accuracies, the accusations, by feeling nothing at all. All that mattered was the goal. The means to that end meant nothing. Control had that effect on him, on us. While everything whirled around him, Cornelius focused on his needs, for he was the eye of the hurricane, calm and still. Narcissist you might say, and you may be right. What does that matter? To identify is not to cure, to realize is not to change. It simply is.

# 9

THE TALL CLOCK at the break in the stairs chimed twelve times. Midnight. Cornelius stopped, looked up from the table that had been continually pounded by everyone's fists but his, and announced that the meeting was over. He gathered the remaining papers and kissed Sarah's cheek.

"Shall we go, my darling?" He extended a hand in pure Southern smoothness, as if he was asking her to waltz. She looked up at him, moved the chair back, and rose unassisted. Her eyes, narrowed by bottled rage, never left his. Cornelius sidestepped Sarah so she could exit first, ever the gentleman. In doing so, he turned to us and gently and assuredly smiled a wry smile.

They exited the room, taking the air with them. I sat in stunned silence, immobile and breathless. We were glued to each other 'til one of the assembly crew came in to place four more Irish Chippendale chairs around the breakfast table. Nasby nodded and left without a word. Madeline rose from the table and hugged Harris in front of the sculpture of Mother and Father, more to be comforted than to comfort. They left hand in hand. Madeline tossed a command to me as she departed.

"Well, my brother, it's been fun, but we must call it a night. So many miles to go before we sleep. By the way, where are you staying while you are here?"

"Here, of course."

"Are you sure that's wise? You're welcome to stay with us," Harris added without hesitation, still holding onto Madeline.

"No, this is my home. We all need to come home eventually, I guess. I'm fine really."

"Cornelius didn't have a problem with it?" Madeline queried, seeming surprised at the arrangements.

"He made some suggestions and I rejected them all. I insisted. I want to be here."

"Can't imagine why. No one stays here anymore since we turned Greyhaven into a base of operations. But if you insist, my dear brother, your wish is my bewildered command. Don't forget, Gorman's at 9:30. There are two frozen hot chocolates with our names on them. Kisses!" Her composure was back, a Southern act. We had each learned those mannered veneers early on, thin and pliable with full coverage.

With the final close of the door on my family, there were still people crawling all over the house and property. It wasn't 'til 2:30 a.m. that the house resumed its stillness, resting from a long day of cosmetic surgery. It pleased me to finally see everyone gone. It was just Titus and me. I visited him again before retiring to my old room. I kept my distance during that moment and then closed the doors of the library. Like a protective father tucking in his child for slumber, I felt fearful of making a sound loud enough to prick the bubble of sleep that surrounded him.

Cognac in hand, I strolled toward my room feeling the details of the stair banister, the wallpapers, the rugs. I drank-in the polished atmosphere of the paintings and the lushness of the collections amassed across the generations. In braille-like wonder, I absorbed my home and it quickly became wonderfully and horribly intertwined with me again. Time's distance melting away, I threw myself on my bed, which had been turned down by the part-time housekeeper who remained behind to look after my needs. Cornelius arranged for Pru to stay with me. She was in the wing off the kitchen, should I need anything.

The stillness enveloped me as the warm breeze from the open French doors rolled in. I slowly removed my clothes so the push of night air could reacquaint itself with my body. I laid back and let it move slowly over my typography. I was conscious at that moment of my age. I remembered how the air had defined my body as a young man. How it once touched the borders of my frame, chilling the high points, crashing against the bottom of my rib cage, swirling around my upright feet and tickling the hairs on my thighs. It was foreplay, aiding in the distraction of my loneliness in the two worlds in which I found myself, one by happenstance and the other by defensive design. I wanted to awaken the memories of other delicate rushes of warm August night airs. No longer protected by clothing, my skin gave birth to a wet veil that draped it unevenly. I became conscious of my body's change at that moment. The territory lay broader; the hairs at the edges took longer to reach. The air that tickled the pinnacles of my body no longer excited me. I went back there for a moment and played the body youthful only to be stopped by the constant gnawing of boredom and sameness of nearing fifty, like a too-familiar and too-removed lover finding excitement elsewhere. My will no longer felt the need to touch and succeed. I partnered with the breeze as if a friend and journeyed with it. My hands followed in gentle mimic only to be stopped by disinterest. It was the first time I noticed my evolution. I had run from this place and all its secrets—my secrets—never to revisit them. New York was the place to be removed from them. The silence of this place, so misused by my family. I had run to the swirl of motion, light. Had run to a place where silence could be, would be, avoided; where whim could mask desire; where planned and predictable associations could hide loneliness. The city absorbed me into its busy isolation.

My mind wandered away from me and played with the layers of a summer night's passing. It was different here at Greyhaven. I had gotten so accustomed to the avoidance of inclement or severe weather that I had buried the subtlety of change. So protected in New York by conditioned air that the feel of what was actually around me was only taken in snippets, between the rushes from cab to lobby or theatre to subway. Those times became my enigmatic reality. Here in South Carolina, the gentle seasons were a part of me. The seasonal changes, though subtle, were gently here for me. I took the gift with gratefulness.

I eventually drifted off into a fitful sleep, not quite captured totally into rest. I fell in and out of dreams that blended fact, fiction, and emotion. I woke to sounds of moaning, many times during the night, not sure whether it was around me, from me, or in dreams. Half awake, in those moments I drifted back, turning so the bed linens could absorb my perspiration and coolness could return to the newly dried spot. In the darkened haze of my room, the starlight delicately reflected half forms all around me. Familiar reflections shimmered like gently scattered diamonds, as the trees outside rustled their leaves between the light's origin and its destination.

BANG! A sudden thump so sharp so intense that the chandelier swayed above me, tinkling the rock crystal. Their faceted cuts warned an alarm of light and sound. I bolted upright to the pounding of hard heels hitting the floor above me and muffled sounds upon their return. I went to the door, and as I got there, Pru, the housekeeper du jour, met me on the other side.

"I am so sorry for the commotion, Mr. Faustus, Cornelius wanted me to pull some…items out of the attic for the morning. So, so sorry."

"More props, I would think. No?"

"Props?"

"Never mind, Pru, it's okay. I wasn't sleeping much anyway. Home is not necessarily, *sweet home*, you know?"

"Yes, sir, I understand. Is there anything that I can get for you now, Mr. Faustus?"

"No, nothing, I'll just go down to the library and find a book to read."

"Let me get it for you. What would you like?"

"I don't know."

"I'll bring you some books and magazines so you can feed a whim. How's that?"

"Okay, sure." It was an odd gesture, but I went with it. Pru returned in a flash, teetering a pile near as high as she, with all sorts of literature, tenuously collected, from *Harpers* to *People* and from Cartland to Shakespeare. This was less a collection for whim than psychosis. Her service was either protective or evasive, but I was too tired to figure out which. At least it would make for good conversation with Madeline at Gorman's. I slept, finally, hovering over a story in *People Magazine* of yet another triumph over adversity concerning a Russian gymnast who overcame the effects of Chernobyl on her liver.

Gorman's Ice Cream Parlor lived out its life as frozen as its confections. It was always first to have the newest desserts invented from across the world–Paris, London, Geneva, Heidelberg. But whenever the chef pushed the newest sweet out of the door of the kitchen, it somehow caught the time and tempo of the place and blended in as if it had always been there.

In our youth, Madeline and I often ran to Gorman's and rendezvoused after a date or movie or a fight with Mother. Sometimes we'd even meet Addie there just to catch up. Throughout the years and as the time came closer to my eventual departure, we saw less and less of Addie. She'd seemed preoccupied with duties that kept her from the main house, either traveling or buried in work at Back Bay House. So Madeline or I would call her and we would meet, usually on a Saturday morning, at Gorman's.

On the main street in Beaufort, it would take each of us over an hour, if there was no traffic, to get there. Leading increasingly separate lives, we rarely traveled together, and usually all three cars would meet in caravan style at the junction of Route 953 and Pickford Street. We would honk and wave and the contingent would storm the town.

Today, however, I was alone. I walked in and stepped onto Gorman's white tiled floor, whose grout lines were alternately stained and bleached for over one-hundred and forty-years. The tiny white tiles showed the signs of settling and cracking and revolt, but still there they were, patched and resealed, replaced and cheated with facsimiles. The tin ceiling, the bentwood chairs, the white and green vinyl booths and black glass tables, the white stucco walls, so shiny that you could see your image in their reflection, all of it still there. Like a three-dimensional scrapbook, it forced you to reminisce. I became invigorated with the sounds and visions from my past. Madeline and I, giggling, talking, screaming delight at secrets and privacies told over ice cream, our booth of black glass and green vinyl, our priests and confessionals.

I sat in the middle booth and faced the door not to miss the street scenes that so differed from Manhattan. Instead of cellphones attached to suits in shades of black speeding by, brightly paled colors passed, as if in an impressionist painting. This blur of soft hues erased the charcoal streaked blur that I'd became used to. Its replacement moved like clouds, pleasantly paced, in a cacophony of yellow and white, pink and white, lavender and rose and white. My heart's pace slowed, as the scene unrolled before my eyes. The colors soothed my senses and cooled the already intense morning sun.

As the pale colors passed, a white-hot summer presence moved within their midst. A study in perfect silhouette across the street, Madeline stood at the edge, ready to cross the tempered but busy boulevard. The largest straw hat that the law would allow surrounded her tightly quaffed hair. It bent over her face as if formed to fit and hide and make mystery out of her slow, assured pace. She was dressed in a whiter-than-white sun dress that gleamed and contrasted in soft angles against her warm, toned skin. Her back, fully exposed to the air in satiny smooth contrast, showed the signs of a body maturing gracefully. A breeze from God and passing cars puckered and rippled the bleached silk of her dress in an accidental shimmer, competing with the sun. Men passing in seersucker and khaki suits spun around as Madeline crossed the thoroughfare, just to keep this vision in their mind's eye. Weaving left to right, right to left, avoiding moving cars and broken pavement, she smoothly maneuvered the flesh-colored heels that banded her feet. She saw me through the white lace curtains and waved, adjusting a long-strapped ostrich clutch. She looked like Mother, in her heyday, willowy, self-assured, ethereal.

A delivery boy, carrying an order from the counter, met Madeline just before she touched the door. He opened it and stood aside as if admiring and respecting royalty.

"Hi there, my darling." Madeline bent over to kiss me on the forehead, the only choice the straw hat would allow.

"Lovely entrance, dear. Still stopping traffic, I see," I offhanded to her sweetly.

"Well, my love, as you know, it takes longer and longer to look worse and worse," she said as she sat down, searched for her compact, and checked the damage that an August street crossing brings. "Have you ordered yet?"

"No, I was just sitting still and catching my breath for a moment. It's been so long since I've been here. I'd forgotten how pleasant this was."

"Twenty-four years, three-hundred-fifty days," checking her Cartier watch, "Nineteen hours and, I don't know, thirteen minutes. But who's counting?" She smiled and studied my eyes for a moment.

"Funny lady."

"I try. So let's order. Buster!"

The man behind the counter glanced a knowing look in Madeline's direction.

"Two you-know-what's. And step on it."

"Right away, Madeline," the soda jerk replied.

"I guess you still come here often?"

"Well, as much as my morning scale and my blood sugar will allow. I keep this little addiction my secret. Can I swear you to secrecy? Aside from the obvious sugar coma, this liquid elixir piles on the pounds in a heartbeat."

"Your secret's safe with me," I whispered, "but be careful, will you? Can't have you dying first."

"I'll outlive everyone except, maybe, Cornelius," she said, as she closed her compact. "The chill factor in his blood will keep him alive for a long time."

"Yeah, there were times I felt I should be looking for a coffin somewhere to find him and get him in his sleep," I mused.

Buster had the frozen hot chocolate on the table almost before I finished the sentence.

"Thanks Buster; don't forget my cream. By the way, meet my brother, Faustus. We all call him Faust. Buster, Faust. Faust, Buster"

"Pleased to make your acquaintance, Faust. Your sister's my favorite," He shook my hand heartily.

"Same here, Buster, on both counts."

The pleasantry exchanged, Buster walked away and I noticed his raucous shock of red hair, a tight but thick body and a limp and a drag from his left foot.

"Madeline, what's...um...wrong with his foot?"

"Us." She again inspected herself in her compact, smoothing her lips with her pinky.

"*Us?*"

"Yes, another casualty from the splits. Let's see, 343 Bridle Way, white split with red shutters." Her eyes searched the air as if it held the information.

"And he talks to us...er...you?"

"Yes, as a matter of fact he does."

"Why?"

"Because." She smiled impishly.

"Fine, I'll drag it out of you. Why does Buster speak to us, Madeline?"

"Because, my darling, without this little freakish turn to his body, he would not have been able to afford to buy this place."

"He owns Gorman's?"

"Yuuuuup! At around the time of the mass moveout, we settled out of court with some of the obviously deformed births, and he was one of them. We put some money in trust for him and his parents, some stock options in our family businesses, and when he came of age, Old-Man Gorman, the Fourth, was selling. Timing, they say, is everything, which is why Buster is the new Old-Man Gorman."

"So money does buy happiness, doesn't it?"

"I'm not sure it buys happiness, Faust, but it sure buys solutions. If it was meant to buy happiness, we'd be giddy in glee, wouldn't we?"

"Our little secret; let's not tell the poor folk. I'd hate to disappoint them. They so believe that they could do better with it." We both laughed, slightly embarrassed.

"How was it at the house last night?"

"A real mix of emotions. Some good, some bad."

"Sleep well?"

"Not really, I was restless. I'm not used to sleeping without the numbing sound of my air conditioner massaging my window frame and my brain."

"I've forgotten how still it gets here at night. Takes some getting used to, I guess," Madeline realized.

"Well that, and the commotion in the attic."

"What commotion?" Her throat dried a bit and it was oddly apparent.

"Pru was upstairs thumping and dragging things. It was so intense that she shook my bed with one drop."

"Ah, Pru. She is a quirky lot. What was she doing?"

"I really don't know. But no sooner had the crash hit when she showed up at my door, apologizing for the commotion. I just don't know. She was up there doing something for Cornelius. Something about getting more things out of the attic."

"Can't imagine what else she could be looking for," Madeline said. "The house is so packed that it might implode under its own weight."

"I just think she was doing crazy busywork, you know?"

"Probably, but I think she is a little crazier than most. I heard her talking to herself, you know, the way people unaware have those conversations with themselves, kinda taking on both sides of the argument."

"I've known a few like that," I said.

"Well, the house is big and lonely. I guess you tend to make friends with yourself, or with your enemies, depending. Just so's someone answers you back." And there it was. The low country drawl that I remembered so well and that Mother hated so much.

"*So's?*"

"Don't you make fun of me, dear brother. You should talk. You're beginning to sound more and more like a Nu Yawka. So don't you get so piss elegant with me, love." She took a phrase familiar to me and a large pearl pin out of her hat and removed the volume of finely woven straw from her head with a flourish, placing it on the empty table next to our booth. She sipped at the red- and white-striped straw and grinned at me.

"What do we do, Madeline, about all of this?"

"I know. It must be hard to be caught up so fast. We've all had time to adjust to this constantly moving line but, I must admit, watching you react brought the full impact to bear for me and Harris, you know," she said, trying to comfort me. "We talked about it on the way home. Faust, can you let the events take their course and get this all over with? Let Cornelius get what he needs and, maybe then, we can bring this chapter of our lives to a close, and all of our pasts can disappear."

"I don't know, Madeline. It all seems wrong, every piece of it. I didn't think that anyone could be more manipulative than Mother. Cornelius sure took that little genetic predisposition and ran with it."

"Yes, he's a lot like Mother. We all have bits and pieces of her, don't we?" Madeline never admitted to that before. "But he loves Greyhaven so much, I guess like Mother. His passion for the place seems to blind him, so just let him have it. We can then get on with our lives, make a little play money, and move on." Her words made the solution feel a little too neat.

"I see that you've written several more books since you came to visit me up in Nu Yawk," I said.

"Well, Greyhaven has so much to offer a writer that I might as well exploit it, no?"

"Absolutely! Your last book, the one about the history of ghosts, how playfully gruesome for children!"

"It was certainly a natural. Almost three hundred years of lives and deaths running through our land and this house, with not a simple one in the lot, on either side of the emancipation, someone had to remain after death, no?"

"I can tell you with all that thumping last night, it did run through my mind. Maybe it wasn't Pru. Maybe it was Addie's mother moving boxes of papers, or better yet, old Wolsley wondering where he put his pipe, his slippers, or his dignity. Or perhaps…perhaps it was Mother, wondering where all the love for her had gone."

"Faust! We loved her. She just didn't know what to do with it." Her defense rang shallow but curiously nervous. "Whores never do."

"I don't believe you," I said. "Can't we find peace somewhere with her?"

"Live by the ways of a whore, die by them," she said, colder than the chocolate.

"Madeline, try to let it rest some. Hasn't time helped at all?"

"The only partial peace that I have known," Madeline stirred her chocolate drink with her straw without looking up, "has been since she disappeared." Her looked hardened. "The one thing about disappearing, though that is troubling for me, is that I cannot confirm her death without seeing the corpse. I need proof to find contentment."

"Wishes don't always come true. You're sure about Mother and the prostitute thing?" I asked the question directly, a skill our family never practiced well.

"Yes, I am. What do you need for proof, old condoms? Remember the rumors spinning around town? Remember when we were kids and we went on that little treasure hunt up in the attic?"

"I remember both all too well. You convinced me that we would find hidden treasure in the eaves under the roof of the upstairs porches. And we could run away and never be found," I said.

"Remember what we *really* found? The journals, the house records? This dynasty was founded on the backs of women and slaves. You know this, Faust," Madeline reprimanded me. "The slaves came from Wolsley

Harcourt, and the women, from Romulus Madigan, a job and career he knew well." She looked at me, "But you know all of this. Why do you keep revisiting the truth? No matter how many times and how many ways you examine it, it'll stay the same, my love. Romulus would easily see no difference between the two, so the addition of prostitution to slavery would be seamless. From its start in that little house on Hamilton Street in Charleston, Romulus built what we are still struggling with right now."

"I know but…Mother?"

"Why do you have such trouble with this? She comes from a long line of women we exploited to feather the business from the beginning of our family's time here, right through the forties. We spanned a couple hundred years getting the Southern men off and taking profit from it. It took Grandfather and Father to divest from this into other more lucrative and public ventures."

"You're right. We were always washing money. Now I know why it comes so easily to Cornelius."

"You never cease to amaze me, my love, how naïve you are." She touched my cheek. "What you do not want to see, you are convinced does not exist."

"Gee, Madeline, I thought you were the one who shallowed out the truths."

"*Au contraire, mon ami.* I know them, all right. But I put them away in dark, little rooms. I know exactly where they are. I just don't open the doors. Where we differ is, I believe what I see and you are constantly surprised by it," She slurped twice through her plastic straw, the maximum allowed by etiquette standards. I upped the ante and slurped thrice.

"Buster, two more!"

"Now, Faust, a little truth telling from the North Country." Madeline hunkered down to the table as if trying to push her words across the black glass table.

"This sounds ominous." Buster had the second round of drinks ready and to our table quickly, bringing the cream for Madeline with him this time.

"How's your love life?" Madeline asked me. Buster froze faster than the chocolate. He didn't know what to do, wait for me to answer, or leave and appear apathetic.

"I've broken up with David," I said, looking at Buster, but speaking to Madeline.

His face blanched. He turned on his bad foot and hightailed it back to the counter. "I'm sorry to hear that. He seemed affable enough. What happened?"

"Prescription drugs. He was addicted to anything in pill form. I made him choose between me and Percodan. Percodan won."

"That's tough. You okay?" She grasped my right hand.

"The toughest. The disease is bad enough, but when you add the element of choice to it, well, it's a dangerous combination." I heard the words myself for the first time. I stirred the liquid chocolate with my straw and watched the ice crystals melt in a tornado of rich brown in a momentary silence. "Anyway, I'm okay. It happened two years ago, around the time you all came up to visit."

"Damn you! You never let on."

"What was I supposed to do? Announce that I'd just broken up with my significant other? My lover? Spend the next three days explaining the terms and testing the atmosphere around us for stormy weather? No thanks. Besides, you're the only one who knows."

"Correction, my love. I'm the only one you told."

"I see. Is it that obvious?"

"No, Faust. It's just that distance doesn't change the barometer of your life. Those who care about you, care all about you. We don't need long conversations, just moments—an errant look, a little action. You were always alone, and sadness crept into your eyes. That's all.

"We love you, we see it. Have you told Addie?"

"No, but it's coming. She's been asking questions for some time now. I guess I owe her an explanation."

"You do. She stepped in where Mother hated to tread. She did it all for us. You owe her."

"I know." I needed to change the subject and get back to the immediate issues. "So, where are those journals and house documents? Still where we left them?"

"I would imagine so. I'm not even sure that Cornelius knows about them."

"How is that even possible?" I felt this to be a little disingenuous.

"You know he doesn't like getting his hands dirty. He sends people to get things. If he did not specifically ask for them, then how would anyone recognize their importance? Besides, Mother didn't know about them. They were Father's documents. If she didn't know about them, neither would Cornelius."

"Interesting. So, you suppose that they're still there?"

"I would suppose."

"What more do you think we can find out?" I asked.

"Can't be sure, but I know that Father had journals. Whenever I passed the library, he was usually writing in one leather-bound book or another. That's how I learned about Mother's career choice before she actually met Father. I know that there were documents about the transfer of Greyhaven, papers on the new companies and documents about the toxicity of the land. Beyond that, there were at least one hundred volumes of personal and financial entries."

"Why don't I remember this? I was on the same treasure hunt."

"Remember, silly, that I was the one who had to hide most of the time, so that's where I hid when I wasn't with you. Rather than waste my time, I read a lot."

"And you concealed it all from Cornelius?"

"My dear, each of us knows about secrets and their necessity. We learned that quite young around here. I don't know whether the secrets come from being a part of our family, being Italian, or being Southern. Quite a toss-up. But, as soon as I found the stash, I knew right away that I needed to keep the contents and location a secret. I haven't read everything. There came a time when I didn't care much. But now, you're here. I'd would rather share the information with you than anyone else." Oddly, her argument was nervously constructed.

"Does Harris know about this find?"

"No," she said abruptly.

"Keeping secrets from your lover?"

"I love him, you know that. But he's not family. You're family," she said, without a blink. "Look, brother dear..."–there it was again–"...I have witnessed betrayal all my life. Individuals changing sides, revealing evil, hiding what they chose to hide or what they needed to hide. I've seen hatreds played out, vendettas, horrible things. You were the only one who has been there for me with any real consistency. Besides which, you've no right throwing stones at my secrets with the one's you've been keeping."

I grabbed at my heart. "Touché!"

"We are so very alike, you and I," she said, surveying my face. "So it's not likely that we could change now, right?" She was almost apologetic.

"Right."

"So, are we going on a treasure hunt?" Madeline peered mischievously through one eye.

"I don't know. It seems intriguing. Oh, what the hell, sure," I caved. "But we have to decide, are we fifty or twelve?"

"Why decide?" Madeline got hold of her seriousness and smiled the impish smile that I remembered, a smile that started every children's book that she penned. She could switch on that childishness at will. She often claimed that writing fantasies kept her in a perpetual state of "picnic." So the adventure that we were to embark upon was just an extension of her inner child, with an adult outcome.

We stayed and talked of other affairs, laughing, crying, and pulling the calloused layers off the core of our bond. Time passed so quickly. Our two hours together seemed to vanish in minutes.

"Oh, my gosh! I must get to Simon's office. He has the plans for our new extension. Harris will be peeved if I don't pick them up. And as you know, *Theatre Absurd* resumes at one."

"How could I forget. What kind of plans are you picking up?"

"We're adding a dining hall to the house."

"Really? That's a switch."

"Yeah, well, Harris feels we need to change our house a bit, and with his new clients, we need to formalize our lives somewhat."

"You okay with that?"

"Absolutely! After Mother's disappearance, I realized that what was devastating about meal time wasn't the room, but her presence in it. With her gone, peace can reign in the food court of our lives."

We both laughed. She stood up, placed her hat atop her head, and gathered her belongings. "Buster, the check, please."

"I've got this, Madeline. You run and grab those plans. You gotta keep your man happy," I said, with genuine sincerity.

"Thanks, sweets. When shall the treasure hunt commence?" Madeline asked, as she swept her enormous straw hat onto her head and pinned it back in place.

"How about tonight, after everyone leaves?" I suggested, innately feeling like this was never going to happen.

"Sounds good," Madeline said, as she checked her face in her compact.

"What about Harris?" I asked.

"After the viewing, he has a meeting with a developer who's trying to find a tract of land to build another mall. We're making the world safe for yet another Walmart. Suffice to say, he'll be home late. You know the good-old-boy connection. Meeting, dinner, sour mash. It'll be early morning before I 'sees my man.'"

"Then tonight it is. Now go!"

I watched her leave, remembering the children we once were. I don't know what turns us into adults. I'm not even sure there is a bridge to cross. It is not a moment or a revelation. It's that same twelve-year-old, but with more information. It is somehow disguised by definition.

Maybe it is more about our level of hope. The more hope we have, the younger we are perceived. The less hope, the older we become. In Manhattan, I somehow lost hope. I saw it right then. I saw it over two frozen hot chocolates and a straw hat. I ran so far and for so long that I aged in the protective cocoon that I spun around me. I wanted to shut my history out and, in the bargain, remained protected from everything and everyone that mattered. I grew older beyond my body, beyond my surroundings. I got what fear designed.

Buster brought the check to my table. He stuttered, a bit unsure about what to say. "I...I overheard your conversation with Madeline," he brazened.

"Which part? The part about our family or the part about my lover?" I became bolder in kind, away from my elemental home.

"The, um, part about your lover."

"I see." The uneasy silence was deafening and my patience quickly expired. "And...?"

"I've heard Madeline speak of her little brother in the big city and always wondered about you."

"Here I am. They say distance always adds to the mystique. Disappointed?"

"No, not at all."

"Must be odd to hear Madeline speak of her little brother and have him turn out to be a fifty-year-old man," I chuckled. "How old are you? Thirty-five? Thirty-eight?"

"Real close. I'm forty next week, as a matter of fact! You're good."

"I used to work the carnival during the summers."

"Look," Buster said, a bit serious, "it's a new town. Leastways, you're new to the town again."

"Yeah, years away does turn one into a stranger."

"I don't know if you're in need of some time away from your family. I know I am, at times."

"Now, who's perceptive?"

"Well, if you do, there's a friendly bar around the corner from the Maiden's Restaurant. Remember where that is?"

"Belicker Street?"

"Yeah. It's called Bellow's. I think you might like it there."

"A local's recommendation. Nothing better."

"Give it a try." His sentence wandered as he backed away from me and the conversation. "I go there, sometimes."

I realized we were now speaking in gay code. A universal arrangement of words that is not dependent on a particular language. He revealed himself to me in his small town, Southern gay fashion, fully in command of revisionist language. I knew to respect it.

A couple dressed in matching pale-green linen, crisp and new as early spring, strolled in with their equally new offspring. They were out of place in their interpretation of what *we* wear on a summer day. This signaled Buster to don a different veneer. His demeanor and his red hair lessened in their intensity, his limp grew more pronounced, his reddened skin seemed to dull as he ushered the patrons to their table with menus in hand.

"What a charming place!" The newcomers' eyes circled like radar over an airport tarmac. "We don't have anything like this back in Chicago, do we honey?" the husband proclaimed as they alternately shushed their petulant child.

"No, we don't. Isn't this delightful!? We should take this idea back home and make a chain out of these! "Buster shot a raised eye in my direction. They believed it was a special place, something that I had forgotten. For them, this was a thing to talk about back home, raising interest and capital for their new idea at a cocktail party high up in a tower along Lakeshore Drive, the right side of the Windy City.

A nod goodbye exited me from Buster's invitation and the tony couple from Chicago. I would keep Bellow's on Belicker and Buster's invitation in mind.

"Hey guy! See y'all tamarra!" I drolled expectedly, waved royally, Southernly, for our visitors. They logged the effect. Southern Code.

# 10

ON THE WAY BACK to Greyhaven, I became more aware of the changes swirling around me. Little haunts and necessities were replaced by chain stores of bland anonymity, reducing the personality of my birth home to an aisle in a supermarket between Asian and Mexican. I became both repelled and defensive of my life and time here. Whittling down the essentials of a familiarity, we could find chitlins and grits, black-eyed peas, and buckwheat, but not the style and grace of slow thoughts and family history, knowledge of neighbors, and their thread in the fabric of local society. To be contenders in this vast machine of commerce we had to condense what we knew and replace it with what was broader, impersonal, and shrink wrapped. Gone were the two hundred acres of Ticer's peach farm and produce stand. A Whole Foods market, bakery, and a Preserves Palace replaced the simpler local jewel, along with severely flattened roofs emulating the evenness of the land. Rice farms were also gone, replaced by chains like Chili's and Barnes and Noble, so you can travel anywhere and buy a book or magazine, dinner, or provisions that were identical to where you left. Coming from South Carolina and moving to New York, this concept of sameness eluded me. I would no more sit in a Starbucks in Manhattan than travel back here to drink coffee in the same place. I came home for what I knew, as well as in spite of it.

The wrong things seemed to be disappearing as I drove back to Greyhaven. It seemed that we were the culprits in our own demise. We had built the blandness and bitched about it over cocktails at lawn parties. We never associated building a better machine with the destruction of our souls and our sense of place and the way we see things. We were no longer separate and apart, but were caught up in the race for sameness. Somehow, to survive in the national obsession, even my own family changed its scope from local to national. The thing that my father and grandfather did to get us out of houses of prostitution and local rumor, catapulted us into another kind of pillage. It was not use and restore, it was rape, plunder, and advance, as if we were our own enemy, compelled to destroy ourselves to succeed. The South, my family, and countless others, no doubt, would live on in a smaller way while their businesses expanded. They would express their roots to other people of the same kind, on acreage once free but now walled in, centered by a country club that resembled houses of our past, built new to look old, adorned with certain trappings that trigger a memory and a fleeting feeling. Greyhaven, steeped in the meaning of the South as it was originally designed, was lost and whittled down to a few acres by measured comparison, a freakish and exaggerated museum holding onto what the recent lineage felt it represented. Had we ever known? Had the distortion started right from the beginning? Were the house and the lands mere time capsules for exploitation of an older kind? Had it been distorted from its inception, or had it always been this way, slowly twisted by the evolution of greed into its present form?

My mind whirled, stirring the broader and lesser details of my trip back here. Fractured thoughts mirrored fractured landmarks as I returned to Salt Marsh. I drove past Parson's Corner as my mind ran with this, Parson's Corner, named after the founder of the First Universal Community of Christ Born Among Us Congregation. In 1790, Reverend Paterson Parson had opened his first chapel at this intersection, which then consisted of two dirt roads. As I approached the building, I realized that its demeanor had changed. It was vacant and dulled, and the windows were covered over. A weathered sign hung on the door of the closed and boarded-up chapel. I stopped to read it.

To Our Faithful Parishioners:

We are pleased to announce our affiliation with United Universalists of Christ Born Among Us, America. We will be moving this historic chapel onto the grounds of the Confederated Universal Museum in Santee, where it will continue to represent the history of our great community and offer to us all a gift shop, so we can develop retail

capabilities. With a grant from the
Pollimers, one of the oldest families in
the region, we will begin construction of
a new chapel on this site, with parking
facilities for two hundred vehicles. It
will house state-of-the-art communications
so we can unite in fellowship and communion
with all Confederated Universalists of
Christ Born Among Us across the land. This
is another success in the long-term goal of
linking us fully to our world and our God.
Thank you for your continued support.

Sincerely,

Rev Arthur Futuris and the Trustees of Par-
sons Universal


The building was pealed and shattered, much like what I had witnessed at Greyhaven the morning before. The lives of this church's
members were buried and joined in the worn stone steps and the jimmy-
rigged hinges that kept the overly nailed and glued doors from falling
off. The stained glass was no doubt removed for display inside the museum. The windows would be replaced by Plexiglas facsimiles, so we
could possibly engender what the founders felt and try the feelings on
like a shirt or a hat from a one-size-fits-all rack.

A board of trustees would pick and choose what was collectively
felt. They would ignore the subtlety of the reasons for the congregation's
birth in favor of a future vision. Similarly, we ignored what we each
brought to Greyhaven, to live out and into what Cornelius, our board of
one, envisioned. His Greyhaven, not mine or Madeline's or Addie's. Perhaps Cornelius aspired to Mother's vision. Did he know Mother's feelings, really? Did Madeline or me? Did Father? Was Cornelius living out
her dream or was he living out the universe he knew, with him as its
center?

Why was Mother so intensely linked to this land, unlike any woman
since Greyhaven's inception? Why had she been so insistent on control?
Wife after wife and mother after mother in our long history used Greyhaven for its excesses and public power. But Mother's use had been different. Its link had somehow morphed. I needed to know.

Perhaps our hunt in the attics of Greyhaven would expose the
links, the differences, the answers. I could only hope. I felt somewhere
within me that this was the key to my decomposition.

Years ago, I'd needed to run from something that I did not understand but had lived through. I was still running. Communication was never the strong suit of families such as ours. Other families of lesser power and money cut their losses at every death. They carried on the subtleties of effect and connection, mentioned offhandedly links and regrets, fortunes and failures. Their scrapbooks were lost in crowded attics and later donated to the Salvation Army in exchange for tax credits. Whereas we held onto everything. Each participant indelibly linked to the next in a long string of decisions and results, like natural pearls strung in a row. Each different and unique but creating the story of the strand and not the single pearl. I stood at Parson's Corner, remembering our Sundays in the quiet pretension of this religious place. We attended services for a while, when Mother felt it was important to mingle. We stopped after Mother had endured as much social snubbing from the women in the congregation as she could stomach. Subtlety was the strong suit of the region. Social standing in the eyes of God and His followers were played out at the coffee hour, religiously performed after Sunday services. This was the proving grounds for a family's importance. Pecking order was established through the offerings brought by the congregants. In biblical times, the sign of a family's wealth was in the plumpness and perfection of a fatted calf or sheep, slaughtered in reverence to God in sight of the villagers.

In the religion of my youth, it became about the Bundt cake. Each Sunday, church elders assigned a woman to make the cakes for the following week's service. It was requested, never voluntary, and was a point of pride and acceptance. In veritable religious equality, the very prominent and the moderately prominent, the rich and the moderately rich alike, showed off their expertise in either baking, or more effectively, hiring the best (and most expensive) baker in the region to do the deed. The congregation included no poor folk and certainly few infamous folk, of which we were the latter. This became clear to me after my morning with Madeline. The pieces and fragments of the puzzle fit all-too comfortably with the mother whom I knew and the woman who was known. As it turned out, Mother was never asked to contribute the fare for the coffee hour. Thus, one less Bundt cake was made and one less fatted socialite was offered to God for sacrifice.

Madeline was right. Mother was forever banished from society for the one thing she could never live down, through, or beyond. It was a carryover from her time in Savannah. She had been a prostitute. Madeline knew it from the time she was very young, and like the congregation, despised her for it.

I stood at the broken door of the chapel, lamenting the loss of what I knew and my family. Finally, the church and my family were oddly the same, even in their differences. Once proud, each struggling for existence and a redefined identity. Standing atop the steps, I was drawn to the graveyard. It had deteriorated as well, with its final art dotting the gentle sweep of the land's curve. The cemetery rolled and twisted behind the chapel, dotted with broken tablets of information appearing more like the rubble and stones when all that remains is the bed floor when a stream dries up. Bordered by a broken stone wall, a rusted iron gate stood as its pinnacle. "The Mercy Of God," written in iron script, stoically welded over the broken entry and managed to complete its thought in rust. I saw the grave stones of Robert Peterson, Grover Johnson, and the elaborate crypt of Alista Pollimer, with its rococo bronze doors, its stone-carved eternal flame, and fallen angels perched on either side of the peaked roof. They permanently lived in fear and protection of the house they were enslaved to secure. Graveyards are the frosting of the church cake. They accompany all chapels. I wondered what would become of all these gravestones and forgotten bodies. The grave art was in disrepair, and the wings of Alista's guardian angels were broken off, lost in the overgrown grass. Would they be moved and repaired to become part of the theme park that the trustees needed to evoke a manipulated emotion and national result? I assumed so.

I picked up the stone wings of Alista's angels and felt their atrophy. Who would protect the angels with the broken wings? Madeline and I had created our angels long ago in the attic in hiding. When I moved to New York, I left my angel here to help protect her. I never found another. We never created gods; we were already surrounded by powerful deities and their histories. We created angels in our myths and stories. I was always sure of angels; they guarded and protected. I was never sure of gods. They struck out with righteousness and planning. Both egos and gods were created through the same mythical and temporal power. Greed and survival created the persona of gods for whatever the need. But in all of the created gods and buildings and religions, it was always the angels that did the work and the protection.

I turned my back on the chapel, the graveyard, the Taco Bell to the right, and the Costco to the left and returned to what I knew. I drove back to my home surrounded by empty houses layered atop filth and mire created by one god, its ornate iron gates at its entrance created by yet another, dancing delicately parallel to this decade's new idea of improved transportation, divided into six lanes, and the country's idea of what was too toxic for human consumption and life yesterday, while marginal today and possibly fine next year. If there was any truth to be found, maybe it was held in the eaves above the porches. Madeline and I would find out, do the work of the angels to free us from this. So, to the gods, the glory; to the angels, the work.

# 11

I ARRIVED AT THE house at 12:30. Cornelius had already arrived and attended to last-minute details. I watched him, as I rounded the carriage house to park the car. He was deep in thought as he walked through the grounds to see if the details appeared authentic. He made notes in his pad but did not record the intense amount of satisfaction that I saw on his face. His power puffed and swelled him at a job well done, a scam well detailed. My stomached turned.

I snuck my way through the arbors that connected the house to the carriage house to avoid running into him. I knew he saw me return. Nothing escaped his view. But we could play the "unnoticed" game, the way one does when recognizing someone at an inappropriate place.

I moved quietly through the kitchen and up the back staircase to my room and began to dress quickly for "Theatre at One," as Madeline called it. I looked out the window at Cornelius who barked last-minute details as the first of the limousines arrived. He briskly walked into the house and let the staff take over for the arrivals. First to arrive were, thankfully, Madeline and Harris. Sarah and my nephews followed. I ran down the main staircase as I had done countless times as a child to greet the people I liked and shun those I disliked.

"Hey, Harris, Madeline." I kissed them both. "Hey Sarah." She appeared with my two nephews. One was the spittin' image of Sarah, and the older had the aloof removed demeanor of Cornelius. "...And look at these two." They came stag. "I cannot believe how much you've grown. Listen to me, saying all those embarrassing things I hated hearing

as a child! You all look terrific." Short and sweet. They removed themselves from the entry hall and took root at the bar, once again open in
the salon.

"Ready?" Madeline and Harris both asked me in an accidental sim-
ilarity.

"Let the games begin."

The cavalcade of vehicles was markedly different today as we
watched the dust rise up from the newly laid gravel drive. Different dust,
richer dust, finer dust than the raucous cloud that followed the path of
my relatives the day before. Drivers pulled up, ran around their vehicles
to let their owners, their bosses, out. There seemed no difference between this moment and one hundred-fifty years earlier, just the conveyance and the contract. Well-coiffed, well-heeled, well-dressed arrogant
men, their wives, and their children. They donned the appropriate de-
meanors, serious faces, as opposed to their country club faces, their
shopping faces, or their acquisition faces. They were well rehearsed, we
were *all* well-rehearsed. They were coming to the head office to view the
man they believed was king. It was a dual visit. Cornelius was right. They
came to pay homage and to look for cracks in the veneer, or tears in the
fabric of a family very diverse and united by little except name. The script
had been laid out and the interaction commenced. We were united and
strong.

"I am sooo sorry for your loss," Adlai Morrisette's daughter, Sophie, cooed. The sound seemed to come from the knuckles of her outstretched hand. "We had not seen much of Titus in the past year or so.
I am sure with his advanced age, he was slowing."

"Yes, I will miss Titus," Adlai chimed in, as if this conversation
had no beginning, just a middle. Such was the privilege of age and wealth.
"I am still not used to it," he continued. "So many years have passed.
They went by so fast. I never thought Titus would die. Somehow, I
thought he would devise a way to live forever."

"Such a long illness. To what did he finally succumb?" Sophie
asked, not necessarily absorbing the answer.

"Pneumonia." I held her hand gently, holding it from underneath,
so as not to cloud her jewels with fingerprints. "Most of his functions
ultimately shut down. Pneumonia was ultimately Father's undoing," I
explained. Page three from Cornelius' Policy and Procedures manual for
this event.

"His death seemed so sudden to have lasted so long. One day we
were on the phone, and then the next he was incapacitated," Adlai said,
a little disoriented by the loss of his friend and cohort.

"We will miss him, absolutely," Sophie added.

"Thank you," I said to her knuckles, as she pulled back her hand. "Titus will certainly be missed."

I noticed the trappings of wealth intertwined on her limbs. A slender woman, Sophie looked the part of wealth. First generation born into it, she was styled right where she needed to be to the expert eye. Dressed perfectly by the book, she wore a simple black, knee-length dress, hair pulled back into a wide clip at the base of the neck, pearls, matched just enough to see the difference. There was, however, a single flaw: she wore too much jewelry. This was always the clue to the generations of wealth. They could copy the magazines, read *Harpers*, or *Town and Country*, but it was something internal about the surety of step and style that the next generation would bring. I looked at Sophie, knowing the secret, whether or not her children had the right stuff, or further, whether they might actually have anything to call wealth when we were done.

This exposed yet another part that I did not like. "Are you in town for long?" I asked.

"No, as soon as we are finished here we are off to the Berkshires. Music festival, you know." Sophie dripped and dropped the location, a test she was ill equipped to pass.

"I understand that they are concentrating on Vivaldi this season, Yo-Yo Ma is the headliner, no?"

"I'm not...not really sure."

Generational wealth has time to read the newspapers, know the cultural highlights, thoroughly, know the top-five restaurants opening this season, and probably have eaten in them before they opened their doors to the public.

"Have you gotten reservations at Pierre's?"

"Pierre's?" Sophie looked pained.

"Yes, Pierre Dulassante. He opened on Madison last year and is doing a stint up in the Berkshires for the summer."

"I must call my agent to get a reservation," Sophie nervously countered.

"Don't bother. Madeline is a personal friend of his, I'm sure she'll help you out."

Another layer of settled wealth missing from Sophie's repertoire. I was starting to get a rhythm for this interaction and wanted Madeline to join in.

"Madeline! Darling, do you have Pierre's number on you?"

"His apartment in the city, or his country house, darling?" She performed beautifully.

"His country house. Sophie needs a reservation in the Berkshires."

"No problem. Consider it done."

She excused herself from another gaggle of groupies, and smoothly joined us, saying hello to the Trilikins and Wally Wilcox on her way.

"He would have been here now, but the season there is overwhelming. Come see the flowers he sent, Sophie."

By the time I handed Sophie off to Madeline, she looked as if she had been hit by a bus. Madeline led away all that remained of her weakened ego to finish her off. She was the master.

Adlai, his seersucker suit, cane, and I remained behind and watched them disappear into the increasing crowd.

"How are you dealing with the transition?" Adlai may have been feeble of limb, but his mind got to the point.

"Pretty smoothly. Cornelius had been running things, as you know."

"Yes, that's why I asked. I'm not sure of his intent. There are so many businesses and so much information that the partners need. He has, how do I say it delicately, not been forthcoming."

This was why my father had been in business with him. He began to sway, unsteady on his cane as much as I was being made unsteady by the conversation.

"Let's sit down over there." I needed time to regroup, and caring about his frailty seemed the right course. We moved to the Celadon silk sofa of the salon.

"I am sure that Cornelius has everything under control," I said, as I helped Adlai rest upon the settee.

"Are you back permanently?"

I didn't know how to answer this. From my heart, I would answer, no; from my head, maybe; from the script, yes.

"Yes, as it stands right now, I am," I kept my answers simple.

"That's good." Adlai leaned both hands on his cane. "We could use some of your father here again."

He was done speaking. He had the information he needed and said what he needed to say. "Let's have lunch when I get back. It's important that we talk."

"Yes, Cornelius and I would like to do that."

"Not with Cornelius. Alone, you and me. No Cornelius, no Sophie. Just you and me." He steadied himself on his feet and summoned his daughter.

"Let's go, Sophie. The Berkshires and your needs await our departure." Adlai was ever astute and aware of people's shortcomings. Sophie's did not escape him. They made their niceties and left, stepping into an opened limousine door. Yo-Yo Ma and Pierre were waiting.

I closed the door on the Morrisettes. Cornelius was fielding Wally Wilcox, the Senator's son and the inheritor of the partnership in the thoroughbred horse farm.

"Yes, Josilyn Benoit is our cousin," I heard Cornelius say. "She is a disgruntled family member who believes that she has a stake in our family's business. There is nothing to what she says." Cornelius was dismissive and firm. I walked over to his little gaggle of financial groupies and joined the conversation.

"Cornelius, did I hear mention of our dear cousin Josilyn?"

"Yes, Faust," Cornelius smoothly added, "I was just telling Wally here that Josilyn has made noise since the day she was born, and that there is nothing to it but an ill-heated breeze."

"But, Cornelius, where there is a breeze there is a storm coming through." Wally turned to me. "Don't you agree, Faust?"

"No, actually I don't, Wally. It's more like flatulence, you know. Always after the fact. But tell me, how are you? I have not seen you since, I can't remember when. The races in Lexington?"

"Why, yes it was. That was so long ago. Eight, maybe ten years."

"I think you're right, Wally. I met Madeline and your sister in town while you were off trading sperm for a position in birth rights. It *was* about birth rights, wasn't it?"

"Good memory, Faust. Yes, it was. We were successful that year."

"So, how's it going, Wally?" Cornelius steered the ship away from Josilyn.

"With…?"

"Sperm sales and stud services, Wally. What else? Have our acquisitions kept up with the needs of the breeding community?"

"Absolutely, Cornelius." He stiffened and stood at attention in the presence of the general.

"That's a funny question coming from the principal stockholder, Cornelius." I decided it was time to take the scrutiny and redirect it.

"Well, never mind, brother. Wally here knows that I trust his decisions. There's been no reason to question his authority. Right, Wally?"

"You're right there, Cornelius. You can come and check the books anytime you'd like."

"Well, thank you kindly, Wally. We have professionals for that, my man. See Faust, we're all on the same page," Cornelius chided me, fawning allegiance and friendship onto Wally. "There's no need, Wally. The standard reports at the end of the quarter are fine."

"So, Faust, is there any reason to be concerned about what I am hearing from that cousin of yours?" Wally sipped his champagne in between words, eyes shifting from me to Cornelius. I understood at that moment the blood theory in the animal kingdom. From miles around, every species can smell the blood of the infirm, the sick, and the weak. The smell swells the nostrils, heats the senses, and peaks the hunger, heightening the need to strike and conquer. The survival of the fittest.

"Ah, she has come to you, has she?" I chuckled. "What a trooper! She just won't give up, will she? Cornelius, did you tell Wally here about her involvement with Reverend Ray Blacksol?"

"Yes, as a matter of fact I did. Such drivel. If there is a scoundrel within a hundred-mile radius, she will either marry him or pray with him. And the fact that they both have hooked up with Reverend Arthur Futuris is...priceless!" This was news to me, and Cornelius' look intensified as if he was trying to communicate telepathically, *Do not react to what you are hearing.*

I always understood Josilyn's involvement with Blacksol. He's a second-rate preacher hooking up to the wrong end of a wealthy family. But Futuris, I couldn't understand this.

"Yes, yes, that is rich!" I played along.

"So, my partners, what's to be done? She is spreading rumors about the land operations. There seem to be oddities surrounding its opening. She told me of midnight crews and trucks coming and going all night long. Please tell me, where is the line is drawn between fact and fiction?"

"There is truth to it, Wally, as you know. It was you who helped Harris meet up with the feds in Chicago. It turned out to be a very successful meeting. The truth is that we are opening the land again for redevelopment. The rules have changed. We're in negotiation with OSHA and the EPA, and it's looking good." Cornelius looked straight into Wally's eyes. "It's looking good for the area, our family, and our business partners." Cornelius spoke directly and with that certain quality of a CEO convincing a room full of employees that the company in which they have invested their lives was strong and solvent.

"I am glad to hear that. When will we be brought up to speed with the details?" Wally pressed.

"We have obvious entanglements here. I would say in about a month, two tops," Cornelius reassured.

"I see. Let me know as soon as possible. I'd also like to know how formidable the religious block is and what their objections might be."

"Trust me, Wally," I said, "their involvement has nothing to do with religion. We'll sort out the whole thing and make it go away."

Cornelius smiled at my interjection as a proud father would smile as his son stole third base in a Saturday Little League game.

I was back. Wally left us after a stiff goodbye. His body language told me that he was unsure but pacified. "Just keep me posted. This kind of thing can get out of hand."

He left as others poured in. The house was filled with nearly two hundred visitors. Each had some association with us, mostly stockholders in all of the public companies. There were thirty companies, or thereabouts, with many stockholders in all but two: Greyhaven Corporation was solely owned by two entities. The majority of its stock was held by my father and mother in trust for the children; Adlai Morrissette also held a minority share. There was also Hidden Wells Corporation, Abigail Delbarton's accounting firm, which held all of the debt of Greyhaven. The company had been formed in exchange for absorbing the lands that Abigail owned so many years ago when the bankruptcy auctions occurred. Father had bought control of the parcels still under Delbarton control. Mother had worked the marriage deals out, mostly in her head and with little involvement from Abigail Delbarton. It was a fair exchange. We married and united with a distinguished family of high regard in the region, and Abigail secured history and finance for her children. Power was the brass ring, and each of them held it, taunting the other to grasp.

Cornelius had explained the night before that one of the dummy corporations established by our father and Abigail Delbarton took care of the books for all of the companies. It kept all of the information of loans and money transfers filtered and managed. Prior to Abigail's death, the transfers and loans had been manageable and a part of doing business. After Abigail's death, the company had morphed into a trust holding, with a board eventually letting Abigail's memory fade. This company guaranteed that Greyhaven could secure the money necessary to convert the contaminated land for redevelopment. Abigail was the original owner of record of these businesses, so that any possible impropriety would go unnoticed. That was the deal. Her name and Southern social standing in exchange for holding her land in trust for Harris and his sister, Cornelius' wife, Sarah. After all, she was part of a pristine Southern family, above the haze of any scandal involving fraud. Local law would ignore improprieties for fear of losing the flow of money into local hands.

And that flow of money made its way regularly into those eagerly waiting hands. Palms sweaty in anticipation of political contributions, touting the transactions as "well-placed investments" from Peaceable all the way to Washington to adjust and purify any state or federal scrutiny. Ah, the political process, slipping all the way up the chain. It all defied gravity.

Cornelius, Madeline, Harris, and I worked the four corners of the house, each keeping the other in eyesight. Nasby, always a secondary player, kept guard and remained reserved, still standing on the break in the stair, perched like an eagle awaiting the flutter of frailty, so he could swoop down to remove the weak. Harris floated around each group, to ensure that nothing legally shaky was discussed. He was the walking cue card for all of us.

Power was its own reward that day and everyone basked in the glory of association with the wealthy coffers of Greyhaven. The demeanor and the pride of the gathered showed in their faces. We gave birth to these people. We created their pride and association. We were responsible for their successes. That felt empowering. I saw in these collected rooms the power of money, the thickening veil of arrogance, and the mystique and allure of history. With few exceptions, the spell had not been altered or broken by Titus' death. Three hundred years of connection. Surely it could go on for three hundred more, unimpeded. A tapping of glasses was heard, and Cornelius quieted the crowd.

"I want to raise a glass. A toast to my father." Silence swept through the room like gravy over biscuits. "Thank you. Thank you for coming. Thank you for your support over the years. Titus is gone, but his memory and accomplishments live on in his family, his companies, and in the people he held dear to him—his partners."

A collective sigh swelled up in the crowd, directed toward Cornelius.

"I look out at y'all and see why Father lived and breathed his life for his companies. 'This isn't business, this is family,' he always said, and I agree. I...we will continue the course that my...our...father set out for us all. We are strong and we are vital. Our father will live on in us and in you. We will forge new heights, achieving the great things that Titus envisioned."

Champagne-filled glasses rose as tide rolling in on the marshes. Silence interrupted subtly by the movements of crystal flute to mouth. Sealing the pact, the bubbly alcoholic bond of people united by a single objective: wealth. A round of applause erupted within the crowd and from room to room amidst the haze of August which punctuated the air like fans pushing heat aside. The applause continued for quite some time, maintained by the Trilikins and the Wilcoxes, the Ruperts and the Johnsons, the Petersons and the Caufields, the Stithers and the Realings. These were faces of attainment, of first generation. They made the deals. And the next in line, their children, hoped the deals would carry them forward through a life that they were accustomed to living. The applause started to die, but there remained an energetic clapper standing at the front door. We all looked toward the commotion and saw a man in black with a flash of white at his Adam's apple and a flash of unruly white at the brow of his eyes and top of his head. It was Reverend Futuris, arms outstretched vigorously clapping.

"May I have a glass as well to raise a toast?" he asked, as the crowd focused. A man dressed in a service tuxedo quickly fulfilled his wish. "So sorry I am late, but I am here to mourn the passing of Titus Madigan and pray for the safe return of his soul to our Lord and Savior."

The demeanor of the silence changed. No longer a silence of reverence, it became a silence demanding answers. The shift was palpable. The crack in the veneer began.

From the four corners of the gathering, we all rushed to be by Futuris' side. Nasby came down from his perch as we all converged on the entry door. Futuris continued to speak. We stood in front of him as a first line of defense, shifting at each of his moves, ready to counter.

"Titus was a dear friend." We knew this not to be true, but the investors did not. "I am saddened by his passing and our loss. I had not seen him for a long time. It never came to pass that I was able to sit with him as his condition worsened, or pray with him on his journey to be with His Savior in Heaven. But I am here now to offer prayer and condolence to the family that surrounded him so thoroughly and securely." He dug a jab to our sides for having been excluded. "Here's to Titus, may his soul live on in peace, in the knowledge that he has left good stewards in his wake to steer the ship he has built. May God bless this house."

We stood frozen in anticipation of worse. I raised my glass and exclaimed, "Titus!" The crowd followed once again and the moment passed. Conversation resumed around us after a pause, and we closed the circle around Futuris, to contain what might come next.

"Reverend, what a pleasant surprise!" Cornelius extended a hand, more to capture than greet.

"I am so sorry that I could not attend yesterday's viewing, but meetings about the growth of our congregation kept me away."

"No matter," Madeline said. "You're here now. Come in and sit with us a spell." She slipped into the vernacular of his own origins.

"I would rather visit with Titus. I am sure that you won't mind. I want to bless the former temple of his spirit, as he embarks on his journey to the light of the Eternal Source of All."

Futuris spoke beyond us in a theatrical tone and timber with his hands stretched out as if reenacting the drama of *The Passion of Jesus*. He would not be captured or steered. He remained in control. Beyond our circle, eyes watched, mesmerized by the exaggeration of the man before them. We needed to shield the crowd from Futuris, so it became our goal to usher him into a quieter and more isolated place.

"Yes, of course," Nasby countered, in surveillance at all times much like a secret service agent. "Let's gather in the library."

"What a wonderful idea," Cornelius added. "You must visit Titus with us as a family for the last time."

Reverend Arthur Futuris came from an old family, much further west in South Carolina; inland people, as we called them. They were different than us. Brackish waters rushed through our veins. Purified, filtered, clear water slipped through theirs. We never trusted clear water people. His family started here some time just after ours. They were involved in cotton and religion. The combination blended well, when you worked all day and had nowhere to find entertainment at night, religion became the substitution. They came from a place of little frivolity, away from big cities like Charleston or Savannah. Prayer replaced theatre. Instead of dinner parties, balls, and orchestras, the night air was filled with healings.

Futuris learned early on that he had a gift for preaching. A bellowing, commanding voice, he could take a simple phrase or word and, by inflection, make it mean more depending on his whim or direction. This served him well. Where we were involved in the business of making power through money, he made power through that which could not be proven or tested–God. He found a way to use the scriptures for his own devises, not unlike the original authors. He captured the attention of the elders in his local parish. They had convinced his parents that sacrificing one child out of their seven to perform in the service of God would be the gift that would return many blessings on their family. They made the deal, placing one of their brood on the sacrificial altar, as was custom to their God and the land on which they lived.

Futuris was admitted into Mount Olive School of Divinity. He flourished there and found his true calling. Upon graduation, tantamount to a slightly lesser sainthood, he was quickly wined and dined by many parishes across the South, and took on three in succession over thirty years before rising to Parson's Corner, a little congregation that had the right demographics, had fallen on hard times, and needed a man of conviction and focus to steer them correctly into the next chapter. Futuris was the man; Parson's Corner, in Peaceable, the epicenter of his storm.

"Thank you so much for your hospitality," Futuris said, "I am so sorry for your loss." We hurried him along, gathering around him like a pack of dogs on a cold night.

"Thank you for your kind words," Madeline said. "I'm grateful that you have shown us the kindness of visiting today."

We all slipped into the library quickly, where we could be alone. The glow of the dimly lit sconces tanned Futuris' skin, as ominous shadows danced upward through his brow, exaggerating his face. He looked like Beelzebub caught in the French paintings seen on a camera trip through the Great Cathedrals of Paris.

"Tell me, Reverend, why are you here? I do not remember Titus mentioning an association with you," Cornelius said, as he closed the doors of the room.

"I am glad we're alone now," Futuris said. He floated over to the coffin and stroked Titus' head in a dramatic sweep of his right hand. "We need to talk."

"Why didn't you come with Josilyn yesterday?" I asked, as if we were at a roundtable forum with Futuris as the guest interviewee. I wasn't buying his *public* reason.

"I felt that this visit should not be about Josilyn or Ray. Their animosity makes me uncomfortable."

"I am glad to hear that from you," Cornelius said, in measured words. We began to stare at the reverend as if he were a high school chemistry experiment that might go awry.

"This is about business that does not concern them."

"With all due respect, Reverend Arthur, what business could you possibly have with us? We stopped coming to Parson's Corner many years ago, when we were, how can I say it politely, *disinvited*," Cornelius added, arching his back in preparedness. He remembered the slight, the pain, and the humiliation that had fueled many stories around the dinner table between Mother and Titus.

"Let's not bring up unpleasantries from the past. That is all done, and I am sorry if the congregation was less than Christian toward you."

"Less than Christian. How delicately put," Harris complimented, while sizing him up. "It was the only *Christian* we knew."

"I see that you are busy," the Reverend focused, "so, I'll make this brief. Josilyn brought me into this. I have had several meetings with her and Reverend Ray. He is a silly man. I sat with them in her God-awful trailer, slapped in the face with shrine after shrine of her dead husband. It was quite an unfortunate incident that caused his demise. Seems if you could survive that environment, you could survive anything,"

It was well known that Reverend Arthur was always discerning about where he visited and with whom he associated.

"She showed me photos of trucks moving dirt and carrying hundreds of barrels away. I told her that she needed to purchase better infrared photo equipment. Like a cheap suit, the impressions that you are left with are poor." Futuris dusted off his lapel for effect. "They are passionate people, Josilyn and Ray, and they make quite a pair. They kept bringin' God into it, as if He would really sign on to this battle. Funny." He chuckled sarcastically. "I didn't give them much credence. You know how petty and small people get when cloaked in jealousy. Through our meetings, and there were more than I could stand, they were persistent." He looked down at the polish of his nails. "There were bits and pieces of what they were saying that didn't make sense, 'til they produced a particular article of clothing."

"*Clothing?*" Harris repeated. "What possible clothing could they have that would interest you?"

"A jumpsuit, actually." Futuris was pleased with his dramatic comeback. "Claimed they snuck up on a guy who decided to take some relief in the woods off the beaten track from the site he was working. When he unzipped his protective gear and undressed, he turned his back to take care of business. With that bit of opportunity, apparently, they ran off with his jumpsuit. It was silver. Made of a material that I could not identify 'til I took it to one of my parishioner's handymen. He knew of such things." Futuris shifted a bit. "You might know him. Bubba Johnson. Used to do night clean up at the hazardous waste plant outside of Greenville."

We continued to listen without interrupting.

"He recognized it immediately and asked where I got it. I told him a cock-and-bull story about wanting to wear it at our next Halloween benefit dinner dance and how I wanted to make sure it looked authentic. Bubba explained the suit to me, right detailed like. I kept an innocent demeanor, very wide eyed."

Futuris mimicked the look that he wore with Bubba. "He told me the reasons for the suit and what it does. It sure does keep nasty things from gettin' inside of y'all. My interest sure was piqued, like seein' lightning when you're on a golf course. But, you know about such stuff. I had a silver suit and not much else."

"I concur. So, what exactly is it that you think you have?" Harris asked.

"Oh, Harris, Harris, Harris, circumstantial, hazy proofs just piss off the local establishment, no?" Harris nodded at Futuris' words. "And then it goes nowhere."

"So is there a point to this little intrigue?" Harris asked.

"Sorry for being such a long-winded storyteller but, I tell ya, it wasn't 'til they showed me a letter from Ivinia that I really felt the heat from that lightning. That is, I suddenly saw some merit to what they were saying."

"And what letter is that?" Harris became the spokesman of this hastily gathered group.

"Ah, I have it somewhere." Futuris feigned a search, surrounded by eyes filled with expectation. But Harris wasn't biting. He knew no letter would be produced...at least not today.

"As I was saying, Josilyn's concerns are petty." Futuris continued the faux search.

"I'm glad you agree with us," Madeline countered to the Reverend, too soon.

"I must have left the letter in my safe." We were being played. "Yes, her concerns and grievances are petty. She tends to continually miss the big picture, she and her little friend, Reverend Ray. If God had to depend on small-time losers like Ray, I wager we'd still be in the desert."

"A reverend with a vault, no one is assured of safety anymore," Madeline said.

"Yes, it's a shame what's going on in this world. God knows I pray daily for Earth's salvation, but until then, a vault does suffice." He raised both hands toward heaven and bellowed, "... '*Til the spirit of God's justice shines through*, I always say."

"With all due respect, Reverend, this justice you speak of, whom might it be for?" Nasby went fishing with a more obvious bait, no subtlety.

"For whom?" Futuris repeated. "Good question, Nasby. By the way, thank you for the job that you did on Selma Peebles. Her face was a mess after that deadly pressure cooker accident. She never looked better. You made her funeral a visual success." Futuris continued. "What was I saying? Ah, yes, justice for the little people, the downtrodden, the abused, the oft-overlooked, those people who money only touches in books and movies. Those people who watch the rich ride by in their shiny cars while they walk. People whose only way to visit foreign lands is to buy a bottle of water packaged in Fiji or France." He stood, right-eous and proud, as if this had been his life's dedication, lo these many years.

"What would you know 'bout the downtrodden and the poor, rev-erend?" Nasby blurted. "You haven't seen anyone poor since your first congregation in the Blue Ridge Mountains. And how long was that gig, six months?"

"Now, Nasby, there's no need to be hostile," Cornelius countered.

"*Hostile?* How can you stand here and listen to what's coming down? This con man is running for office, at a funeral no less!"

"Nasby, calm down," Harris added.

"I will not calm down. He is threatening us, and no one wants to say the words."

"You're not threatening us, are you, Reverend Arthur?" I asked, as I touched Nasby on the shoulder. He was pushed beyond what his Ma-rine training could tolerate.

"Oh my, now I've gone and done it. I have given you the wrong impression," Futuris said, in feigned apology. "I have always been a heartfelt and loyal supporter of your family, despite what others have said about you."

"These are the same Christians of which you speak?" I said.

"Unfortunately, yes. But, with all the tragedy and rumor that has surrounded you over the years, I sympathize and give you my total sup-port. What kind of person would I be if I did anything less?"

"Thank you kindly, Reverend. With such graciousness being shown us now, in our hour of mourning, I'm driven beyond words into feelings of warmth and spiritual generosity," Madeline said.

"Let me get to my point. I see great things happening for this re-gion, new developments, new opportunities, and great political ad-vantages."

There it was. This was a new direction for Reverend Arthur Futuris and his thirst for power.

"And how would any of that be of concern to us?" Harris asked, with a knowing look already on his face. Madeline grabbed at his hand and he pushed it aside, taking a more protective stance in front of her. Harris's lawyerly instincts were piqued.

"I am concerned for my constituen…parishioners, that the land where all those unfortunate people lived is about to reopen. I am also concerned for their future health issues. I might add that if news of these mysteriously disappearing barrels leaks prematurely, let's say, before y'all work your *magic* on the government agencies, then I can't imagine how the surrounding neighborhoods might respond. They may fear that those barrels might just wind up under their own houses."

He continued, even more sure of himself. "And let us not forget the way news travels so quickly, with a well-placed phone call to, let's say, the local TV stations, and we all know about the speed of the information highway, that is what they call it, no? The internet? I more than suspect that you know people in high places, and it would seem that you might want to avoid this kind of trouble." Futuris puffed with pride at the trap he believed he was setting.

"And how would we avoid *this kind of trouble*?" Cornelius got in the way of Futuris and Titus as he asked the question that brought all this into focus.

"Why, I just don't know, right now, but I will put my thinking cap on for you. I know that we all want what's right for this area. I know that I am not alone in this. After all, Titus and y'all loved this land. You have history here, and I'm sure you would not want that history marred by another scandal. There have been so many that you have already lived through with Ivinia, you, Faustus…the lot of you, really. I don't want that ever to happen again and I would do my utmost to prevent it."

The light from the sconces flickered against the walls with a seemingly collective shudder. The shadows of the books appeared to tremor and retreat, as if to protect the secrets held within. I could not help but look at Titus, laying in the coffin, trying to catch a reaction. Why didn't he rise up and defend us from this marauder, this carpetbagger? Why were we left to be manipulated and challenged in a fashion that might very well destroy what remained? I remembered so often that the subtle defenses my father mustered up were never enough to satisfy the hurt or prevent the danger ahead. He just stood there, depending on his stature, integrity, or righteousness to change the course of events. A silent pride. If he orchestrated a big, behind-the-scenes involvement, it was hardly ever evident. This was his style. In a family where trouble and turmoil were always so obvious, it seemed that the response should be as dramatic as the act. Such was never the case.

"I want to thank y'all for your concern," the Reverend said.

"Get back to us when you have a recommendation," Harris answered. "We are certainly receptive to anything a man with his finger on the pulse of the county might have to say."

"I am glad that I could be of service. I'm looking forward to a fruitful relationship. After all, we all are just foot soldiers in the army of God, are we not?"

He left the library. But as he walked through the door and entered the crowded reception hall, Reverend Arthur Futuris turned dramatically, raised his arms like Jesus at the Sermon on the Mount, and said, "Bless y'all for honoring Titus. He is with God in heaven, and Titus knows that I'm at your service in God's name."

The act was profound and the scene convincing to the crowd. It was certainly not reflective of his true posture, only the public face that Futuris needed to dramatize. We closed the doors of the library as if to be alone with our father.

"Did that really just happen?" I asked.

"Helluva performance!" Madeline chimed in.

"Yes, quite a piece of theater. I think we'll be sending him on out-of-town tryouts," Cornelius said. He wasn't joking. Cornelius' eyes bounced frantically in his head as if he were playing out an imagery conclusion to the Futuris complication in his mind's eye. I didn't care to know what Cornelius was thinking, nor did Cornelius appear anxious to share his thoughts.

"Let's see how this plays out, Cornelius. It may just be a play for some money, a piece of the action, something not as public as it might seem." Harris tried to diffuse the obvious so that we could continue with the business of the day.

"Come on, Harris, you heard him. He's going to be a lot more dangerous than Josilyn and Reverend Ray," Nasby said. "They have been mouthing off for years. Everyone dismisses them, but Arthur, he's another matter. He is head of a powerful parish, rebuilt from nothing. He's surrounded by supporters who would not have our best interests at heart."

"These are the same people who rejected us socially yet their hands are still out and grabbin' at our pockets," Madeline added.

"I know. Let him reach out to us again. Let's not move too quickly," Harris said.

"You don't know how it felt to be shunned," Madeline remembered.

"I know, dear, but patience is power," Harris moved to console.

"No," Cornelius shot back. "Patience is power to you, but it is business as usual for me. I do not have the temperament to wait this out." Cornelius opened the door to the library and Sarah entered.

"What's going on?" Sarah looked confused. "I just watched Reverend Futuris grandstand his way out the door, passing out his calling cards to all our partners. He made a lunch date with Wally Wilcox before Wally goes back to the ranch. Anyone care to tell me what's going on? I smell trouble."

"We received a veiled but serious threat to expose the land deal prematurely to the locals," Harris said. "We may be in for some serious complications."

"We've weathered worse," Cornelius said, returning to his measured and unruffled tones as he exited as if floating on automatic pilot.

"What now?" Sarah asked, then turned to her children who stood at the library door. "I'll be right out boys," she said, shooing them away to perhaps keep the cancer within from spreading to her offspring.

"What now? There seems to be a crack in the dam, no? Not one of us expected this?" I couldn't hold back. "This is why I left. I constantly feel dirty here. I get sucked in to an arena where the lions are underfed."

"Cut the dramatics, darling, and let's just get through this," Madeline said, surprisingly. "I'm not particularly in love with the thought of getting in a pissing contest with a man of the cloth, but I have to admit I am intrigued by the prospects of finding out what's in our reverend's mind." She walked over to kiss me and soften the blow of her words. "Sorry, love, I just can't have this drag on anymore. I need this to be done. We all do." She touched my cheek and I saw Madeline change right before my eyes. She put my fears on red alert.

"I hope you're right," I said.

"I'm as right as I can be at the moment."

We left the library in single file as if a fire alarm had sounded. I gazed at the crowd standing in the August heat and the melting gold and red around them. The heated color created halos that banded everyone's head. The crowd seemed to move in slow motion, staring alternately down at Futuris' card then up toward us, questioningly. They searched our eyes for an answer. These same faces that, years ago, started out so innocently, had developed a language and a business savvy that smelled deceits and secrets.

Madeline and I rushed out to the veranda with the family in tow, sweeping through the crowd in gracious but nervous demeanor, to find cards strewn everywhere—the courtyard, the flowerbeds, caught between the wipers and the windshields of limousines and personally driven BMWs, Mercedes, and Lexuses. Futuris had spread his cards like rice at a wedding. For him, it was the start of a new partnership that held promise. A late-afternoon breeze blew down the path from the road and caught errant cards in flight like paper airplanes. We frantically began picking up the mischievous kites that shone in the angular sun. Picking, picking, and picking, and then even more picking, all the while unaware of the gathering crowd on the veranda that watched us reenact cotton harvesting as if we were actors in a revival play about the early South.

Those we knew gaped in shock at our behavior.

Ted Willikin spoke first. "What in the hell are y'all doing?"

We emerged from our collective trance.

"That preacher never lets up," Cornelius said, regaining his composure almost immediately while the rest of us looked as though we'd been caught with our hands in the pie keeper.

"Yes, sometimes Reverend Futuris' zeal overcomes him and overwhelms everyone around him," Harris said. "He misses Titus so much that he assumes everyone around him feels the same pain. He is only too willing to help spiritually with everyone's sadness."

"He is a little over the top," Ted said. "He invited everyone to a service next week, even promised a dinner would follow afterwards."

"There will be no such thing," Madeline said. "This is our father, not his. I'm sorry, Ted. As much as I am fond of Reverend Futuris, I will not abide such an intrusion on our mourning. I will respectfully ask you, all of you, to kindly disregard any overtures by Arthur. He has become a little unglued by...by all of this. He means well, but this cannot continue."

"Okay, Madeline," Ted replied. The crowd grunted and nodded in agreement. "He was a little extreme. We'll honor your wishes. Just seems that a man professing to be as spiritually close to y'all should be minded."

"Thanks for your input, old chap, but I'm going to insist that you stand behind us on this," Harris said.

"To...Titus!" Andrew Carson, our partner in pork belly futures yelled from behind the crowd to transition us away from the awkwardness.

"I'll miss Titus, but remember that it is the family that remains and the family that I respect," Ben Bosworth, our partner in the Kick Rump Chickin' franchise, added.

"Here, here!" Ted said.

As the crowd filtered back into the house, it dropped its paper clues, leaving us standing in the confetti-like aftermath of Futuris' helter-skelter carding. We looked at each other in silence and followed our partners into the house, picking up more cards as we walked.

It took another hour before the visitors started to leave and longer still for our fragile confidence to return. We bid goodbye to the last of our partners at shortly past 6:30 p.m., turned off the lights, and pushed the help to go on their way, ensuring that they would arrive a bit earlier the following day.

Cornelius closed the door as the last staffer departed. He pressed his forehead against the shiny mahogany door and bolted it. His exhaustion showed for a split second and we watched as our alpha leader regrouped. He turned to look at us.

"Thank you for all of your assistance today," he said. It was then that I knew that this bit of theatre, this charade, was not for the preservation of the *family* history, or for Titus, or for any of us. An uncomfortable air filled the entry hall as we stood around and stared at each other in our collective emotional nakedness. Cornelius exposed the truth behind his façade. He owned the moment. Madeline would have none of it.

"Cornelius," she said. "We are all in this together because of the exposure *and* the payoff. Remember that. So, in actuality, I thank *you* for a job quite well done." Madeline's words threw me off course. Was her bravado genuine? I withdrew silently to think.

"I, for one, am tired. Let's go, kids." Sarah draped her shawl around her shoulders and secured it to a diamond brooch. She ushered her children, as if toddlers. They left with her behind them, shielding them further from any more Madigan infection.

"Aren't you waiting for me, dear?" Cornelius asked, surprised by her exit.

"No."

Sarah's sudden exit left Cornelius isolated, exposed, and staring at her back. The momentary silence swelled up from the floor like a fog that rolled in beneath our feet, invisible at first but slowly swirling thicker and thicker, fixing us to our places. I stood alone at that moment, knowing that I felt the same as ever, the same hollow ache in my stomach. I wished Sarah had included me in her protective exit.

Cornelius turned, red faced, from the humiliation. "Anyone else want to leave?"

"No, Cornelius, we still have stones in our pockets. Apparently my sister has emptied hers."

Harris' comment brought back memories. Ages ago, we used to play games out in Back Bay with Addie. This happened during Mother's interminable garden parties where she sought to muster social acceptance. The only way she could entice visitors from the local gentry was by throwing so much money at a charity that they would comply with her wishes to host a dinner, Sunday social, or ball. Otherwise, our only visitors were family members, a few business partners, or people she knew from the West Coast—movie people. When one of those times came around—and they came around as often as Mother could arrange—she would cart us off to Addie's and drop us in her welcoming lap.

"Stop what you're doing, Addie, and take care of these for me, will you?" Mother refused to speak of us by name. It was as though we were a sack of potatoes. Cornelius, of course, was never part of the drop off. She would hardly stop the car before we were covered in the dust of her speedy exit. Addie would sweep us up in her apron and sit us down on her back porch that overlooked the bridge connecting all the little islands together. There we would play one of her games. She invented games all the time to keep us occupied.

One of the games Addie taught us had, she said, come from her great grandmother, who had taught her grandmother, who had taught her mother, who had taught Addie. She would set a pile of colored stones on the table. They glistened like precious gems, all different colors and shades. She said they came from Senegambia, her ancestral home. Then we played cards, and the winner of the throw would place a stone in his pocket. If you lost a card throw, then you removed a stone from your pocket and placed it in a tea cup on the table. If you matched the color of a stone in the tea cup, you would take two stones back. This game lasted for hours as we'd laugh the time away on Addie's porch, eating her cranberry biscuits and ham hocks, while the feel of salt water air, sweet and tangy as perfumed oranges, brushed against our skin.

"What do you mean *stones in your pocket?*" Cornelius was in the dark.

"Nothing, Cornelius. It was part of life that you missed," Harris said. He'd heard this, and many more stories over the years, so much so that he was closer to being family than Cornelius. "Need a ride home, Cornelius?"

"No thanks. I'll get Huxley's Service to take me. I'll wait outside."

"I don't know who gets more tortured with Huxley's Service, Honor Huxley or Cornelius, who insists on using him," Harris said.

Honor Huxley and his wife, Betty Lou, had lived in a little house on Arcadian Way in our development, Greyhaven Estates years ago. While residing there, Betty Lou gave birth to two stillborn children and two more who were so seriously deformed that they had to be institutionalized before hitting puberty. Years later, when the news went public, we settled with Huxley and they moved further up county, as far away from this trouble that his business would allow. Cornelius felt that our family had settled the issue and that in doing so, he had the right to avail himself of any service he needed in the county. "After all," he'd said, "we dealt honestly with all parties concerned."

Cornelius called the taxi from the hall phone, then adjusted his tie and his pride as he walked out the door and to the end of the drive. He knew that although Honor would pick him up, he refused to step foot on any Greyhaven property. After all, a fare was a fare. Honor was the only game in town.

"Before I meet with the developer, I'm going to head home and get to work," Harris said. He scratched his head in amazement.

"What work, my love?" Madeline asked, as she adjusted his hair and stroked his cheek.

"I think we are going to need some background material on our Reverend Futuris."

"Tonight?" I asked.

"If he has a secret, I'm going to find it." Harris picked up a briefcase that he kept in the coat closet of the reception hall.

"What kind of secret are you looking for?" I asked.

"Anything that will make it unprofitable for him to pursue his current track." Harris donned his straw hat. He was striking. This was the Harris of which Madeline and I spoke, when we both wished for our ideal partners. She found it in him. He stood face to face next to his wife. I followed the arch of his back and the curve of his neck, as he looked down at Madeline to kiss her goodbye. It reminded me of the photo I received from them when they first announced their engagement. They were fuller, more mature people now, but retained a connection that increased by layers and years. Their lives grew parallel, with the roots of what they'd planted, intertwined so that the origins were no longer apparent. Each protected the strengths of the other and nurtured their weaker sides. They worked their personal corporation with a goal in mind: survival.

"Think there's something?" I interrupted their moment.

"There is always something," Harris said, his eyes never leaving Madeline's. He kissed her on the forehead and held her arms. I watched her close her eyes and lean into him just a little and saw their connection. "I'll be at home, if you need me."

"See you tomorrow, my love."

Harris left us to our devices for the night. We watched as he stepped into his car and drove away, gravel spitting off rear tires like spray from a sprinkler.

# 12

THE SUN HIT a spot in the sky where it starts to pay attention to its next destination. Now the only occupants of the house, except for Pru, the housekeeper whom Cornelius had planted, were Madeline and me. We started to relax and plan our evening. After all, we had much to do. There were corners of the attic that had not seen the light of eyes in many years, or so we hoped. Father had multiple hiding places that no one knew but us.

"I have to get out of this black stuff. You know, our old clothes are still in our rooms." Madeline began to reenter her childhood.

"Don't we have to start looking for the papers up in the eaves?" I asked.

"Haven't you had enough seriousness for one day? Can't you have a little fun?"

"Madeline, I have been back for two days. I have not seen this place for thirty years. I come back and, except for a few wrinkles and an old corpse, nothing much has changed. The intrigue, the heat, the dust, and the people are all the same. And now you want me to not only get absorbed into the workings of our family, but to dress the part. It's a big ask. Besides, I hated myself in that stuff when it was new. What makes you think it will look any better?" I protested her scathingly brilliant idea, but chuckled privately at the thought of bell bottoms and hot colors.

"Oh poo, just do it. We need to have a little fun in spite of this whole thing. Come on! "She pushed me toward our old rooms and we rummaged through the armoires and the dressers, the chifforobes and chests. Wire and wood hangers clanged as we quickly threw together our fashion statements. It all slept there, waiting to be nudged awake. What we did not take with us upon our departures lay patiently as if we were coming right back. The family threw nothing away. We nurtured the notion of dynasty. This is, in part, what makes dynasties. We do not just have necessary possessions. We have collections of every imaginable sort. We closet and box, categorize and log, sort and move, and dispose of little. We create catalogues and history at auction houses when pieces and parts of human creation surface just when they seem lost forever. It is part hubris, part arrogance, that we assume that anyone is interested. It is the theory that those who die with the most toys win. So, actually, it will always continue. The next generation will rush breathlessly to collect what the past generations have acquired, to create a memory, to capture a feeling, but mostly to win and surpass, kicking sand in the face of the last best, to be the next greatest. This seemed isolated to the eighties, but it was not. Wealth always believed this notion. It just filtered down to a segment of the populace that heretofore never dreamed of such accumulation and accessibility. Our greed became the goal of the masses. We taught them more about ourselves than we bargained. We showed them how to covet things when the joy left on the exhale.

Giggles and shrieks came from behind each of our doors, laced with utterings ranging from "Oh, my God, I can't believe I wore this!" to "What the hell was I thinking?" We quickly changed into costumes covered in the heady smells of mothballs. We dragged out clothing that was so out of fashion that we were on the cutting edge of what was coming. Madeline appeared in a lime-green and yellow-plaid André Courrèges dress with a sailor's collar and thick-soled magenta boots. I found navy-check pants and a blue nylon Yves St Laurent shirt with a large pointed collar and electric-navy platform shoes. We simultaneously ran into the hallway that adjoined our rooms.

"Do you believe this? Do you believe that I *wore* this? I told you that this stuff wouldn't have a shelf life. And by the way, look at you!"

I roared at the sight of my sister in her period outfit with zippers that didn't zip, buckles that didn't buckle, and belts that didn't complete their round-trip excursions. She could not stop laughing at my costume either. My nylon shirt strained at the tension created between button and hole. The plaid of my pants bellied and curved in strained contortions, covering a body it was no longer designed to fit.

"Don't you wish you still fit into that thing?" Madeline pointed to the half-buttoned shirt whose opening surrounded my thickened stomach, years in the making. She struck poses from one end of the hallway to the other. I ran back to the armoire and pulled out a broad-brimmed hat and cocked it to the side of my head feeling very natty. Each of us wobbled and wiggled on and off the platform shoes of our past.

I'd taken none of these belongings from home when I left because they reminded me of the arrogance and extremity of the times and of this place. When I left, I did so with only a few pairs of jeans, loafers, plain shirts, and a business suit. New York was a fashion town and the birthplace of the seventies fashion scene. It shared the spotlight with Carnaby Street in London. Most of our clothes and fashion *must haves* came from there, as well as the Left Bank in Paris. With all the plaid, sharp lime, navy, and shades of orange, I'd found a small circle of hold-outs in New York who wore black. Always timeless, a little held over from the beat generation, anti-war, intellectuals, the coffee house sect left to their own time warp. Even though black took on the severe silhouettes and proportions of the times, it still read black. Extreme, blank, basic, and monk-like in its simplicity. Mine was a smaller club, with fewer members, surrounded by a prison of colorful uniforms. To a select few, everything else was just a shade away from correct. I became comfortable in that translation, found my group, and settled in. For all the traveling that our family did, I had thought the garish colors I wore at home were the colors of the South and the heat and the wet. I was myopic in my distaste for all my Southern experience. It was the first lesson I learned about my ancestral home. I had created a nonexistent vacuum for myself, a singularly distorted vision.

Summer and heat, in and around Beaufort, did not bring out the colors that would seem garish further north. Fashion, politics, and affluence were the culprits; war, the emotional motivator; and political consciousness, the fuel. Color bleached against the heat and looked pale and wistful here. Up north, the same colors intensified in front of the gray backdrop and made those of us who wore shadows stand out. Purples, reds, and psychedelic color irradiated the landscape and mirrored the dreams that drugs caused. Still, people looked to those in black for the insight, the wisdom. We had much to offer in the way of discourse, solution, and intellectual anarchy. Our silence often resembled pensive wisdom. We had nothing to offer by way of action. We determined early on that we just conceptualized, we didn't implement. Implementing was left to those who could not form whole sentences, but could use our thoughts to form their lives. So, until we found such a small-minded contingency of people, we partied and danced our night lives away, spouting political postures and predilections while snorting, sniffing, and inhaling an alphabet soup of drugs. We kept the colors in our heads.

"What else is hiding in that room of yours?" Madeline woke me from my reverie and I ran into her room. We pulled everything out, held it up, and told stories attached to each item as if a script had been sewn into every seam. The clothes revealed a scrapbook that softened over time. We did not remember the hurts and dramas but, rather, for a moment, the bits of fun attached to our lives. Clothes leapt into the air as we trashed the pristine room, scattering cotton, wool, and nylon everywhere. I think we began to hope that by covering our rooms with these former belongings we could change what was and mask it with a layer of sweetness. The noises we made became increasingly childlike and I took Madeline by the hand and rushed her into the hall again, throwing an ostrich feather boa around her neck.

"Do you think there's anything left to eat?" I asked. "I'm ravenous."

"I think the caterers moved everything into the refrigerators," Madeline surmised. "Let's go downstairs and make the biggest sandwiches known to mankind."

"Sounds like a plan. Let's go."

Platformed and pinched, we wobbled and wended our way down the stairs. As we hit the break in the stair the loudest bang erupted from the attic above our heads, followed by a dragging sound. It startled us so that we became still unsteadier in our abrupt stop.

"What the hell was that?" Madeline squealed.

"That's the noise that I heard last night."

"That's no spirit of the past."

"So sorry I scared ya," Pru peeked around the stair wall. "I was up in the attic gettin' things for Cornelius."

Once again, Pru descended the attic stairs and opened the door in front of us.

"What exactly are you getting up there? You have been rummaging around ever since I arrived."

I felt annoyed, not only at the intrusion into my time with Madeline, but at the violation by Pru's seemingly incessant pillaging of my stored family history. As much as I ran from the bits and pieces of my family puzzle, I resented an outsider rummaging through it all, no matter who paid her salary. It was sacrosanct in that place up the back stairs and I wanted no one outside the bloodline to touch it.

"I am sorry, but Cornelius, he gives me strict orders to git this done." She held papers and scrapbooks close to her chest.

"Know what, Pru? You need to go downstairs, 'git' yourself comfortable, and stay as far away from the upper floors as possible, got it?" I spoke New York, fast and direct.

"Okay, but…" Pru tried.

"No *buts* about it. You have done enough for one night. We are going downstairs to make ourselves something to eat. Would you like something?" Madeline registered a pleased surprise on her face. She liked me curt.

"Thank ya kindly, but I brought my own stuff. I'll just git on to my room," Pru resigned.

"Yes, that would be wise," I assured her. "You'll need your rest for tomorrow. It'll be a big day."

"Yes…all those people from far away, and the locals." Pru looked like the Cheshire cat, smiling through her knowledge of the guestlist for the third and final day.

"What do you mean, *far away*?" Madeline asked, as much surprised as I was.

"Oh, I has spoken outta turn," Pru smiled impishly at her revelation. "I'm getting things ready for some outta towners…all the way from Hollywood. Movie people, you know." She looked side to side, mouthing the words louder than the sound that came out, like old biddies in black sheer head shawls who, over afternoon tea or juleps, whisper words like *cancer* or *affair* at recreational funerals or *in the family way* when gossiping about a young woman having a child without an *in-town* husband. She said *movie people* this way, resembling a fox that had been given the key to the lock on the hen house door. After a moment, Pru continued.

"Cornelius felt it right necessary to include some of his, that is, *your mama's*, friends from way over on the West Coast, see'n as they all knew your father and all."

"There are any left?" I asked the air, coming down from my perch of superiority of absence and command. I expected no answer from the blank look on Madeline's face. "Exactly who is coming?" I asked insistently.

"Don't know for sure. I was just told how many were coming and to get some of the old picture books down from the attic."

"Let me get this straight. Cornelius invited Mother's friends on the West Coast to the funeral?" I asked incredulously.

"It's news to me." Madeline searched the air for a clue to this new turn, "I can't imagine Cornelius wanting any of them here."

"You know more," Madeline insisted. "Fess up, Pru, or I'll wup you this side of heaven's outhouse, I swear!"

Pru knew that Madeline's words meant business. She was from a family where corporal punishment was doled out as often as blue ribbons at a county fair. Pru's daddy, Alias Stern, often used harsh talk. Pru was born in what every class above her station in life called the *back side* of the county. It edged the lands either at the end of old plantation markers long since plowed under, or at the outskirts of towns where Walmart feared to tread, where roads had no exits, where there were no stores, not even abandoned ones. No one ever built anything there that could be abandoned or depressed. The back side became its own small country, its own territory, self-governed and forgotten. Bits and pieces of scrub pine and swamp that were neither rich enough to support new growth crops nor fresh enough to supply proper irrigation for nearby farms. The land was not wet enough, dry enough, fertile enough, or situated well enough to be of any use to anyone except for a small collection of social misfits who were not even successful at skullduggery. Like my father's family, not ne'er-do-wells, not thieves, not scam artists, not shiftless.

Back side residents were known as "bits and scraps" by people who availed themselves of their services. They performed little jobs of short duration that did not fall into the category of handymen or house servants, mister fix-its or temporary help. Just...bits and scraps. They were nomads of sorts without wanderlust. Uneducated and silently desperate, Cornelius used Pru Stern and her family because they needed the work. Her ilk did the work because they needed the money. They lived vicariously through the people that hired them, and accepted little bits of money, and scraps and remnants of items that were going to be thrown out anyway.

Cornelius found Pru and her kind extremely loyal for the exchange of work and silence for pay. They did not talk the way other help in the region talked. The underground of gossip was always spread by the service class of the area and was established when the first settlers arrived. It flowed gentle but steadily from the third floors and the dirt cellars of every home, exchanged in the marketplaces and stores where *agents* would meet to hand off their stash of gossip, so the daily news would envelop the far reaches of every household in the county by evening. Pru and her clan were not part of this. So even the service class had no use for them socially.

I had known Pru's family on and off through my youth and adolescent years. Like my family, hers had been here for many generations. We became interdependent as the years went on. We neither liked nor accepted each other. It was situational détente. They came and went at our will and were trustworthy because they adhered to a strict code of ethics that were born from remnants of ostracized Shakers from Penn-

sylvania, distracted rural mountain Christians, and purported Indian relics all mixed together like the leftover autumn fruit of a medley pie. They
met through their difference and intermarried because of the dominant
"misfit" gene that appeared in all of them. Their lack of identity identi-
fied them.

They took little solace in blending socially as a group but were always ready to adopt one stranger at a time, which expanded into a family
that turned into a herd that grew into a region. They lived in shacks that
had a mix of cardboard and old wooden crates on their sides, tin on their
roofs, and shredded pieces of brocade knotted over windows sporadically missing panes of glass, therefore not completely sealed from the
elements. They lived on dirt roads, collecting discarded pieces of everyone else's lives. Their outhouses, crudely dug, sat next to their congrega-
tional meeting halls, each of similar construction, hard to discern one
from the other. Their land was where scrap metal from junkyard cars
became the fences that defined their plantings, scattered with limp corn
and twisted debris. They squatted on, but did not own, their land, and
did not care to learn that no one would have them, but for toil and task,
keeping to their jumbled traditions of baking good bread in communal
stone ovens with their lives kept honest not only by the venom of peoples' disregard, but also by the venom of a religion of snake bites and
soul purging.

"I think Madeline means it, Pru. Let go some now!" I added, double teaming her and walking her nose-to-nose to the nearest wall. Several
buttons popped from the side of Madeline's dress as she swelled from
anger, too much for the memory she wore to withstand.

"I swear I don't know nuthin' more, just that they be comin' tonight. They's hold up at the Four Season's in Charleston and some at
your hotel in Beaufort. That's what I know. And that Cornelius is puttin'
em up to keep an eye on 'em. And that Cornelius just wanted the locals
and Addie's family to be the only one's here tomorrow. That's all I know,
I swear. But that woman, Ivinia's best friend from California, said she
was coming with some people. I don't know who. Just people, she said.
Don't tell Cornelius I tolds ya."

"That isn't all you know, but it's enough for me right now. Let her
go, Faust." Madeline leaned against the newel post of the stairs, weak
more from the news than from the platform shoes. I thought her reaction to the news odd, but I let it go. Pru scurried down the stairs, knowing that she would have been punished for holding back, but now feared
the repercussions for having told too much. Immediacy formed her decision to tell. She would deal with Cornelius later and the snake venom

even later still.

We didn't know what to do with this new information. Hunger for completion, hunger for still more information, and plain hunger crashed within us. Plain hunger won out.

"Let's just get something to eat," Madeline said. "We'll figure the rest out later."

We clomped and clumped our way down the stairs, the buffer of the oriental runners not offering any solace to the bullying of our platform shoes against the treads. We hit the hallway with a pounce and Madeline walked over to the door to turn out the porch lights and lock us in for the night. She gazed mindlessly out the side glass and jumped back.

"Someone's out there!"

"Who?"

"I don't know. I can only see a silhouette."

She backed off. I grabbed a walking stick from the umbrella stand and swung the door open. I rushed the mysterious figure, hoping to send him or her away.

"That's no way to receive a guest, is it Faust?" Addie said, standing there looking up at a madman in bell bottoms and plaid, holding a cane over his head, in lock step with Madeline, dressed in a sailor dress, an ostrich boa, and my broad-brimmed hat.

"Rather festive garb for the occasion, don't you think?" Addie looked askance at us from top to bottom.

"Oh my, God." I dropped the cane. "What are you doing here? We thought you were an intruder. How did you get here?"

"I didn't call first, but I'm hardly an intruder." Addie smiled up at us, holding a basket covered in a checkered cloth. "Thought you might like some real cooking tonight after all of that fancy stuff you two have been eating today. I had Jed drop me off while he was going into town. What...um...are you doing, exactly?"

"Just seeing if the past still fits. It doesn't." Madeline embraced Addie with words and hugs. "How are you?"

"I'm well." Addie seemed oddly dismissive. "I see that you are taking care of each other. Nice. It's been a long time since I've seen this here. Y'all even wearin' things I...sadly remember." Addie surveyed us up one side and down the other with a familiar, disapproving eye. "It all looks a little shop worn." She passed us to enter the kitchen. "Hated 'em then, hate 'em now," she mumbled, shaking her head.

"Gee, thanks, Momma, I thought we could pull it off," I lamented.

"Thought wrong," Addie said, rolling her eyes as she dropped the basket of food on the center hall table.

"What did you bring us?" I asked, like a child waiting to know what's inside a wrapped box.

"Double-fried chicken, biscuits, gravy, and sweet potato pie."

"Terrific! It beats the hell outta leftover 'anything between two slices of bread.'"

Addie smacked my fingers as I nosed around under the red checkered cloth that covered her fixins.

Walking from the entry to the kitchen, I watched Addie look around slowly, gingerly putting one foot in front of the other as much because of wonderment as age.

"I see Cornelius' handiwork all around. How long did this all take?" Addie asked, askance at all the changes.

"Less than an overnight to do all of this," I said, still marveling at the feat.

"He's a man of many accomplishments. He certainly can achieve anything if he sets his mind to it," Addie said as her eyes caught all the refurbished details. She paused to absorb the house. "Brings back old memories." She looked uncomfortable. "Turned 'roun though," she decided, gingerly twisting her body. She faced the front door, back to the butler's pantry. "There now, that looks right."

"What are you doing?" I asked, unsure.

"Just seein' this tired old house the way it's familiar to me, is all." Addie touched the draperies and ran her hand over the woodwork. The look in her eye wasn't tender, but I could see that the edges of her memory pulled at her. I thought I knew the movements and the shifts and the truths about the face that raised me, but I couldn't read her now. The only thing that I could see was that her look didn't caress the memory, it repelled it.

"What do you mean?" Madeline added.

"When the house looked like this, I never entered it from the front door. Comin' through the front's like backing up down a highway. Long time since it looked like this." Addie thought for a moment and gave us a little history lesson. "Funny how walking through the front door changes your perspective on things. Ivinia always insisted that we use the kitchen door."

"Even you?" I asked, incredulously.

"*Especially* me." She kept busy and didn't look up.

"I never knew that." My shame surfaced and I wanted to embrace the little woman who meant so much to me and meant so little to

Mother, but I no longer knew how. She'd grown not only older but different to me.

"There's lots you don't know." Addie turned around and continued setting up. We watched 'til she finished emptying the basket and then followed her lead and sat at the kitchen tin top. She gently unwrapped the food and took plates from the cupboard and shakily heaped mounds of her cooking onto them. The aroma spilled out like a fog that enveloped the simply painted walls and the all-too-spare furnishings.

"Can we help?" Madeline asked.

"I been doing this for well over seventy years. There's no help that can catch me."

So we sat like children waiting for dinner, as we had done in this kitchen all of our early days. I recalled the shine of the pale green walls and the scrub of the soapstone counters, the hollow of the butcher block, and the domed handles of the drawers. Not the kitchen of a fancy twentieth-century home, this one held efficiency as its only tenant, practical and serviceable, not luxurious. Adults never cared about these kitchens, especially the master and mistress of this house, but the children sure did. We'd sat here, watching life pass, and were made ready by people held in little regard except for the way they made life easier for the people on the other side of the butler's pantry door. Their faces didn't matter. Their lives didn't matter. Fired or quit, they'd be replaced like a broken glass or dish. But these faces had been important to us. Madeline and I grew up here. We matured here with a cookie in our hands, and a kind expression or touch, a story told and a face wiped, a scraped knee healed, a broken heart mended with a 'thank you' and a 'you're welcome' in reply. With an outstretched hand to catch a tear, when the words were meant, they were spoken from the heart. We would sneak in when Mother was not around and visit with Addie and our "friends" regularly. We would spend time with the faceless people who became the parents of our everyday. They became more our family than the one into which we'd been born.

Addie gave us our plates; and as we ate, she told us stories, little things that tweaked a tickle and a laugh, to soften the path we were on. Like the time I fell head first into a stand of freshly baked blueberry pies because I was in hot pursuit of a ginger cookie in the jar on the top shelf. Or, when Madeline wanted so desperately to have a "twin cousin" like the one she saw on a TV show that she convinced me to pool our allowances so she could buy a wig and special clothes that would help her look like a long lost cousin from England. We dismissed the flaw that we had forgotten that we were of Italian extraction. Addie reminded us of the hours we'd spent helping each other speak with a British accent and work out the details just to make sure that everything would go smoothly and no one would expose the "scam." Addie even gave us a map so we could plot the places that Madeline, or "Corine" (as she was known) descended from and had family. We never brought this act on the road. Addie knew that this would be the case all along. But she was right there with us while Mother attended yet another charity thing or was in town buying a dress or a hat.

"Now isn't this better than strange-made food?" Addie asked us.

"It does carry me back some. Why isn't life as simple as this anymore?" I asked. I thought between the three of us we could come up with an answer.

"Well, the sun comes up and it goes down. Everything turns as well as it should. I don't know. I suppose it never lived as simple as our memory allows. You know," Addie continued in between bites of her own food, "it takes longer and longer for me to do the same things. I would've whipped this dinner up in two shakes of a cat's tail, but now it takes me hours with Jed helping me. So…" Addie took a drink of her 'powerful good' lemonade and thought a spell, shaking her head, "…I guess it was never simple; it's just us that got weaker."

We ate, talked, and ate some more. There were moments of silence where I drank in the quiet and the ticking of the clock over the big porcelain sink and the peripheral sounds of cars carrying strangers all too closely now past our gates, who know nothing of us. I listened to the sound of our breathing, and felt the cooling of the air as it brushed against my moistened skin. I felt satisfied finally. I missed this. The price that I paid for my exodus overwhelmed me. I began to understand the person I grew into here and, therefore, the person I'd left behind. "Run where it's foul run, where it's fair…no matter where I run, I always find myself there," as the song goes, and, although I adopted that line which remained in my head from long ago, I knew, right then, that in my travels and escape I did leave something behind. I did effect a change with my absence and, therefore, my presence. The balance shifted in my family structure. I left and, in the sweep of emotion and trail of debris, Madeline and Addie scrambled silently for repair and regrouping.

Madeline married Harris shortly after my departure. Addie convinced my father to put his offices in the main house and she became a permanent resident in Back Bay House. They each created their own fortress. I knew nothing but the faces now. I had to find out who they were, over sweet potato pie and wills, frozen hot chocolate, and land.

This life bore down so differently on me than my life in New York.

When I arrived up north, raw and broken, I pruned myself of the dead wood, the diseased limbs that Spanish moss, so beautiful, so deadly, all but completely strangles. I cut back as far as I could and looked for new growth by severing ties to most of my family. Not fully formed with voids and hollows that needed to be filled, I accepted rawness and fragility, strangeness and vulnerability, and hoped to alter my ego. I was ready for change. I had hoped to be a blank canvas whose colors and forms, newly painted, could tell a different story. I succeeded. During the day, I worked, building new and rigid routines to protect the void not yet filled in, to heal over it like a callous, tougher, instead of open, clean, and ready for the new growth I had wanted. At night I clung to a regimen of free abandon, shaking off everything that did not fall loose by itself. I ran with a crowd of young elite, using a weakened drawl and a twinkle in my eye that hid a past. The more I concealed, the more the allure and the curiosity. I played this game so effectively that I am not sure that either they or I cared to break the allusion that swirled around me. I was mysterious. Here, I was able to use my family to my advantage. Mystery became more intriguing than truth. I ran away and became a different me.

"Now that we're alone, just us," Madeline began, swallowing her last fork full of sweet potato pie and adjusting her feather boa, "why did you really leave here, sweetie?" I recognized her impish smile, offered when she was fishing for something that she hadn't heard before or didn't want to volunteer information herself. She was pushing me to tell the truth to Addie.

"We've been over this time and again," I breathed out, leaning into the table with sticky hands and greasy mouth, my old shirt straining at the button holes, almost nose to nose with Madeline. We were kids again and Addie was presiding.

"Yes, Faust, why did you leave?" Addie asked, emphasizing the moment.

"It wasn't all about family, was it?" Madeline was pushing me to say the words that Addie hadn't heard, words I was afraid to speak. Of all the loss and change that life permits and randomness creates, this was the final fear, the rejection of the person who had given me growth and solace. Although she was now frail and old, I was still fearful of words that would alter another relationship. I had quickly learned that my course of personal exposure took on experimentation, isolation. Alone inside my head so long that each road of self-exposure and public knowledge felt like the first, but with increasing stakes in the gamble of loss. I plodded ahead years ago, starting with the peripheral, easily disposable people, the ones who would never be missed. I then worked my way into the core, testing with each layer challenged, weakened by shock or dismay or rejection or surprise. Stabilizing, then moving toward the center, which I never actually reached. Reaching it now, my Addie, I swallowed the lump of fear as a finish to dinner and dove in. Before this very moment, as long as the relationship stayed intact, what did a secret or two matter? Now it mattered. I suddenly realized that my return had to be on different terms. Running just delayed the necessary things.

"What do you want me to say, Madeline? It was equally about our immediate family and some legal complications."

"Now I'm thoroughly intrigued. I always thought it was about leaving behind our crazy relatives. But now I don't know what to think." Madeline became almost clinical in her dissection, trying to expose me and finally leaving the emotion to be dealt with or not on possibly another day. She wanted the control of this, though I did not know why.

"Let it go, Madeline. Please." I was not yet ready for a clinical analysis.

"No, Faust, you let it go," Addie said gently, and placed a shaking hand on my arm. She looked up at me and said, "It's time. Tell me what's on your mind. Use the words. I need to hear the words from you that maybe can confirm what I've felt all these years."

"Momma…" I called her that much to hear it myself as to remind her how I felt about her, trying to brace against a terrible outcome, "…it's still hard. I don't know if it's that I am born into all this deception and it's easy to hide out, or it's what I am used to. Maybe it's just fear that stops me. I don't want to lose you."

"If secrets kept you away from me then I've already lost you, no?"

"Okay, Momma. I left years ago because of many complications all surrounding the fact that I'm…gay. I was about to be exposed in a very negative way and I felt that my move to New York was my best option." I deflated, heard no explosions, surrounded by unchanged faces. These words still had import to me after all these years. These words still had power to change relationships. Almost thirty years in New York, establishing a life of raucous peace if not contentment, I was still struck with the simplicity and strength that these offered to the people who love you despite the parts of you that are unknown, unspoken, and perhaps unconfirmed, but for whispers and incidences that the mind explains away. Still, in the end, I did not really know that I could be loved in spite of eyes that hoped that these words were not true, that they were not part

of me, reasoning a choice, a decision that can be discussed away or undone with prayer, therapy, or meds. Wars abounding, scandals of inter-
national import occur, and the words "I'm gay" turns families upside
down, as eyes search some variation of a Bible, intent on proving where
their level of hatred can be confirmed, where the separation can be up-
held, where ties can be severed, where unqualified love becomes quali-
fied and severed. Thirty years, immense knowledge and resources built,
and still those two words became caught in my throat.

"I left not only because of what you saw to be the craziness of this
family, but because I had to."

"I knew you were gay from the time you were three. You were
sensitive and different and unique, with the face of a boy who had a
secret. You saw the beauty of the night sky, the beauty of the grasses
poking through the water's heavy fog, the joy of times spent and stories
told. That's one of the reasons I stayed close by your side. We had different words for it then, as with most things, and I knew those words
and I wanted to shield you from them. Words hurt, people hurt. No one
knows this better than me. And, from where I stood, I could protect
you." Momma reached over the checkered cloth strewn with the devoured bones of her food laid bare by our hunger, and touched my face.
"But I, too, did not think that there was anything to talk about, long as I
was there. Besides, whenever I tried, you would change the subject. I
couldn't know for sure what you wouldn't tell me." She gave me a different perspective. "I could not learn to love that part of you without
you letting me in."

"You knew?" It got to both Madeline and me.

"Yes. Always. But the words needed to be said between us. So, that
was what drove you away?"

"Well, several factors figured in on my departure. I guess you knew
that part. But the biggest one was the disappearance of Christian Benoit."

"You can't mean our cousin Joslyn's husband?" Madeline stuttered, surprised.

"It was just enough to make the decision for me, especially when
Ivinia found out.

"Tell us more; don't stop," Madeline chided me. She leaned forward on her elbows, starting a second feast on chicken parts and Southern gossip.

"How did Christian figure in on this?" Addie jumped on the band-
wagon of interest.

"We ran into each other…at a gay bar in Charleston where I sometimes met with some local guys for beer and a conversation."

"What was he doing there? Must have been by accident," Madeline added.

"There was no accident about it. He would...how do I put this politely..." I searched for words that would carefully and gently tell my story to Addie. "He would bed anyone—man or woman. He had allegiance to no one or for that matter, any sexuality. He called it free spirit. I called it selfish. But then again, no one asked me at the time. Anyway, he sauntered into the bar, you know the one, it was called Sammy's Downtown, and he already felt little pain from previous watering holes." Christian had a reputation for cruising from bar to bar 'til he had snagged his catch for the night. Josilyn Benoit chose to ignore this flaw in her husband, which was among many of his less admirable qualities. Her ability to ignore the suspicious or the obvious was a gift passed on from her mother and before her and again like her mother before her.

"There was so much to hate about that man," Madeline chimed in.

"So true," I added. "So, anyway, I watched him sleaze his way to the corner of the bar, picking off the first barfly he could find, making their deal in the corner in the dark. Just before he left, though, his loose eyes focused and he saw me there."

"'Hey Faust, how yur doin'?' Christian hollered loud enough to wake up the dead in the city morgue across the street."

"What did you do?" Addie asked, trying to stay in on a conversation that was at best uneasy for all of us. Southerners don't like exposure. We don't like earthquakes that show soft underbellies and jagged edges. We don't like emotional landslides. But Addie, Madeline, and I kept at it.

"I waved politely. The man I was with waved as well. I instantly became aware that my dinner companion's discomfort gave away his history with Christian. At that moment I realized that my dating instincts needed to be honed. Christian came over with Barfly on his arm and started the inevitable conversation, 'Hey guy, what you doin' here?' He didn't wait for me to answer. 'Same as me I guess. Pickin' up one o' these here fruit flies to buzz around your crops.' He tussled Barfly's hair as a gesture of friendship and lighthearted joking. Barfly was so numb that he thought that he had landed a good one and had just been complimented. Christian always had a way with words. I said, 'Not really. This is a friend of mine.' I tried to avoid a confrontation and shorten this sudden intrusion. But his mental acuity wasn't as shaky as his walk. 'You come here with friends? Wait a minute. He...I know you. How ya doin'? Hey, Faust, you're one o' *them*?'

"I froze, unable to speak. After all the years of hiding and delicately avoiding the land mines of small-town gossip, I knew that no matter what I said it would get back to the family. I also knew at that moment that running away was easier than this. Running away shielded me from this. All of a sudden my world stalled at a crossroads. I could no longer coast. I had to take a direction. I was about to be outed by the dregs of the county."

"Outed?" Madeline questioned the lingo of the moment, having not kept abreast of the current terms of a life that she only knew peripherally.

"Yes, outed; about to be exposed, like what we do to enemy agents and CIA operatives," I said, hoping that this conversation would not turn into a lesson in gay subtext and language.

"So running away would be the safest thing to do," Addie said, focusing on the heart of the issue as her eyes looked away, drifting to another place. It's that look that you recognize in someone you know well, when sent on an unwanted journey by the possible outcomes of something that you've just heard.

"I hadn't quite decided to do that right then. After all, I was twenty. I thought I was an adult who could make a rational decision about my life. The sexual revolution was in full swing and I thought with a bit of courage I could weather any storm that might come up and be stronger for it. That, however, did not turn out to be the case. Christian came over to me, pushed his evening's catch away and said–Addie, I don't know if you should be hearin' this."

"Faust, I didn't get here by being shielded. I've heard my share of things. It's time for us both to know you."

"Well, Momma, he wanted to know if I would be interested in taking Barfly's place. 'What y'say me and you take it somewhere private and…keep it in the family?'" Addie and Madeline breathed shallowly and started to fit together what they previously knew with what they were hearing now.

"I reacted swiftly. I stood up and pushed the table out of my way. My date raised his glass and his hands as if to seamlessly avoid being swept away in the undercurrent of moving furniture. I reached for Christian's hair, locked on and slugged him square in the jaw. I heard his lip crack against his teeth as my fist connected to his face and blood spewed everywhere. He fell backwards and started to laugh, obviously numb to the pain, "C'mon boy. Make me feel glad I stopped in…" He grabbed his crotch and that was the last thing I remembered. I jumped on him and, as told to me by the bartender, I beat him so hard that people were pulling at me to separate us. He tried to fight back, but his surprise at my anger prevented him from changing from laughter and defense to survival and offense quickly enough. Finally, he lay unconscious bleeding profusely, starting to swell from the pummeling. Sammy, the owner of the bar, tried to clean the mess up quickly without involving me and his place. He'd had too many run-ins with the local law and church groups and knew that a fight would be the excuse needed to close him down, even if it was the low-life Christian Benoit bleeding on his floor. He picked Christian up and delivered him to the outskirts of town, you know, the 'easy side,' where people wantin' meet people sellin'. That's the night he disappeared."

"That's why the police came over that night," Madeline remembered.

"Yes. Father asked Sheriff Gofferd if the questioning could be kept quiet. The words *fairy* and *faggot* were sprinkled liberally through the conversation between them as I sat waiting for the outcome in the salon. Father reminded Gofferd that we had quietly helped him get elected, feeding him campaign money and information against his opponent. Gofferd said that only goes so far. He had stuck his neck out for us when everyone who bought houses in our development tried to tear down the head office. He drawled, 'I gotta worry about reelection. Land scandals are one thing but homosexual shit…why…in this county…that's a mule kick to the political balls, if ya catch my drift. I'd lose big time.'

"'Goff, my man,' Titus went into action, 'you know you have strong opposition growing in the town council. They don't like your *off-hours antics*. You know the rumors…that *late-night* warehouse transfer stuff,' Titus paused to let it sink in. 'So despite what I know about the facts behind the rumors, keeping this thing *under wraps* is the least of your worries. Besides, you need to worry more about your financial security after public office.' Then Father went for the jugular. 'You know, your finances have always been adjustable according to your cooperation with this family. And I'm sure that your new wife would like to continue to live in a nice house and drive new cars and wear fine dresses after you retire. As you know, a consultant's salary always comes in handy, wouldn't you agree? Remember, it wasn't your youthful good looks or your smarts that got you that sweet pretty young thing of a wife.' Father chucked Goff's belly with a clenched, but joking fist, jiggling his rotund stomach that pressed and popped over his 'In God We Trust' belt buckle. He followed that with a tap on Goff's large, bald head, 'And we all know that public service doesn't pay for many dreams. Unless you're a senator or better, the cards don't play in your favor.'"

"He blackmailed Gofferd," Madeline confirmed unsurprised.

"He persuaded a lot of people the same way," I reminded them both. "You know that everyone in the county, except for family, got a regular stipend from Titus and his father before him for one reason or another. And this was the scandal that lay in the balance."

Although I continually felt embarrassed by my birthright, it always amazed me that we could be alternately shunned and the payor of "pleasant money," as Mother called it. Sometimes it felt through the years as if people streamed into our front door on empty and poured back out full, like the homeless and indigents on the breadlines during the Great Depression. Inside our door, everyone collected their "contractual" payouts for various necessary secrets and needs, courteously greeting us and considering us their equals. Outside, the smiles dropped from their faces and the plots strengthened the food chain at war with the hierarchy.

"Titus, God rest his soul, hated the ritual that he was born into," Addie spoke from her wealth of knowledge about my father. She worked many deals with and for him and had to be the go-between and intermediary at times.

"But Titus negotiated the terms. Why did you leave so abruptly? Weren't the 'negotiations' going the right way?" Madeline moved the chess pieces in her mind.

"Well, it wasn't Titus that pushed me onto that train going north; it was Mother."

"Ivinia?" Addie was caught off guard.

"Ivinia." I said, putting to rest any questions.

"She had always said that Titus thought it was better for you to leave and start living in a northern city, perhaps New York, so's to get 'a harder shell,' he said." Addie voiced her thoughts as if turning the pages and reading from the family diary in her head. "Titus would arrange it and you would return after a time."

"I remember that, too," Madeline was embarrassed to say.

"Truth was, Momma, I was sent away by Ivinia so that the people and the police might look to another direction, especially since the car filled with drugs was found on Christian's car lot a few weeks earlier. With him gone, everything would be blamed on the drugs. Ivinia insisted and Titus, given the circumstances, had no other choice but to comply with her wishes."

"Maybe it's a good thing Titus held that from me," Addie mused.

"Why's that?" Madeline asked.

"Had I known the root of the hair, I would have killed her with my bare hands, is why," Addie said with not a shred of doubt in her words. "And now, I see from what I'm hearin' that Titus had more to do with this than he told me." Addie grew visibly upset for having not known the full details of the last scene before my departure. "He never would lie to me. He couldn't; he didn't." Her process of purifying the memory of Titus hit a snag. It's something that we all do. The dead can do no wrong, and time and need twist the memories into a gentler, more forgiving place.

"Well, apparently he did this one time," I forged on. "Late that evening, after everyone had gone, I had my final run-in with Mother. Titus was already off to Chicago with you, Addie; the help had retired. You, Madeline, were off for a weekend with Shannie Palmer to New Orleans. Ivinia sat in the dining room, lined up all the martini glasses on the table, and slowly drank down the line. She stayed in there most of the evening. Then about two in the morning, I awoke to glasses crashing against the dining room wall. I heard Ivinia stomp up the stairs in a liquored rage, falling into walls and cursing. She pushed the door to my room open as she held on to the doorframe. I froze atop my bed in anticipation of what her next move could be. She tore into my armoire and started throwing my clothes over the balcony, down the stairs, screaming for the servants to gather them up and send them away from here.

"I'll never forget her words. 'These dirty things have sullied the family for the last time. Get out and get gone!' she screamed. The servants came from everywhere: falling down from the third floor, spilling out from the wing off the kitchen, jumping up from the cellar. They scrambled barefoot, still half asleep, picking up my belongings as if that act would calm my mother. Desperate to satisfy her rage they tried to catch my things in mid-air. The commotion shook the moss on the oaks lining the drive.

She screamed, 'You are not my son, and I am done with you!

"Ivinia would not take any more embarrassment from me and Titus' family. I was the reason she was shunned. I was the cause of her isolation from society. I was the punishment that she bore for being in this family. She hated my father and Madeline as well, wanting to burn the house down to be rid of everyone and build a new 'empire' with Cornelius, 'the way it should be run.' As she raged, I could see Cornelius across the hall, half-hidden behind the door of his room, watching Ivinia as if checking on her performance, smiling calmly and contentedly at the unfolding scene. 'You bastard! You spoiler! Get out! Get out of my house and take your faggot ass out of here before I kill you!' This was the last thing that Mother yelled at me before I jumped into the car with a few belongings and raced to the airport."

"You left that weekend, didn't you?" Madeline asked. Both she and Addie looked more uneasy that Ivinia had orchestrated my departure without their knowledge, rather than with the rest of the story that I was unveiling.

"It was Ivinia. I suspected it," Addie proclaimed. "Tell me, when you made it to New York, why didn't you call me?"

"I couldn't, Momma. I was so full of...I guess...shame. I was twenty and convinced that I had destroyed my family, crushed my mother. I didn't know where you stood. I couldn't take the risk to find out. So it was better to leave for a while. At least 'til you and Father returned from Chicago. You were unreachable. There was nowhere to turn. So I ran. A little time away turned into a long time. I fit in quickly, met someone in the first week. I set up life and gave you and Madeline a place to visit, to have fun and give the whole mess a rest."

"You weren't troublin' me, nor did you cause this family any trouble. We have lots to chew, Faust, I just don't know where to begin." Addie studied my face and I, hers. She returned from her thoughts and asked, "So, the man that you lived with...Judge, that was his name, right? Did you love him?" The words seemed to come easy to Addie. With all that was staring at her from the past, it was this simple detail she wanted to know.

"Yes. No. I mean...I don't know. Eleven years counts for something. But was it love, or need? I still can't tell after all these years. I've given up trying."

"How could you not know?" Madeline asked. "Eleven years should tell you something, no?"

"You would think. I felt *something*. I guess our getting together was more a reaction to family than anything else." I looked into the ripple of the lemonade in my glass.

"Years don't make the book, they just fill the pages," Addie said, "Made a new life, right?"

"Right. At least I could be me. I could control my world and he accepted it. Who I was no longer was an issue," I continued. " Judge needed me. So for him it was easy. He was in awful financial trouble. I knew I could help. I was resourceful and clever in my youth. I had seen so many financial shenanigans around here that his money problems were a piece of cake. I brought a fresh perspective to someone older than me. I was his second wind and he was my first stop."

"Much older. Hmmm. I seem to remember about ten years, right?" Madeline counted in the air.

"Why did it end?" Addie asked.

"You know." I reminded her of the men who had brought her two daughters. "His need ended. I solved the problems and I was not as interesting on the coast as I was on the climb. He needed fresh and younger. He found it quickly. You can't imagine how available young men are when replacement parts are wanted. Younger, thinner, wide eyed. On every corner, in every restaurant, office buildings, theatres. I could only be in one place at a time. *They* were everywhere."

"Pretty's everywhere, we all learn that one." Addie's reply was pulled from her own story, I was sure.

"After ten years, I had heard all of Judge's lines before and most of his thoughts, and he, mine. I found routine comfortable; he found it boring. He needed to see surprise as the reaction in my face to his words, not familiarity. When we fell into silence, I felt warm and included. I don't know. A shared secret somehow. I guess he felt nothing in silence but silence. Pretty, young men are clever, you know. Their thoughts are only one-line deep, glittering jewelry to older gay men. A narrow window. *Perfect age.* Not unlike straight counterparts, I suppose. Slowly, I turned from being jewelry to being a saddle; practical and sturdy. My wit became thoughtful and introspect, not off the cuff and frivolous. Judge became acerbic and withdrawn until one day he was gone—a sparkling new twenty-year-old to his forty-two."

"Just like that...gone?" Madeline asked.

"Madeline, honey, you're lucky you missed it," I admonished her, as if punishing my sister for having found happiness. "You got married and stayed married. Lucky you."

"I'm sorry Faust. I didn't mean..." Madeline blushed.

"Oh, love, I know. Don't worry," I said. "I thought we could weather the drought, then maybe it would rain and something would begin to grow again. But it was so much easier for him to leave than to wait and fix. It's a lot easier to put energy into something new than to rustle up enough energy to fix a relationship that has caring, abuse, anger, and history built in. We even tried therapy. Two sessions and he was done."

"You ran away from here for all the same reasons," Addie challenged. "You left without a single word, without fighting back. You left me and your sister without talking to us...to me...Momma." Addie showed me her anger, old and pent up. "You didn't let me comfort you. That was my job, my life. You took that away from me." She shook from a combination of frailty and frustration, hitting her chest with her withered hands.

"I'm sorry," I said, looking at Addie as she caught her anger and withdrew.

"Sometimes the dam breaks no matter how much you shore it up. Why didn't you trust me, Faust?"

I had no answer.

"Why do we keep so much bottled up, so close to the vest?" Madeline asked. "We edit our lives according to other people's needs just so that we don't make waves. That's the system here, I guess."

"Oh, Madeline, it's everywhere, not just here. I edited so much of myself out when I got to New York that I hardly recognized my reflection in the mirror. It just seemed required for the job. At the time it suited me. Except for my easy speech and gentle manner, the only way Judge would recognize Southern was if it was fried in a pan and served with grits. I stared sometimes in amazement that he never asked me about my family. Never."

"And we're so colorful," Madeline added.

"Can you imagine?" I laughed back at her, the hurt so long ago done and settled. "He never cared to meet anyone. When you came up to visit he'd find a reason to be gone. Relegated to a footnote in our conversations, or a picture on a nightstand, suited him. He missed the biggest part of me and didn't care. I never took it as unusual. I guess I was so used to hiding that it felt normal not to talk about something. It took time for me to realize that this was different. That it wasn't about him. It just wasn't."

"Then who were you to him?" Madeline asked.

"I was the blank canvas that I so desperately wanted to be. I submerged myself in his family. I hid out in his arena. It's so easy to do when you have had years of practice. I made it my business to know everything about them, all their little nuances, their likes and dislikes, their preferences, their friends, even family tensions. I shared holidays and gifts, gave loans and advice, but never did I find out the truth—that they'd been taught to care only about themselves. That they could only take and would resent the return of the favor, as if any need I might have would far outweigh the gifts I had given."

"Home away from home," Addie concluded.

"Yeah, I could see it so plainly in his family and in him, and yet missed it when I looked at my own family. I knew there were secrets here, but it was clouded by history and tradition, land…even legacy. I felt what we did and what we hid contributed to a cause, a future that needed to include us, that depended on us. It was our responsibility somehow. But with Judge, there was no land, no family history to speak of, except maybe a few forgettable generations, recorded largely by accident with the greeting card errantly saved, or a picture in a dusty incomplete album that someone forgot to discard. It's not about the South, the North, the East, the West, or China, for that matter. It's about our pride, hubris, about self-absorption, learned as a trade like a county fair huckster. I traded affection and interest for peace and secrecy, like that huckster, selling trinkets, waiting for the big score, hoping that what I would offer would be enough."

I woke suddenly from my tirade. "I'm sorry. I get a little intense when this part of me is pried open."

"Was there something different out there?" Addie asked, ferreting out what was important. "Did you find what you were looking for away from us?"

"No. It took a while, but I had soon discovered that I had run to the same thing only dressed differently, with different manners and a quicker, more obvious, style. Funny how that works. I found familiar. I only *thought* it was different. I didn't take the time to understand the subtlety."

"I never knew," Madeline said, sadly amazed, head slowly shaking back and forth. "I...didn't know. I thought I stayed connected. I thought that my visits and phone calls could give me what I needed to know about you."

"Madeline, it's impossible to know enough about you—or about me, for that matter."

Addie's face, a mixture of cognac and cream, valleys and ridges. Her words, slow but oddly with abandon, spoken from the heart. "There are things we choose to show about ourselves that tell a story about who we think we are. I remember as a little girl playing in the marsh grasses. I found a perfectly still pool of water out behind Back Bay. There, resting on a matt of fallen thickets and pine straw, I found three frogs, frozen in time like they were made of wax, lookin' at their own reflections. So perfect, so still, that I's sure they thought they were staring at another one of their own kind. Then, I tapped the water and they woke up from their trance, like in a fairy tale. Their reflection wrinkled right in front of them, and poof...they were gone." Addie animated her words with a delicate hand gesture so familiar to me. "That's what we're afraid of. If someone taps what we see or disturbs it in any way, it'll shatter our reflection and those we love'll run away, shun us. So we hide early on, as babies, sure that we're seen one way and not the other. It sure does unsettle the nerves to be mistaken of our own reflection. Silly frogs. Silly us."

The full import of what Addie spoke of had yet to be fully revealed. "And you'd better believe that those reflections change depending on the ripple in the pool. Ashamed o' you? No, Faust. I'm ashamed o' myself most. I weighed you down with troubles. Forgive me." Addie looked up as if to say more but stopped. She stood up gingerly and cleaned up the mess on the table.

"I'd better get movin'," she said, as she busily put the remains in the basket. "We need to talk some, I'm a card's throw away from where Titus is right now. And you know something? It brings you a heap of freedom. I'm tired now. This old body don't hold up to too much serious talk anymore. It's too much like plowing fields all day."

Madeline and I joined in on the cleanup.

"You going to be with Titus tomorrow? Or can I come steal you away from him just for a little bit? You'll be back up New York soon and I need some o' your time." Addie spoke directly to me, as if Madeline was no longer in the room.

"Don't mind me," Madeline said winking, "I can hold down the fort. After all, it's just some of Mother's friends from LA and some locals, whoever's left. Between Cornelius and me, I think we can handle it. You can have him, Addie."

"*Friends from LA?* Interesting. Let's see what tomorrow's sun brings," Addie said, and turned to Madeline. "Thanks, Madeline. I'll show up early to say goodbye. I just can't do it yet. By the way, you're goin' on a treasure hunt up in the attic?"

"That's the plan," Madeline giggled, but a disingenuous laugh at that. It registered on Addie's face as soon as she heard it, but she pressed onward.

"You might want to look up in the eves over the servant's quarters. Nobody ever went there, 'cept Titus. He always said to me that if he ever wanted to keep something from the family that's where he'd put it. I'm not even sure that Cornelius knows about what's up there. I know what I need to know; any more is useless to me now. But you might find something you need."

And then she was gone. No sooner did Addie put everything in her basket, than Jed picked her up. She left, never closing the front door, as if doing so would break the spell.

Madeline and I stood there as Addie and Jed drove off in his old cream-colored '60 Cadillac. She stared at me 'til the car faded in the white wet of the night air. I closed the door.

"Shall we start our mission?"

"What are we looking for?" Madeline asked.

"Pieces," I added.

"Of…?"

"Since this was your idea, I suppose pieces that make everything fit."

# 13

THE URGENCY TO PUT the pieces together became over-whelming to me, and although Madeline originated the idea I ran with it after Addie left. Returning to Greyhaven had an unexpected effect. I became enmeshed in the goings on and realized that part of me was still here. I still reacted to my family and I quickly caught up to speed in all things devious. There was so much left out—with Father's death, Mother's disappearance, and Cornelius' agenda—that I didn't know where to begin. Things "didn't sit in the chair right," as Addie once said.

In our determined mindset, we ascended the staircase unsure, as if for the first time, up through the hallways and down the aged corridors designed like a confusing rat maze. This house was too large even for its day. Built to prove that we were important, that we had a place, and that we had a stake in decisions larger than ourselves. Now we were turning every corner with the determination to explain all of this, like a joke that loses its laughter when it is pulled apart.

"I had forgotten how uselessly big this house is," I mused. "Aren't the places you return to supposed to feel *smaller* when you return after many years?"

"No, this one gets bigger. Like a tumor. Until it's lanced, it will keep getting bigger, maybe until it bursts." Madeline's words rang in my ears.

There were two ways to reach the third floor: from the main staircase and from the servant's wing that led to the kitchen. We chose to ascend the main staircase. Grand right from the bottom, the steps stayed important right to the top. Madeline and I walked comfortably side by side. This was always the staircase used to transport furniture and large paintings up and down. We stored many things up there; some for seasonal change, some for disregard, and the rest waiting either for fashion to reignite their interest or for inheritance to kick in and be moved away. The attic also housed Mother's auction purchases. Once upon a time she pondered going into business selling fine antiques and paintings. But since she was neither liked nor respected, the merchandise might as well have been valueless. She often thought she was being punished for the many backroom deals she negotiated at the close of many area plantations, her son-in-law Harris Delbarton's included. As we all knew, that reason was just the tip of the iceberg.

When the parties were lavish, many visitors from California, Virginia, and other points stayed in the first section of the top floor if the rest of the guest suites were full. At times we had upward of thirty weekend guests staying here for every reason *except* liking us. There were business deals that needed seeding and charitable causes that needed financial guarantees, mortgaging of big-old plantations that were sure to go bust, and hosts of other situations that required our family's funding. We became responsible to entertain these needy entrepreneurs, only to realize that we were never socially involved with any of them, except cyclically when money became the issue. They politely tolerated us for cash, nothing more.

As we ascended the stairs, Madeline's cellphone rang, startling both of us.

"What's that?" I asked.

"Oh, shit. I forgot I had my cell on me!" Madeline patted her sides and found the pocket.

"Yes? Snoop Team at your service," Madeline quipped, then turned serious. "Harris, honey, what's up?" Silence followed her opener for many seconds. "I see. Are you sure? Well, that's why I married a lawyer. A whole profession ready to ferret out evil and thwart thine enemies. Yes, talk to you later, sweets." She pressed the disconnect button with a flourish. "That was Harris, my dahling Faust, and he has gotten some dirt on our friend, the very holy Reverend Arthur Futuris."

"And that would be?"

"Seems as though he's been sending checks to two women; one in Savannah and one in Shreveport. Harris isn't sure why Futuris is funding the Savannah gal, but he's going to check it out. He does, however, know for sure that there's an Arthur Junior in Shreveport cuttin' his teeth on a silver rattle supplied by Futuris, which would be changin' the plans of the current Mrs. Carina Mae Futuris if that news got out."

"A baby?"

"I'm not sure that that's what you call the devil's offspring, but there you have it."

"So what do we do now?"

"Harris wants me home. He needs me to help him collate all the papers for tomorrow. They're coming in by fax and e-mail from everywhere. Apparently Futuris has made some interesting enemies along the way. I'll fill you in when I get more information. Harris asked me to apologize for messin' up our plans, but he hopes that you'll understand."

"Yes, of course, by all means go to your bloodhound and reward him," I said, unconvinced of her need to run to Harris' side for this.

"He heard from Cornelius that Futuris wants to give the eulogy at the cemetery. *That* cannot happen if we want this all to end."

"You're right, leave now!" I said.

"Shit. Harris took the car."

"Madeline, there are three cars in the garage for God's sakes. Take one."

"Right. Super." She didn't know what to do first. "I gotta get outta these duds." She ran to her room, stripping and hopping as she went. "Faust, honey, I'm sorry I can't stay and carry out our scathingly brilliant plan, but first things first."

"No sweat, Natasha. Boris here will be ready to spy another day. Maybe tomorrow night?"

"Sounds like a plan, my love." Madeline's voice trailed as she left a line of old clothes to the door. I followed her through the front door and onto the porch.

"Don't do anything without me. Hey, why don't you go into town and have some fun?" Madeline always needed to have things settled before she exited. "If you get outta those clothes and put on something…I don't know…something *mysterious*…I'm sure you'll attract only interesting people. Act very New Yawk." She arched her back and waved her hand regally as she opened the door to the car.

"Yeah, that'll work," I said dryly. "Thanks for the dating tips, oh sis 'o mine."

Madeline took the convertible and backed out as if shot out of a cannon. She kept the ostrich feather boa on and it waved and flapped in the rippling air as she sped off. Isadora Duncan minus the Bugatti.

Closing the door, I did feel the need to leave for the night. The sudden ring of the phone startled me and temporarily dissuaded me from my escape. Planned business, planned company, now postponed, filled the house with an unexpected agitation as if it bristled in annoyance at my continued presence. I didn't want to answer it, but unanswered phones cause me more stress than answered ones, so I conjured up reasons why it might be for me and took the bait.

"Is she still there?"

"Addie, is that you?"

"Of course it is. Is your sister still there?"

"No, as a matter of fact, she had to leave."

"I thought as much."

"What? What's going on, Addie? How'd you know she was going to leave?"

"Tomorrow is another day, Faust. We've had enough Madigan intrigue for right now. Good night."

Addie hung up abruptly.

I became unsettled as I rested the receiver back on the cradle. Why would Addie care? More importantly, how would she know that Madeline left before we went on our exploration? The phone rang again.

"Are you alright?"

"Addie, I was just about to get changed and go out. Why?"

"Good, I need you to trust me and go. Okay?"

"What's going on, Addie?"

"There's little time for hanging clothes on this line. Just leave, okay? Besides, the less time you spend in that house the better. I don't like that you're there."

"It's my home, Momma, but I'll leave, I promise. Soon as I change."

"Good. Go have a good time. Your visit needs to be filled with fun things, too."

"You're more optimistic than me."

"That's how I got to this age, my love."

"Good night, Momma."

"Good hours." She always said that whenever we spoke by phone. It came from her family and meant time well spent wherever you go.

Addie's call upended me, but I listened to her. Enough Madigan shenanigans. I didn't know why she insisted that I leave, but when she insisted on something it was pointless to argue or disengage. Madeline's behavior started to nudge at me as well. I no longer knew what to believe or whom to trust. I ran upstairs and removed the old duds, dressed in something *mysterious*, and left the house in Pru's care.

I pulled open the garage doors to see what car was left for me to drive—an antique silver Jaguar and fire-engine red pickup truck awaited. I decided to take the pickup into town instead of the old Jag. Shiny and red, it didn't fit the profile of a Backwater working-class pickup, but it'd do. It didn't look like it was used for hauling, just the passing thought of it. Almost perfect and more theatrical than real. I certainly felt caught somewhere between being Backwater needing a pickup and East River needing opera tickets and dinner reservations. Everyone has their list, and mine was shifting minute by minute. I jumped into the cab of the pickup, wishing for a layer of grime, some scratches along the side, a bumper or two missing and a cracked windshield, instead of this gleaming red cream puff. I needed authentic pickup attitude, history on four wheels, worked 'til it was about to drop like a loyal horse familiar to the harness of a plow. But, alas, there was no time to make the transformation unless I called Cornelius to come over. He's good at such things on short notice, but I decided against it.

Country music low in the background, windows open and sweat forming rings under my arms on the dark t-shirt gave me the personality I wanted. The cicadas chirped and snapped a rhythmic pulse over the hum of the engine as I drove. I felt part of something even in exaggeration, studied and intense. The stars shone above, their light adding to the heat of the breeze. Pointing the way, a star flashed high above my head and lay over Beaufort. Destination: Bellow's on Bellicker Street.

---

Near eleven o'clock, I pulled in front of the dimly lit bar called Bellow's. It had a familiar gay feel, as if part of a gay bar franchise. It had an unassuming front and would be passed by out-of-towners and ignored by locals unlikely to cheat on their relationship with their own watering hole. I took a deep breath, for unfamiliar always catches me off guard, and pushed the door open with the self-assurance of a sheriff entering a saloon in Dodge. All heads turned in a collective curiosity, as if their neck muscles were attached to the springs of the front door. Expecting to fit in, I was met with a wall of men in khakis and white t-shirts, madras, and jeans, fresh and scrubbed, close-cropped hair, trim youth or youthful wannabees standing three deep around the pretty if only slightly available bartender. The air hung easier than the atmosphere of the bars that I frequent up north, a sort of slower tension. I stood in the doorway and I cast a darker shadow than the fractured lighting could fight. Although entering from the night, my eyes still needed seconds to adjust to the shadows. I stood frozen in the entry, knowing that I did not fit in, once again not reading memory or, for that matter, my present, correctly. I was still in costume. It made my strangeness stranger. Losing my nerve and deciding to leave quickly, I turned and rushed the exit only to knock someone into the frame of the door.

"Wo ho, cool your jets, guy!" he said, brushing himself off.

"Sorry, I changed my mind," I weakened in apology, head buried.

"Faust?" The stranger grabbed me by my shoulders and looked under my bowed head to confirm my identity. "I'd recognize that accent anywhere."

"Buster! Thank God, a familiar face! Wait...what's wrong with my accent?"

"Well, sir, it's not quite SoCar and not quite SoHo."

"Don't call me sir. I feel old enough already."

"Yer not old at all..." he assured me, "...'cept maybe in your head. Where're ya going so fast?"

"I'm not comfortable all of a sudden. Guess I'm going home."

"Wow. Doesn't take much to spook you. You're looking fine tonight. Kinda mysterious and sexy." He grabbed my arm, "Stay?"

"You certainly know what to say. Are...you single? Just a joke, sorry. Not prying." I wanted to know.

"Funny," Buster said with a laugh, "as a matter of fact, I am. I just came in to see if some friends're here, but," he looked around, scanning the crowd, "they're not," He paused. "Could I twist your arm so's you'll stay? I'll...buy you a drink."

"Hmm." I wanted it to seem as if I at least thought a little about it. "Good offer. I'll take you up on it." I didn't need to be asked twice.

As we made our way through the crowd, Buster said "Hey" to most of the guys we passed.

"You know a lot of people." I assessed the lay of his territory.

"Well, you meet guys everywhere. You run into them all over, ya know. Dinner parties, Home Depot, they come into my shop and we shoot the shit a little. Get...right friendly...and it sticks. Look who I'm telling."

"No, please. I'd forgotten the familiarity. It's not something I practice anymore. I have a well-defined group up north. We party, we dine, we talk; break off into subsets but don't stray much from the core."

"Sounds not so friendly. Hey, Keep! Two!" Buster ordered for me from the tap.

"How do you know what I want?"

"I know."

The conversation between us flowed smoothly. I watched his movements as he spoke, his lips curling around each word so softly, so lightly, adjusting to fit his story by strong hand movements. He was a guy in every sense of the word, selling his point, moving with confidence, eyes glistening at each of my reactions. We spoke of how he knew Madeline, and how he and she had struck up a friendship after the court case involving his family house in our tainted development on Bridle Way.

"Madeline came into the ice cream parlor just before we went to trial. She sat at one of my tables, I think deliberately, although she tried acting surprised."

"That's certainly Madeline's style."

"Yup, it is. She looked up over her sunglasses and said, 'Why, I think that you're one of the people that are suing our ass! Am I mistaken?' And I just broke out laughing. She asked me to sit down and talk. We talked for hours. Next thing I knew, my lawyer called and said that there was a settlement offer. And I accepted. However, there was a side offer that surprised even my lawyer. It seems Madeline had arranged for the sale of Gorman's Ice Cream Parlor and put my name on the deed of the building, business, everything. We had been in court for over ten years and it was just this one meeting and the whole thing was settled, over iced drinks."

"Iced hot chocolate, right?"

"You know your sister," Buster shrugged. "I've owned the place ever since."

"I think she took a shine to you." I said, winking.

"Well, I'm very fond of her. She speaks well and often of you," he said, tapping the bottom of his glass with the top of mine.

"…and she of you." I met his tap with another.

"But, I must say, the one who speaks even more about you is Addie."

"Does she? I didn't know that she came into your place that often."

"Whew. She comes in all the time," Buster said without hesitation. "Well, not as much recently," he corrected his recollection. "She stops in as often as she can get into town. She keeps complaining about the rheumatism 'grippin' her means of conveyance'."

"She is pretty stiff, I've noticed," I said. "She's slowed up a lot."

"Yeah, walkin' gets tough for her sometimes. She calls it 'the creaks'." Buster spoke in such familiar terms of Addie that jealousy started brewing in my stomach. He heard all this instead of me. "But anyway, I don't know who's your biggest fan."

"Well, there you have it. The complete list of fans. My sister and Momma, my biggest and only. I miss them both."

"Well maybe they'll have some competition in that arena." God he was smooth. I blushed and changed the subject.

"How long've they been makin' Gorman's their home away from home?"

"After the whole mess with the lawyers was over, Madeline became a regular customer. Then Addie started coming in with her. That didn't last too long though." He paused and found the connection of their separation as curious as I did. "Now Addie comes in by herself most times. Gets dropped off by Jed. Apparently Madeline and Addie's schedules don't jive anymore. But I just love those stories of hers, that Addie! She got more stories than I got cherries on top of whipped cream." Buster's smile beamed and caught the whole room. He wasn't handsome in the classic sense of beautiful men, but he had a style and a charm, a sort of rhythm that drew you in.

"How long're you staying?"

"I don't really know anymore. I love being in Manhattan. I love the pace, the small-scale pockets of neighborhoods within a larger framework. I love the night life, the dating. Such an expanded pool of applicants." I laughed as I spoke.

"Anyone...special?" His curiosity held no embarrassment.

"I'm dating some. No one special for a couple of years. It gets tougher as you get older. You know, more baggage and less interest in helping to carry it."

"So, I'm askin' again. How long you staying?"

"And I'm begging the question again. I thought I knew when I came here, but now... I don't know. I bought an open ticket. I expect I'll stay five days or so. Peaceable is a small town. There's not much to do around here. When I got into town I didn't even want to unpack. But now with what's going on, I've become a little more flexible. There seems to be more to do and I'm feeling a little different." I found myself opening up to this man who I met only a day ago. "There're some complications at the house, with my family. And, well, Addie's getting older and frailer and I realize that I miss my sister so much after all these years. Besides, there are no cicadas in New York and I prefer the sound of their call lulling me to sleep rather than the hum of my air conditioner back home all of a sudden. Aw, shit. Listen to me roll on. Blah, blah, blah."

"No, no. Go on. I like the sound of your voice." He leaned in.

"Anyway, who knows?"

"I'm glad to hear that the jury is still out."

"We'll see. The jury is still looking at the ties I have in the Big Apple."

"Jury decisions get over turned all the time." Buster leaned back and studied my face. "You know, I've been trying to see who it is you look like. I see some Titus and your sister in you, but I don't see hide nor hair of Ivinia in that face of yours."

"How would you know what Ivinia looked like? She never came in to Gorman's, did she?"

"No, never. But didn't Madeline tell you that I was the one who found Ivinia wandering the old development one day, sort of at dusk?"

"No, that little nugget slipped by without tellin'."

"It happened just before Madeline came in to meet me. I didn't know who Ivinia was at the time." He realized that he may have overreached. "I hope that I haven't said anything out o' turn."

"Not at all. I've been gone so long that it's hard to get caught up on everything. Most times Madeline and I just try to start where we left off and pretend that it was just yesterday since we last spoke. It's a silly game, but everyone has some sort of pattern they fall into. So, how'd you run into Ivinia?"

"I was visiting my old house on Bridle Way. You know, there were good times still to remember. Every once in a while I need to go back to that little house and sit and remember. Sort of a comfort when I get stressed."

"Aren't you afraid to be there for any length of time? I know I would be."

"The damage is already done." Buster slapped his left leg. "Besides, I've got a peace worked out with it. I sit on the porch out front and just try to remember us kids playing, my friends...all grown up now and moved away...the basketball hoop at the end of the Cul-de-sac that all the dads put up so's we could play outside. My best friend and I played for hours."

"If you don't mind me askin', how'd you play?" I rudely pointed to his leg but tried to keep the tone inquisitive and light.

"Well, everyone cruises around their shortcomings eventually. You know same as, I dunno," he looked around a bit, "like DJs and news anchors. Do you know how many of them have lisps or stutters? Or, you know, even paralyzed people swooshing down ski slopes."

"Okay," I said, getting it.

"And then there's me," Buster said proudly. "Besides, if you must know, everyone called me Hop.

"Hop?"

"Yeah, 'cause I pivoted and hopped on my good leg. I would be the point man. I was sneaky and fast."

"I would've loved to have seen that!"

"Yeah, I was wicked out there! So much so, that…someone or another's parent was screaming at us to stop the game and get in to supper." He turned serious. "Sad. Teddy's gone now."

"Teddy?"

"Yeah, he was my best friend."

I was afraid to ask. "Moved away?"

"No. Gone now. Dead. Died five, six years ago."

I was sure it had something to do with us, with my family.

"AIDS took him real quick."

I felt guilty for feeling relieved that it wasn't us, but it was good to see Buster's sensitivity. "So, where was Ivinia?" I altered the direction of the conversation back to my newfound interest.

"Oh, right. I found her rummaging through my old house. She was full of dirt and barefoot. She had on a torn, sorta silky, nightgown. Her hair was all curled and piled on top of her head with mud tangled in, like a fancy starlet gone loco. She had a pile of papers in her arms and she looked as if she was trying to hide them. She musta been battin' the hell out of the walls in the basement, I guess, cause she had a sledge hammer with her and there were so many holes and broken cement and plaster everywhere. She was passed out when I found her. Her feet were bleeding. When I woke her up, she was clearly disoriented."

"What did she say?"

"She kept saying that she needed to find a place to hide. I asked her what was it that she wanted to hide and she yelled at me for being stupid, and to just shut up and help her 'keep hittin' the wall' so she could 'hide the papers.' Then she passed out again. I called the sheriff, but instead'a him coming, Addie came with Jed. That's how I first met Addie."

"Did she ever tell you what kind of papers they were?"

"No, but it seemed that Addie knew. She took 'em before I got to look at 'em. Cornelius called me the next day. There's no other way to describe his demeanor but to say it was…intensely curious. He politely badgered me with questions 'til I said, 'enough is enough.' Told him if he had any questions to ask Addie. 'All I did was find her,' I said. 'That's all. Ask Addie.'"

"I'm not surprised at Cornelius but…Addie knew?"

"Yeah, Addie didn't talk about it much but that was the sense I got after the whole thing blew over. When I'd ask after Ivinia, Addie would say just that she was fine and that Titus was taking good care of her. Then, just as quick as an ice melt in August, one day Ivinia disappeared. News traveled all over the county. I heard that they dragged the bay behind your house but found nothing. And now your father's dead, too."

"Well, they found a shawl, and her footprints led to the water, but nothing else. So everyone just thought that time just stopped for her," I added, not realizing I was speaking aloud. "That's why Addie wanted me to go into the attic."

"What attic?"

"Oh, uh, never mind. Just something I forgot to do tonight."

"Well, anyway, it was a shame. Seemed like a wild lady," Buster said, trying to find something nice to say without lying.

"Thanks for your kindness. She *was* wild." I shifted the conversation and my eyes from Buster then to him again. "So, you come in here a lot?"

"It's part of the mix, not a habit. I like the dark and the camaraderie. You know, opposite world."

"I'm a stranger in these here parts. What's that mean?" I added a little extra Southern drawl for him.

"Opposite world. You know, outside I can shake your hand and not get noticed, but if I did this," he leaned over and kissed me slow like molasses slippin' down the side of a short stack, "it would raise an eyebrow or two."

"It raised mine, just for different reasons."

It had been a long time since I felt that twist and surge inside my body, that hollow ache that wakes up inside when possibilities change by a sudden act.

"Life's just full of surprises, isn't it?" Buster paused to let his actions sink in. He swallowed the last of his lager. "Well, it's getting late. I gotta run." I thought it possible that he planned this all out. "I open the store at six most mornin's for the early birders."

"Pretty early."

"I have a brew that I call *black tar* that makes espresso seem like iced tea. Takes extra-long to triple brew that sucker."

"Well then, you better go." I got on board the program right away.

"Hope to see you again; it'd be right nice."

"Back at ya. Thanks for the drink." I tipped my glass and watched him walk away. His almost-red hair took shards of light with it. Buster's limp and drag less noticeable, he walked prouder. I stayed for a while, watching the crowd rise and wane, mingle and freeze, couples and singles, men of all permutations. So natural, so indistinguishable from straight bars. The same televisions hanging from the corners, the same stale smell, the same camaraderie, and the same acceptance given to those who enter. Just the object of their desire–theirs and mine–altered.

I left lighter and happier than I had felt in a very long time, the drive home not so monotonous, the night air not so heavy, and my mind freer to sort out who I really was.

# 14

MORNING CAME SLOWLY. Throughout the night until the sun pushed against the dark, I thought of my family, what had happened at Bellow's, and about Addie.

Sleeping was not an option. Soon it would be time to ready for the final day of this ordeal. My father would be shown for the last time, like the ice sculpture around which a party is planned. He would be eulogized, memorialized, and steered into his final home. A boat pushed in to drydock for winter.

We would get over and around this somehow. Death is the ultimate challenge, the last task; just get to the finish line. It's nature's lesson. Nothing lasts beyond its intended design or need, be it tree, animal, human, or dynasties. It is a quiet massacre, one thing, one person at a time in quick succession evenly dispersed so little notice is given to the change or the cycle. Like the space between heartbeats, nature secures a rest for itself, healing just a little from the onslaught of all living things.

I wondered if the passing of my father was the actual call of the Siren of Death for Greyhaven, so seductive its song. Did she warn us of the need for all things to end? Would we heed her call? There was so much to fix, change, hide, and distort to keep it alive. It appeared to be too much energy to expend. The only one who seemed to have the energy to continue the fight against this passing was Cornelius. I wondered if he knew something that the rest of us didn't.

He had a vision for this place, so lacking in me. I understood why Madeline despised Greyhaven, or so I thought. But I could not understand my disdain for this place beyond the obvious that I had reasoned.

It went so much deeper, as if a natural trait like hair color or nose shape.

We came from the same place, Cornelius and I, but differed in every available category. What was it about the warmth of that womb that affected us so completely differently? What nurture, what nourishment, differed for him and me? Did we not bounce to the same joys, did we not feel the same stresses inside Mother's taught skin? Did she not laugh and cry so that we could feel the vibration? Like armor, it should have protected us equally, but it instead came between us. We did not share the same egg, but we did share the same womb. Why didn't that give us a more complete bond? Beyond the physical differences, there should have been an intuitive link, a reading of our souls. There was none of this. I can't say that I was saddened, I was just aware of it.

Long ago, sadness passed for us. Cornelius would say the same, but from another direction. The only difference that I could see was that I was disappointed by the failure of the possibilities. He, however, would say, "There it is, it's different, and I will not waste time on *what ifs*."

I thought about Buster as I dressed that morning. Addie would soon arrive to steal me away for a while. I felt the need to ask her about him, what she thought of him; about life here for the years I was gone. So much had been left to imagining that I needed the details from the storyteller. And there were the documents. She needed to tell me as much as she could remember before the chance to hear it disappeared.

I dressed for the funeral just in case plans changed and I was caught short for time. I donned my suit, polished my shoes, did all the little details that routine attaches to your day. I wanted to remember walking from my room this morning. It struck me that I should record this feeling, the smells, the texture of the place, for I might never return. I wanted to move in slow motion so I could catch different angles and certain vistas that might possibly help me remember.

Something drew me to desperately remember all of this, an unformed feeling, a thought. Something. I shook it off, but recorded it.

Addie appeared in her mourning regalia, looking oddly out of place in her finery.

Although stately, I was used to seeing her in simpler attire. She struck a different image this day, worldlier than I remembered, more accustomed to that which money purchases. I never put that together, 'til now. I met her at the door and helped her in.

"It's time for me to say goodbye to Titus. Escort me, won't you?"

"It'd be my pleasure, Momma." I took her arm and placed it on mine. She was even unsteadier than I remembered. We walked, slow and proud, as if a crowd was forming to see us bear up. As we stood in front of the doors to the library, Momma turned to me and said, "I'll be fine now."

"Do you want me to come in with you?"

"No. I have been with your father for so many years that the hands have spun off the clock. I want to be with him now, alone, the way we always were."

I stepped back, surprised, and said, "I'll be in the hall if you need me."

"Suit yourself." She turned and slipped into the room.

I closed the French doors just slightly to give us little more distance and watched through the old glass panes as she steadied herself upon approaching the coffin. I strained to listen like a child sent to bed early before the guests arrived. The light from the candles gave glitter to her silhouette. And, I'm sure that this was my imagination, but my father's prone face lit up as if he had been expecting her and was happy.

Addie placed a hand on the coffin and I watched her feel the metal and touch the satin that lined my father's bed. She gingerly knelt in front of him on the velvet pad and spoke. I felt like a voyeur but stayed for selfish reasons. I needed to know what I thought I would never be told.

"Well," her eyes followed his rigid terrain, a typography she knew well, "here we are, my friend." Addie touched the pillow that my father's head rested on. "You've gone without me." Time stood still while she looked at my father's body. I drank in the moments, watching what I didn't know. "You got your wish. Always said that you didn't want to be the one who's left. That was always funny to me till now."

Addie adjusted the sweep of my father's hair across the pillow. "Now, I know what *you* didn't want to feel." She touched his head and stroked his silvery white hair, pausing for a moment. "I don't think that I'm strong enough for what I need to do. We were almost there, you and me. It was almost the end. Why couldn't you hold out just a little longer?"

Did she mean Greyhaven? Addie breathed in a sweeping torrent of air and looked up. "Why is it that we get the hardest challenges when we're at our weakest? God damn you for leaving, Titus. God damn you, God, for taking him!" She cursed God from a higher place. She hit the edge of the metal with the palm of her hand then rested both hands on his coffin. "I don't rightly know what to do next, I just know that I have loved you for fifty years. A lifetime to some, a minute to me. I felt it back, you know…the love. Words always failed you, but I felt it just the same."

I fell back onto the hall chair as if all power had left my legs. I knew that my father and Addie had a special relationship. Adept and savvy, she could see business matters a lot more clearly than Mother because Mother's lists of resentments always got in the way. Addie gave me the mothering that I needed, as well, which pleased Titus, for he knew that Ivinia was incapable of such attention. Somehow, I never put the signals together. I didn't know this. The words clarified what I always thought I saw, and I was both pleased and saddened for the loss.

So much of what happened fit better now. Addie was always there, Titus was always there, and now I realized that they were there for each other. Then it hit me. I didn't know how Mother fit into all of this. I didn't understand her role, although I was oddly pleased by what I was seeing and hearing. Was this why Mother would not let Addie into the house? Had she known? As questions raced through my mind, Addie broke the silence in the library again.

"The bargains we made so long ago don't hardly feel worth the trouble anymore. What would've happened if we just let it all go?" She addressed Titus as if she wanted to start an argument with him. "What Titus? What did we gain from all of this? I hate that we're over. I hate that you're gone. I hate that I'm old. I hate that my children are scattered in all directions, pointing away from me. Would that we could start again now. Can you imagine, Titus? Can you see us?" Addie started to weave a tale so alluring, wanting to convince him one last time of her vision, leaning into his face.

"Opening wedding gifts, having friends, raising children, struggling together for something good. Not fearin' financial ruin and not protecting the one thing that mattered to only your father: a contract, a legacy that's all but ruined now anyway." She stopped in the middle of it all. "Look at me, still trying to convince you and you still won't answer me." Addie started to laugh and cry at the same time. She paused in her tears and regained composure. "I will keep my bargain." Addie turned from the casket and started for the doors, as she did, she chuckled, shaking her head, as if all of this was unbelievable to her, as unbelievable as it was to me.

"You all right, Momma?"

"I'm fine, Faust."

"Are you done?

"Yes, Faust, I'm finished. *It's* finished. Let's go."

We pulled away from the house in silence with Jed at the wheel, as the first of the limousines arrived to let the remaining people who had not yet paid their respects do their thing. I looked out of the back window to see Cornelius greeting the first group. The guests started to pour in, more exaggerated than any before them. The West Coast contingency had arrived. Older and painted up, like geriatric peacocks, finding a style so long ago and letting their mirrors tell them a lie. "Mirror, mirror, on the wall, you'll never change me, after all."

# 15

THE RIDE TO CRUMPET Island on Back Bay was quiet and somber, as if we continued without pause the ceremony of burying my father. I chose not to break the silence, for it would interrupt the prayer for the dead. We drove over the bridge that connected us to Addie's house and Jed pulled into the gravel drive off the road that led to the more-developed islands for snowbirds and newer financial achievers. Addie's house, down the long gravel path, looked different in the early afternoon light. I now saw its protection differently.

Addie waited for Jed to open the car door for her. I followed them into the house as Jed said his goodbyes.

"Addie, if ya need me, I'll be out back hittin' some cords"

"I don't sees as I'll need you anytime soon, Jed, but thanks. Faust and I are just goin' to spend some time together catchin' up."

Addie and I walked to the sunporch where we'd spent many a year watchin' grass grow. As I walked through the rooms, I became more aware of the pictures scattered on tabletops, on chests of drawers, on every mantlepiece in the house. I'd never before noticed how many of them contained my father's image. Travel photos, group shots, single images. I saw a story being told for the first time. It gave me both startle and peace, first for my lack of awareness all these years, and then for my happiness. A place existed for Titus where he found solace. Madeline and I always knew that it was never at home, but we had no idea that it existed here.

Addie brushed past all of the delicately slip-covered furniture and strategically used them as tools to steady her determined walk as she forded her way to the sun parlor. We entered the sunporch with its divided panes and sat on the settee where we'd rested many times before. It was covered in a barrage of large-leaved prints, still vibrant under their subtle fade of greens and wine, blue and mustard. A tray, already on the tea table in front of us, held a large pitcher of lemonade, a tin of ice protected from the sun, two glasses etched with delicately intertwining vines dancing around the tumblers, a dish of shortbreads, and an envelope. The items lay arranged in an apparent plan.

"Something to drink, my love?" Addie asked me.

"Yes, please." She started to pour both glasses shakily. I noticed more effort spent than I'd remembered.

"There's something you need to know," she said, wasting little time in getting to the point. "The information I'm about to give you is not an easy thing for me to do." She handed me the envelope and let me open it without explanation. I quietly read the documents, paying careful attention to the highlighted area. It was the final court case involving the lawsuit that Josilyn and Reverend Ray Blacksol brought against our family.

"Pay particular attention to the wording of the judge's findings. For now, just read the summary written by the lawyers." She wanted to make sure I understood where she was going.

I carefully read the documents, knowing that in these pages lay something important. I quickly found the lawyers' conclusions.

"There's little that I don't know already, Momma. These papers still talk of the firstborn male descendant of Titus Madigan," I said.

"Those are the words he used, 'the first male born.' No, you can't make those things up, but there's more." There was an efficiency to how she spoke.

"How much more could there be? We have been over this continually through the years." I felt the familiar exhaustion in my words. I knew more was coming but pushed my ignorance as far as I could to stave off the effects of possible new information.

"Look at these." Addie reached for a small box by the leg of the tea table and handed me the wooden locker.

"What are these?" I asked, as I opened the cover and flipped through torn and dirty pages from three different law firms.

"I got these from Ivinia a while ago," she said slowly.

"Are you sure of this?" I said, after quickly reviewing the findings.

"Quite...sure." She looked straight into my eyes without blinking. "It means that you own Greyhaven and all the land."

"You mean Cornelius *and* I, don't you?"

"No. You own Greyhaven."

"Twins are considered simultaneous births, we already know that, no?"

"No. We were so caught up in winning against Benoit and Blacksol that we missed the very specific wording," Addie said, almost as if I had said nothing. "And Ivinia found it out."

"Why didn't you tell me this sooner?"

"I didn't want you to get involved. Ivinia broke down a while back and these papers were the reason. When she read them she went crazy." Addie winced through this memory. "I had never seen her so out of control. She tore through the house and threatened Titus. Then she came here and threatened me. That's why Jed moved in."

"Why do you say *I* own it?" It was like a hot potato that I wanted to drop before the music stopped.

"Because you were the firstborn, by three hours."

"Again, Momma, he and I are twins; simultaneous births. What more needs to be said? Knowing this, what has it got to do with owning Greyhaven?" I glanced at the wording again.

"I'm quite sure I know when my baby was born, so did your father," Her words were meant to stun. How could they not?

"*Your* baby?" I asked, incredulously, not yet making the connection.

"Faust, as you know," Addie hesitated, stuttering the first few words 'til she comforted in the truth, "the will states very specifically that the lineage of the father is the only thing that counts to the ownership of Greyhaven. The mother is of no concern to this corporation and never did mean anything."

"What is it you're saying, Mamma?"

"I am your mother, Faust," Addie stuttered again. "I am your mother," she repeated as if relieved.

"Of course you are, Momma," I patted her on the leg, thinking she would move on.

"No, Faust. I *am* your mother. Ivinia is not. I gave birth to you, the man that I am so proud of." She tried to touch my face with her shaky hand. "The man who gave me Titus back."

I froze in disbelief.

She handed me a large photograph that was hidden in an album sitting on a bookshelf beside her chair. Through my echoes of shock I saw her frailty, even more pronounced now, as she handed me the photo from the yellowed pages of a scrapbook of frozen images, proving what she said. I looked at it and saw a familiar pose of two peoples' arms, holding a baby. I then recalled the album Addie had prepared for me and had given me just a few days ago.

"This is the photo on the album you gave me," I said. "The same photo?"

"Yes, the same photo, only...the whole photo." Addie gathered more strength.

"These...these are your hands, and Titus' hands, holding me," I stuttered. I always assumed they were Ivinia's hands. Addie's skin, so fair from generation after generation of inter-relations, and ours, so olive, originally designed to weather the heat of Sicily, passed down birth after birth, grew to match in hue. Little discernable difference. Ivinia, rich and dark, so exotic she shimmered in the sun. Addie, fair and radiant, paled into creamy softness. Descriptions so unalike explained more of their similarities rather than their differences.

A sudden din blanketed the room. It enveloped over the delicate slipcovers and hit the travel photos in their silver frames with a thud. There it was. Titus and Addie holding me for the eager camera lens. I sat there numb.

"Jed took that photo of us at your second christening."

"The *second* Christening?"

"Yes the public one, then the second one that counted for your father and me."

Addie spoke through my shock, not wanting to stop until she was done. "A whirlwind surrounded your birth, to no one's surprise. So much so that Cornelius' birth went almost unnoticed. There were things to do, moves to be made, and egos to pacify. You were born and life on Crumpet Island sheltered us from the storms on the mainland.

"I can't believe what I am hearing." A surge of rage pushed its way up from my stomach.

"You were born not because of Ivinia but in spite of her. When she found out about my pregnancy, she wanted you aborted. I refused."

"What about Titus? Did he want me gone?"

"I can only tell you that he never asked."

"But you don't know for sure?"

"I'm long past telling you anything but the truth. I know what I saw. He loved you, protected you. He saw to it that every day you were safe."

"Why did I live at the house with Ivinia?" It amazed me what questions came first to my mind.

"That was the deal. If I did not agree to that charade, then Ivinia would have told everyone. And in 1952 that would have been a scandal that Titus and the corporation could not withstand. He would have been destroyed. The family would have been destroyed. Anyway, I have kept my promise now."

"What promise?" I asked.

"Listen to me." Addie saw that I was in another place. Grabbing me by my shoulders, her bony fingers dug into my flesh as much for emphasis as to steady herself. "I have kept a promise that I made to your father some fifty years ago. I have told you who you are. We made a pact that whomever survived would tell you what you needed to know."

"You calculated this, years ago?"

"I don't have time to debate our planning. We are in a bad time, now, worse than when you were born. Things need to change and you need to hear the words I'm tellin' you. I told you there were secrets. Cornelius may even know by now. Even he was kept in the dark. That's why Ivinia was found in one of the splits."

"You mean by Buster, don't you?"

"Ah, he told you. Good."

I felt numb. I felt foolish. So much pointed to this moment but custom and daily routine had hidden the obvious so well. I thought of Cornelius and wondered why. Why, when we saw our father's complexion in each other, the shape of his eyes, had we not been suspect to our differences? When we did not bond as brothers early on, why had we not seen the loose threads of our weave instead of the sparsely knitted ones, thinking 'separated by a gene or two?' We were enough alike to get by to fool everyone around us. I felt foolish and defrauded, robbed of a better time, a time of peace, a haven embraced by what would have been more familiar surroundings than the atmosphere in which I grew up.

"How could you not tell me, Momma?" It started to hit me. "Looking me in the eyes when you played with me out back, all those years? How could you let me return to that house every night, knowing that I was hated...hated for being the seed of what she feared?"

"Couldn't I lay the same thing at your feet?" Addie struck hard. "You left. Leastways I stayed. You didn't do the same thing for me."

"As far as I knew, you were my nanny! How could I know?"

She touched my leg, apologetically, as her hand shook with the weight of her secrets. "Faust, I love you. I always have. I have given up two children. I never get to see much of them because of that. I gave birth to them and gave them up, so's they were protected, well before you were born. I wouldn't let your half-sisters stay here and be the next in line for this twisted fate. I was sure that it would happen to them as it happened to me, and every female Waters before me. It ripped my innards out, bare hands inside pullin' raw. But when I saw your face and you had the glow of Titus and his shock of hair, I said to myself, I said, 'Not this boy; he is not leaving.'"

"You chose this, didn't you? You loved him or needed me, which was it?" I didn't get the connection to the past as I heard it.

"I chose from the ways available to me. I loved your father, but that didn't matter as much as the fact that he loved me." Addie's eyes hardened as she pounded her chest. "He started on the same path as the rest of the men before him, but ended up lovin' me. I made him love me. Men are weak like swamp mosquitoes. They are both fragile, last but for a short while, only to sting and disrupt. Namah had such a chance when…"

"*Namah?*"

"Yes, Noah's wife. You're not up on your Bible passages, I see."

"Oh yeah, two of everything."

"Namah had such a chance, I reckon, to get those two mosquitoes and those men so this would not continue. Mosquitoes and men, I always say, would've helped if they were gone. But we need to deal with them both. Now look at what we all have to do."

"I guess it is written in stone, right Momma?" I asked.

She looked up at me. "Written in stone, all right, but the stone was thrown in a different direction. I picked it up and threw it for our benefit. I made any kind of compromise, any promise, any deal, to keep you here."

"I was a business deal?" I shot up out of my seat and paced the floor, no longer sure of this place.

"My God, yes. So you could have Greyhaven!"

Heretofore, Addie's house was a haven. Now it felt strange and disloyal. The room blushed at the afternoon sun as if embarrassed by the tales they told too late.

"A business deal!" I repeated, looking up at the ceiling.

"Yes, and so what to the excuse? Pay attention to the reason!" She managed to defend herself and reprimand me at the same time. "It turned out to be the smallest part of the bargain. I had to do it. Didn't you hear me? You became the best thing in my life. You gave me Greyhaven and you gave me Titus." Addie shook her hand to the sky. "And this time I was dealing from a stronger position than Ivinia. You were his. Titus' first son. Not hers, mine." Addie swelled with a frail pride, again pounding her chest. "But Ivinia swore that she would 'give this backwater town a run for its money.' She promised to make life, that already seemed like hell…how did she put it…'seem like an afternoon garden party in comparison.'"

In my shock I let Momma exhale the breath she was holding for more than fifty years. She continued. "Ivinia said, 'I have endured this loveless marriage, never been accepted by anyone, and I bore you children. You owe me. You both owe me and you will pay starting today.' Rage poured out of her when she found out I was pregnant, a bull seein' red. The upset of my givin' birth forced her situation to be early. She gave birth to Cornelius some three hours later, a month premature. When she woke up a week later, she surrounded herself with allies and made the deal…your grandfather, for one." Addie looked drained, like a weight had been lifted from her shoulder.

"Momma, I know enough. Stop." I leaned against the mantlepiece in the parlor and it struck me. "Does…does Madeline know?"

"No, of that I am sure."

"How could this happen? What will she think?"

"If she knew, things would be different. Besides, she's changed somehow. I am not sure of her intent anymore, Faust."

"*Madeline?* What do you mean?"

"She has not been the Madeline that I knew, not since we all met up in New York. I noticed some things. That's one of the reasons I was gone for a few hours when I was up visitin' you. I needed to see some people that could help me."

"What did you see in her?"

"Not so much see, maybe *feel*. She became more aligned with Cornelius. And Harris' demeanor changed towards me. He became more guarded, more involved with Cornelius. Sarah became more distant. Planets just started shiftin'." Addie's eyes kept on moving, like her eyes were showing what her brain was saying.

"Enough, Momma." I held my hand between our faces. I didn't want to hear anymore. I realized that I had been dealing with this all my life, the incongruity of the situation, the miss of the fit. I'd always run to Crumpet Island to feel settled, connected. Now I know why. It was more than a safe place, it was my home, unlike Greyhaven and the big house, the circus big top. My 'family' always danced around me. As much as I wanted to belong, it was like forcing a piece of a jigsaw puzzle to fit when it clearly didn't. I didn't.

"Faust, please let me finish. You need to know all of this now. I don't have time to walk you through this like a trainin' horse."

"Oh, for God's sake. Alright." I couldn't refuse her even now.

"You were absorbed into that household. Titus made the deal with

Ivinia. You became part of that family. But there was more pain involved in seeing you there, and Ivinia knew it. She was the mother o' record and I would have to make peace with that. But I never could. She won. It turned into a contest of wills. She named you, over my objections. She dressed you, saw all the first times I missed throughout the years. She took the last thing from me that she could and dangled it in front of me just far enough so I could touch but not embrace, see but not be seen."

"Why didn't we just run away and start new?" I begged.

"I couldn't. There was nowhere to run. She threatened my other two children as well. Ivinia would have destroyed you and your two half-sisters while she aimed at me. She was despised in this town, but even hatred has its pecking order. Prostitutes carry the weight of being shunned, but a mixed tryst and an offspring, pretty soon you have lynching. I still would have been on the bottom. Also, she had connections up river north o' here where you're sisters were growing up. I couldn't take the chance. I was trapped. Titus was trapped. We made the deal and she demanded more."

"How much more could she have gotten?"

"It was clear what she wanted. She always coveted Greyhaven and looked at its history and the mistresses that held court but no title. Deep in her heart she searched for an opportunity, and this was it. She wanted control over the land, and she wanted to develop it."

"I can't believe that Titus would give in to her."

"Oh, your mother was smarter than that. She demanded, not the owning of the land. Forced Titus into developing the north parcel of land into Greyhaven Estates. She had been able to develop the parcel further north, upstream from what she wanted next. She had already started to develop the northern section for manufacturing of building materials and used all the tributaries and the streams to hide the waste. Ivinia was entrepreneurial but uncaring about the devastation."

"Titus agreed to this?"

"Actually, *we* agreed to it. It seemed harmless at the time and it would keep peace. It would keep Titus, you, and me together."

"But look what all of it did." I ran the movie in my mind's eye, watching the devastation caused over the years to the community, the families affected, the anger and the loss.

"We know now that Ivinia not only destroyed the land, but also extracted a massive amount of profit for herself. It took her years to develop the plan but she was dogged. Then she found out how to do it. And build it she did, with some well-meaning advice from several high-powered friends. She was building her future on the backs of every person born into Greyhaven. All this for what we had done to her." Addie paused in a swell of emotion. "Just please forgive me for not telling you. I cannot undo years of loss, but I can protect you now."

"What do you want from me, Addie? I'm pretty spent right now." I did not want to roll this off my back as if it were nothing, but I would have found it hard to muster up the indignant rage of a child finding out that he was switched at birth. I would have found it hard to be angered by the years given over to bad parenting and lost affection and deal making. Nearing fifty, I had a better perspective on choices and what they achieve, given my own life and its result. My whole life was based on this family dynamic, this struggle for power. Everyone had something to protect in the context in which they belonged. Now I was not only the pawn but the player.

"I know," Addie said. "And you should be done right through to the bone now. But you know that I was always there for you and never left your side. Don't let go of that. Please. I did all the things that I should have but was just not the mother of record. That's all."

"That's *not* all, Momma. Everything has a different meaning now. I'm not going to go running off screaming, but I'm devastated at the lack of courage. I gave this all up willingly years ago. You should have done the same thing when I was born. Now I'm back, and right in the thick of things all over again." I stood at the mantle of the fireplace and stared at the pictures, each of which told a distorted story of vengeance and deals. How different would the pictures have been if the truth had prevailed?

"We were as courageous as we could have been at the time," Addie insisted. "Times were very different then. Again, we were misfits of the lowest order. I had no status, without your father and my own strength to manipulate. We would've fit nowhere."

"I'm sure you're right," I relented, "but I can't help thinking of the possibilities if you had stood your ground. I am a product of my parents." I knew at this moment that my running was almost predestined to happen given the emotional genetics of my family. I did by leaving what they did by staying. They ran emotionally from a fight and I ran physically.

Something happened to me at that moment. Knowing the why of my incongruity and how it planted me here, right here, on Crumpet Island. I became enraged. I paced as if a caged animal. Rage suddenly turned into resolve.

Addie noticed the change in my face. She took a gamble and kept going. "We have more work to do. We cannot waste any time."

I awoke from my trance. "What?" I asked.

Addie held my hand and patted it as she had always done when I needed reassurance, reminding me that some things never change.

"There is more I need to tell you before you make a move in any other direction. I'm sick."

"Sick, with what?" I asked. "Have you seen a doctor?"

"I have seen the doctor." Raising her eyebrows, Addie continued. "And the doctor has seen me." Her slowed and thoughtful tone no longer tried to reassure me.

"Well, we'll see another doctor," I said. "I know some people in New York. We'll go."

"I have seen *all* the doctors that I'm going to see." She tapped the top of my hand. "There's nothing to be done."

"That's silly, Momma, we'll go…"

"There's *nothing* to be done." Addie stopped me by pressing harder on my hand. "My bones're brittle and it's takin' over my body."

"But, Momma…"

"No buts about it, I'm done. Faust, you have to die of something. I'm old, I've learned what I can learn here. God knows when…and its now. I'd rather die here from the disease than in the hospital from the cure. I've seen and done more in this life than anyone could've done three times 'round. I wake up and I'm here, surrounded by the grass and the mist, seeing the sun color the sky as it wants every day. It's part of me, like…like…an organ or a limb. I's born here, and it's settled; I'll die here."

"Who'll take care of you?"

"You're here now and Jed is taking good care. It's where I want to be."

"Does Madeline know?"

"Not yet. It was important for me to tell you first. So much has been hid from you in the past, I wanted t' change that somehow. But there're things…more important things that you must tend to before too long."

"What could be more important?"

"Cornelius is more important right now. I don't know much of what is going on with him. And that worries me. I never saw your father again after the accident. Cornelius and Ivinia kept me away. The workers at the house told me that there was more activity than usual; boxes and papers going in and coming out. Then they were all fired. I figure he found out that I been talkin' to them. Then, new faces started pickin' things up in Peaceable. You know, at the Minute-Stop Market, and droppin' things off for mailin' at Sam's Post and Script Pharmacy. Strange faces, all mysterious like, started showing up. I've smelled many things in my lifetime, but this'n here was way beyond bad fish. Then Ivinia disappeared. Again I tried to reach Titus. I kept getting Cornelius." Addie shook her head in resignation.

"What about Sarah or the kids? Did you try to talk to them?"

"Of course. I even went to Savannah to visit Sarah at her office. When she was told I was there, she sent her secretary out to apologize to me that she had an emergency and had to go to the hospital to see a patient. I'm afraid that everything that your father had built away from this place is in jeopardy. Something more about Titus that you need to know. He wanted to end Greyhaven."

"End Greyhaven?" I froze at the thought of a future without Greyhaven. A flood of emotions swept over me—fear, loss, anticipation, revenge, satisfaction, guilt, emptiness, peace. Years of living from within, years of living bound by the same ties from without, that miles and time tested, strained, but couldn't break. I took it everywhere I went, like spice added to a recipe, forever changing its texture and taste, never able to extract it once blended.

Would ending Greyhaven ever really *end* Greyhaven? Altered lives stay altered. Father wanted the land to rest. His guilt over the desecration loomed justifiably. His remedies, as remedies go, were far too little too late. Did he recognize that he allowed the land to be poisoned because of the one decision that he made many years ago—the decision to marry Mother, now just "Ivinia" to me? One man could not satisfy the claims of generations toward this misdirected course. But was this union orchestrated by his defiance? If he loved Addie, then why not marry her?

Seems like an easy choice now. Interracial is little surprise in the twenty-first century, but what would have been the reaction decades ago? Intolerable love, impossible to sustain, but in pockets of secrecy surrounded by an amount of land that was as big as a country. Thousands of acres surrounding this possible union was enough for at least a while. I needed to find out the reasons beyond conjecture. Was this the only penance he could pay, to let this land spend the rest of time getting over our family? Even though he had three children to help navigate the future and repair the damage, he wanted to be Titus Madigan, The Last.

Addie touched my arm. "Faust, he grew to see Greyhaven as a symbol for a lot of bad. He and I started to divest from the seed many years ago. It seemed natural. During the last two years of his life it became a quest. He wanted it ended for us, for him…for us." I realized that the second *us* included me.

"Why, Momma?"

"Look at him and me." Addie became more aware of time with each word. "We came to realize our end. There was nothing here that symbolized his love for me but the secret of it." And there it was. Addie let the feelings of so many years flow like gentle rain down the edge of a cliff. "He saw Cornelius and Ivinia trying to gain control. He knew that Ivinia was racing toward a different end, an end that even Cornelius did not know. Titus wanted to end Greyhaven as a center of the family business, shift it away from here. Ivinia wanted to own it all and him in the process. He saw it from the beginning, just after Cornelius was born. She groomed him like a minion o' the devil. He knew, in his heart, that this time, no deed restriction, no inheritance, and certainly no will would alter the determination of a woman like Ivinia. She would succeed where all others had failed. So he built a world outside of Greyhaven, many worlds with many partners, other than Ivinia. You know, one of the last things your father said to me, we was sittin' right here, was that Cornelius was 'the bad seed from a diseased tree; it must all be ended.' I'll never forget those words as tears filled his eyes. He wanted to change the legacy and give the land to a higher purpose. He wanted to turn this into a learning center for everyone, documenting the start and finish of a bad system. His penance for his family's sins, from slavery and the birth of this place till today. It was important to Titus to show not only how hatred starts but how it never ends, how it just changes to survive. How this inbred hatred lived in the hearts of the *Confederate South* and how it existed everywhere, rooted in code and outright acts of prejudice and hatred. He wanted to apologize to me for the years he spent in fear. He wanted this place to be about him and me and you and let the world know of the struggle. Then the accident happened. And I never saw him again."

"Did you try every way to reach him?"

"I wrote letters. I called on Titus' personal line. Nothing. I even went to the house and tried to get in. A man in a uniform, a stranger, refused to let me in and threatened to call the police. I even tried to stare him down. But Cornelius owns Peaceable—every building, every person. Police officers escorted me back to Crumpet Island."

"Addie, if Father gets his wish and this all ends, how will you live? What will you do for money? I have long ago written off the loss and I'm happy with what I have. Madeline and Harris are taken care of each in their own right. But you, Momma. What about you?"

"Don't worry about me. There's enough. I've been frugal. I have watched my pennies. Besides, how much and for how long do I need anything? I own Crumpet Island and that's a chunk more than I dreamed of from the beginning." She dismissed my concern with the wave of a hand. "And there is plenty more, more than I would ever need in three life times."

"What can I do?"

"First off, I need you to stay." Addie shook off helpless and became the business woman, the business woman Titus must have known.

"How long?" I asked, looking at my watch as if that would put a comfortable limit on my exposure.

"It's not 'bout how long, my love, it's 'bout doin' business and 'bout business done."

I watched Addie turn from the protectorate I knew to the business woman who'd survived generations of my family. I sometimes forgot that she and many other servant mothers before her survived my family, while living through the worst times of our country and its piquant for prejudice that stronger laws would, at best, only twist the devil into a new shape. From Lincoln on, it turned from enslaved people to the trapped desperate; those destined for low salaries, separate lives, poorer schools, limiting futures, and fading aspirations while living in cast-off housing, wearing hand-me-down clothes, and trapped within a system of compromised rights.

"You could be white and mediocre and have a life's worth of successes," Addie would always say. "Any part of African and you must be extraordinary just to survive." And there it was. My clue about not only her mixed lineage but mine. No matter how watered down the Waters, it would never be enough here. This, and the shackles of our family dynamics, proved to be what kept the Addie's people here, what kept Addie here. She became the new paradigm and stayed for very different reasons.

"It's time to go." Addie drifted back to the present. "Your father needs to be settled."

"Is it that time already?" I looked at my watch and helped Addie out of her chair. "It's hard, isn't it, Momma?"

"Faust, you have no idea."

# 16

WE TALKED ON OUR WAY to the cemetery. I chose to ride with Momma and meet the rest of my family there. I let Madeline know of this plan and asked that she relay the message to Cornelius. Addie asked Jed not to come. He agreed to her wishes, very willing to grant Momma's request.

As we left Back Bay, Jed payed his sax. We could hear his throaty notes fade in the distance, filling the car with a diminishing sound that would prepare Momma for what she needed to say next.

"We must put an end to this right here and now."

"You mean Greyhaven, don't you?

"It's a cancer that defies cure, like mine. Help me do it, Faust. Please." I never heard Momma plead so deeply. "It needs to end while I am still here to see it happen."

"I will, Momma. What do you want to do?" She became the one to finally draw me in.

"We need to stop Cornelius. He has the whole family convinced that the land can be reopened. Titus wanted this land to go back to seed and I will do what I can to make that happen for him." She wore a determined look, one that I had seen when she protected me from Ivinia and her rage. "Cornelius is calling a last meeting tomorrow night for the family. We can't trust anyone now, not even Madeline."

"*Not even Madeline*, Momma?"

"No. You know I'm right. Something has happened to her and Harris. You will stay for the meeting?"

"Yes, I will." I promised.

"Find out what you can, today." She looked up at me.

"What if it's late, Momma? You need to rest."

"I haven't rested in quite some time. My bones don't take kindly to the bed, so no matter that you fetch me."

"Consider it done."

We traveled together the rest of the way in silence. Driving ahead of the dust that we raised on the drive that led to the Heaven's Gate Cemetery, I turned the car under the rusted arch of its threshold and continued toward our family crypt. In a knit-and-purl twist of the car, we edged and dodged former friends, enemies, and the few that never knew us but by reputation, all driven into silence by time and nature, with only markers to punctuate and prove their existence. A large marker for Mr. and Mrs. Relegante, with a sword and cross at its top. To the right, Hanna Harabel, alone in death as she was in life, choosing not to be buried in her family plot.

The cemetery was laid out much like a town with better and worse sections, a small section for the very poor with overgrown grass; the promise of perpetual care lacked consistency. Looming in the distance, the place where the elite came to gather as if at a country club or trendy new restaurant, in stone houses that would stand the test of time. All donned bronze doors and the smell of spent fuel from their eternal flames as if these components would keep them alive and remembered somehow. No matter how grand the edifice or small the marker, the pattern of loss would be the same. Some family and friends would visit shortly after the newest member was interred. But they would eventually stop coming, faded emotions and other duties filling the hole in their lives, keeping them away. Equalized by death, forgotten is forgotten no matter what the legacy.

But today a crowd of the dedicated surrounded our stone house. The groundskeeper opened the bronze doors on cue. These twisted bronze guardians stroked our egos with their cast of characters arrogantly acting their role in the story. Melted and forged to depict a Greek tragedy of obscure origin, the doors told their story but only partially—the myth of sorrow and redemption completed on every window and door that surrounded the building as if the residents might want to look out at the views or venture forth into this forced garden and be fooled as to their place in history.

And there they were—the mourners. Each attired in their interpretation of appropriate sadness. Our immediate family dressed in hard and soft veneers, all blacks and all whites, dramatic in the glimmer of appropriateness; our extended family dressed in what the closet had to offer, begged, borrowed, or tasteless; partners and friends in varying degrees of the same. But then there was the contingency from the West Coast. Peacocks and ostriches of color and exaggeration, their plumage trembled at their tips, old and dusty but stiff to the awareness of strangeness and threat. These were the people Ivinia made her friends. Always alert to the danger around them, they responded like a herd unaccustomed to its environment. They perched and looked around, each covering another direction, ready to alert the rest if just one sensed a threat.

They never belonged on the West Coast; they were transplanted from here to there, and before that from somewhere else to here. Vagabonds with dramatically sweeping fronds and shallow roots, like the palm trees that surrounded them, both equally strange to the air that they breathed. They were all part of the red-light districts that my family created in and around the fringes of Charleston, Savannah, and New Orleans. Grandfather's pedigrees, and his grandfather's before him. They hailed from Italy and Iowa, Portugal and Pittsburgh. Anywhere innocence gathered in lonely places of desperation. These were the people, the sexual servants, prostitutes, and whores, depending on your needs and your finances. Like cars, they took you to where you needed to go, but the more options you could afford, the better the ride. This last generation of paid flesh finally broke free.

Freed by Titus' business savvy and moral conversion, he divested our business into lucrative and more reasonable ventures and, as our troops had done in France during the war, liberated the downtrodden, dressed not in rags but in plumes and sequins, allowing them to prosper or fester somewhere else, becoming troubadours, bards, and pipers of another sort. Most survived and some even remained Ivinia's friends.

And in the papers in the attic over the servant porches, Madeline found early on that Ivinia was one of them, a prostitute that Father met when he was sent by Grandfather to inspect the *troops* in one of his first trips without the *boss*. He found her lively and interesting, ignoring the prostitute aspect for public record. Always rebellious, he fancied her. So while the story he told varied little in scope, the details were as twisted as the land we occupied. All this clever storytelling because I found one of their wedding albums squirreled away in the bottom drawer of his dresser. I often thought back to that time and swore that he tried convincing himself more than me of the reason for their union. It all started making sense, piecing what I felt with what I had just been revealed to me by Addie.

I helped Addie out of the car and the muffled commotion of the assembling crowd froze and fell silent in its tracks. We walked together.

Helping this fragile woman, I watched as the crowd parted to Cornelius' dismay.

"Come, Faust," Addie said, "we'll be in front today."

"Are you sure, Momma?"

"It's time for me to stand up for your father," Addie said, her words steadier than her steps.

Addie's body jerked forward, using all of her strength to walk through this reluctant receiving line. She pushed onward, determined to be at the head of this. The scene had a drama that appeared surreal, like Georges Seurat's *A Sunday Afternoon on the Island of La Grande Jatte*. As in the painting, everyone shared the experience but reacted differently. Some concentrated on our family's loss, some on the freedom that it engendered. Some were there to ensure that we registered their presence, some were there to make sure that Titus was dead. I saw this in Cornelius' eyes. He dreamed on to another place at that moment.

All this changed as we moved to the mound of flowers surrounding Titus' coffin. We strolled arm in arm as we passed *the family Miserable*. They stared anew, as if Addie was a prop invented for the day just to irritate the already irritated family. They exhaled like angry bulls in the dead of winter, steam escaping from their noses to add a layer of humidity to an already sweltering day. Even the clouds thinned out, losing their water to the increasing scorch of the sun. The grass that we walked upon, drought stressed, would not rise again from its flattened state. We forged ahead, feeling the eyes of family and friends locked upon us as we inched our way along. I touched Madeline and kissed her on the cheek as we passed, and I nodded to Harris, grasping at his arm for support. He lightly grasped back. I needed to feel the underpinning of peripheral shoring up, so needed for the storm that was about to rage at Addie's request.

We passed the gaggle of "Westies," as Ivinia used to call them. That colorful bunch, what remained, stood mostly together as if a tether rope prevented them from straying. There was Buddy Blakely, character actor whose sidekicks were usually horses with nasty attitudes; Bedelia Lennette, a B-film star who appeared in second features at the theatres before they were eliminated in favor of late-night television broadcasts that aired seconds before the flag and the anthem signed us off to bed. I recognized several others from the pack that descended on our home periodically through the years before being picked off by nature, one by one. They registered scorn for us and quiet support for Ivinia, the woman I called Mother 'til that day. Roger Dallimund, swarthy ladies' man brought in to the fold by all of these former beauties, whose career disappeared in the fifties and surfaced anew, in notoriety, because he'd invested heavily in Malibu real estate, by way of his wife's money, acre by acre, making him richer than his film residuals ever would, complicated by the murder of his estranged last wife, leaving him millions more because of her failure to sign the final divorce papers. It remains a Hollywood mystery. Sarah Rush, Feona Louis, Jessica Bennet; each had sexual specialties, honed at my family's court, that held them in high esteem and let them reign as "cream of my grandfather's crop of beauties." I shook my head at that thought, trying to rip it from my mind, as I looked upon these bent creatures of the night. I recognized their faces, though they cut a more jagged rug now. Then, as the crowd opened up, I saw a fierce red vision that drew me to her like an accident scene: Tatiana Paskaya, sometime business partner and fierce defender of Ivinia.

Tatiana Paskaya stood there like a gladiator ready to fight. Father had told me about her once after he orchestrated a clean-up from a party she had attended at our house. Days after her departure we would routinely send messages to antique dealers and furniture suppliers to replace the items she had broken, torn, or damaged in her drunken antics with Ivinia as her sidekick.

Parties at our house always signaled a shift in family policy or the creation of a new venture. Like masked balls, they hid the truth. Ivinia gained strength over the years and learned that making her ventures public ensured success. Not only did she negotiate this success throughout an area that disliked her, but it also guaranteed that Father would be dragged in publicly as well. Although hated, degree being moot, the county could not ignore the increase in jobs for its citizens, so an uneasy alliance formed, for it was always customary for the people of the South to make up its mind and never change it. So each side would extract what they needed and then retreat to their corners of fixed alliances and emotions. It was the oddest weapon in her arsenal, but it worked seamlessly.

One party stands out in my memory. It was 1960 and vinyl was the new emerging product in the building industry for siding. Ivinia had insisted on building a vinyl siding plant to add to the arsenal of factories she owned that supplied product for the housing and commercial buildings that my father's company constructed. She controlled and separately owned production plants that made many of the parts—asbestos flooring, ceiling tiles, paint, insulations, and now vinyl siding. These plants skirted and framed the bucolic neighborhoods that Titus built. Titus did not want any more factories in the area. He felt uneasy about their impact. So a struggle ensued and Ivinia solicited the help of Tatiana and her money to do this business deal, once again. Ivinia reasoned that if Titus could have partners, then so could she. So periodically, Tatiana served as Ivinia's ace in the hole. This event launched vinyl production for siding and, as we learned, the continuation of the poisoning of our land.

It had been Ivinia's custom to host several balls each year, sifting through the local who's who, reaching from our county to the bigger cities, then finally to the "Westies" for balance. Charity was always the front; tense acceptance was always the result.

Tatiana had learned that the Barnum circus was in town, so Ivinia decided to blow out the entertainment and have an African Safari theme, complete with circus animals. She cooked up this event with Tatiana, who had some dealings with the Barnum clan. Tatiana set up the meeting between Mother and the marketing people for Barnum. By the time Tatiana finally arrived to attend this extravaganza, there were three hundred attendees, town officials, local notoriety, key partners of my father's. Not just monkeys and bearded ladies, but deformed actors who gave freakish physicality to the already distorted scene, all borrowed from smaller and more local circuses. There were elephants, lions, tigers, and bears in silly hats, walking either free or on leashes, not only through the estate but, for added intensity and drama, freely through the house. This resulted in mass destruction and an unhealthy level of animal waste on the stairs, in the halls, and throughout the rooms of our manse. No one had considered this part of the scenario. Trays of food knocked over and eaten, the help scurried picking up food and dung. It all added a new meaning to "circus atmosphere." One particular problem was the giraffe. Spooked by one of the children, it wedged itself in the corner of the solarium attached to the dining room. It chewed on the rare flora and fauna as if attending an all-you-can-eat buffet. All the specimen trees and plants went from blossoming spring to bare winter in a matter of twenty minutes. Tatiana saw the devastation and left early, telling Ivinia that she felt ill from the odor in the house. And in a dramatic sweep of safari clothing and netting, she was gone. This was typical of Tatiana Paskaya. But who was she? Tatiana Paskaya had an interesting past. She passed through Russia on a gambling junket as an escort while working for us and, deciding to be born there, had changed her name from Gladys Plunket. She hailed from South Bend, Indiana. She added an Eastern European accent to her repertoire, married the sugar baron that she escorted, Pla Verison from Cuba, and settled in Bel Air. Bel Air was the perfect place for Tatiana. It was a place where instant success finds roots, buys family antiquity, and pretends longevity. With this short, dark man of equally questionable lineage, she gained legitimacy and talked of loving Mother Russia and hating what Castro did to her profit margin. She spoke of sneaking her fortunes out of Cuba while expounding on travel, fashion, possessions, and the loss of her mysterious husband years ago to a suspicious overdose of pills and vodka (or as she said it, *wadka*). Fear of her daughter, her only child, took over most of Tatania's days from then on, as Ivinia told us frequently. This ungainly woman of odd parenting, who had an unnatural affinity for thoroughbred horses and the gambling circuit, spent the rest of her inheritance trying to have her mother committed. This was a battle worth fighting. The daughter stood to inherit hundreds of millions. And, even with Tatiana's advancing age, soon was not soon enough.

This was Ivinia's closest friend. Now a caricature of herself, she knew Ivinia like no other.

For Titus' funeral she dressed in red, the mourning color of another country, with a hat brimmed and bent over one eye with a long sweep of coke feathers dyed in shades of red to "aubergine," as I could hear her say in my memory. The crevices lacing her face exposed her age and journey. She spackled them smooth for the distant dramatic impact. No more close ups for her. She was formidable in her youth and her presence here brought that back to mind. Coming with great fanfare to my father's funeral, she would leave a path of destruction like a twister through a Tennessee trailer park. The plot thickened by her presence. Before her arrival, the intrigue and chaos at Greyhaven had followed a predictable path. But by her presence a new complication would arise, tension ratcheted up to a new level. Madeline and I insisted on calling her *Gladys*.

"Faust, I missed you at the house," Gladys, aka Tatiana, grimaced.

"Ah, Gladys, but I'm seeing you here. You are looking, um, well," I said, as I escorted Addie through this mine field. Gladys twisted her face at the sound of her past.

"Addie," she acknowledged Momma with a vocal contempt that audibly hurt all those near. Addie looked up, stared at her without a hint of recognition on her face, a deliberate act; paused to emphasize the affront and moved on.

As we passed, Gladys quickly grabbed my shoulder and made her predictable move. "You might want to talk to me about your Ivinia."

I stopped and made my eyes meet hers. "What more can be added, Gladys?" I would not back down.

"You know we kept in touch as if we were next door neighbors," she confided.

"Yes, I was painfully aware of that," I sighed.

She breathed out and shook her head. "I loved your mother like a sister. We spoke three days before she disappeared." She became impatient.

"What did you speak of, Gladys?" I took the bait.

"Not now, darling." Her Russian accent became drawn and dramatic. "First things first." She turned her head forward and nodded toward the coffin. She controlled the environment that she inhabited still. "There's no rush to have this conversation. It just needs to be said, if not in defense of Ivinia, then in spite of her."

"If not now, when?"

"Later. After. Meet me by my limo," she said, while retrieving a compact from her purse to check for cracks in the veneer.

"Death doesn't distract you, does it? Isn't it your habit to infect other places once death has occurred?" I asked without caring for a response.

"Ah, Faust darling." She moved close and touched my cheek, scanning my face in search of familiarity. "So old, yet so naïve. Will you ever connect the dots in your life?"

Addie pulled me along, weary from our tête-à-tête. "I need to sit down, Faust."

I looked back at Gladys and watched a bowed grin appear on her face as she turned to grab the attention of another victim.

Others faded in and out of my recognition as we cut a path to the front of the gathering, 'til we reached and ran headlong into Cornelius. He formed a one-man protective wall to prevent or, better yet, persuade us to reconsider.

"Addie, how do...Faust...this isn't really necessary, is it?"

"Yes, apparently it is." I turned in deference to Addie.

"Cornelius, I have known you since you drew your second breath." Addie stepped into his face and shook as she stood firm. "You have gotten in my way for some time now. And this ends it right here." She pushed him aside. The seats in front, reserved for the immediate family, were now one short. The attendants scrambled to make adjustments, Addie sat down first, front-row center, the best seat in the house.

I stood with Cornelius and watched him watch Addie. "So, Cornelius, where is Reverend Futuris? I thought he wanted to head the service?"

"I haven't seen him yet, but I know he's skulking around here somewhere."

At that moment a limo pulled up near a tent erected to protect the immediate family from the distress of South Carolina heat. The door flung open and, pausing for effect, Futuris stepped out for the show-down. Three faces that shone like copper accompanied him. The trio wore long, electric-blue robes with gold scarves wrapped around their necks and trailing behind them. Cornelius spun around in response to the look on my face.

"Harris got you the information?" I asked.

"Whatever are you talking about?" Cornelius removed a piece of paper from his pocket, balled it up in his hand, and threw it on the eternal flame that sat in front of the crypt. It flashed its last energy and disappeared in ashes.

"Follow me," Cornelius said, as we brushed past everyone to head Futuris off at the pass.

The reverend stood erect at the side of the car and eyed our approach. He knew that a settlement was forthcoming; he just didn't know what form it would take.

"Reverend, it's good to see you." Cornelius extended a hand but Futuris hesitated, as if returning the gesture might be a losing proposition.

"Top of the day to you, sir," Futuris said. "As I explained yester-day, I wanted to come here and sing the praises of this man and his God." Futuris was not a subtle man, and his voice projected over the increasingly aware crowd. "Are we ready to start?" He adjusted his collar and slicked his hair with the palms of both hands as he walked forward. "I just want to tell the good people here about Titus and his family and what a future yo'all have secured for the county."

"There will be no speeches," Cornelius whispered in Futuris' ear.

"No speeches? He rebounded. "I have prepared a wonderful send-off for you people."

"That's just it," I said. "We're not going anywhere and you are not running for any political office off our backs."

"The hell I'm not." Futuris' face grayed and turned dead serious.

"The hell you *are*," Cornelius countered. "I have some things to talk over with you that might change your mind about staying in this neck of the woods. Excuse us, Faust, would you?"

I had no time to answer. Cornelius took his frozen elbow and escorted Futuris around to the other side of the car past the startled backup singers. I overheard bits of conversation and choice words.

*bastard children*
*affairs*
*accounts*
*offshore*

*payoffs*

Futuris tried to deny it all. As he did, Cornelius withdrew an envelope from his breast pocket and shared what appeared to be photographs and, for extra effect, a notarized document that contained an official seal. Futuris fell silent. Cornelius escorted him back to the other side of the car and released his arm.

"As I was saying, I wanted to give a proper send off to Titus, but alas, I have forgotten a pressing engagement that needs my prompt attention." Purple rage ran through Futuris' voice as he realized he'd been caught in the vortex of his own tornado of human frailty. "I just wanted to stop by and give my condolences before we rush off to perform for a church in Charleston," he pivoted.

"Thank you so much for coming," Cornelius said. He then embraced Futuris and whispered in his ear loud enough for me to hear. "If I ever see or hear that you are interfering with this family or any friend or partner, even once, I will do what I promised and there will be another funeral of an unexpected nature. Do we have an understanding?"

"We do." Futuris turned to his car. The radiant robes lost their glimmer and retreated to a fallback position in the rear of the overly stretched vehicle.

Cornelius and I watched as the black car sped from the scene as if Futuris was gunning the accelerator himself.

"We'll not be hearing from him again," Cornelius turned to me and said. "By the way, there is one last meeting at the house tomorrow evening, but I'm sure you're already aware of it. We have many things to discuss; important things. Addie will *not* be attending."

As he walked to his seat at the service, Cornelius returned the documents to his breast pocket. A smile grew on his face at a job well done, like the child I remembered at the dinner table, much more for his own satisfaction than for anyone else.

I joined Addie in the front row of the service, ahead of the whispers and the amazement.

She straightened her back and adjusted herself. The din of the mumbling swept through the crowd and died down as Madeline and Harris took their places.

"I gather Cornelius had his way with Futuris," Madeline leaned across Addie to whisper to me.

"Indeed. Did you hear about the meeting Cornelius wants tomorrow night?" I whispered back.

"You mean the meeting that will go on without me?" Addie added, unprompted.

"You knew?" Madeline asked, somewhat embarrassed by the affront.

"Oh, Madeline," Addie patted her knee, "there's little I don't know."

Addie straightened and looked forward as the service began. I grabbed her hand and she held onto mine, far tighter than ever before.

"Meet us an hour before the time that Cornelius has called the meeting," Addie whispered, her eyes forward. "Make sure Harris is there. Please convince Sarah to come." Addie whispered, her eyes forward.

"Why would Sarah come?" Madeline asked.

"I somehow doubt that she would miss this. Just tell her." Addie saved her strength for moments like these.

The service droned on, led by a generic preacher supplied by the funeral director at Cornelius' preemptory request. He sprinkled the formulaic sermon with bits of information supplied in the worn-out blanks of his monologue. Air trickled by in a rhythmic beat as hand-held fans pushed wet air under our chins. More than one hundred people sat rustling their clothes to find comfort in the heat, linen—even polyester—wrinkling with the assault. Black clouds formed over our heads in an explosion of steam and movement. A storm from the west gathered strength as it swept in.

As the service drew to a close, the sound of thunder rolled in from the horizon and brought with it lightning bolts and increasing darkness. The preacher spoke faster as the ensuing storm approached. He quickly brought his words to a close, asking us to throw a bit of dirt on the coffin before we departed. He mistakenly asked for the widow to start the procession, not knowing the technicalities and nuances of this gathering. Addie rose to her feet and the occasion. I tried to help her up but she refused it. I jerked and stopped and jerked and stopped to catch her as she steadied herself on her feet. She bent over and took the clay in her hands, kissed it and threw it on the shiny metal box that contained her lover and their secrets. The sound hurt.

I helped Addie back to the car. "Momma, sit tight. I need to take care of something."

"If 'something' has anything to do with Gladys, take careful steps, please." Addie's hand grasped my arm as I pulled away, shifting my attention to the task at hand. Large drops of water, spread far apart, hit the paths that laced through the three- by seven-foot plots of individually owned land. I walked to the limousine, its black interrupted by dust kicked up in its face by cars ahead. Large drops of water punctuated the brown haze as if diseased. I approached the side and stared into black-ened windows. I knocked and waited as if it would take some time for Gladys to get to the door. It took pregnant seconds for her to respond. The window retreated slowly. Gladys did not turn my way 'til it was com-pletely down.

"What brings you to me?" she asked, as if our conversation had played out only in my head. Her beauty, now fragile and on the rough edge of handsome; her mind missing those things that help the young to be sharply duplicitous.

"You had wanted to speak to me about Ivinia."

"Ah yes, my friend Ivinia. I received a call from her just before she *disappeared*," Gladys said, emphasizing the word with a very disapproving tone. "She complained of many things. She had a lot to complain about. It is hard to be an outsider everywhere you go." Gladys slipped in and out of her theatrical accent.

"She did little to be included," I countered.

"You want to have this pissing contest right now, darling, I will. But I would rather spend my time with other pursuits," she said, in her best Russian accent.

"What about the phone call?" I asked.

"Well, it seems Ivinia and Cornelius had a little parting of the ways."

"*Parting of the ways?* She and Cornelius were locked at the hips like a strange set of twins…stranger than he and I."

"Yes, twins. Funny how unlikely people are paired off by nature and other propositions, isn't it?

"You're referring to our family contracts?" I said.

"How is Addie?" she asked, avoiding my question. "She's looking frailer than I expected. Is she unwell?"

"Nothing that a break from all of this nonsense wouldn't cure. I'm thinking of taking her up to New York for a while. A change of scenery would do her some good." I refused to let Gladys in on the extent of Addie's frailty. Gladys sought out weakness like a bomb with heat-seek-ing capabilities. "What parting of the ways were you referring to?"

"Ah, yes, Ivinia and Cornelius. It appears there was a slight detour in Cornelius' plans and Ivinia did not seem to see it his way. She no sooner began to tell me than she was interrupted and had to go."

"What do you think she was trying to say?"

"Cannot say that I know," Gladys said, aloud but not really to me. "But, soon after our brief conversation, I tried to reach her. She was not available. I called daily for a week and finally I reached your sister, Madeline, who told me that Ivinia was missing. That's all she told me; nothing more."

"Oh, the dramatics! You're too used to dramatics, Gladys."

"Really, Faust? Well..." she paused to gain her composure and her command, "I will tell you that your lovely Madeline has something to do with it."

"Oh, please, Gladys," I rebuked her.

"Don't take that tone with me, Faust. I have seen all of this from a different vantage point than you, an aerial view so to speak. You would think that the distance you kept from your family would have given you the same advantage. Your loyalties blind you, my dear. They always have."

"You mistake blindness for caution, Gladys."

"*Caution?* How amusing. Well, I will give you one last bit of information to feed your caution. I received a voice message from Ivinia three days after she supposedly disappeared."

"That couldn't be."

"Faust, I am, if nothing else, Ivinia's closest and most loyal friend. We have survived many things in life, most with either profit or satisfaction. I would have no reason to tell you this unless it was true. You all are in a serious complication, to put it mildly. I will not be here to see it played out, nor would I want to be."

"More complicated than I already know? There couldn't be more."

"Darling Faust, thirty years of naiveté and distance should have changed the landscape for you. I've only been away for five years, but it's obvious that everything has changed. The clean horizon has disappeared, replaced by a jagged line that cuts into the sky like a knife. You think that the horizon is all that's changed and gotten edgier? The players have become older and more desperate." Gladys spoke with sureness. "Aging brings on a sense of timeliness at jobs left unfinished. There is a changing of the guard afoot." She stopped to let me absorb her meaning.

"Sounds like the royals are watching the guardhouse," I returned.

"My dear boy, you have no idea. Ivinia grew to resent Greyhaven early on. She felt trapped here. I tried to get her to move West before she married your father, but she would not listen to reason. At first she loved Titus, but then she saw that he was tied to the land. Later she found out about Addie and how much Titus loved her. She spent much time and energy trying to break those bonds, but they couldn't be broken. It was as if Titus had two mistresses, neither of which was Ivinia. She could never fit in except as dressing for the plantation. That's when she became determined to beat Titus at his own game."

"What kind of game? I knew that she elicited Cornelius, even early on she trained him. But, in my heart, I thought they were both bent on total control." I looked at Gladys less harshly. Her red flamboyancy assumed a softer demeanor. *Aubergine.*

"*What kind of game?*" She repeated the question with practiced disdain. "Ask Madeline."

"What do you mean ask Madeline? What does she have to do with it?" I was taken by how closely her information aligned with the present. I began to hear her.

"You're being played, Faust. And as usual, it's by your nearest and dearest. I am not going to handfeed you everything. I know what I know from Ivinia. That being said, I am a better judge of the things that have transpired than are you. I loved Ivinia, but I was not clouded by that emotion."

"Love never got in your way did it, Gladys?"

"No, Faust." She breathed in as if made tired by the exchange. "And if you meant that as a less-than-subtle insult, I don't feel those things. That's where I surpass my adversaries. I always identify the players first, then the game. You, however do neither. You just feel the effects of the result, like a dog wounded in a fight and then surprised by the blood."

"Now who's trying to insult?

"I don't have time to be mildly insulting. That has never been my style." She looked at the mirror that she pulled from her purse. "I always knew Ivinia's goal. Something has changed, and it is Madeline. Be, of this, frightened. She is a tougher adversary than Cornelius. I increasingly am aware of winter in the air." She inhaled deeply. "And now you know. The game has changed."

"Why didn't Ivinia tell me?"

"*Why* Faust? You are Addie's son, not hers."

"Gladys, it's always a blood thing." I tried to act as if I knew this for a longer time than I did.

"Ah, a blood thing. Oh, Faust." Gladys shook her head in exasperation. "She saw the bond that Addie and Titus had in you. She could see nothing else. It clouded her judgement. She missed the littlest detail."

It began to rain hard, as if the sky might finally purge the earth of this. "Come inside." She opened the limo door. I brought the rain in with me. "There's one thing more," Gladys said, and opened the jeweled cover on the watch that hung from its diamond lariat, "then, I must go."

"What more could you add?" I sat there, bracing myself.

"Madeline discovered what Ivinia's hatred for Titus and Greyhaven finally meant all along. When Madeline became aware of her mother's long-held feelings, and worse yet, her plans, she became enraged. She felt excluded. Ivinia told me this the last time that we spoke. Madeline thought that she would finally get something from this empire." Gladys put away her mirror and fingered the ruby solitaire that weighted her hand. "But that was never in Ivinia's plan. And I believe that to be her biggest miscalculation."

"Madeline couldn't..." I started, in defense of my sister.

"I do not have time for this defensive nonsense. I have said what I had intended to say. I must go now."

I was dismissed. The air in the limo was no longer something I felt I could share. As I was about to open the door to exit, Gladys grabbed my arm.

"You know all of this from me because of Ivinia, nothing more. I am afraid for her...still. As far as I am concerned, the balance of this God-awful place could become the parking lot for one of your Southern flea markets. And I wouldn't blink at its passing."

"Thank you, Gladys," I softened at her cold warmth.

"There will be a headstone for all of us, Faust," she said as I exited her mobile fortress. "Look around you; it's all that is left, my darling, and on them only names and dates. We think birth and death are the markers." She looked straight ahead. "It's what is held in the dash between that holds all the secrets.

"Driver!" She pressed the intercom button. "Open the door for Mr. Madigan. He needs to leave. It's been, how do I say, interesting to see you again." The driver did as instructed.

"I might say the same." I looked back at her as I exited and saw a momentary fragility. There it was—the fear, maybe the sadness that built her empire. She sped off.

I stood there for a moment to refocus.

"Are you all right?" Addie stood behind me with moistened eyes, her cane, and her pride.

"Yes, I am. Let's go."

The ride back to Addie's house was filled with a silence that only endings could achieve. Each of us stood wrapped in our own course. I dropped Addie off at her house. As the car slowed to a stop she sat for a minute.

"I don't know how much longer I have here," Addie said, her words unmistakably clear.

"Oh, Momma."

"Don't," she said, a finger pressed to her lips. "Just stay near."

And, with that, she left. I watched Addie shakily disappear into the always-open front door of her home.

# 17

THAT NIGHT I SLEPT fitfully. Too much ran through my mind, much the way free association grabs you and takes you on a roller coaster ride. Two, three, four o'clock with only alternate minutes in shallow half sleep. The past, both here and in New York; the present, with situations abounding; the future, now so uncertain, all merged into one stream of thought. The harsh ring of the phone startled me, spilling over me like an accidentally tipped glass of red wine. I knocked over the clock in the pursuit of the receiver only to hear Jed's voice.

"She needs you now."

"I'll be right there," I said, fully aware of the meaning of his words.

I drove to Addie's house in a breathless screech of tires and twisting roads, both complaining about their treatment. The closer I got to her house the more I didn't want this chapter to start. On the long stretch of marsh road between the bridges I found myself doing triple the speed limit. I started to panic and sweat. I felt the hanging moss choking me. I could see little as the mist rolled in from the struggle of disagreeing temperatures. The faster I drove the less I could see.

Suddenly, glaring red eyes caught my headlights and I slammed on the brakes without thinking. Out of the corner of my eye I caught the tail of a scurrying deer that decided not to challenge the assault of the oncoming metal beast which had dared to infiltrate its territory. I swerved and jerked the car to avoid it. The car, breaking from my control as I slammed into the muddy marsh, plunged into the brown slip. My head slammed against the windshield. As I catapulted back, the car sprayed a wave of brown onto the unexpecting grasses and trees. It took a few moments to settle into its unnerved position. As it did, I felt a welt running across my forehead. Dazed, I tried to open my door, but to no avail. My car angled nose-deep in the mud, tail up. As I tried once more to open the car door, it hit annoyingly at a large tree, which, had my vehicle veered inches to the left, would have resulted in a dramatically altered outcome.

I sat stunned and motionless, unsure of what to do. I searched for a moment for the cellphone that I had left on the nightstand. I looked at my watch. It was four-thirty in the morning. No one would be driving by for at least two hours. Six o'clock church bells always signaled the start of life on these roads and the groan of worn pickups carrying their cargo of parishioners. I remained frantic, aware that Addie awaited my arrival, possibly for the last time. My heart did the pacing that my feet could not. I tried again to open the door and then the window, but, its electronics were drenched by muddy water. I kept slamming the door against the tree in a rage of upset and fear. I didn't know how long I'd remain trapped or how much longer Addie could wait. The door would no longer close from my manic pounding, and then the mud came oozing in. Thoughts of gators crept into my mind I saw the reflections of lights scattering off the rear-view mirror, bouncing off the edges of the steering wheel and the chrome. It was accompanied by a voice.

"Hey you down there!! Hey! Anyone there? Need help?"

"Yeah! I'm down here. Please help!" I was silent for a moment; the lights stayed fixed where they landed on the metal. I heard a rushing and pushing of water and mud from behind, glad to be in the sight line of my rescuer.

"Holy shit. Faust?"

"You know me. Whose there?" I asked, as I turned to the suddenly familiar voice. "Fuck. Buster! It's you! Oh, thank God!"

"What the hell are you doing dippin' your car into this brown batter like a corn dawg?" he asked, as he tried to open the same impossible door.

"Ya know. I always like to give my car a mud bath in the early morning hours. What the hell are *you* doing out here?" I asked, a little too exasperated instead of grateful. "What time is it?"

"Funny question coming from a man ass-end up in a mudhole at, let's see, four-fifty to be exact." Buster moved around the car to the passenger-side door. "I was going to check my shrimp traps out on the jetty when I saw taillights stickin' outta the marsh."

Buster pulled the door with such force that he slipped under the car, but he managed to open it enough to get in. "Are you free enough to climb over?"

"I don't know. The shift is bent up. let me try...wait... yeah, give me a pull." I grasped his hand as he yanked me out in one easy motion. I landed on top of him in the mud and started to laugh nervously.

"You think this is funny?"

"This goes way beyond a bad night. Addie needs me."

"What's wrong?" Buster asked.

"I don't know, but I can guess. Jed called me and said *now*."

"Let's go then. Hop in my truck."

We both swayed in the mud rushing toward Buster's truck, pushing our legs and swinging our arms like characters in a 1950s horror flick. I was too frantic to assess my injuries, but it appeared that I had no broken bones, just bruised skin and ego. I once knew these roads well. But it became clear to me at that moment that if you stay away long enough from anywhere, even your birthplace, its nuances, tricks, and secrets re-align and gather anew, finding new hiding places, demanding pursuit and attention, roads notwithstanding.

We stumbled into the truck, wet and focused. Buster down shifted, accelerating in tune with the shift and spin of his tires. Grabbing the road, we took off fast. The speed of the truck lay in contrast to the stillness of the inside. We could only look forward, hoping the journey would be shorter than it was.

Finally arriving, Buster spun his truck into Addie's courtyard, skidding to a stop. As I jumped out, he grabbed my arm and said, "I'll wait here. You should go alone."

"It might be quite a while," I said, hoping that Buster would leave me be. I used him, I knew, but I just wanted to be alone with this right now.

"I'll have Clarence open the store and I'll wait for you here." He leaned in to kiss my cheek. I knew right then that he would be there when I needed him. It was more than I could handle.

"Please go."

"Not a chance."

"I'll ask again. Please go."

"And again, no. You don't handle being alone very well. You've proven that already today."

"Buster, why're you doing this?"

"Because I can sense a situation. And besides that, I don't take kindly to being pushed away 'specially since you clearly need someone right about now."

"Stalkers use those lines," I quipped.

"Good one. Now go. Addie needs you and, like I said, I'll be out here."

The door, pushed back and held by Addie's cast iron doorstop, was still open. This iron basket of flowers had been holding the door back in the same position for as long as I could remember, always quietly inviting you in. This time, however, the invitation was cautionary.

I entered into a stillness for which I was unprepared. Jed's silhouette in the distance motioned me to Addie's bedroom. I approached and felt the increased dread of ending. Not of a chapter, but of her story. She lay there, withered and drawn, breathing heavily as a winded soprano, desperately sucking in air in between her fragile notes. I approached, hoping she would see me, grabbing at each straw of hope.

"Is she conscious? Is she awake? Will she recognize me?"

"What happened to you?" Jed looked me over and saw the mud and the bruise on my face.

"The car...the marsh. I'll tell you later," I slipped past Jed as he tried to tenderly brush me off. I did not have the ability to be gracious. I reached Addie's side. Jed handed me a towel and sat on the edge of the bed. I pulled up a chair and sat close to her.

"Momma." No response. "Momma...Addie." She flinched a recognition to her name and opened her eyes with as much energy as she could muster.

"Faust. What're you doin' here? It's the middle of the night." She focused on my forehead. "What happened to your face?"

"A little accident, Buster helped me. Don't worry about it. Looks worse than it is. Momma, Jed called me to come over. He said you needed me."

"Ah, yes," she remembered, and exhaled. "I asked him to get you. Jed, would you leave us alone for a spell?"

"Sure, Addie. Call me if you need anything." Jed backed out of the room, not wanting to set his eyes away from her.

"Such a good man." Her eyes stayed on Jed as he left.

"Faustus, I think it's time. I think it's time for me to go." She looked up at me.

"Nonsense. We'll get the doctor and..."

"Faust, my love, let's not waste any more time. There's something that needs saying." Addie moved her hand in search of mine. "You are my son. My son. I've waited a long time to say that to you, or to even speak it aloud." She smiled and searched my face.

"Yes, Momma." The words still hit my ears like waves against rocks.

"You're my son. My son…my son." She drifted in and out with relief.

"I know, Momma." I didn't know whether she repeated herself from a guilt so entrenched or a failing memory.

"Time is running out, my love."

"No, it's not. We still have time. I just met my momma; you're not going away so soon." I was not ready to let go.

"Sometimes you get blinded by the sunlight and the important things make shadows that slip too easily behind. I am sorry that I was blinded by what was in front of me is all." She held on to my hand as if I would pull away and run. "I kept making excuses, pushing things off, letting other things be more important somehow…'til there wasn't another day." She ached to apologize, to have forgiveness, to do the business of a parent that should never have been left undone.

"I just wished that I'd known this sooner, that's all," I said, thinking of the possibilities and holding her hand to keep the connection. It was all I could say at that moment. I wanted to feel rage, even then, anger beyond the lightyears it takes to get to another universe, but I couldn't. I was too old for dramatics, too tired to expend the emotional energy, too unseated by what it all meant. Addie's death loomed—a much more immediate issue.

"I know, my love, but there were promises to be kept and agreements to follow."

"I was compromised because of an agreement?" And on that I did pull away.

"There was much in between then and now, Faust. The line kept moving and I did the best I could. But, right now," she coughed from the center of her being and winced in pain, "I wish we had told you. It doesn't seem such an important secret anymore. It's just the quiet place where secrets go when the time passes for their telling."

"You know, Momma, sometimes when things got really bad, I would imagine that I was your son, and I have to admit I often believed my imagination, especially during some of the roughest times. It gave me a place to go." I held Addie's hand close. "I wanted a place to go, wished so intensely for escape, the way Madeline ran to her books and her imaginings. I did, too, I guess. But I signed on to the way it was."

"No, no. This wasn't your fault. How could you fight for something that you didn't know, couldn't really ever know? Things just never look the same from the front end, y' know?"

"I wish that things were different, Momma."

"Me too." Her breathing labored. "Maybe, just maybe, I could have helped make you stronger or happier or…" She became lost in her words and drifted in and out for a moment. "…safer."

"Momma, don't. I'm okay," I lied, just to move the moment forward.

"No, I let you down. I sacrificed you, thinking it a greater good, when it was *you* that was the greater good. I see that now. I was too young to see it then, but now I'm too late." She seemed preoccupied for a moment. I saw her paying attention to something else, maybe death, giving into leaving. Addie broke from her distraction. "I'm sorry for all of the years. I'm sorry for the wasted moments. I'm sorry for keeping you at a distance."

"Momma, please, not now."

"It's all we have, my love…right now."

"No." My eyes blurred from the tears.

"Ya know, I remember," she wet her lips to fend off the dryness, "when your grandma died, I was thirteen, a wisp of a thing, and we lived in the old sharecropper's house, you know the one. It's still there. By Shrimp Crabby's Shack. Silly ole house. The walls were so thin and cracked that the light, y' know what I mean, that light in the early morning, so fine, so thin." She raised a hand and tried to touch the memory of that light with her fingers. "It crissed and crossed and laid on the walls an' floor in a plaid of gold. White gold and yellow gold and pink gold, mixin' with the dew. It made our shabby house look glorious, like the Angel of God was knockin' on our door. Wait. What was I sayin?" The sound of her breathing reverberated and Jed reentered the room.

"I…is everything okay in here?" he stuttered, hanging from the frame of Momma's bedroom door, afraid to step closer. I could see it, but I couldn't help him. I wanted Addie to myself.

"Oh…yeah." Addie focused. "My Momma, she lay there and she'd talk an' talk to me and Jed, so afraid that she was leavin' out something, something that we'd need. We were so young. 'Don't forget,' she'd say, wagging her bony finger. Sometimes she'd drift off; sometimes she'd talk to someone else an' she'd go off as if she was bein' called somewhere else, you know. And Jed and I'd look at each other an' wonder what was goin' on. Well, she was trying to tell us not to forget 'who we were and are, and, by God, will be,' she said. 'We are *the Waters* and don't you forget it. We built everything you see and everything you work at, the house, the land, the Pride of the County. That's your pride, not theirs. It may look like it was for someone else. But it's for you. It is your legacy. Promise me you won't forget,' she said. just before she left us."

I lifted Addie and gave her a sip of water. She took a little bit but was too occupied to indulge.

"You are a Madigan, but more than that you are the son of Addie Waters. Don't you forget that. I promised my momma that I'd make this my legacy, and I did it." She looked away for a moment. "I did it, Momma, I did it." She looked back at me. "Now it's yours." She gazed around as if searching for something. "I've written some things down, nice and legal-like. There, in the cedar chest under the window. Over there, under the quiltin'. Read it all carefully. Jed knows the rest." She made me get it and hold it between us, "I gave you no family to depend on, to build on, but here's the interest on your investment. You'll read it real soon, promise."

It was then that I realized what she had done. Addie had taken the promise that she had made to her momma and joined the pride of her family history and the pride of the ownership of the land together, in me. I became aware that the love she had for my father became the right course for her. Love or contract, love or something like it. Love or business, it secured the joining of two legacies. The final payoff.

"I promise I will," I said. I felt like I had so many years to make up right then. Although almost fifty, I felt twelve. I felt the pureness of bond, the essence of lineage. Finally, I felt a connection to everything in front of me. I fit, if for just a moment, in a family context, not an outsider anymore. This satisfaction pulled against the emptiness of being the "bartered." And then it bubbled up, and I could no longer stop the feeling. I was my mother's son. I was my grandma's currency. Did she know what she was saying to Addie so many years ago? Of course she did. I was indentured, like my ancestors, brought in to service without sanction or bill of sale. I was a slave to the cause. Was there any difference in us? Does it matter who does the selling? No.

I heard Jed behind me again. I turned to see that he was pulled back into the room like metal on a magnet. He whimpered and wiped tears from his cheeks with one of his 'Sunday cloth whites.' That's what Momma called the carefully starched linen handkerchiefs reserved for Sunday.

"Oh, hush Jed," Addie said sternly. "We knew this was comin' an' you promised."

"I know, Addie, but talkin' and preparin' don't change nuthin' inside. You know that."

"That silly man." She leaned into me so he would not hear. "That silly man has a heart o' mush. Watch out for him, will you?"

"Sure, Momma." I tried to be careful of the promises that I would make. Emotions bind the words to promises that cannot be broken.

"I need you to promise me that you will bury me in the Clearing."

"Where we played all those years?"

"Yes. That's where all the Waters are buried, but you knew that. Remember I showed you their stones." She drifted again. I did remember. I spent more time there with Addie and Madeline, playing, dreaming, imagining…a family without words…a family beyond public view. I had known these private bonds many times after in the closed society of loving another man, in the repetition over the years of the secrecy and the words dropped from sentences to make them more general, coding them so only the members would know. So automatic, that it would take looking back to see. We were connected after all, Addie and I, beyond blood, beyond lineage, but by the fear of the loss and the consequences of loving…just loving.

The morning sun began its rise. New light pierced the room ever so gently through the window panes and the lace curtains, and mixed with the dewy mist. It filled Momma's bedroom with a golden haze. I looked out of the window, responding to nature's call of waking birds singing out in concert, and saw Buster leaning against the car, creating a white stream of exhale from his cigarette, his free hand holding the underside of his elbow. I felt no impatience from him, only my own.

I turned back to Momma, but she was preoccupied with someone else. "Yes…I won't," she said to the air.

"Momma…what're you saying?" I startled her out of the private conversation.

"Nothing. My momma…seems to be standin' over there. She wants me to go to the Clearing and be with her." I turned to look, to placate, but of course saw nothing.

"There's no one there, Momma."

"Yes…I know," she answered, perhaps to placate me. "Faust, please remember you're my son. You've traveled too far because o' what I've done and fo'ever I'll make amends. I'm sorry. I only hope that you find what you want. Stop running; there's no need." She reached for my hand and found it. "All you need is right here. Just see it. It's yours now. I…give it…to you."

"Do I really want it?"

"Some things are just the way they are. Now just get on with it," she said to me. Her eyes fixed themselves on mine and looked at me as if I was further away. She squeezed my hand to signal her departure. Her eyes, richly brown, released her soul and lost their focus. The rigidity of her hand and arm relaxed and the grace and gentleness of her body returned to her for a moment.

In that mist and morning light Addie slipped away from me. I saw her leave and watched her body settle into its rest. A paleness and a stillness replaced the life that she bore. The birds stopped their call. She had answered them.

# 18

I STAYED BY ADDIE'S SIDE watching, waiting, as if staying there would stop the progression of death. It does progress, you know. Death entered her body cell by cell and I imagined that a silent struggle ensued. She wouldn't have voluntarily left. She always had things to do–things to start and certainly things to finish.

Jed entered the room and wept openly. We sat there, he and I, in a new relationship. No words, just family now. An hour passed as if it were a minute, knowing what to do but not wanting to start the process. We exchanged words after a time, filled with directions, duties; each of us volunteering who would do them. We pushed the important things behind the sun, as Momma would say. We promised to talk later. I left the room and turned to see Jed holding Addie's lifeless hand against his face, rocking back and forth asking, "What do I do now?"

The sound of the tires on Buster's truck ground the gravel road like spice against a pestle as we drove back to Greyhaven. It was an irritation every bit as grating as the silence between us. My claustrophobia sat there like an overweight passenger, filling all the available room in the truck. Although Buster tried to help at every juncture, it felt like an intrusion.

"Are you okay?" he asked as we drove. My silence persisted. "When we get back to the house, do ya need me to do anything? Are there any calls that you want me to make for ya?" He switched gears. "She was such a terrific lady. I'm gonna miss her."

"*You're gonna miss her?* Who *are* you? What right do you have to miss her? Why are you even here right now?"

"Faust, I only..." he responded with surprise.

"Only nothing. What are you doing here? What do you know of my family? What do you want from me?"

"I don't want anything, Faust. You needed help. I was there. That's all." Buster kept his responses measured, suddenly aware that he was dealing with a crazy man.

"I don't want help from you. My mother's dead. Addie is dead. Dead. Dead. Dead."

"You've had quite a few losses. I am sure it hurts." He still tried to make peace.

"What are you talking about? *A few losses?* You know nothing."

"What don't I know?" There was more to prove on the grounds of those words.

"Nothing. Just keep driving," I barked at him as if he were a chauffeur. The truck tires squealed around the turns, fighting Buster's downshifting.

"Hey guy, what's wrong?"

He read me and it hurt my head. He let go of the shift and tried to touch my arm. I recoiled.

"Don't touch me," I barked, short and tense. "*What's wrong*, you ask? *What's wrong?* I found out that the life that I fought to ignore wasn't the life that I was born into. That's what's wrong. I've lived all my life defending myself from an enemy that was damn near a stranger to me. And all this because no one could step up to the plate and take charge. Seems they had more important fish to fry."

"What're you talkin' about?"

"Addie's my momma. She told me yesterday. And she's dead today. That's what I'm talkin' about." I started to mimic Buster's drawl but omitted the kindness. "She left me in that house and I struggled everyday trying to fit in, trying to negotiate a kind word, trying to do whatever I could do to get some affection." I started to punch the truck's dashboard. "I tried everything I knew to get something from that miserable woman, Ivinia. I was left with...Ivinia...*Mother*. Hah! For so many years I tried to form some bond...something...anything that would make the days not seem so long, so fucking long. I lived in an armed camp, captured by the enemy. She hated me every day of my life! Every day! And now I finally know the reason. Because I wasn't Ivinia's. Every day she looked at me through the eyes of someone who knew I was the one who screwed her chances to own her husband's empire. Nice stuff, don't you think? It's the fuckin' *Brady Bunch* on steroids." I watched Buster's eyes widen as he tried to steer the truck from a position a little further from this madness to the right of him. "I'm fuckin' angry at…at…at the loss, the time wasted, the years spent in a lie. And for what? For this? A big house, some land, for fucking what? Maybe a cook and a maid. Status! Status and a goddamn garden party!"

I held my head because it was about to burst. "Why didn't Addie just take me and leave? Why did she give up everything to get this? It's…nothing? That's what all this is—nothing! We could have had a better life away from here. I am only *half* of anything. Don't you get it? I am only half to everything around me. But I own this…this mess. What comic justice! What payback for leaving, for running. Now, not only am I here, but this place is attached to me like a barnacle!"

"You'll figure it out. You have friends, you'll get through." Buster tried to be the idea man in this meeting of the board, this new board of directors.

"There's nothing left as I know it. Don't you get it? Even…fuck…even Madeline, all my life my sister…now half of that. Sisters in Virginia, half. Titus used me as barter. Addie kept a promise to her momma, my grandmother…sold me, like her, like me. It never ends. It never ends. Sisters in fucking Virginia. They got away. She let them leave; more so, she pushed them away. Why not me…us? I served a purpose! That's why. I had to stay, don't you see?"

"Well, poor you. What do you mean *gave up everything*? Oh you mean, *your* loss, right?"

"Shut up!"

"Fuck, I will. You've been flappin' your gums, feelin' sorry for yourself, longer than a man should." Buster continued to take the turns of the road a little later than they were designed. "Well, *she's* dead, not you. She made the hard choice. Not you. You may have had to live a part of it out, but you left. She had to stay here and face the humiliation every single day."

"What are you talking about? How do you know this?"

"Because I knew her, that's why."

"What do you mean you *knew her*. How? Served her some coffee, told her a joke or two?"

"Actually, it was tea, not coffee, and it wasn't a joke. I listened to stories. Many stories as a matter of fact. She came in a lot, more and more."

"And because of that, you think you know her?"

"A hell of a lot more than you do."

"Sure of that, huh?"

"Yeah, damn sure. I've been hearin' you over the past several days and I keep wondering, how much did you actually know about her? She knew you alright. And don't think for a minute because you didn't officially call her 'Mom' that she wasn't. She was as proud of you as brass buttons."

*Brass buttons.* How did he know that phrase? It stopped me cold. That was Addie's way of talking.

"*Brass buttons?*"

"Oh yeah. Point proven?"

"One phrase does not a lifetime make."

Buster jammed on the brakes and the truck spun into the soft part of the road.

"Look, there's an incredible amount of stuff for you to do with Titus gone, now Addie, too. So much before you go back." Buster shook his head, knowing that it might all be too impossible to do. "Such a short time for so much. I have an idea. Stay and find out what you can only find out in time, about your father, Greyhaven, Addie...about me." Buster's eyes went from his lap to meet my gaze in his presumption. He knew the risk he was taking. To counter this check, this assumption of knowing me, he offered a challenge. "Just that. Though I'm not sure that you have the guts to stay."

He showed his cards. Well, at least he showed that he had some, but they were face down.

The fence I sat on began to hurt. I was undecided about whether to return to New York or not. This would all be over soon, I philosophized, and I could go back into hiding, resuming the city life that I designed, with its veneer of self-confidence, attitude, a mysterious albeit faded Southern accent that intrigued the circles in which I traveled. I could slip back into my niche as if I had never left. But he made me angry.

"*Guts to stay?*" I asked incredulously. "Who're you? For that matter, how did you get involved?" I searched his face for the answer.

I asked these questions rhetorically, but Buster felt compelled to answer. I held some power, something that made what he did and what he said weightier to him then what appeared to be on the surface. Buster continued, delaying my decision about him for a while.

"I met Addie through Madeline. After I signed the papers, transferring Gorman's to me, I changed hats. I went from lackey to CEO in the slam of a door. By that time I had known Madeline for a while, but only superficially. Month after month, your sister came in and paid more attention to me, and I became increasingly enamored of her. She always denied her involvement with my gettin' Gorman's, but with a sly smile. She was certainly different than the rest of the locals. She was smarter, savvier…I don't know…smooth. She helped me a lot. She brought in lots of people from here, in fact, from all over."

I listened intently, looking for something, some information about Buster that would give me what I needed.

"When we first met," he continued, "I was just a soda jerk, but when we got to know each other, and Madeline found out where I grew up and the stuff about me and my laig," he poked at his thigh as if it was something he just carried around that wasn't part of him, "it took a while, but we could finally talk about your family, my family, and her involvement with me and my gittin' Gorman's.

"Turns out, she worked out the deal for me with your family, nice and quiet, like I said, never saying diddly to me. It was all done through lawyers. I was overwhelmed. One day, the Friday before Easter, I remember old-man Gorman just hung up his apron and said to me, 'Son, we're closing early today, bein' Good Friday an' all.' And he stopped, took a second to turn to me, and said, 'By the way, you're the new owner here, if ya want it. You know more about this place than the last six guys I had workin' here. I'm tired and I want to get some fishin' in before my ass-end goes horizontal.' He said it as if he were saying, 'See ya tomorrow.' He gave me a card with six last names and five commas on it. Turns out they were some of the most powerful lawyers in SoCa. He ticked his finger off his brow and was gone saying, 'They got the books, they got papers, and you got the key. See ya kid.'" Buster edged closer to me. "After I took over and owned the place a while, Madeline introduced me to Addie. They used to meet here. Then Addie started comin' in by herself. We talked and, more than that, I listened."

"So you said. What exactly did she have to say?" I asked, too sarcastic even for my taste.

"What? You want a synopsis of a life right now? You're a piece o' work! You want to know her, you stay and find out. I'm done footin' around. Where do you want to go right now? I'll get you there, then I'm done for a while." He trumped my annoyance.

"Okay," I said, backing down a little. "If you know so much, take me to the place that Addie, Madeline, and I would go almost every Sunday morning." If he knew.

"You're on."

That said it all. If he knew the Clearing, he knew about Momma, my Addie, and I needed to know the cards he held, and force him to roll 'em face up. I wanted to see them right then.

Buster took a hard right and beat his dust down Time Line Road. It was low tide and he knew it. Time Line Road showed its tar only twice a day. High tide covered its path most of the time. Few locals knew this road, except for graffiti artists of late, it seemed, by the trail of spray paint and litter. It was mostly known only to the Madigans. Addie and her family kept it in their itinerary, for they built it, many years and many generations ago. It was the picnic grounds for the original owners prior to the war. There was only one war for us folk–not World Wars or Revolutionary Wars–just Our War. And it obliterated not only the pleasant pasture of the Clearing, but the desire to enjoy it, enjoy life, for life changed forever with the first shot fired of *that* war.

Father discovered the path one day while duck hunting in the marshes. He did some research, not only uncovering the history but also the bucolic pasture and the remnants of a decaying gazebo that had the initials of every couple, every one-night lover carved into it, each trying to be more important, more permanent than the carver who preceded them. These generations of carvings overlapped each other, some quickly scratched and some delicately carved as if in and of itself the evidence of a layered history of love.

Once Titus uncovered this piece of history, he'd wasted no time in securing the path from the brackish tide, restoring its private pasture and gazebo for the family to enjoy. Addie wanted it. It was the first public gift that he gave to her. He'd painted over the carvings, leaving only faint impressions, "...so the ghosts of love would protect us," he said, as he dug into the Sunday picnic baskets. Above sea level, if only a few feet, this piece of land gave respite to the heat because this little clearing cornered four winds that gently crossed almost all year round. It looked over the place where the river met the sea. The view went on forever. Birds and small animals flocked and sheltered here from the beginning. Addie called it Eden. Being there called its history to mind.

"You're here, okay?" Buster said.

"You know about this place," I said cautiously, not wanting to show my displeasure in what I believed to be a violation of my private memory.

"Addie told me about the Clearing one day when she came into the store," Buster reminisced. "She took me here. Then after a time, we'd meet here at dusk, when the tide allowed, and we'd talk some and listen to the birds. I'd eat her chicken and she'd eat my shoofly pie." Buster exited the truck, walking and kicking the dirt. I followed him.

"I didn't know."

"I could see it on your face. By the way, never play poker," he remarked.

"Damn, I thought I was years smoother than that," I said, trying to ease into trusting him.

"Yer not so sophisticated, you being in the Big Apple for so long." He stood close to me and looked me up and down real slow.

"It seems to be wearing off quickly," I said, frozen to the spot upon which I stood. "That's one of the reasons I don't like coming back."

"That's not anywheres near close to the reason, now is it?" He turned and looked me straight in the eye.

"I feel like I didn't know her at all," he forced me to admit. "And that doesn't make me feel any better, ya know."

"I know that too, somehow, but I have an idea." Buster diminished the distance between us to within inches and grabbed my face. He looked at me awhile as if searching for something. "Stay. There's so much to find out. I can help with that, some." He kissed me, at first gently, as if asking permission, then again with assuredness. "The rest can only be ticked out by time."

I joined all the others who felt compelled to carve their initials in the witnessing columns of the gazebo. He knew me more than I knew myself, and I felt it in the grab of his hand and touch of his lips. I never felt that before, or I had forgotten it. Somehow, I felt kissed by my history. But then it came over me. I had been hit with so much information that changed my life. What could I trust?

I recoiled. I pulled back and looked into Buster's eyes. I couldn't see what I needed to see to feel safe. No one here tells. No one here gives. No one here does anything without barter. I needed someone with no agenda. What does he like? What does he want? Is it me he wants, liking me, even knowing my history? He was so affected by my family's hubris and still he stayed a stronger ally to Addie...and to Madeline. An odd coupling. Was that what Addie did in talking to him? Did she use him in my absence? Did she prepare his way to me? Who was using him, if anyone?

I felt the wash of apprehension, jealousy, mistrust. It ran over my body, thick with heat on the entry and thin like ice water on the retreat. Did she give him the preliminaries so that time could be used effectively, efficiently? Was Addie that calculating? Was this her parting gift or her parting shot? I fought against my flight reflex and then gave in.

"You don't know what's in store for you." I warned.

"Try me. I know that there's something to finish. Addie was adamant about that. She wanted it done her way." Another hint to how much he wasn't telling, how much she may have told him. A juggler's act.

"I guess she got to you, right?" I baited.

"Well, I've been drawn into many adventures over the years, sometimes whether I wanted to be or not. This is one I took on gladly. She drew me in, convinced me. She was compelling, you know. It all happened slowly, right over here as a matter of fact." Buster pointed to a large, flat rock that was as strange to this place as he and I. He grabbed my hand and pulled me. I tugged back, an errant child, fighting against everything, it appeared, everything that Addie may have tried to lay out.

Buster forced me to sit on the rock's moss-edged platform, as if scripted. I wanted to suppose that his insistence was out of seduction, but I resisted everything about it. However, since he held the keys to his truck and my escape, I used the time, avoiding his stare, to sit in silence 'til the sun hit the highest spot in the sky, dragging shadows into hiding. Nature stood tallest then, taller than either its future or its past. I sat impatiently, absorbing it all, desperately running in my mind from here to there, reviewing memories of Addie, Madeline, and this place. Buster didn't figure in my reverie, only in the layer of claustrophobia that pushed against me again. It would be the only time for me to reflect, for like summer and its final blast of August heat, the swelling breeze would shift the seasons soon in its cycle of change.

We sat in silence. I used the quiet to give reverence to the dead. It would be the only memorial service I would attend that year for Addie.

# 19

WE DROVE BACK TO Greyhaven in silence. Buster had pulled all the emotional plugs he could, sitting alongside of me on Flat Rock back at the Clearing. I'd resisted everyone, so proud I felt, so lonely. Riding next to him in his truck we rolled and pitched over every stone in the road, punctuating the absence of banter with granular sounds. So many times during the ride I felt the heat of his emerging words, only to have them abort before their birth. He sensed something ominous in me; I felt it, and he conserved his moves. This created a friction in the air, frenetic molecules stinging, pounding, hitting each other, every syllable bouncing back and forth unstructured and unfortunate as Buster's decision to go for broke would be replaced by one of apprehension and retreat.

Occasionally, I stole a glance at him, slyly, throughout the drive, and watched the trapped words form beads of sweat on his upper lip, near explosions of desperate tension. While the trees twisted in the distortion of the windshield, and the tires rolled their incessant groan, I made him nervous. How sweet. He liked me, possibly more, for his reaction to my silence overwhelmed me. Or could it be my scintillating wit or possibly my aging boyish charm? I didn't know which, I didn't know how, I didn't know why. Maybe Addie convinced him to love, like, or be intrigued by me. Her words planned and so knowing, so sure. She had time to work on him, recruit him. Knowing what I wanted, would need. But she had no time to work on me.

Could it have been for her purposes only? Maybe through Madeline, her words so funny and filled with our history of schemes and mayhem perhaps beguiled him. She ultimately bought him off. But was that because she liked Buster and wanted him for me? This couldn't be possible from what I discovered from Addie and, finally, from Gladys. Both Madeline and Addie fought over Buster and made him the bait for me to capture, devour, ingest. What a nice gift, and oh what different reasons and certainly how old South, people giving people...well...people.

Madeline designed so much, had the imagination of a castle builder, a writer, whose childlike readers lived a better life through time spent with her words. Did she lure him gently for the Madigans? Days, weeks, months tick away slowly here, allowing all things to happen in their time. Was I the honored guest for whom the clock ticked? Which *she* moved gently, cunningly, like an animal onto its prey, seeing the goal, knowing outside help necessary, spending the time slowly and methodically, each move in response to the opponent's, so the feast of wealth could begin? Which *she* wetted his appetite? Did Buster feel the hunger before the feast spilled out before him? Which plate looked the most tempting?

Buster wooed me in absentia, the careful eyes of the hunters fawning over the prey, the puncture of the wound ever so slight, seeping the paralyzing venom into the vein to stun and lay silent any resistance. Seemed like a high price for a date. So, the likelihood that Madeline designed her choreography for and about me seemed barely on the radar. Maybe I just swept him off his feet, the least convincing of the scenarios. For I realized then, in that awkward silence, that I knew so little about Buster but least of all about me, finding so little to love.

I looked in the mirror year after year and saw only a stranger seeking my past, searching for someone to love in that reflection. Not knowing how to love the stranger in me. Here it was, the springboard for my flight, the realized fantasy of a new life in New York, finding a script I could control and write. I mixed a frenetic pace of night fun and the tamed organized work day, seamlessly united by minutes and a shower with no room for my complaints, for the days were filled with them—in folders, in wastepaper baskets about ribbon and trim, at Vastigone Tie and Trim Company, purveyors and manufacturers of trims and ribbons and fluff, used to make life colorful for other people. For the daredevils or the desperate, the more ribbons, the more festive, assuming that all is plain without them. Everything disappears unless trimmed and punctured with a needle painfully, like heroin, fastening it to the tired fabrics, transforming them from boring and transparent to glowing and happy, making a wanton luxury a necessity, a necessity a need, and a need an ache.

For my life, and those lives of my enlisted Manhattan compatriots, so much needed to be forgotten, if only in the night hours. And we worked hard at it, filling the dance floors, then the bars, as we aged reluctantly in this arena of youth, then later the restaurants and cabarets so we could reminisce about the good times we'd had, erasing the reasons for the run and the chase, for it was to forget then, and now it was to remember in folklore, transfixed on the lie that it all created, just to prove it the truth. I had accomplices, I made sure, for all of my time in Manhattan, and when they did not suit my purposes I cast them off, and when I did not suit their purposes they, likewise, cast me off. None of this ever spoken, we drew on animal instinct, creating emotional détente in an unspoken struggle to survive. I became an equal.

I had carried this style, my family's style, with me, right into Buster's truck, reluctantly using my genetic predisposition to manipulate and survive in my transplant and now my return, for relationship is a game of advantages, where one ponders his steps to get the best result. I am my family. I am my father and my mother...Momma...Addie...no longer Ivinia, repeating this mantra of connection, and so it would dissolve in my head and form new configurations. I felt singularly uncomfortable as the road twisted in front of us. I even believed for a moment that I had said the formerly unthinkable aloud, punctuating the silence in that metal box with windows, with no real captain at the helm, just borrowed hands.

Never before had I sat long enough to think about all of this. I reacted daily over the years, the cart controlling the horse, minute by minute, hour by hour, day by day, and never sat silently to really sort, for I feared the outcome. And that dreaded outcome shifted more severely than I could have ever imagined, or for that matter, Madeline could have ever written, or Addie could have ever wished.

I now trusted no one. That became the legacy of Addie's admissions. Not wealth, not power, not position, but mistrust. And again I wanted to retreat to the structured pressures and cares that hid themselves in the corners of my flat in Manhattan, five floors up, pushing against the old plaster walls as if trapped and looking for a way out. In truth I was comforted by the tension. Was this my way out? Mistrust. Was *"What's in it for me?"* the formula for emotional success? Was Buster it? Was he my way out? Or was I his way in?

I spent many years hiding here, dodging, and even more years, in

New York, running. And to this, Buster clung. To this, he directed affection, saw a future, or sought connection. It felt oddly incongruent. That's what mistrust feels like, pressing and incongruent, hot and incongruent, leaning against me like a heavily perfumed fat woman in a coach seat on Delta, where I swore I would be sitting in five days, no more, back on Delta to Kennedy, Kennedy to taxi, taxi to the West Side, through the door of my refuge, up the stairs to my flat with the last door bolted from the inside, keeping the incongruity at bay.

"Turn right," I said

"I know," Buster overlapped, irritated, leaning into the uncomfortable air, saying no more. The distance between us grew further than the truck seat allowed. I felt intrigued by the flattery, put off by the attention, tickled by his frustration, peeked by the energy. He felt the rush to commit. I heard it in his words, saw it in every one of his moves, everywhere we were.

I kept revisiting possibilities for this anomaly. Could it be, simply, the exaggerated existence of a gay man, living out his emotional life in dog years, so he can reach the finish line and be done with what he thought he cherished? For it can only be inevitably flawed, clinging to the evolved sense of our damaged selves. Our desires pinned to our *peni*, which sounds better than *penises*, for in the "ses" I imagine only bubble-headed foot-soldiers dressed in the grayness of sexual hunger masked as relationship, ever-starved, running a mad dash for release and satisfaction, as close to a one-minute mile as possible; enter and conquer, exit and move on; a quick rise, shoot, and wither, five minutes, three hours, two weeks, little more.

I had one relationship of duration through all of this and, in truth, the journey artificially stretched out through too many years for the sake of our "evolution" as a community, certainly not as a couple, for I reluctantly became part of community in my exile from my family, without a vote, but, in unison spouting allegiance, nonetheless, hands on hearts swear new truths to us, tired fashion to those of straighter legal holdings, to them who owned the rights by law, who secretly covet our desires and randomness. We rush to the struggle to test a new happiness, shielded from the truth by the victims in its wake, made to deal with the forced permanence, a gift, a right, a harness, a chain. "We will make them fight hard for what they do not want," the *others* say at secret meetings. So, in the end and as we ended, years later, I paled at the prospect of yet another, shedding darkened shadows on every union or start, date, or tryst that I could pick from in the acres of bars in the "partner grove."

So now I asked, looking at Buster, how much did he know of me?

What kind of relationship was in the design, in the want? Did Addie tell him of my ownership here? Would he try to compete like all the others in this quagmire? What wish did he have? What jewel did he see hidden in the rubble? Did he justify this endeavor as payback for his condition, his leg, his life? After all, he was affected by Greyhaven and the captains of the ship, pulling and tugging selfishly, not minding the inconvenience of a shattered life if what they (we) got, what they (we) needed to get—an acquisition, a pearl of power—added to the string of poisoned *pop its*, a strand to choke the neck prettily, a vine wrapped so invasively that only equal or greater deviousness could eradicate it.

What was equitable for this damage, this twisted twist of a life, if that be the truth? Did Buster want a piece? Did he seek additional power for the peripheral hurt? Did he want it all? How much was there and did he know the accuracy of the numbers? Were the choices he was forced to make, based on the selling of his life by silent bid and offers of others unknown, fair exchange for our continued wealth, a new wealth added to the old, pressed in archeological layers, diamond pressing against coal against agate against crude? Would he satisfy the anger deep inside when all was settled? What was deep inside? Would he try to be the next Mrs. Madigan? There was no time to speak, even if I felt the compunction, for in between minutes and grouped within seconds of an exhaled breath my fortunes increased two-fold and forced the silence of any words that I could utter, mute silent as a cancerous voice box, adrift silently in dangerous waters boating sometimes with the current and oft times against with no oar and a torrid undertow. The ride was long and my questions prevailed over the awkward answers.

Pulling up to Greyhaven, everything looked different somehow. Addie had figured in its struggle, and it knew she was gone, like an enemy reconfiguring its plan as each event occurs. Stiffening in front of me, the house, brittle as old bones, braced against another storm; not a leaf rustled on the trees, standing like soldiers, flanking the path ready for another day, another battle, an identifiable adversary and not the womb where I was born anymore.

Addie and Titus placed me here, the wampum in a barter system. They threw me into the fray, a reverse refugee running into harm's way instead of away from it. The reasons for my life at Greyhaven were all new to me now, fitting me like a suit still needing alteration. Although uncomfortable and strange, I knew that I owned it, at least in the words. I owned this history to be sure, but could anyone actually own Greyhaven? Instead, Greyhaven owned its people, tenants with checkered pasts and uncertain futures, at the mercy of the landlord, gathered and

selected for its amusement. All applicants saw great potential in the contract, but none of them read the fine print, for in the fine print lay the
destruction of all who signed on the dotted line.

That was the deal.

All the memories of this place, of course, struck a familiar cord,
but their vantage point shifted now. I became the sole tenant before Addie reached the period at the end of her final sentence, passing the
choices and the punishments to me. This sentence of a dying woman
changed my life, one single sentence from one little dying woman. Now
everything angled more abruptly, alliances more tenuous. I now had
something to protect. My path to survival here, less obvious, and my
family bond, more fragile, as the reasons for events and decisions,
needed to be viewed from a different window.

"Are you all right? You haven't said a word since we started driving
back," Buster remarked, his discomfort apparent, as he tried to reenter
into my radar again.

"I'm okay. Just organizing some new information is all." I couldn't
look at him. Buster's truck became the temporary fortress for my emotions and I wouldn't add, subtract, or change anything with the utterance
of more words than felt comfortable. I realized as I sat there that every
move I made from that moment on would reshape my future. I was no
longer safe using my pattern of running from here, from my family, from
the fight, because the deed to this place had become my anchor, making
it impossible to run with this added weight.

Keeping my suitcase unpacked certainly would not settle my issues
of safety either, for the players in this struggle were that much closer and
would be forever snapping at my heels, seeking weakness, clawing their
way up over me, around and through me if necessary. I had something
to steal now. It would take planning to protect, not just shoring up
against a random city break-in for easily pawned electronics and replace-
able jewelry. I now protected real possession, not pawnable, not replace-
able, not half, much more than all. Who was capable of stealing this from
me? Who? Who next to watch? For years, I'd lived a life of singular escape in New York and did not feel the effects of the game, but, because
of my absenteeism, I had to accept the result. And while I disappeared,
all those years Addie worked very hard to move the pieces on the chess-
board to her advantage, for she did not ask me. She assumed, she
planned, and somehow her child's welfare became of little concern to
her as the years paid their toll and the reason for her struggle blurred. I
don't know when it became clear that none of this was done for me. It
seeped in like the tide salting the fresh waters. I went from useless son

to unfortunate ally to tentative adversary. Was it here in Buster's truck or was it minutes after Addie's death that I took on the yoke? It just appeared and I accepted it like I accept sunrise, sunset, or three-dollar coffee. It called quietly to me, no great revelation. It fit seamlessly in the scheme of things. I sat there, in a pick-up truck, having nothing to do with Addie's years spent in check and checkmate. Her moves began a generation or two before her, her mother, her grandmother, feeling the effects of "less than" in a "more than" society, dreaming the scheme, waiting, watching the nuance, the smallest of openings to pour in, bleeding their blood, drying, then staining, then bleeding some more, just to get the presence and the stake, always there, never not there, part of the fabric unnoticed 'til strongly rooted.

Addie, then, loomed as formidable as Ivinia in the powerplay for this place. She held me in the balance, bait on a tender hook, dangling me between the struggle to identify her and Titus' union, the blood stake Addie's primary mission, owned and operated from time already spent.

And this was at the core of my flight reflex, I now knew. I wanted to jump out of Buster's truck without him coming to a full stop, disappear, find a new place to hide, and have it be like it was, not like it had become. I would stay. I would go. I would stay. I jumped from manic decision to manic decision, knowing that I did not have the power to decide. It would not let me decide. I shifted, convincingly, in a useless mind game, convinced from one second to the next that each was justified. Old behavior. New. Which would it be? Which was which? As I flung open the truck door, ambivalent to the decision for war, Buster grabbed my arm.

"Don't fight the wrong battle." I looked at his hand and saw the veins and arteries that carried blood to his heart, pulsed the energy to his brain, and I wondered of what alchemy, of what component, of what molecule should I be wary? I trusted few things in life, blaming myself for this genetic weakness. The little trust that I had in things that I knew lost whatever power they had left. I trusted no one now, for I realized my body's instinct was not a genetic weakness but was, in fact, a protective trigger beginning to serve me well.

"*Wrong battle?* I don't know what that means." I searched his face for the flaw.

"I'm on your side."

"Thing is, I don't know which side that is anymore." I was acutely aware of the flatness in my voice. He winced at my words as they punctured his eardrum.

"Okay then," he sighed, "I'll be *Southerning up* the tourists at Gorman's all day. Call if you get the inclination or the need."

"Um, okay." The words, a fishbone on the jab before a last look at his face. I let go of the heated metal of his truck's door, seeing neither truth nor lie. All I can remember to this day is the sound of the door closing, possibly the sound of the Sirens calling fate.

Buster drove off, exhausting every move that he had. I knew then that I would not make a decision about him for a long time. Therefore, Buster would dangle from my line for some while. I wanted to feel what it would be like to be on the other end of the bait, and not be the bait.

Rejection, even if temporary, matures the soul faster than acceptance. Nearing forty, Buster found himself late in life by circumstance, not unlike most, yet quicker than me with all my advantages. I would never let him know that. Silence gave me this advantage. I saw his red hair settle then into the embers of brown like a wild fire that finally gets to the core and slow burns quietly, so much stronger than the flare. He moved the truck slowly, in case I needed him to stay, in case *he* needed to stay. I watched him gaze in the truck's rearview mirror, cautiously pitching the subtle edges of the drive, awaiting a call or wave from me that never came. He crossed the gates and turned left toward town, paused on the tar, one last chance, then gunned it gone.

# 20

"WHERE HAVE YOU BEEN?" Cornelius yelled at the back of my head in a rare fit of uncontrolled impatience. "There's too much to do and you're holding me up!" Shrill, Cornelius broke my extended moment of control. I began to amass emotional possessions. His interruption annoyed me.

"What the hell are you talking about?" I turned and barked. "Addie died this morning, I'm not interested in your schemes at the moment." I threw the words at him like a bad pitch.

"Ah...she's dead." He paused, knowing the game had shifted. "I suppose I should offer you my condolences." Cornelius paused with no condolences offered. His face registered nothing but strategy.

"What?"

"Oh, nothing. It's just, things got a lot easier, s'all. Sometimes you just wait and *what is* changes right there in front of you and gets better." Invigorated, he turned to reenter the house.

After all these years, I still didn't see it coming. He stunned me, a sucker punch to my stomach. I followed Cornelius incredulously, slipping back into my family role for a moment. Up the front porch stairs and through the door, I marched into the dining room following his scent only to meet with the rest of my half-clan. Sarah, Madeline, Harris, we, the five musketeers, joined by familial chains. Again, a party started without me.

"Madeline," I embraced her though merely by rote, "Addie's gone."

"Oh, my. I'm sorry, Faust." Madeline, in abbreviated sadness, patted me on the back. It felt cautious. Sarah's face mirrored a kind sympathetic feeling without saying anything. "I'll fill you in later. After this," I said.

"Let's get going," Cornelius said, not looking up from the head of the table where he positioned himself once again. We appeared smaller around him, all important people in our own right. Madeline, famous writer; Sarah, well-known surgeon; Harris, nationally known lawyer; all looked humbled, heated.

"Since our last meeting, there have been a few developments, some good, some bad." Cornelius shuffled the papers in front of him, trying to ignore the elephants in the room for they were mounting. He recapped, like minutes of a meeting with no end. "We've held off the partners, distracted their focus, quite well, I might add. They're unaware at this point that the books have been…manipulated…to look profitable. The funeral went well. We dodged the Futuris bullet." We sat not in our dining room but in an operations room briefing, surveying the result of a successful battle in an ongoing war. "But this won't last for long. We need to solidify our base and make sure that enough of the 'remuneration' of the land is done so the Feds will give us a revised clean bill of health in two weeks."

I floated a test balloon. "You're very optimistic that this will go unfettered. The thing about crimes, you know, is that criminals always slip up."

"Look, Faust, you've been gone for so long, I can't pretend that anything you have to offer is important. Stay involved or stay away." He continued nonplused, and what was more important, he didn't seem to know about the reality of his ownership of Greyhaven. I was not about to tell him just yet. "I've ordered more payloaders from one of our building divisions. They arrive in two days."

"How long, on the outside, will it take to accomplish the soil exchange?" Madeline offered a question that surprised me. I looked at her face and it changed in front of me. No longer a victim of this place, she became a player.

"The foreman said that it will take six days around the clock to finish the disbursement of the toxic soil, five days for the tunnel mix to be incorporated into six random spots." Cornelius had the vision tightly in hand.

"A *tunnel mix*?" I asked.

"Yeah," Harris offered the explanation. "The Feds check soil from differing levels. We need to *water down* the toxicity. It's a new procedure;

its effective. We are instrumental in developing it. If successful, it'll become the new standard and will be used as a model nationwide."

"You mean that we found another way to swindle. What a surprise! And we'll go national with it. What a legacy! What about groundwater?" I threw back.

"It seems to have settled in to the right range," Harris explained further. "Don't know what's down at the other end, but silt covers the worst offenders and we've already dredged most of the worst silt."

"It's really the soil that is our problem and our focus," Cornelius clarified. "Soil doesn't move."

"What about the waterbeds, then? They don't move?" It seemed obvious to ask. Secure in my own knowledge, I began to enjoy this.

"Took care of some of them," Madeline said, looking up from her nailbeds to talk about riverbeds. "The right ones." She knew more than she ever told, and then I remembered her having said, *"I don't know nothin' about land opening. I just write children's books."* The developments grew more interesting.

Madeline clearly understood more about the land deal than she previously let on. Although disappointed, I became sure that she did not know of my ownership as well. Therefore, Harris was also in the dark. My body ached from the loss of my investment in my sister. She had remained a part of my life no matter where we were, how far, how long absent, and I misread the innocence, didn't follow the words, each syllable twisting her away from what I knew of her. I loved a ghost, a manufactured character, like in her books. She wrote her own character study, just for me. I'd read it and bought it. Addie's death brought me knowledge and ownership of secrets. I wasn't sure that I wanted this, but I felt oddly stronger in this conference.

"Some key beds were cleaned up. The ones they'll check, anyway," Harris offered.

I played devil's advocate. "Who's to say the Feds will pick those spots? I need clarity and assurances."

"You know we have an ally on the team that's coming," Harris said. "He's assured me of their intent and what they are looking for. I'm confident that the money we're spending on him is worth it."

I replied sarcastically, jumping into the murky waters with my clothes on. "Okay, then my question to you is, when will he turn? We all know that no one stays in line forever."

"His payout is across thirty years and amounts to several million. A pension, so to speak. Works better than a lump sum, and we can well afford it, based on the numbers. He won't *turn*, as you put it." Cornelius impatiently pulled me through some of the important details.

"I'm sorry if I'm pissing you off, brother, but I need to know what's going on. You brought me back here. You could have done this whole thing without me. But, no, your plans involved me. I'm here, now continue." I was no longer interested in the play of brotherly tensions. I wanted facts.

"We also need to secure the loans from the outside investors," Cornelius resumed, a little more apprehensively than before, apparently unsure of where I was going with my newfound attitude. "We'll get the money back into the coffers before anyone is the wiser."

"You mean like Adlai Morrisette?" I asked.

"For one," Cornelius said, looking curiously. "Why do you bring him up, specifically?"

"He pulled me aside at the wake and, to paraphrase the sharpest mind in the oldest body that I know, his instincts were 'not to trust you.'" I loved saying those words. They felt like a kiss from the gods on my lips. "My guess is that right now," I looked at my watch for affect, "he's probably sent Sophie on to the Berkshires alone and is arranging a legal look-see into our dealings. Right as we speak. Trust me, he will take no prisoners."

"Why didn't you tell me this sooner? You stupid bastard." The crack in Cornelius' veneer widened to a fissure. "I could have headed him off."

"Oops," I said, even more sarcastic than my tastes allowed. The 'bastard' remark hit a little too close to home. "Watch the name calling, Cornelius. You need me more and more. Besides, you're so good at this." I pushed back in my chair for a broader view of his squirming. "I don't know, just call it a little plot point in your autobiography of divide and conquer." It was becoming harder to contain my animus for this man and it grew in me, spilling on to the rest of my family.

Our separation was completed right then. Just knowing that he was half a brother made him half a threat. "I'm sure you'll smooth out the rug that you pulled over his eyes just long enough to see him dead or destroyed. Right, Cornelius?"

"*Dead?* What are you talking about?"

"You don't let anyone stand in your way, do you? Not even Ivinia." That hit a nerve. He burst open like a volcano that had spent years in building its pressure.

"Don't you *ever* bring up her name again." His fear was palpable, "She's gone. I don't know where. Wait...you don't think I had anything to do with her disappearance, do you?" He chuckled, an incredulous, nervous chuckle. "You can't possibly think that." The room grew restless.

Madeline backed up in her chair. "Faust, what makes you think anyone had anything to do with Mother's disappearance?"

Harris absorbed every word to see where the weakness lay. Sarah sat frozen, refusing to claim Cornelius as her husband or for that matter, us as her family. She sat isolated and away.

"I didn't say *anyone*, Madeline." My antennae registered a hit. "I said Cornelius." Had she slipped?

"If you think that, then, you are an even sorrier excuse for a brother than I thought," Cornelius continued.

I couldn't resist. "You mean *half-brother*, don't you?" I couldn't resist.

"What?" Sarah registered the only surprise to be found in the room.

"What the hell are you talking about?" Stunned, Cornelius laughed through his words. He always laughed insidiously when nervous. I looked around and noticed nothing else. No one moved. No reaction from Harris. Madeline starred at her nail quicks, solidly listening. No gaping jaws, no glaring, no inward draws of sharp breaths. Nothing. A quartet of faces, frozen as the flowers on the wallpaper, the cleverly placed furniture, and the untended mantle clock.

"That doesn't matter right about now, does it?" I wouldn't give him, any of them now, the satisfaction of knowing the timeline.

"When did you find out?" Madeline finally moved the words from her throat and reiterated, touching my arm as she asked. Her touch felt cautious and indifferent. My connection to her kept eroding. In that touch, I felt her connection to Cornelius. I saw it in her face. Blood percentages matter.

"Addie told me before she died, Madeline. I'm sorry, but there was no time to sit this down with you."

"I see." Madeline shot Harris a look that gave me pause.

"It changes nothing," Cornelius blasted, like a coal furnace on high. "Have your fun. You're enjoying this? You're pretty brave, toying with the futures of the rest of the family." The urgency in Cornelius' voice loomed thick in the slowness. "You'll follow the plan. I know it. Right? Harris, Madeline, Sarah, I *am* right, aren't I?"

"What does he have that could hold you?" I asked everyone, assuming a master plan that forced the players to play. Sarah confirmed a piece of the player's list.

"I took Titus home from the accident," Sarah said, piercing the silence. "Cornelius convinced me to hold back information from the medics at the accident site concerning the severity of his injuries. He said that it would better serve Titus if he were home and mending. He played me, he sounded so concerned. It had not been an easy time for us, and I thought maybe there beat the heart of a sensitive man all along, under there. I was wrong. He set a trap. It wasn't long before he laid it out for me. One phone call to Cornelius' friends on the emergency service and they will be forced to report the incident to the authorities. My license to practice medicine would be pulled, immediately, and determining the findings, I could possibly, in a worst-case scenario, be held over for board review. It very rarely turns out well." The words escaped Sarah's lips as if by remote. She didn't move a muscle. She kept her head down, staring at the grain of the dining table all the while. "I'd be ruined."

"Why, Officer, how would I know the severity of his injuries?" Cornelius broke in and feigned an innocent voice talking to an imaginary lawman. "I trusted my wife to do the right thing, Officer. How could I know that she could make such an error? It feels almost…almost deliberate, you say?" Cornelius exaggerated his every word like a B-movie actor. "Oh, I'm sorry, not Sarah. Well, we have been estranged. Yes, I live at my parents' home. We've been separated for a while. Well, you know the history of her family, Officer. Resentment? Revenge? I don't know, Officer, what do you think?" His voice turned brittle and flat. "Is that enough or should I continue?"

"How could you?" I said, horrified by the revelation.

"*How could I?* Well, well, well, turns out it's easier than you could ever imagine. It would be my word against hers as to who was at fault. And as we know, the fault always lies with the doctor. I guess that's why they call it *practicing* medicine."

"She made a bad decision," Madeline offered, a small consolation for listening to Cornelius. "I'm not sure what I would have done in her shoes."

I felt the coldness in the room toward Sarah. The herd forced her into isolation, much like the wounded or the weak, allowing the predators to attack and devour for distraction, allowing the rest to escape. Harris' lack of involvement was the most shocking thing of all. He allowed his only sister to be held for sacrifice.

"For God's sake, she's the mother of your children. That should account for something," I shrieked in a nervous desperation at the possibility of this scenario. "You couldn't possibly do this, to her…to them?"

"They're young, they'll survive. It's a risk I'll take. It would give me such great pleasure to take the love they have for her away, if just a little. Let them doubt something about her, if only a moment." Cornelius turned to Sarah and spoke over her shoulder right next to her ear, desperately slow. "Question it...just...a little. Let her know what it feels like to have someone look at you with disdain. Someone you loved so much, never to feel it back, right Sarah? That would be terrible, wouldn't it?" He moved so close to her that the skin on her ear bristled red. "Right...Sarah? Tell them Sarah, how much you...love...me?" I could see that he had said all of this before in private, so many times in fact, that in public, it felt smooth. The sound and the hurt of those words were familiar to me. Then it hit me, blaring out of my mind's loudspeaker, screams, plaintive and angry, desperate and high pitched, words coming from my father's bedroom. Ivinia's voice pierced my brain. Had history repeated itself? Yes. I remember Ivinia spewing these words like molten lava pouring out over my father, a threat, real and hot, through the door of his room, his only sanctuary, where she'd barge in so often, so loud and abusive, letting him run nowhere for escape and quiet and refuge. She screamed as much for effect as for her need to let the whole house hear. Looking back, the words made little sense to me, then, but I think that she needed to let us all in on her desperation, to know the pain.

That pain also lived in Cornelius. I heard many of these monologues directed at my father and now, when awakened here, spoken again, they fit like the genetics of features passed down randomly, without fault. Cornelius had my father's eyes and his smile and his command. He had Ivinia's high cheekbones, her lips, and on them, her hatred of lost love, lost opportunity, a powerlessness seeded in circumstance, position. So much continued generation after generation, beyond the obvious; so much passed to us that would never be called a gift.

The silence broke. Sarah broke it. It can only break, as I know now, when tornados of ache and sorrow gather strength, when the abyss opens and there is no other decision to be made but to face the fall.

Sarah looked at Cornelius as if a stranger. Something happened inside of her, right then, and she looked up, focused and slow, chopping each word into its syllabic content. "Love you? Who... could...ev...er...think...that? You? Momma's...boy? How could I even try? Love you?" Her anger broke for a second in memory.

"So...long...ago." She heated her words as the strike of a match across a stone. "I wanted to, once. I thought I knew you, had you figured out. But you had too many secrets, and there were too many bad situations with you as the core. You want to have this conversation in front of your family? Fine, we'll have it."

"Darling," Madeline said, "you might want to think this through a bit. We don't need to do this now, no?" She formalized her thoughts into placation and condescension.

"She's right, Sarah. Don't." Harris tried to soften the intent.

"Shut up! Both of you! You two are as slippery as the mud this place was built upon!" Sarah gathered her strength and focused on Cornelius. "And as for you, Cornelius, you and your mother destroyed my family. We survived disease and war, survived depression and famine over many generations, countless years. I watched your Mother, and then you, systematically obliterate my family name and drag it down to the lowest level...the level where you live." She seethed. "My mother was right. You are *common*. Abigail never thought that you would, or could, rise above the street thugs and pimps of your beginnings. I tried to convince her she was wrong. She was tempted to agree. We were desperate. And in that moment of desperation, we planned you. We planned with Ivinia, knowing the risk. All the calculations and the agreements meant nothing. We needed to be powerful and strong to ensure our safety, our survival. We were none of those things anymore. We were wrong to get involved. I was wrong." She beat her chest in punishment. "Money doesn't change who you are. My mother would have let it all go, every acre, every piece of wood that built Fallen Timbers, my home...*my* home...not yours." Although she'd never let on for countless years, at that moment it became clear that Sarah's hurt over the loss of her home had stung–and continued to sting–like a thousand angry bees. "When it came time to sign the deal, Abigail recanted her wishes and reversed, knowing the quagmire that would be created. But, I kept going, how foolish. She begged me. Everything. She would have given up everything, if only I would not marry you. But it was too late. She begged me. She woke to the fear. She begged me." Sarah shook her head in disbelief at the present existence.

"For the last time, Sarah, must we...must we do this now?" Madeline droned dryly, bored, and impatient. "We all know this."

"Madeline, you are the most contemptible of all." Sarah did have new information for me at least. "Your scheming pushed Cornelius into these waters and I will abide this no longer. Not one more minute!"

"Sarah, can't we do this at home?" Cornelius tried to dissuade her from her tract.

"No, we can't. This is the last time that I want to see your face, and I want to say this to you. I married you hoping that with our name and your land, you would become a man of integrity and heart. Land should build character. Family history shows you the way to maturity. These were gifts, and your family squandered them, wasted them. You couldn't follow a decent path if it was tarred in front of you." There was a release of venom that pleased Sarah. She shook her head in a tremor. "Sometimes…sometimes on the lowest days, when you absorbed our last bits of land, sold off our house for parts, I realized that you were no different than your mother. We could not stop you. And you continued the humiliation, year after year." She thought for a moment, holding the command of the room. "There were times I wanted to…to…choke the life out of you. I hated the air you exhale. It is diseased. Everything you touch withers." Sarah looked down and spoke from an intimate place. "I fear the life of my children." She was taken aback by her unleashed anger. "I will *not* let them be who you are. I would sooner kill them both then see them turn into you." She choked back tears at the thought of such an act. "I despise every move that you make, every thought…" Her diatribe broke with a stunning thought. All of the emotion inside of her exploded and drained. At the end of the tirade, a stunning realization came to her. "Wait a minute. If Ivinia is not Faust's mother," she erupted in a volcanic laugh trapped for so long but finally released, "then you don't own Greyhaven! You have no hold on this property!"

"No! That isn't true!" Harris stepped in, trying to stop the dyke from breaking. His effort was too little too late. Sarah's laugh shook the very foundation of the house.

"Of course it's true, Harris! Faust was born before Cornelius!" Tears came to her eyes as she released years of hatred and anger. "The mother doesn't matter but the father does. Hah!" Sarah looked liberated. She turned with this release and raised her eyes to meet those of Cornelius. She saw her way out, her escape, and her energy and resolve returned. "I will survive you, now, knowing that all you've worked for has been lost this day. It's like fucking Christmas." Sarah bolted from her seat, depleted yet energized with new spirit, satiated, "Half-brother…that's rich! This makes leaving all the easier! Whatever you do, you'll do. I no longer care what happens." Sarah arched her back and adjusted her pride in an eloquence I'd thought lost to her.

Walking away and toward the door, she said coolly, "Harris, you knew all of this, didn't you?" She didn't bother turning to see the response, for she knew the truth now.

"I…I…" Harris stumbled for words to steer him through this challenge. This truly was a rare moment for him for he could find none.

"Maybe then," she put the pieces quickly together, looking alternately at Madeline and Harris, "since I know little of these affairs, maybe

Harris, you and Madeline should tell Faust of your involvement here. I'm finally free of yo'all. Oh…" Sarah restarted, almost forgetting so important a feeling which she could not overlook, "Harris, I no longer have a brother. And just to keep matters absolutely clear, stay away from me and my children. There's nothing holding us together, anymore. It's all yours."

"You don't mean that, Sarah. Sarah….!" Harris watched in disbelief as she started to exit, holding out his hands, twisting them in mid-air as if they could shape a reason, an excuse that his mind could not.

"Don't I? Well here's the bargain. Stay away from me and my children and I will remain the innocent. I have had a great teacher all these years. Cornelius, show them how's its done. Oh, wait, you already have." She turned.

"Don't you leave, Sarah!" Cornelius threatened in a tone more desperate than determined.

Sarah pivoted back one last time before walking through the archway. "Leave?" You did that years ago. I'm just doing the paperwork." With that, she flung the front door open and disappeared from sight. A sudden stillness followed, as if everything needed to catch a breath. But there was none to be found, for Sarah took the air with her.

"Thank you, Sarah, for that illuminating monologue," Cornelius said to her absence, fingers tugging at his collar as if it had grown tighter. "Nothing new. Boohoo. I'm a scoundrel. We're duplicitous. But it changes nothing," Cornelius declared.

"Madeline, what did Sarah mean by *your involvement?*" I ignored Cornelius, so focused on the changed Madeline. I needed to arrange the pieces of this jigsaw puzzle according to color. "What's going on here? Madeline?" She could not look at me for a split second. Then she regrouped.

"Well, Faust, honey, we were going to tell you anyway, but at a slight bit better time. But this might be perfect, no, Harris?" Light as ever, Madeline glazed over and poised.

"I think you're right, babe," Harris said, looking directly at her. "I want a piece of this as much as Cornelius does, though for my own reasons. It's a pie, love, and I'm taking a couple o'slices for myself while it's still hot."

"Why, Madeline, why?" I asked, already knowing the answer. "I thought you wanted to be done with this place."

"No, Faust, honey. Yo'all misunderstood. I wanted it over. I said, 'Let Cornelius have his way.' I guess I just didn't finish the sentence." Her eyes firmed.

"So finish it," I said.

"...so's I can have mine."

"What could it all possibly do for you?" I stared at her, incredulously. We shared the same animus, I thought. The same resolve. Her softened beauty edged toward a harder veneer. Everything halved at that moment, yet again.

"Honey, I've made millions off this place," Madeline said. She eased back in her chair and twisted her body, putting her arm over its back. She shaped into the chair fluidly and self-assured. "I wrote about every nook and cranny. And this opportunity is just what we need, right Harris?" She smiled at him.

"When did you know this?" Cornelius, now almost invisible in the room, asked Madeline defeatedly. "When, Madeline?"

"Oh, my sweet. Early. I really don't remember when exactly, do you, Harris?" Madeline arched her back and the diamond clip in her hair shimmered in the light of the room.

"It's just a deal, Faust," Harris said, trying to reassure Cornelius and me that it was all on the up and up. "We get the house and some of the land, and Cornelius and you get the old development and the connectors to do malls, office complexes, and whatever the hell else you want to do with it. We split all the stock in the rest of the businesses, getting out of all of them before they slide. It's just a deal, but a damn lucrative one! You are figured in on this as well, Faust."

"I want none of it, Harris. What could possibly make you think that I would sign on to this?" I said, as Cornelius seemed to slowly deflate. Before him lay the history and the future. And that future no longer depended on him.

"You're not seeing it, Faust." Madeline focused her attention on me. After all, I was the final battle. "Layered marketing, mass appeal. This house is a goldmine." She needed me on board and she knew it, perhaps even if only for a while. They were a team, Madeline and Harris, and I saw in them what had happened for generations before. Greyhaven finally owned them, probably always did. It's just that I didn't want to see it. They never escaped and never would. She glistened and waved her hands, so like Mother during the heyday of her schemes. "Tourists, cocktail table books, reproduction furniture, character costumes, games, even fucking cookbooks, darling, you see? Trinkets, giftshops, demonstrations, reenactments, satellite stores in malls across America, even foreign distribution! The top has no top, my love. I have even contracted with a factory in Austria to reproduce the crystals on that fucking chandelier above the staircase. A mail-order catalogue is being proofread right now, for Christ's sake! I will exploit e-ve-ry inch of this place. I want it all! It should be mine, and it will be mine. Right, Cornelius?" Madeline finally turned her attention to him. He looked incidental now to the whole picture. Madeline glared at the prospect and at him as she leaned into the table to reinforce her words. "*Right*, Cornelius?" She needed reassurance that the contract was intact. Her eyes chilled and she leaned back, like a snake that recoils after its assault, pausing while its next meal still squirms.

Madeline dropped the final ball in front of me. She controlled the room. I sat motionless, as if awaiting the retraction.

"Your idea? Madeline, you hid this all from me?" Cornelius said at last. "How could you? I thought…you and I…" Cornelius' voice trailed off as he slumped into his chair.

"We hate this place, Madeline," I said. "It holds no fond memories for you, for me. I can't believe that you want to stay and hold on."

"Oh, Faust. Naïve Faust. I don't want to just hold on, honey. I want to take it where I need it to go, not the other way around. This is a new chapter for Greyhaven. It's a chameleon. You always knew that. It can have life again. We can make it happen! The millions more that this place will bring me will transform my shitty memories into cherished moments," she rationalized. "Besides, we grew up here, for whatever that's worth." She shrugged slightly. "I am locked to it the way all notables are locked to their props. This one is mine. Like a hat or a well-turned phrase." She mocked innocence. "A little Southern drawl, a little wide-eyed, slow-talkin' memory, and a pen to paper." Madeline wiggled her shoulders demurely. "Wrap that around a children's story and voila, a formula for success." She turned deadly serious. "And it's *my* success. No one's gonna ruin it now."

She looked at me real close and touched my face with a gentleness that mocked instead of providing reassurance. All the warmth that her touch held froze over. "So be a sweet boy and let me run with it." Madeline's tone changed and all the things that I held dear about her shifted and collapsed, an emotional landslide. "You don't really care about this place, or for that matter what we do with it, Faust. Let us have it, please." Her eyes widened. "Please. We'll make you richer than you could ever imagine. You won't even have to be involved. We'll do it all! Cornelius has it all worked out and with Harris running the front, it'll be finished soon. It'll mean hundreds of millions for you, too. Please, Faust?"

She pleaded one time too many. She risked everything on my feelings for her and was cashing it all in at that moment. I felt bankable but, more seriously, expendable. Suddenly, I was horrified and fearful that she forgot to hide the little twist of desperation left in her voice. I had them in my hands, yet I knew that with a hint of a false move on my part I could unleash personal risk and harm. It became my decision. I could leave this place and say no when safely away. Or, I could crash this continually rising phoenix, once and for all. Or...I could say yes. Each choice had its own elements of devastation.

I thought for a moment. It put their lives on hold for longer than they could stand. "Madeline, you're in on all the schemes?" I asked, wanting to be clear. "All the shifting of monies back and forth? You and Cornelius and Harris? How masterful. You really did it," I said slowly, filled with the wonderment of someone in awe of his surroundings. "I am impressed!"

Their expressions revealed caution about what they saw and heard. It looked like I could be convinced. Dare they hope? At that moment, I struck. "How could you Harris? How could you sign on to this?"

*"How could I?"* Harris thought for a moment, stunned by the switching of tracks. "It got easier over the years. The line just kept moving and the stakes...oh, the stakes got higher."

He must have started out the reluctant partner, for I saw the uneasiness in his eyes. Doubtless the allure of beauty, love, of success that my sister held in her and her resolve could not let him refuse her. "As Titus got older, he changed somehow, saw this place differently. But then as he separated from here, I began to see the potential for this place eluding him. It became clearer that something had to be done. Madeline woke us up to it."

"When did you know about Faust?" Cornelius asked Madeline and Harris both, for it seemed they were one now.

"What does it matter, Cornelius?" Madeline said. "Harris is a lawyer for Christ's sake, Cornelius. Did you expect him to accept what he saw?"

It was completed. Madeline had orchestrated all of this. All the marionettes changed. The master cleverly disguised as just one of the puppets. I became enraged at the scam. All of it seemed lethal, but not 'til the one person I thought of as sure, that I thought I knew beyond a shadow of a doubt, came up not only blurred but a stranger to me. She became more than damaged by Greyhaven, she became diseased by it. I realized, sadly, that I'd wasted years of longing for our relationship, years of offering silent support.

"How do you look each and every partner we have in the eye, Harris, or for that matter, you, Madeline? I expected this and more from Cornelius, but you? These are people who trusted us over the years. How

can you begin to entertain the thought of making their businesses worthless, Titus' memory worthless?" The world that I built in my head, and
the categories in which I placed everyone in my family, disintegrated before me.

"Do you actually think I give a shit about their businesses, Faust?"
Madeline bolted out of her chair. "We built those businesses, not them.
We funded their successes, not them. And now we're taking our due. Do
you think that they cared about us when there were lean times over the
years? Every one of those sons o' bitches threatened lawsuits and injunc-
tions and investigations over the years. And then they come here once a
year to smile over our food and laugh while they consume our liquor. If
you think I care about any last one of them, you're wrong," she spewed.
"There's no way to stop this, so don't even try." As she spoke, she
moved toward Cornelius slowly and embraced him, kissing the side of
his head while looking at me without blinking. Cornelius winced as the
whole affair came into focus, clearly crestfallen at having been diminished to a partner instead of in control.

There it was. This was the South that I knew. The strength of its
people and their resolve, and the ability to surmount every obstacle put
in their way. It was as steady and smooth as the rain that quietly accu-
mulates in its stillness 'til it floods and envelops all in its path, sweeping
everything clean away, leaving nothing in its wake.

"How long have you known about my ownership, Madeline…Har-
ris?"

"I wasn't sure, at first," Harris started. "Titus and Addie held the
reigns on the information tightly. Cornelius worked on Ivinia. She's the
one who dropped loose hints and snippets throughout her worsening
dementia, but she was too far gone when we realized what was going on
and what she could possibly know. Then I took it to some legal buddies
in Chicago. They confirmed it. I found some precedence and realized
you were *it*." He almost looked relieved at the admission.

"And you, Cornelius?" He became a small man. He was no longer
the moving force in this debacle. Where he had accomplices before, now
he was but a minor player. The world shifted as he watched.

"Hard to imagine, huh?" Cornelius tried to reclaim his composure,
"But, opportunity makes for strange alliances. I never discount any turn
in the road. You never know who's gonna help further the journey." He
issued a weak smile. "So what do you say? Let's talk percentages." As he
spoke, I started to see the fragility of the corporation in front of me.
There was a transfer of strengths. I held the biggest key to the strongest
lock, opening the door to the richest room. I knew it and they knew it.

Madeline, somewhere in the middle of this power. Cornelius, now a sad third in the food chain.

I liked it. I became the center of their universe and I swelled in the knowledge and the power of it. No one moved. I looked at Madeline coldly, pushing away the remnants of my feelings for her. The Madeline I knew was no more. The queen was dead, long live the queen.

Harris, a withering pawn in defense of the royalty before him, became nothing. Sarah saw it, too, and I could see how she could leave Cornelius, for there was so little to leave. What would I do with this collection of misfits? I no longer envied Harris' feelings for my sister. I could look at them at the very least, pathetically. The aura of love and affection was as much a fantasy as the books Madeline wrote.

Sensing resistance, Madeline continued. "The wheels of this project are turning, faster than you can imagine, Faust." She flexed her jaw muscles, and struck hard. "Don't get in the way. It...*we*...will run over you so fast and hard that you won't even know what hit you. There isn't one of us who will step on the brakes to save you."

The last pane of glass shattered. Nothing survived of what I knew. It all changed. The house shuddered and perked, invigorated. Chains of history held them to this place, the links coated in the greed of the vision, like so many others who thought they could succeed, thought they could survive intact. Once again, it didn't happen. Greyhaven won, but I rose to the challenge.

"Don't you dare threaten me! I've got what you want. I hold the cards here. Me. How funny. Long departed but not counted out. How funny! No one else. *Me!*" I loved this. A sudden feeling arose within me. "You know what? I need to go and think on this a spell. Masticate, rejuvenate, commiserate, et cetera. So, now, if you'll excuse me, I have some thinkin' to do."

"Don't take too long," Madeline said, seeming to have lost her ability to create. Creation takes time and careful planning, and both turned against her now, as well as me.

"Madeline," I reiterated, "like I said, I really need to think on it. I'm not in as much of a rush as you are, but I'll get back to you, right soon."

"Well..." Harris didn't take long to put the parts together. He spoke as if I'd already left the room. He searched the air, pulling together what he now knew. "What do we do?" He asked it as a child who does not see the ramifications.

"Looks like we must deal with Faust after all," Cornelius said, getting the joke. "You cooked the books for nothing, it seems, unless we all can convince our dear brother, Faust, to come along for the ride." Cornelius reminisced. "How you helped me 'pull a fast one' on dear old dad." Cornelius wanted to put each infraction where it belonged, strategic brilliance. "Poor Titus, give him wide-eyed innocence and he would believe anything."

"Shut up, Cornelius," Madeline became stern. "Faust, it's not what it seems." She looked at me with the eyes of an honest woman who'd made a mistake.

"Yes, it is, Faust," Cornelius interrupted.

"Shut up, Cornelius!" She turned to me to see if an explanation would fly. "I asked Cornelius if we could squeeze some funds out of the hotel business, so Harris could repay some investors when a bond came due on the land. I knew Cornelius would understand, but Sarah made it conditional that he would leave the children and her alone. With Sarah out of the picture, the rest came slowly, business by business, till we had all the debt paid and the businesses were damn near worthless. We stretched the truth about the worth of everything."

"Ah, Harris, in for a penny, in for a pound." Cornelius' sarcasm rang like a deafening bell. "Once you have someone help you open the door, it's amazing how easy it is to push it wide open."

"Knowing how to do it," Madeline continued, "I found lots of cash held by all of our companies. I didn't need Harris to do it anymore. Titus was pretty good at what he did. We just took the profit."

"Harris' fingerprints are on the first one," Cornelius hastened to add, as if it wasn't clear to me. "What do you think the Feds will say about the others? *Ahh, it is the frailty of human nature, isn't it? He was so eager to help, so willing to go out on a limb...for family...for bargaining.* Right, Harris?"

Harris stared at Cornelius and Madeline, realizing at that moment he didn't figure in this at all, doubtless wondering if he'd been played. "You continue to meet my expectations."

"What do you want, Cornelius?" I asked.

"You know what I want...what we want. Control of Greyhaven, pretty simple."

"I'm not ready to give it to you. And it's mine to give, Cornelius."

"Look," Madeline became practical, "what do you want in exchange?"

"I don't know yet. I need to think about what Addie might have wanted, since she is the only one that I am predisposed to trust right now, alive or dead. So, as I said, time is what I need."

"Don't take too long. We need closure and decisions. Quick is the only way," Madeline said. "Figure out what you want in exchange."

"Well, that does it for me now. I need to rest some, so I'll leave yo'll and go to my room." As I turned, the discord in the dining room increased. I suppose they never expected my lack of involvement here to be a question. I was a sure bet. I would agree to anything. *Give him a stipend send him back to his New York hideout where he'll be quiet enough with the constant flow of a retirement fund.* They banked on cut-and-run. They figured wrong. With all of the other variables, I became the riskiest element, the most disruptive of the lot. They figured wrong.

———

I phoned Buster on the cordless as I cautiously walked up the stairs. He didn't pick up so I left a message as I closed the door to my room. It felt hard to do. The pressure from outside seemed to make it heavier, more resistant. I sat on my bed and wondered what to do, aware that I'd sounded a lot surer of myself downstairs than I actually felt. There were too many enemies around me now, knowing that I was the weakest link in their chain of planned events. No one figured on my "thinking things over."

I opened the French doors to the porch off my room and the slight breeze enveloped me and carried my mind to Buster. I went with the feeling and phoned him again. This time he answered.

"What's up?" His voice sounded more unsure than cold.

"I been giving you...us...a lot of thought. Things are getting heated here. Can you pick me up?"

"When?"

"How does now work for you?"

"Umm...sure. Where?"

"How 'bout at the big gates up front. I don't think you should come in."

"Okay. See you in twenty."

# 21

AS SOON AS I HUNG UP with Buster there was a knock on the door. I opened it slowly to see Madeline. This was not her usual entry into my room. She never showed timidity when barging in. All changed this day.

"Can I come in?"

"Sure. Never stopped you before."

"We need to talk." She ignored my play to establish normalcy.

"I think enough was said downstairs, don't you?"

"No. I can't let this go. We need to have resolution today, now. Time is running out." She stepped close to my face and I felt claustrophobic.

"Madeline, I'm not prepared to give you an answer yet. Buster's picking me up in a bit. I need to get some space between us for a while."

"Buster. Hmm…how's that working out?" She tried to get an inside track by getting personal.

"Nothing to work out. Besides, what do you actually care?"

"I guess that's true enough. Just feels odd." She felt a little pang of lamented change.

"To me, too. Truth is, we played at so much over the years that this just feels like a little wrinkle in the fabric is all. Don't you agree?" I looked at her blankly.

"I suppose so."

"I have to go." I patted her on the shoulder as I left, hearing the hollowness of it.

"Don't be long, please." She tried one last time to evoke a promise from me.

"It'll be what it'll be." There was nothing more to say.

I followed the trail of the staircase as it led to the front door and, from the corner of my eye, caught Harris and Cornelius watching my moves. I overheard Harris whisper to Cornelius, "Where's he going?"

There was no response from Cornelius, just the silence of calculation. As I hit the front door, a bird flew in. It raced into the dining room, slamming into the delicately carved statue of Ivinia and Titus. Shaking back and forth on its marble stand in slow motion, teetering to save itself, and then, giving over to a greater force, changed its mind, and fell to the ground, crashing like an egg against the floor. It split in half, between their two images.

Titus spent years facing Ivinia in exquisite marble form, forced to look on her in a conjured-up pose, perceived by the artist to project love and union. Titus was finally free. They now lay looking in separate directions for the first time. The sound echoed through the house like an alarm. Cornelius picked up the head of Ivinia and caressed it, as if in some Shakespearean twist, and slowly walked out of the room. He met me on the veranda.

"This meeting is over," he said to me, as if he still controlled the arena. "You know what I want."

Cornelius studied Ivinia's marble likeness as he strolled down the porch steps and onto the path. He disappeared, as if swallowed up by his own wash of acid and venom.

"Give it to them, Faust. Just give it to them. And we'll all be free," Harris pleaded from behind me as I'd never had heard him before. "Please, Faust, they take human frailty, turn it on its side, and use it against anyone in their way. You can return to New York. I can get out of here and transfer to Chicago. There's a firm that owes me. I could be a partner there. Please do it. Please."

"You'd leave Madeline?" I asked him.

"I just want this pain to go away." He shifted back and forth on his feet. "Let it go. You never wanted it anyway. What's your loss?"

"I don't know that now. All I know is I need to figure out what I want, Harris. For the first time, it's what *I* want."

I was about to head toward the gates to meet Buster. At that moment, Harris and I heard that same thump that had haunted me all the nights since my arrival. We were the only ones left in the house. Cornelius and Sarah were gone and Madeline remained upstairs.

"What the hell was that?" Harris heard it for the first time.

"It's exactly what I have heard every night since my arrival.

"Where is it coming from?" Harris looked in the direction of the upper landing.

"It's always the attic. I thought that Pru was the one knocking around up there. She's not still here is she?" I asked.

"No, I saw her speed off in her pickup just as I arrived," Harris confirmed.

A revelation struck me. "The attic, right now!" I bolted through the front door with Harris on my trail. Through the entry and up to the first landing, we rounded the stairs as if they were a raceway. As we did, we called for Madeline, but she was nowhere to be found. The thumping hit again and we reached the top of the third-floor landing and stood in front of the doorway that led to the servant's wings. We stood there for a moment, each hesitant to touch the handle. I finally opened the double doors and we peered down the unlit hallway, catching the light between the shadows. I tried the lights, but they failed to go on.

The smell of wet permeated the air. Even walls sweat in this heat, and the smell of mold stung my nostrils as we rushed toward the source of the curious noise.

With each nervous step, we felt our way while feeling the evidence of our history, our movement. But no Madeline. The movement of our possessions. But no Madeline. Back and forth, in good times for storage, for there was so much. In lean times, when we had to hide their evidence. But no Madeline. Each doorway that we passed held secrets of the people upstairs—housemen, maids, hired help, trapped victims, layers of people, nameless and forgotten, coerced by various reasons to promote this experiment. But no Madeline. We searched as quickly as we ran. Where was Madeline? What was the source of the noise? Flashes of our hatred jolted me with every touch of a wall or a door, the punishment for our abuse. But no Madeline. What is the punishment for our abuse? What is the reward for a victim's endurance? How different the goals, ours from theirs? How different our approach to survival? It was all here, within these walls. We could tell our story with its achievements and challenges, and it would be instantly diminished by the sadness worn into these walls as if an endlessly patterned wallpaper documented its painful truth. But. No. Madeline.

As we raced to the noise, my mind went to Addie telling me again of the plan that she and Father had dreamed. Should I refuse to let it go? Could I pull it off? If I gave this all to them, the land to Cornelius and the house to Madeline, would they let me go or forever hold me libel for his folly? I didn't know. I just didn't know.

The hallway twisted and turned going on, it seemed, further than the house actually did.

We opened each doorway that we came upon, only to expose more cobwebs and more faded wallpaper, boxes, crates, and old trunks. Remnants of people past and their graffiti colored the withered walls in a chaptered pattern, one that exposed and did not 'make pretty' the struggle. This debris documented the slaves and servants of this house, carved and painted like the art of cave dwellers. It haunted this place and us. Old pictures left in fragile wood frames rotting, ashes to ashes. Harris and I were both struck by this time capsule. Madeline and I had crept through these rooms and rafters as children for safety and discovery both. Harris had not. Instead, he heard the stories in more colorful and humorous a turn.

But there was no Madeline. We opened every door that we passed, each seal harder to break than the last, if not for the age and its condition but for the dread of what the next door might reveal. But where was she? Tattered lampshades tilted on bent lamps, old clothes and dusty Sunday hats, single shoes and old papers thrown helter-skelter in the corners of open closet doors. We searched. Drawers, in broken chests, hung out askew with the last thing touched draped over the edges.

And then we stood in front of a door, larger than the others. The door opened to the old head housekeeper's room, where the muffled sounds of life had pushed their way through night after night, year after year. Looming defiant against intruders, this room still held the uneasy blend of downstairs and upstairs and, for its experience, looked and stood stronger than the others. Bolted shut, the locks hung like barnacles from the edges of the metal straps and nailed boards.

"Help me, Harris," I said, as I tugged at the metal straps that bound the door. They surrendered, much like a bully showing more muscle than he ever used.

We pushed against the door with our shoulders, straining the lock on the handle. The frame broke on the third attempt and the door swung open, squealing an alarm from its hinges. We stood there knowing that we had just entered a world made deliberately secret from the rest, not ancestral or organic, more recent.

And in that room, in the mist of the mold and the humidity, appeared a figure, sitting at her looking glass, ghostlike, for there appeared to be little left of her. She did not startle to the intrusion but kept busily preparing and adjusting ratty and twisted curls matted and swelling in an unkempt order. We stood there frozen, forgetting for a moment the object of our mission.

The ghostly woman wore a torn peignoir, silken and pale, faded. It flowed away from her as gently as the sea grasses rustle in the breeze at the night's change to day. Her shoulder stuck out shapely from its silken cocoon, blossoming in welts as she rubbed cream on it. Spilled food on tarnished trays surrounded her. Old pictures in jeweled frames of better days sat among open jars of cream and rouge and powder. She leaned into the mirror and adjusted the harsh swath of red on her cheek.

It was Ivinia.

She suddenly caught our intrusion next to her reflection and spoke. "Who are you? What do you want?" She seemed to use all her energy to control what remained of her world. She continued to adjust, only glancing at me sporadically in agitation as she trowelled on the color...pink, red, and aubergine.

"It's me. It's Faustus." I didn't know how to address her. So I chose not to make that decision. How could I?

"Faustus? Faustus? I'm sorry, I don't know you. You're not family." And I had my answer. My stomach jumped at the sound of her denial of me. I wanted to leave this place and never turn back, but the weight of these words transformed me into stone. I welled up in tears. Harris shielded his eyes from the sight of her, shaking his head.

"What is it that you want? I cannot be disturbed. I must get ready. What time is it?"

"It's around four o'clock, Ivinia," Harris said, staring at the floor.

"Is that you, Harris? Where is my daughter?

"We don't know, but she's around," he said, hoping to ease some information from her.

"I hope so. My clock has stopped. I know that she has been playing with it again." The crystal face, cracked through, had only its bronze frame holding it together. "How many times have I told her that if you want things to last you must take care of them? How many times?" Ivinia shook her head as if Madeline would never learn. "Harris, be a dear and hand me my brush. I can't seem to reach it."

She could not move. She wobbled in her chair. I scanned the room and saw the tray of medicines, a dozen bottles if one, one more powerful than the next. The task of administering them must have been delegated to Pru. Was this Cornelius' grand scheme or his attempt to postpone a decision? I could hear my brother's voice inside my head: *What to do? What to do? What to do with Ivinia?*" I could hear him say.

"This is Cornelius' doing, I'm sure," Harris said in disgust.

Bolts dripped from the balcony door on the other side of the room as well. Dirt prevented Ivinia from seeing through its glass to the front drive without considerable effort. Her isolation was complete.

"Are you sure he could do this?" I wanted not to believe what I was thinking.

"Who else could do this? Are you thinking Madeline?" Harris said, incredulously.

Had Cornelius imprisoned Ivinia here? If not for his private pleasure, then for her torture? Or was it Madeline? Cornelius must hold the hand of this, I truly thought. He hid the things that he discarded here, for future reference, for necessary debris not quite ready for Pru to take away. What to do with the woman he adored? The woman he fashioned his male courage after. He absorbed the parts of her that built this vision and trapped her in this room, discarded when their purposes took different direction. His all-consuming anger, revenge, desperation, letting her know, just enough, that life would go on without her. Her dearest friend, Gladys, came to mind, and three words she said to me at Titus' funeral: "She wouldn't leave."

"Madeline is picking me up very soon now." Ivinia continued to brush her hair through her delusion.

The news of Ivinia waiting for Madeline to "pick her up" shocked me. "Isn't Cornelius picking you up?" I asked.

"No, certainly not." She fingered her makeup. "I haven't seen Cornelius for weeks," she said in her reflection. "He's with Titus on the job. Madeline keeps me aware." She looked at the mirror, adjusting her makeup as we adjusted our fears. Madeline had created all of this.

"We are going to visit Titus on that new project. I am very proud of this one, you know. I created it. That's why Cornelius is there...to protect my interests. And now, there is so much to do. So much. There are guests to attend to, dinner tables to set." Her list drifted off. "I hope that Addie has prepared everything just right. You know, that girl can really mess up. The last party we hosted, she never even showed. Titus spent the entire evening searching for her, while I entertained and looked after the help." She suddenly looked overwhelmed at the task at hand. "There just is no one to trust." Then, in a glimpse of reality, she put down her brush and lowered her head and said, "No one to trust."

A door slammed downstairs and we heard hollering. It was Madeline. She bolted through the front door and we heard the noise from where we stood. We raced out of the room and down the halls to reach her. The smell of moldy memories and attic treasures turned into the heated smell of smoke mixed with the pungent acrid smell of gasoline. As we hit the entry to the attic we saw Madeline.

"Where have you been?" Harris, befuddled, asked her.

"You'll never let me have this, will you?" Madeline yelled. We stood frozen on the attic stairs, not knowing what to do.

"Yes, Madeline, I'll give it to you. All of it. I promise." Automatically I answered, quite sure of the severity of the threat. Cornelius' threats were frequent, and we were numb to them. They shallowed out in time. Madeline threatened, and we paid attention. Neither Harris nor I knew what Madeline might be thinking. How could she bring herself to destroy the one thing for which she worked? She appeared disheveled and frantic. She reacted to the loss in front of her. I stood at the landing with Harris and smoke permeated the air.

"No, you won't. You found Ivinia, didn't you? Didn't you?" She blurted out almost as if relieved. "This is all yours. I have no stake here."

She held a dozen old pop bottles with wet rags hanging out of them. She had a lighter. And she lit the dampened rag ends and threw the bottles, one by one, continuing the path of destruction she swathed through the dining room and salon, not waiting for additional answers, no more decisions to be made beyond this one. She threw lit Molotovs, her cocktail of choice now, in opposing directions like party favors on New Year's Eve. Lite, throw. Lite, throw.

"This will make a great story, don't you think, Harris? Faust?" Her eyes stared frozen and dead.

She swung the gasoline bottles as far as she could. They crashed against the carpeted stairs and the wallpapered walls and the pedestalled art. They burst on impact and flames flared and danced like carnival lights traveling the frame of a rollercoaster. The flames consumed the fibers and the threads holding our house together, attempting to fill its insatiable hunger. The flames danced rapidly, running and hopping in choreographed destruction, obeying Madeline's orders to choose an alternate course for our history. It would never belong to her so destroy it she would, taking nothing and letting nothing remain. Ivinia had a plan that developed over the years, financial, ruthless, seeping like poison through the veins of our family's heart.

Her plan calculated and twisted our weakness. Madeline's final plan, born out of a quicker desperation, seeped from a crack in her psychic veneer.

So be it. It would never belong to her now. She knew it. I knew it. It would belong to no one. She had Ivinia's eyes, her calculating coldness, her determination, but not her ability to go the distance in the face of hopelessness.

Titus had called Cornelius the bad seed, but he'd called Madeline nothing. He could not foresee this end. Madeline would finally emerge important in this struggle called Greyhaven. She was no longer caught in between. She emerged the final player, the final leader, or just the final. Titus wanted to save this place, to purge it of its guilt, not burn it in effigy. He wanted an end with Addie, wanted different, wanted over, wanted to tell the story of this place to anyone who would listen, clinically, controlling the outcome of the message.

Dance dancing, light lighting, jump jumping. Flames licking and moving as quickly as they could, in, around, and through, behind, around, and up the furniture and the curtains, up the walls, wilting the patterns of flowers and leaves woven, printed, embossed, and embroidered, blackening what defined our family. We tore down the stairs and circled around Madeline. Harris grabbed for her as she ran toward the staircase.

"What are you doing?" Harris screamed, "We were almost there!"

"It would never happen. I know Faust better than you, better than all of you." She cursed at the air. "If I don't get it, no one will. Do you understand? No one!"

Madeline broke free and picked up more bottles, throwing them as she ascended the stairs.

With a throw born out of contempt, Madeline lobbed a bottle our way. Harris tried to catch it, but it hit the window and flashed behind us, enveloping the silk hangings and the sashes. It melted the stairs leading up to the landing, separating her in a final attempt to divide the family the way she saw fit. She ran up the stairs and stood on the top of the landing, laughing, consumed, satiated. The flames traveled up the carpet and swallowed the banister and the paintings that lined the stairs. Madeline disappeared behind a wall of flames.

"Quick! We have to get to them through the back staircase!" Harris pushed me toward the kitchen. We tried to climb the rear stair. We got half-way up, but the smoke from the advancing flames pushed down at us with an intensity only slightly greater than the increasing heat. We retreated back through to the entry. At that moment I thought an exorcism was taking place. We ran for our lives, Harris more reluctantly. I tugged at him.

"It's hopeless, let it go!" I said.

"I can't, she's up there! We need to save her!" He pulled away, but I held tight and dragged him over to the doorway and out over the porch and on to the drive. We hit the gravel as a great explosion erupted from the center of the house. The force threw us to the ground and we covered our heads from the flying debris. The fire consumed the outside, licking the boards and the columns, charring everything it touched.

"Are you okay?" I asked.

"Yeah, I think so."

Shaking, we stood up and turned toward the house. The flames enveloped the entire interior, making the glass of the window panes glimmer, then shatter, too hot to fight the heat's resolve. We searched for Madeline through a sea of smoke and fire, certain that we could get to her if only we could see her. But she did not appear. Flames crackled and laughed at us from every window of every floor, 'til we looked way above the front door to the housekeeper's windows.

There at the balcony Ivinia pressed against the heated window glass, the reluctant Joan of Arc of her decisions. She scratched at the glass, trying to pierce it, a final moment of lucidity, then in a turn of resolve. She disappeared as if pulled back. Madeline stood at the balcony door, calm and regal, as if just noticing that she was being watched. She adjusted her dress and hair, turned and stopped for a second, arched her back, and disappeared.

The house shook in every corner of its foundation, not wanting to relinquish its power to the flames. Another explosion catapulted the interior of the library forward out through the shattering French doors. Furniture, porcelain, and bottles spilled onto the front veranda. Furniture tumbled onto the driveway, the house vomiting from the torture. Out came the statue of Dionysus, broken before it landed, and the celadon-colored silk divan covered in a halo of flames of brilliant reds and gold, landing upside down, outside for the first time since it arrived. In the house's final attempt to withstand this assault, its columns began to wobble in a vain effort to hold on to what it remembered, a command given so long ago. One by one they collapsed inward in surrender.

Buster arrived, screeching to a halt behind where we were standing, and jumped out of the pickup.

"Are you alright? Where are the others? I saw the flames from a few miles down the road!" He spoke breathlessly, as if he had run the distance. "Is there anyone still in the house?"

"We couldn't save Madeline," I said, as the swells of tears pushed out of me.

"Oh, my God." Buster tried to console me, grabbing on to me. I did not resist. Harris just stood there with a framed old daguerreotype in his hand of the house in its heyday, looking at the photo and again at the reality, back and forth.

"It's all gone. She's gone. What will I do now?"

I could say nothing to console him, for I didn't know whether he felt broken or confused.

Minutes played like hours while waiting for the fire department to appear. They finally arrived and surmised the futility of the situation, content to allow the fire to play itself out. They stood by, unknowingly duplicitous with Madeline, and watched the final demise of this regal phoenix, crushed beneath its own weight.

It took minutes for the house to disappear but hours for the embers to die. The firemen pumped water from the hydrants to wet down the glowing debris, fearing the embers could be captured by the winds of August and take light somewhere else. I am not sure to this day if it were the embers of fire they tried to prevent rekindling or the essence of Greyhaven they wanted to finally extinguish. The intense fire singed the drape of the moss and torched the under layer of green leaves which the moss did not already choke away.

Now at rest, the house became only the charred sum of its parts resting in a heap of blackened wet debris.

Nothing to save, it was all gone: history, architecture, a family's material legacy, as if the figurehead never existed. A long gravel drive elegantly twisted toward nothing, all landscaped and proper, ending to reveal a distant mound of debris. The family effects were gone, but the effects of the family lingered, indelibly scarring the past and forever shaping its present and future.

The police banded what was left of my home in yellow tape that was repeatedly printed with the words:

## CRIME SCENE. DO NOT ENTER.

I always imagined the yellow tape there, in my mind's eye somehow, a fitting ribbon to this gift that the Madigans left to me. I didn't want it touched after the firemen and the police finished their work. Cutting it would release the evil contained within. Evil doesn't itself burn; it burns whoever or whatever gets in its path. It doesn't disappear; it reconfigures and transforms and regroups.

—

Months have passed since the fire. Harris buried Madeline in the family plot. He kept his silence publicly. What more could he add to the story? To the police, he fashioned a psychic break for Madeline, which wasn't far from the truth. He kept it simple for legalities, press, and closure. He used his legal acumen to weave a possibility, a supposition, and they bought it. There was a small ceremony with a few close friends. No relatives came.

I buried Ivinia in California. Gladys came alone from the West Coast and, for once, we were united. She took the body to LA. There was no one willing to fight the decision, least of all Cornelius. He remained silent. We gave Gladys a gold locket that we found in the rubble with the photos of Ivinia's two children, Madeline and Cornelius, with a promise that she would place it in her coffin before her burial. We trusted it would be done. Gladys left as she had arrived, in silence and aubergine.

Madeline's stories and books continued to sell; all the notoriety made them sell faster as adults now looked for clues to her past. Internet cults sprang up, discussing the fortunes, details, and hubris of her and my family. I was glad that our misfortune and history could fill the lives of the empty and those starving for the notoriety that their own existence failed to give them.

Harris moved to Chicago and abandoned any claim to what was left, content to live on the royalties that his wife's estate mustered. He took on her literary empire and worked it. It was easier than Madeline ever thought.

Cornelius took the Madigan holdings in all of the companies and settled every debt, leaving him a substantial cushion to keep him in the style to which he had become accustomed. He took private those companies where we held majorities, again easier to manipulate all of this without involvement from anyone. I sold out to him and left him alone. It became easy to let go, for exactly how much money defines affluence? What amount makes you safe? What amount makes the locker-room antics of male achievement worth the ordeal?

I took what I got and returned to Back Bay—Momma's house. It was bequeathed to me from her will. Yes, I made the grand decision. I returned to New York for a few weeks just to close up shop there. I returned to Peaceable quickly because, well, it now suited me more, somehow. New York was no longer a place where I could be lost. I no longer needed to be lost.

Addie left me a major stock holder in Vastigone Tie and Trim Company, a little piece of the puzzle that she failed to disclose before her death. Turns out she collected more than just ribbons from the company to which I dedicated my time. I left the complaints department and ascended to CEO and chairman of the board of Vastigone.

I decided that the board of directors and, in fact, the entire company, needed to move down here. It was cost effective and more competitive with overseas markets. So I settled in among the pictures and the faded fabrics and the open door, the birds of paradise and the bougainvillea.

Today, I live here and I write the stories of my family as it was affected—*infected*—from both sides of this Southern struggle. I am both families. I am the balance. I am the truthteller, more able to see what was real and what wasn't. My stories are not fantasy, no longer hidden in castles and wishing wells, golden doors with brittle iron locks. These are the stories of Addie, my momma, and her quest, instead of the stories centered on the Madigans.

I negotiated ownership of the land where we built the debacle called Greyhaven Estates. It will finally be able to rest and return to whatever nature allows, the gift that I wanted to give to Titus. No one will scheme for its development. I saw to that.

The Feds backed off, you don't need to pay attention to land left alone. The police narrowed their focus on the dead, leaving the living to their own devices.

Sarah finally left Cornelius and settled for her children, her career, and what remained of her own family legacy. She also took a buyout from Cornelius. She is the Southern survivor that we read about, that those of us born here know exists, often despite us.

It is the women who make the South, not the men. "They muck it up," Momma wrote, in one of her diaries. "What was Noah's wife thinking?" she wrote. "She had such a chance to make it all be better. She coulda changed it all by swattin' those two mosquitoes and those two men, put them in their place from the start. Mosquitoes and men. Mosquitoes and men. That's all she needed to do."

It's clear that I didn't know Momma as well as I might. That's one of the reasons I stayed here. I felt that if I could just absorb her surroundings, see what she saw, and hear the balance of the stories from the last great storyteller, Jedidiah (her brother and my uncle), I could maybe piece a life together, finally whole.

I travel often to see my half-sisters in Virginia. I'm getting to know their circle of family…my family.

As for Buster, well, he sometimes brings me flowers awkwardly, in vain attempts to be the kind of romantic he thinks I need. We decide between going to dinner or Home Depot, which has become our Paris. Where will it go I have thoughts, but, well…

Is there ever an end?

POLO

## MARK ALAN POLO

When not writing, Mark Alan Polo works as an interior designer. He is President and Owner of The Urban Dweller/Polo M.A. Inc., with offices in Northern New Jersey and a satellite office in Delaware. Mark has resided in Delaware since 2014.

Mark's published stories include "Fifty-Five" (*Beach Nights*, Cat and Mouse Press). He has contributed to the DPP anthologies HALLOWEEN PARTY, SOLSTICE, EQUINOX, AURORA, and SUSPICIOUS ACTIVITY.

MOSQUITOES AND MEN is his debut novel. Mark is presently at work on a second novel.

# Award-winning anthologies so engaging, it would be a crime NOT to read them...

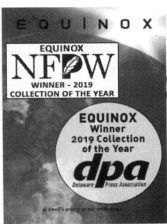

Whether you're in the mood for something scary or something seasonal, we've got you covered. Devil's Party Press anthologies contain engaging, original works by talented voices from across the globe. Our authors are a diverse group of over-forty creators who bring to the page their unique talents.
We'll make sure your reading time is well spent. Visit us on the web for ordering info.

## devilspartypress.com

# Does this look familiar?

photo credit: Valerina Solaris

If so, chances are you're over 40, so perhaps you might consider submitting a short story, poem, or memoir piece to one of our upcoming anthologies. DPP grew out of our belief that your work deserves a better life than a file on your laptop.

Our main criteria are fairly simple:

1. Your work must be original and compelling.
2. You must be 40 years of age or older.

We publish two anthologies per year, typically in the spring and the fall.

For complete submission information visit
**devilspartypress.com/submissions**

If you wow us with your skills, you'll join a unique group of writers, each a compelling, original voice.

We look forward to hearing from you.

## devilspartypress.com